runaways

a novel

RACHEL SAWDEN

Visit my website: www.rachelsawden.com

Follow me on Instagram: @rachelsawden

Twenty years from now you will be more disappointed by the things that you didn't do, than the ones you did. So throw off the bowlines. Sail away from the safe harbour. Catch the trade winds in your sails. Explore. Dream. Discover.

- Mark Twain*

To my Mom and Dad.
Thank you for never telling me to get a real job.

(Oh Mom and Dad, if you could skip chapters 27 and 28,
that would save us all a lot of awkwardness.)

runaways

a novel

RACHEL SAWDEN

Chapter 1

Date: January 8, 2010
Toronto, Canada

Where would you go if you could run away? Trek the tangled jungles of Thailand? Camp under the constellations in the Australian outback? Or run wild with your lover on white sand beaches in the South Pacific?

"Nowhere," I whispered. My heels clicked on the linoleum floor, punctuating the spiel from my presentation echoing in my head. "I am exactly where I am supposed to be."

How could I not be positive? I was one of the lucky few to gain and maintain employment in the shadow of the Great Recession. Fresh out of university, I might add. Granted, my working unpaid for TMI Marketing during my summer years gave me a leg up on the competition. While my job consisted mainly of making coffee, filing papers, and having my ideas ignored, I worked my ass off for the past three years. And today was the day my hard work would pay off. It was the day it all would change. The career side of my five-year plan was on schedule.

A fresh wave of adrenaline pulsed through me as I made my way down the hallway of very unflattering lighting to my boss's office to discuss the presentation I'd given that morning. A discussion that would hopefully lead to a new position in the company. One where I could take on actual responsibility and express my creativity. Perhaps be involved in art direction. A business card with a title: Harper Rodrigues, Marketing Executive.

I would actually manage my very own accounts.

We had secured a new client, a travel website, Madcap Travels, who was looking to reevaluate their social media marketing plan and contracted my company to manage it. Myself and a colleague had made competing presentations for the job. Only one of us could gain the account. Only one of us could be promoted. Only one of us could win today, and I wanted it to be me.

I had never been so excited about a project, and so damn scared about presenting.

Inspired by my friends' upcoming "gap year" travels, I created the *Run Away* campaign harnessing the power of this growing thing called social media. When Facebook became a buzzword a few years back, my father said it was just a passing fad used by horny college students too lazy to go to the bar and talk to each other. He may have been right, but once it had been opened up to anyone with an email address there were millions of lazy, horny people of all ages across the world skulking around on confined areas of cyberspace. And that is gold to a marketer.

In a nutshell, the campaign would focus on incentivizing both amateur and professional photographers who were traveling the globe to connect and share their stories and photographs on social media platforms. Top entrants would not only gain recognition on the website but also chances to win prizes from partner sponsors such as airlines, tour companies, and hotels. I poured myself into this presentation. Putting myself in the shoes of one of the many runaways, I imagined my life living out of a backpack, seeing a new city every week, learning from other photographers, finding remote waterfalls and villages from the whispers of other vagabonds.

It was what I hoped to do had I not abandoned my plans to become a world-famous travel photographer.

It was what I could do if I abandoned my carefully crafted five-year plan and took off with Jade and Lana.

It was what I wanted to do with my sister, Audrey, since we were little girls.

It was what we could have done if she were still alive.

Pausing with my gaze focused on the grain of the wooden door, I flexed my fingers and inhaled the scent of varnish. Her image filled my mind, and I imagined her telling me that whatever happened, I would be alright. Everything would be alright. God I missed her. She was my anchor, and I spent the past three years adrift I lost her, slipping into depression. With the help of therapy through that time I graduated university, gained employment, and surfaced from the depths. Waves of depression knock me down from time to time, but it's been quite some time since I've drowned.

My counselor taught me the keys to finding happiness again with two simple principles, gratitude and goal setting. Gratitude, as no matter how bad things get, we all have something to be thankful for, even if it's just the fact that we live in a world where Brad Pitt exists. (Never underestimate the healing power of humour.) And setting goals to regain a sense of control.

"Fail to plan, plan to fail" became my new mantra to handle the ebb and flow of my emotions.

Raising my fist to the door, I set my jaw. As I rapped my knuckles on it, I repeated more affirmations. Even if I didn't win the promotion, I was grateful for the opportunity. I was grateful to have a job. I was grateful for the breath in my lungs.

"Come in," my boss's voice called.

An acidic tang hit the back of my throat as I turned the knob and swung the door open. To my surprise, the HR manager, Karen, perched in a chair next to my boss, Ms. Hatching. I supposed it wouldn't be too odd for the HR manager to be present if I were negotiating the terms of my promotion.

It all seemed a little rushed, though. I had only just given my presentation a few hours ago.

"Ms. Rodrigues," Ms. Hatching said gesturing at the chair in front of the desk. "Please, take a seat."

I plastered a smile on my face, but there was something about her formal address that made me wary. Perhaps we were not about to negotiate my new contract.

"Thank you very much for your presentation today. I can appreciate the amount of time and effort you put into it." Ms. Hatching took a step forward and removed her glasses. "We have decided, however, that Victoria will be taking the Madcap Travels account."

I bit my lip as disappointment washed over me. But it wasn't the end of the world. I still had a job. "I understand. So what does that mean for me?"

On cue, my affirmations repeated in my head. *I'm grateful for my life. I'm grateful for the breath in my lungs. I'm grateful for all of the wonderful opportunities afforded to me.*

"We are going to have to let you go."

I'm grateful for my…wait, what?!

I squeezed my eyes shut, hoping that I was having one of those horrible false awakening dreams. But when I opened them again, I was still sitting in the office. Karen wore a strong poker face, and Ms. Hatching looked infuriatingly indifferent.

Naturally I asked the reasons for why I was being let go. Phrases were tossed out like "creative eye" and "great ideas" along with, "control freak," and "inflexibility."

I sunk deeper in my chair. My afternoon so wasn't going according to plan.

"I enjoyed your presentation, but it didn't seem as if you took it entirely seriously," Ms. Hatching said. "It seemed as if you were trying to line yourself up to be a content provider for the campaign than to run the marketing end of it."

My mouth hung open. Sure, who wouldn't want to travel the world taking photographs? But that's what made me perfect to run the campaign — I could see it from both sides.

"The bottom line is we had to make cuts," Karen cut in before I could make my case, "and given that you are the least experienced on the team made you a weak link."

"Weak link?" I sputtered.

I'm grateful there's a desk between us.

Now, I want to say that I fought for my job. Any rational person would. When news of redundancies and unemployment became regular headlines I always thought that if I had been one of those unfortunate many, I would have refused to leave. Proved that I deserved my place in the company. Showed them the scars from when I had burned my hands with their cheap coffee, brought up how I went along with some of the most harebrained marketing ideas you can imagine (a cell phone built specifically for women, for our "small hands" and "delicate hearing." Guess how well that went down in the test markets.); and endured the constant barrage of sexual harassment from the accountant, Pervy Percy.

Reminded them that while the others lounged on beaches in Cuba or went skiing in Whistler I stayed behind picking up everyone's slack, except on the anniversaries of Audrey's birth and death.

I want to say that I leapt from my chair after my proclamations of what an asset I was. How I bent over backwards at every opportunity. Told them that they did not deserve me, and any other company would thank their lucky stars to have me. I want to say that I strode from the room, gathering employees while waxing poetic about my new company manifesto.

Launching a rallying battle cry, "Who's coming with me? Who's coming with me?"

But alas, I did not have my Jerry McGuire moment.

With shock shutting my senses down, she droned on and on sounding more and more like the teacher from Charlie Brown — wha wha wha whaaaa wha wha whaaaaa. My gaze zeroed in on a mock-up ad for a perfume brand on the desk for a new fragrance, *Lover's Embrace*. At first, it looked like an abstract image, but it was a black and white bodyscape of two figures embracing. It was an image that the viewer would need to stare at for a while to see, like a sexy stereogram. The composition was striking, the lighting impeccable, the mood, sensual, teasing and playful. A pang of envy hit me each time I saw it. The photographer was an incredible talent. One day, perhaps, I could create images as beautifully executed. It was too bad that *Lover's Embrace* smelled like an awkward hug.

But advising the client of top and bottom notes was not my job. My job was to sell it. Or it used to be anyways.

Used to be.

"Harper, are you listening?"

The sound of my name jolted me back to reality. I flicked my eyes to Karen's. Stars danced in front of me. My vision became a tunnel, narrowing faster and faster. Karen's cat-eye glasses spun in the center. Then everything went black.

***

When I came to, three people stood over me. My vision focused as the scent of menthol burned its way up my nose.

"I know CPR." All of my muscles clenched when I recognized that voice. Pervy Percy. "I should give her mouth to mouth…as a precautionary measure."

"That's not necessary," my boss said with a huff. Never had I been more grateful to her. "Look her eyes are open."

I sat up, and both Karen and Ms. Hatching reached for my arms. As they pulled me to my feet, Percy reached for my torso. Thankfully they stepped in front of him before he could touch me.

"Percy, we have this under control," Ms. Hatching snapped, as I slumped into the chair.

Giving a slight pout, he nodded and left the room. A welcome rush of cool air swept over me as the door swung closed.

"Are you alright?"

I nodded. Still feeling shaky, I took deep and deliberate breaths. The memory of the moments before I passed out washed over me. My life was about to change.

"As I said, the company will give you a generous severance package," Karen said, as I forced myself to focus. "But you must pack up your things and vacate the office immediately." The moment she finished speaking there was a knock on the door. "Security is here to show you out."

Security? Were they expecting me to run through the office popping off staples screaming, "Yippy kay yay?"

On cue, there was a soft knock on the door and it creaked open. The kind face of the gentle giant we affectionately called Security Steve peered around the door. I pushed myself to my feet, knees still wobbly, and turned by back on my former boss and colleague.

"It's just protocol," Security Steve whispered when I passed him in the doorway.

Mortified and humiliated by losing consciousness as I was losing my job, I needed to get the hell out of that office. Stat. Even though my feet moved as fast as my shaky legs would allow, the hallway seemed twice as long as usual. My desk felt so far away. The walls narrower. The fluorescent lights unbearably bright.

When I reached my cubicle, I grabbed the first box I saw from my trash can and threw in the few personal items from my desk: my phone charger, five romance novels, my mail. Carefully I placed in it the last photograph of my family before we lost Audrey. As I gathered my things, none of my cubicle neighbours dared to look at me. Out of the corner of my eye, I saw Pervy Percy lurking in the shadows. Gaze on me, stirring his cheap coffee. Willing myself not to cry in public, with all of six-foot-four Security Steve looming over me I set my jaw and held my head high. Voices fell to silence as I passed through the hallway carrying my cardboard box. The usual idle chatter and gossip now turned to keyboards clicking.

Standing in front of the silver elevator doors clutching the box to my chest, hot tears pooled in my eyes. A cough just behind me caught my attention and when I turned a single tear broke free. Pervy Percy stood there, watching the tear streak down my cheek. His eyes flicked back up to meet mine. Sympathy etched on his face. He reached out and my entire body went rigid as he enveloped me in his arms.

"My days won't be the same without you," he whispered in my ear.

With wide eyes, I searched for Security Steve, and mouthed "help!" A bear claw of a hand landed on Pervy Percy's shoulder. "That's kind of you, but I think that's enough."

Slowly the creepy accountant released me, gave me one last lingering nod and shuffled off down the hallway. A *ding* sounded, and the doors to the elevator opened. Steve gestured to let me walk in first. I leaned back against the metal wall and once the doors closed I let out a loud sigh.

After stewing in awkward silence for ten floors Steve said, "I know it sucks, and it's too soon to see, but this could be a blessing in disguise."

I snorted a wry laugh. "Right, I never have to deal with Pervy Percy again."

A smile carved his face. Two floors later, the doors opened, and we stepped into the lobby.

After removing my security pass, I held it up to him.

"Seriously, Harper," he said as the card disappeared in his grip, "this is the beginning of anything you want."

With a nod I didn't quite believe in, we exchanged farewells and I crossed the bank of security turnstiles. It was then that I thought it odd that the company had made such a big decision within hours of my presentation. Crossing the sprawling foyer on the ground floor, I played the last few months in my head. As I pushed open the doors leading to downtown

Toronto, the realization hit me: they had known for weeks that they were going to let me go. Instead of telling me in advance, they made me go through all of that stress, all of that work, and now they were going to use my ideas.

They used me.

Like a wild moose freed from a trap, I tore through the streets, the sub-zero wind chill licking my burning cheeks. I pulled out my cellphone and dialed Adam's number. If anyone could make me feel better it was him. He worked from home, so he should have picked up, but the call rang out. At Bloor and Spadina a face peered out from a shivering bundle of blankets next to the metro station entrance. An empty Starbucks cup sat in front of a sign that read, "Smile if you're horny."

In spite of my mood, a smirk tugged at my lips. I took a better look at the hapless comic. He was perhaps in his mid-forties, or maybe younger. There was a glint of youth in his eyes, but stories of a harsh life written in his skin.

Our eyes met.

"Hey, you're like the hottest girl I've seen all day."

My face flushed more and my smile widened. Even though I was having a bad day, at least I had a roof over my head. Stopping, I fumbled in my purse with my mitten-clad hands. I pulled out a five-dollar note and dropped it into the cup. He needed it more than I did, and this gal needed that compliment.

"Thanks, doll," he said with a nod.

I descended the staircase amongst the crowd of commuters. Over the din of echoing voices I swore I heard his voice again, "Hey, you're like the hottest girl I've seen all day."

I slumped in the cold plastic seat clutching the box containing my personal effects and fixated my gaze on a wad of gum on the floor. Anger bubbled in me as I thought of their reasoning of choosing Victoria over me. My boss didn't say that she had done a better job than me; it was that she had more experience. Which meant that I could never get ahead in this industry without more experience — exactly what I was being deprived of. And I was about to join the unemployment line with others like me, most of whom would be more qualified *and* more experienced.

I sighed and thought of my teenaged self, who constantly wished she was older, and looked forward to that miraculous time where she could call herself an adult. Times of independence and income, Sunday brunches and girls' trips, Manolo Blahniks and museum openings, just like the women of *Sex and the City*. And as I crossed the stage at my university graduation, diploma in hand, I took my next step into life, looking forward to my newfound autonomy. Only to realize that I felt no more of an adult than I did beforehand, and that TV and movies cut out all of the worst parts of being a grown-up: bills, taxes, corporate bottom-feeding, random body parts aching for no apparent reason.

I quickly realized that being an adult meant little more than making life up as you went along. Nobody ever tells you that no one has any idea what they're doing.

And on top of that, my generation entered the workforce in the worst economic time since the Great Depression. My mother always said that when she was my age she, as a woman, had three career options:

teacher, secretary, and nurse. I thought we had it better, as the Information Age brought an explosion of options, but the economic collapse of 2007, the year I entered the workforce, obliterated opportunity.

The car lurched, waking me from my angst-ridden contemplation. I glanced up, and all eyes were on me. Perhaps they saw me as another casualty of the Great Recession, sympathizing or worrying if it was going to be their turn next. Or perhaps it was because I was rocking violently, muttering aloud with the occasional expletive clutching a bulk sized tampon box to my chest while staring at a wad of gum on the ground. You would think people would be used to seeing that sort of thing on public transportation by now. Must be tourists.

An envelope poking out of my box scratched at my chin. I had found it wedged in my door that morning and didn't have the chance to read it. Resting the box in my lap, I pulled it out and tore it open.

Dear Tenant,

Please be advised that you have thirty days to sign your lease for the upcoming rental period. If you fail to sign or chose not to renew your lease, you will need to vacate the premises within thirty days.

Kind regards,

David Bryson,

Landlord

Great, more good news.

I winced at the thought of telling my parents of losing my job. They would insist that I move back in with them, but it made them so happy to see me stand on my own two feet. I also knew finding a new job was

13

going to be a long and depressing road, and the last thing I wanted was for them to worry about me more than they already did. After we lost Audrey, they seemed to be conditioned to fear that the same may happen to me.

Anxiety clutched at my throat, and instead of letting it control me, I acknowledged my feelings of losing control and centered myself with three deep breaths. After exhaling the third, I whispered what I was grateful for. "I am grateful for my family; I am grateful for the breath in my lungs; I am grateful for my friends; I am grateful for the chance to start each day anew, I am grateful for the love of my boyfriend."

Then it hit me. Maybe this letter didn't have to be a bad thing. Adam and I had been together for two wonderful years. I loved him beyond measure, and he loved me too. I wasn't sure of many things, but I knew that I wanted to spend the rest of my life with him. We had discussed the idea of moving in together a few times, though in passing, so maybe this letter was delivered to me to push us towards taking our relationship to the next level. Maybe it was a sign. It was fate. Kismet, if you will.

Flying out of the car at the next stop, I made my way to Adam's place.

Chapter 2

The terror of presenting that morning paled in comparison to asking him to move in together. Though the question was few in words, it was a big question with a big answer. He had to say yes.

I rapped on the door three times, and as I waited for him to answer, I feared I would faint from sheer nerves. At that moment I understood the horrors of boyhood having to ask a girl out to the prom. When Lana, my best friend, asked a guy to prom, she didn't seem nervous at all, but she had a chest so large it heaved, and there wasn't a single boy would say no to that. Hell, the same probably went for the male teachers too and, *oh God*, the door was opening…

"Hi, baby," Adam cooed, leaning in for a kiss.

He was average height and in my sensible heels, I stood three inches shorter than him. The perfect height for kissing. When his lips touched mine, I instantly felt grounded, and my nerves dissipated. No matter how bad a day I might have, his touch never failed to comfort me.

"I wasn't expecting you so early," he said as I stepped over the threshold. "I'm just in the middle of a *World of Warcraft* level. Can you give me a minute?"

"Okay, but have you taken your insulin today?"

"Not yet," he called back as he scuttled across the room to his computer in the corner.

I hated that answer.

Walking into the kitchen, I searched for a clean glass. I reached up into the cupboard and found no glasses but a sleeve of red solo cups. I pulled one out and sniffed it to see if it had been used. Thankfully it was clean. Tilting the cup between the faucet and pile of crusty dishes I filled it with water. After draining it my mind cleared, and a stench assaulted me. With burning nostrils, I looked around. Bottles and cans spilled out of the trash, old food grew new life on the counter, and I swore I saw the sponge move.

Adam *had* to want to get out of here, didn't he? He owned and ran a successful telemarketing business; how could he live and work in a place fit for a slobby college kid?

I shrugged off my coat as I crossed the living room and sank into the stained Ikea couch. After moving the stack of *Men's Health* magazines and three empty Cup Noodle soup containers, I set down my water and the pack of Oreos I had picked up for him. They were his favorite, but I decided to hang onto them until I saw him take his insulin. Glancing at the mop of ash brown hair bobbing wildly above the back of the shaking chair, I knew I was going to be on this couch for the long haul. The things you do for love.

We had met on my first day of group grief therapy. I'd been struggling to come to terms with Audrey's death, and he was fighting the demons that haunted him over his mother's suicide from five years earlier.

There were ten of us in the room including the counselor, but when I first saw him, it was like a little switch turned on. Like a little voice said that he was going to be really important to me. I ugly cried through the entire session and was all red and puffy when he introduced himself at the end of the session. We sat next to each other for the next sessions, and on session four, he asked me out to dinner. Even though I was twenty-three, no boy had ever taken me on a date before. I was pretty awkward looking through high school, riddled with insecurities, too focused on sports, and school and photography, and blossomed in the summer between senior year and university. Why I didn't date in university is a long story. Then when Audrey died in my final year, my depression stole my attention.

I lived believing I would never feel happy again.

On our date, Adam took me to an Italian restaurant in the Eaton Center, it was the dead of winter so we could get there with minimal time outdoors. During that evening with him, I smiled more and laughed harder than I had in a year, and I cared so deeply for him from that night. And as we grew closer, we broke away from the group sessions and supported each other as we fought grief and depression and found happiness and joy, falling in love along the way.

The front door swung opened, startling me. His housemate, Jeff, strolled in, snow dusting his puffy jacket. We exchanged greetings, and then he grabbed a *Maxim* magazine with Jessica Alba on the cover from the coffee table and disappeared into his room.

I grabbed the *Men's Health* magazine. Oh, hello Zac Efron. I think *I'll read this one*. For the articles. Only for the articles.

I smiled as I wondered why there were even *Men's Health* magazines in the apartment. His roommate ate Cup Noodles every meal (not exactly a health food fanatic), and Adam, rather than being a hard-bodied gym rat, was more of a soft around the edges Sunday stroll in the summertime kind of guy. Not that there was anything wrong with that, soft was perfect for cuddling. I wouldn't trade him in for the world.

By the time I learned how to get rock hard abs in seventeen days, power up my diet and speak her sex language, I heard the shuffling sounds of a level completed.

It was time.

"Sorry about that babe," he said walking over to me. "How did the presentation go?"

Rising to my feet, I wrapped my arms around him, buried my face in his chest, and he kissed the top of my head. As I inhaled the scent of his freshly laundered sweater vest I listened to the slow and steady beating of his heart. He ran his fingers through my hair, and I stifled a sob. "That bad, huh?"

"I lost my job today."

I nuzzled into his chest and he stroked my hair to soothe me. When I pulled myself together, I released myself from his grip.

"Baby, what happened?"

"They used me…." I then gave him a rundown of the day from my presentation to Security Steve taking my pass. "I finally felt like I had my place in the world.

Maybe it wasn't about the experience. Maybe I wasn't as good at my job as I thought."

He took me in his arms again. "No, baby, you are smart and capable, and your ideas were amazing. It's their loss."

I looked up into his brown eyes. "I'm grateful for you."

"I'm grateful for you," he said back.

I sank back onto the couch, and he joined me. I nestled into the nook under his arm and reached for the envelope from my box. "So, to make matters worse, I got this in the mail today."

He pulled out the letter from the ripped envelope and scanned it. His forehead scrunched, and he said, "At least you didn't lose your job after you resigned your lease."

And that was one of the reasons why I loved him; he was level headed and logical. "That's true."

"Have you spoken with your parents? They'll let you move back in, no questions asked."

"Well baby, I was thinking, what if we moved in together instead?"

His face froze like a pained gargoyle. It wasn't exactly the look of joy I was hoping for, but I know I did shock him.

Dammit, Adam, just say yes already.

After what seemed like an eternity he finally spoke, "I…I…I don't know. I need time to think."

"What do you mean you don't know?" I said, pushing myself to sit upright. "We're going to get married, have babies, do all of that stuff *we* talked about. I love you. I want to spend my life with you."

He wanted a future together, too. He said he did. Didn't he?

He stood and paced the room raking his hands through his hair, muttering and stumbling to get the words out while I sat there frozen with the realization of what he was possibly thinking. Finally, he stopped, looked me in the eyes and said the last words I expected him to say:

"I'm just not sure about us."

It was my turn to look, and feel, like a pained gargoyle.

"What do you mean you're not sure about us? How can you not be sure?"

How could we go from choosing baby names just a month ago, to him not being sure about us?

He pushed his glasses to the top of his head and pinched the space between his eyes. "I don't know."

It shouldn't be that difficult to decide — if you want something, you know. If he wanted this, he would have said yes. And that meant he didn't want us. He didn't want me.

"Don't you love me?"

"Of course I love you, but we're still so young. It's such a big step. Are we sure we're ready for this?"

Tears of anger pooled in my eyes. I was ready a year ago.

Then he said, "Are you sure this is it for us?"

Did he really just suggest the possibility that I wasn't The One?

I was angry and mortified. I had visions of our life together, and they were so real, so vivid. It was unthinkable that it wouldn't become a reality. I had been not only dreaming for our life together but preparing for it. I had even been setting money aside to buy a place together. For years I gushed to my parents and best friends about him, about us, and about his excitement for our future. We helped each other through the darkest periods in our lives. I shudder to think what would have happened if we didn't find one another. I knew he loved me, but now I realized just not enough. Our relationship had become comfortable, maybe too comfortable. Perhaps all of those talks we had about our future were to placate me, keep the peace, and stop life from changing. The talks were abstractions of the future, but when it was time to face it, it wasn't what he wanted.

I pressed my face in my hands. These past years with him were all a waste of time. I had to get out of there.

"I am sure," I said, rising to my feet and grabbing my coat, worried I might go ballistic and shove the kitchen sponge down his throat.

"Baby, stop, let's talk about this," he said, placing his hand on my waist.

I pushed his hand away. I didn't want him to touch me. I didn't want to look at him. I didn't want him to tell me that he didn't want to commit to me. I already knew.

"No. Let me rephrase that, I *was* sure this was it for me. I *was* sure about us. I *was* sure you were The One," I said, ramming my hands through the sleeves of my coat. "But I can't be with someone who doesn't feel the same way about me."

I loved him so much, and I hated that I did. Part of me wanted to stay and talk. Maybe try and change his mind. But my self-respect wouldn't let me.

Instead, I snatched the Oreos from the coffee table, and stormed from his apartment.

***

With eyes that stung from crying myself to sleep, I trundled off my bed and sat at my stub of a desk. I'm always curious how people's minds work when they encounter a crisis. Everyone is different, and my mind forces me into strategy mode. I always needed a needed next move. Regardless of what happens, life goes on and you don't want to be dragged along face down in the mud wondering, where am I going? Why is my face muddy?

I clung to my five-year plan even though it was slipping from my grasp. There was not much I could do about the marriage and babies side of things. I was either too much in denial, or numb from shock, to be able to process what happened with Adam yesterday. As I felt tears resurfacing, I decided to keep my mind busy by beginning my job search. Pressing a button, my laptop blinked to life. I rifled through the job boards on Craigslist, Workopolis, Monster and whatever Google fetched for me. But after three hours, my patience had been exhausted. I read job description after job description, but nothing spoke to me. Nothing screamed: Harper Rodrigues, come on down! This is your life!

Regardless, once I began applying I would need to stand out from the CV slush pile. Leaving the browser open in the background I pulled up the Word document for the first time in years. The only change I needed to make was the end date of my latest job. The blank spaces glared at me demanding words, demanding experiences. I searched my memory hoping that there was something I could add, something to spice up my boiled chicken breast of a resume. I let my mind drift, and my fingers typed a pinch of paprika on the page: dive master in the Maldives. Then a dash of dill: former acrobat in Cirque Du Soleil, and finally a sprinkling of saffron: retired panda handler. I stifled a laugh and deleted the words. Without thinking, I replaced them with "photographer."

I sighed and closed the document without saving.

Standing and stretching I wandered through the room hoping a plan would coalesce. I only had to take twelve steps before reaching the door, having to turn back again. Though small, I made my studio apartment my sanctuary, my escape from the Canadian winters.

Decorated in a minimalistic tropical-tiki-chic kind of way, I employed all of the colours of the spectrum except greys, browns, and black. Posters of paradisiac land and seascapes I had bought in U of T's poster sales hung on the walls, shells in glass vases adorned the counters, and deep pink fabric flowers were scattered across all surfaces. I rolled a silky petal in my fingertips before grabbing a pack of matches and lighting the 'Caribbean Breeze' Yankee Candle on my desk. As the scent that made me think of Piña Coladas and beachside romances wafted into the air, a flashing orange square on my computer screen caught my attention:

Amateur Travel Photography Competition!
$10,000 in Prizes!

I clicked through to the website. It was one of Madcap Travel's competitors, Awesome Adventures, a smaller company also based out of Toronto, geared towards the Canadian market. It was part of the inspiration for my campaign vision, but I hadn't paid it much attention as their Facebook page had less than a couple thousand likes and barely any activity. Scrolling down, I read the contest information:

Rules:

- Only amateur photographers are eligible;

- Photographers must be Canadian citizens and/or residents;

- Photographs must be taken outside of Canada within a year of the closing deadline and never previously published;

- Photographers are to submit no more than three separate entries.

Prizes

- Grand prize: $7,000, a feature on our website and the opportunity to join our content creation team;

- Three runner-up prizes of $1,000 each.

Pretty straightforward.

I clicked the link to see the past winners. Nothing particularly extraordinary, but they did show a high level of technicality for amateurs. A Google search of the past winner returned with his official website, articles about his win and subsequent accomplishments as he made the jump from amateur to professional. All hailed him as the one to watch in the travel photography world.

He was living my dream.

Photography had been my dream ever since my grandparents gave me my very first camera when I was ten. It was no Hasselblad, but I loved it nonetheless. Shortly after I received my camera, I discovered legendary travel photographer, and my idol, Steve McCurry. More specifically, I discovered his famous photograph, "Afghan Girl" from an old stack of my father's National Geographic magazines. Audrey possessed similar striking hazel eyes and olive skin, so I wanted to recreate the image. She sat patiently as I shrouded her in red fabric and took my time lining up each shot. With Audrey as my muse and cheerleader, I amassed shoeboxes full of images over the years as I searched for my artistic voice.

When I was in high school, I begged my father to let me go to art school, but he considered himself "pragmatic" (I called him "old school") and refused to pay for it. Being the child of immigrants from Brazil, he believed in the Canadian dream of getting a practical degree and a stable government job. I had the choice to run myself into debt and go to art school, or take my father's offer to pay for a business degree. I chose the latter and took photography classes at the student center, dreaming of going pro and traveling the world when I graduated. But Audrey's death in the middle of my final year changed everything. My parents needed me here, and I needed them to be happy. I ended up staying in Toronto, burying my idealistic fantasies, and living a more stable, and sensible life accepting that not all dreams can come true. And so, my artistic voice fell silent.

I squeezed my eyes shut and tried to still my thoughts. After a minute I opened them and saw my Digital SLR-Hybrid camera glaring at me from its perch on a stack of books and papers behind my computer. Audrey had given it to me on my twenty-first birthday. The last birthday I spent with her. I reached out and cradled it in my hands, letting my fingers skate over the cool plastic, clearing off the film of dust that had collected in its curves and grooves. I pressed the power button, but it remained in its slumber.

My mind wandered to fantasies of traipsing across Asia, camera in hand, lazing on untouched beaches, exploring ancient ruins and tasting exotic foods with my two best friends.

In that moment, my heart broke for the third time in two days.

They were leaving me. Jade was already in India, and once Lana leaves next week to join her, I'd be alone.

My eyes heated as I wished I could talk to the one person who could help. I plucked my cell phone from my bag and searched for her number. A rogue tear made its way down my face as my thumb hovered over the call button.

"I need you," I whispered.

Its sudden vibrating shot a feverish fluttering through me.

Audrey?

My pulse pounded in my ears, and I lowered myself to the bed, letting my eyes drop to the screen. It was a text from Lana alerting me that she would be knocking my door down in an hour with a male stripper to cheer me up. I exhaled the breath I didn't realize I had been holding and stood to shake the tingling. I was going insane. I needed to get away, and there was one way I could get a vacation that afternoon.

Crouching down, I reached under my bed. Stashed in a shoebox hid my collection of trashy romance novels. I was a world of zippy one-liners, adventure, and toe-curling romance with hot men who were sure about their women. A small but dirty, dirty smile spread across my face as I pulled out my favorite, *Tahitian Heat*. Snuggling into bed, I kicked out the jitters, opened the cover and escaped.

Five chapters later, a violent knocking on my door startled me, bringing me back to Canada from my fantasies in the South Pacific.

Chapter 3

"When life hands you lemons," Lana said as she pulled a bottle from her handbag. "Get Tequila."

Plunking the Jose Cuervo on the counter, she pulled me in for a hug. Her strawberry blond hair swept across my face, and I inhaled the apricot and sandalwood notes of her Victoria's Secret *Sexual Star* perfume. She had always dreamed of becoming an Angel and though she had the looks and the body she was a thumb-width too short. But when a television producer scouted her during our freshman year of university, she dropped out of school and became "Canada's Favourite Weathergirl", who more recently became "Canada's Most Notorious Weathergirl" when she was discovered in flagrante with the news anchor. By his wife. It should have been her fall from grace but infamy brought some very lucrative opportunities.

"It's two in the afternoon," I said, releasing her.

"Oh, honey, you're hurting. You need to drink 'till you can't feel feelings," she said, producing wine from her purse like Mary Poppin' Bottles. "Red or White."

I paused and let her words roll around in my mind. I would like to not feel feelings. "White," I replied. It was more appropriate for the hour. "And where is my male stripper?"

"Sadly, the guys they could offer short notice weren't hot enough," she said pouring the wine. "I only want the best for you, honey."

I didn't know what I'd do if I didn't have her.

"Oh, so how was the other night by the way?" I asked before the attention could turn to my worries. I had accompanied her to a happy hour before going to "date night" with Adam that consisted of our favorite Italian takeout, and a movie from his Adam Sandler collection. I didn't ask for much from our date nights, and it was a perfect way to spend a cold winter's evening. "Get lucky?"

"Yah, that guy, Neil." A cheeky smile spread her across her face as she handed me the glass. With a wistful look, she said, "He performed admirably."

"His name was Nick," I said, taking the glass from her hand.

"Seriously?"

I nodded.

She paused as a memory seemed to hit her. "Oh... That's why he told me to call him that."

"Why did you think he wanted you to call him by another name?"

"I thought he was just trying to be kinky." As her eyes widened she covered her gaping mouth with her freshly manicured hand. "That explains so much." Then, with a shrug, she continued with life. "So what the hell, you and Adam broke up?"

With glasses of Sauvignon Blanc in hand we moved to the bed. As I tore open the pack of Oreos I began my dramatic retelling of when I popped the question. She cringed, pouted and got angry at all the right moments as we worked our way through bottle number one.

"And then he said," I spilled my wine as I raised my hands to make air-quotes, "I'm just not sure about us."

"Noooo!" she cried, recoiling. "What an ass!"

"Yah. *He* wasn't sure about *me*." I repeated those words over and over, each time with more indignation. And volume. "After investing two years of my life on him. That's nearly ten percent of my life!"

She dumped the remainder of the Sauv Blanc into each glass, filling them to the brim. "Tell me you punched him in the bifocals."

"Hah, no. I had to get out of there. So I told him that I gave him the best years of my life and slapped him across the face."

"You didn't!"

"Of course I didn't, I'm not a soap opera character. I told him I couldn't be with someone who wasn't sure about me. And then I took the Oreos and left."

"Good call," she said, holding one up and devouring it. "Did he try and stop you?"

"No, he just stood there gaping. I should have shoved the Oreo package down his throat, but I think he may have liked that."

Lana paused as we both mused over my words. After a minute of silence, she said, "This is a good thing."

I quirked an eyebrow at her, "I fail to see the positives."

"Seriously, it was time to shit or get off the pot. Or else you'd just be sitting on the toilet with life passing you by." I stared at her. She had such a unique way with words. "So let's pull your pants up and find you a new man."

The depressing thought of joining the singles scene hit me. I had to start over, go on awkward dates and struggle to make small talk, put myself there and invest in someone new for the potential of heartbreak. *Ugh.* But the worst part was, "No new men, I still love Adam."

It was time for bottle number two. I could still feel feelings.

"Oh my God," she shrieked as she sat back down with the bottle of red. "This means you can come traveling with us."

"No, I can't," I said as tears began to prick my eyes. I willed myself not to be the emotional drunk at the party. No one likes her.

"Yes, you can. You have money saved. You just got a severance package."

The girls had kept me CC'ed in on all of their emails about the trip. I had been putting money aside for years to make the grown-up move of buying property. According to their budget, with my severance package and savings, I had enough to cover the trip.

"It's not the money." I wiped a tear that had escaped. "I just... Audrey died while traveling. I... my parents... I just can't. I can't come."

"What happened to her won't happen to you." She rubbed my knee. "Honey, you of all people deserve some fun in your life.

"I can travel when I retire," I said with a sigh.

She slapped my knee. "Repeat after me: I deserve fun."

I stared at her, and she threatened to slap me again if I didn't do what she said. She was the dominant one in her relationships and what the whips and nipple clamps to prove it.

"Alright, alright," I said, "I deserve fun."

"Louder!" she screamed.

I said it again.

"With meaning this time!" She grabbed my hand and pulled me to stand. Jumping on the bed we yelled the words over and over, spilling wine and laughing with reckless abandon. And when we collapsed in a giggle fit, I finally felt it: didn't we all deserve a little fun in our lives?

She reached for my laptop, pulled it to the bed, and opened the travel agency website. After entering the booking code she set it back on the desk, "For when you change your mind."

As the day rolled on we polished off the bottle of red and then went shot for shot finishing the tequila. No lemons needed. Takeout was ordered, and Lana tried to get the deliveryman to strip for us nearly landing us on a sexual offenders list. But when I told the police officer and restaurant manager my sob story of losing my job and the love of my life in the same day we were only banned from ever ordering from there again.

And that was when my memory became a little patchy…

***

A wise man once said, "Drinking today is stealing happiness from tomorrow," and I was the Prince of Thieves last night. In my hangover haze, I grabbed my phone and stumbled to the bathroom. Squinting as light sliced through my brain, I looked to see if I had any messages from Adam.

Not a single word.

However, there was an unread email. When I opened it my knees buckled. I steadied myself against the sink as I registered the words.

I had booked the plane ticket. I had booked an around the world plane ticket. I had never left the continent of North America before, and I was booked on a plane to India. In seven days, I'm supposed to board a plane bound for Mumbai. After India, we'll go to Thailand, Laos, Vietnam, Cambodia, Australia, New Zealand, and then nearly five months later I'm supposed to leave Fiji, our last port of call, and return home.

Bile surged. It was serious about looking for an exit this time. I collapsed next to the toilet bowl and proceeded to relive the day's drinking in reverse. It was much less fun.

After splashing cold water on my face, I checked my email history for any further horrors. It turned out I had sent a barely coherent email to my landlord telling him that I was a soon-to-be sex offender who had to flee the country and therefore couldn't renew my lease. Also, the apartment smelled of a man who wasn't sure about me and should be burned to the ground.

I crawled back under my red wine stained duvet hoping it was all a dream.

I wasn't.

I threw the sheets from me.

Plan. I needed a plan.

"Okay, breathe breathe breathe," I said to myself as I grabbed a notebook from my bedside table and started my to do list:

1.   Stop freaking out.

2.   Talk to parents.

My fingers stopped. How was I supposed to tell my parents?

Think.

It was all about selling it to them. Hell, I worked in marketing. I could do this. Most importantly, they needed to know that I wouldn't be alone; I will give them a copy of my itinerary and keep them abreast of any changes, and I will check in with them as often as I can, preferably every day.

Then I needed them to see it from my perspective. What was the point of staying here? It was a tough job market, and this would look great on my C.V. if the whole travel photographer thing didn't work out. I already had a plan and a vision for what I would do if I were a content creator for Madcap Travels, why couldn't I do it on my own? I was taking a calculated risk investing my life savings into this, but I didn't have a mortgage or children, so it was the best time for me to do this.

But then they'll say, "Look at what happened to your sister."

And I'll tell them that she got unlucky. Terribly, terribly unlucky. But she spent so much of her short adult life in an office dreaming of more, dreaming of seeing the world. Yes her life ended with a random, senseless act, and yes it happened when she too left the continent for the first time, but I don't want to be held captive by my fear anymore. I could stay here and live a "safe life" and be struck down in the road tomorrow, having never truly lived. And Audrey, despite what happened to her, would want me to go.

I paused as my vision narrowed in on the last sentence.

Slumping at my desk, I reached out for my favorite photograph. It never failed to center me. My breathing slowed as I studied the image as I had done a million times before. Two teenaged girls separated in age by half a decade sitting on an ATV, spackled in dust, smiles as wide as the desert behind them.

I sighed and asked her, "Audrey, what should I do?"

A feeling of warmth washed over me, and something inside me, perhaps it was my subconscious, that part of me that yearned to be true to myself, that part of me that craved to resurrect the dreams I had abandoned years ago, told me I was making the right choice.

I knew I was taking a big gamble, and the odds were against me as I started a long road towards a new goal, but I thought, why not me? Why couldn't I live my dreams?

In that moment, I knew in my heart that I wanted to do this for myself. And I hoped I could get my parents support.

Checking of bullet point number one, however, would take all week.

And then I allowed myself to get really, really excited.

***

After a shower, a litre of water and two painkillers I stood in my apartment, ready to pack up my life. Scanning my room trying to figure out where to begin was a sobering feeling. My eyes stopped at a tan-colored U of T sweatshirt. Not mine. My legs began to tingle and heat spread through me like wildfire. Then I decided that I would start with all of his shit. I needed it all out of my life as soon as possible.

I ransacked the place, grabbing whatever I could find that belonged to him, along with everything that he had ever given me, and threw it all into a plastic shopping bag. The birthday cards written in barely legible handwriting, the t-shirts that reeked of him, the stupid *Girlfriend's Guide to the World of Warcraft* book, the jewelry…

Maybe keep the jewelry.

I snatched the teddy bear he had given me on our first anniversary and as I looked into its black button eyes memories of our first date at the Italian place, our first kiss a week later after taking me to see a Maple Leaf's game, our first fight that started over the difference between ice cream and frozen yogurt, our first time making up after a fight, and the first time he said, "I love you." It was my first non-family "I love you." He had taken me to a U of T photography exhibit, and when I pointed out the photograph I loved the most, he told me that he loved me the most.

It dripped with cheese, but it was everything I could ever hope for.

The soft knocking on my door brought me back to reality. I placed the bear down on my bed.

I opened it, and standing in the hallway was the love of my life with puffy red-rimmed eyes that matched mine.

"Can we talk?" His voice crackled.

I kept my poker face firm. I wanted to slam the door, but it was only right that we got closure. I said nothing and gestured for him to come in.

As he leaned against the kitchen counter, I walked to my bed, grabbed the bag of his belongings, and marched back, handing it to him before he could say a word.

"You're breaking up with me?" Shock flashed in his face.

For someone so smart, he could really be dumb. "We broke up, remember?"

"No, I remember having a discussion and you stormed out."

"You told me you weren't sure about us."

"Let me explain."

"I'm leaving Canada," I cut him off. I didn't care for an explanation as to how he thought I wasn't enough for him.

"What?! When?!"

"Next week," I said, in a tone that could chill a polar bear.

"You...you can't leave." He took a step towards me.

I took one back. "I can, and I am. Maybe I'll find someone who is sure about me."

He froze and his beautiful mouth hung open. I knew my last sentence hit below the belt, but my pride was wounded. And I was hung-over. Bad combination. I remained still and held out the bag, waiting for him to take it and walk out of my life.

Raking his hands through his hair, he gave that look when he was searching for words. When he found them, he said, "I came to tell you that I was an idiot. I don't know what I was thinking. I was scared, but I *am* sure about you. I can't lose you. I need you. You are The One."

The tears I had been holding back broke loose. Why couldn't he have said this a day ago? A single day ago. Everything would have been different.

I wanted to scream, to hug him, to slap him to cuddle in bed, to throw the empty tequila bottle at him, to kiss him but most of all, I wanted to go back in time and undo everything.

And then he did the one thing I had dreamed about since I was a little girl. The thing I had been dreaming about him doing since our first date.

On the linoleum tile of my kitchen, amongst the fallout of my breakup party, he lowered to one knee and asked me to marry him.

Chapter 4

I spent the next seven days setting up my blog and convincing Adam that we could make the relationship work long distance. We had overcome so much together over the years, what were a few months apart in the grand scheme of things? He respected my desires to chase my dreams, and I loved him even more for his support, but I knew it was going to be tough. Even before leaving I missed him terribly. My parents, however, were not entirely convinced of my plans but knew that they couldn't stop me. I bid a tearful farewell to them the day before leaving, promising to check in with them as often as I could. As snow fell on the 15th day of the New Year, Adam drove Lana and me to the airport.

"When you come home, we'll get you the best ring money can buy," Adam said as we held up the security line.

"I don't care about the ring. I just want you."

He wrapped his arms around me, and as I bit back the tears and also the desire to stay with him.

"I'm grateful for you," I said looking up at him.

"I'm grateful for you."

As I followed the line of travelers past the frosted glass doors to the security check Adam remained in the crowd, waving until I walked through the X-Ray machine. Once on the other side we heard the boarding announcement for our flight to Mumbai via London. I waved to him for the last time, and the fear crept in that I had just made the biggest mistake of my life.

***

Date: January 23, 2010
Goa, India

After a morning of sleeping in, I waited outside of our beachside hut with my camera in my hand, waiting for Lana to fix her makeup, and reflected on our past week in India. After a flight to, and short layover in, London, we made it to our flight to Mumbai within minutes of the gate closing. Exotic and intense, the city was home to Bollywood and beggars, colonial architecture and congested traffic, street art, stray dogs, and staring men who had rarely seen leggy pale skinned women with strawberry-blond hair. Yes, despite my protests Lana insisted on wearing short shorts out and about. My parents had given us a send-off gift of two nights in a five-star hotel, mainly for their peace of mind, and I was grateful for the security. The hotel's high-speed Wi-Fi meant easy communication with Adam. During our evening downtime, I spent hours on Skype with him, just letting the chat idol as I organized my belongings and he played his video games, just as if we were hanging out at his place.

After our whirlwind two days in Mumbai, Lana and I boarded a bus southbound for Goa and spent four days beach hopping from such whimsically named beaches as Arambol, Baga and Anjuna. The guest houses and beachside huts we stayed in were a far cry from the opulent hotel of Mumbai, but Adam and I worked around the absence of high speed Wi-Fi with scheduled times at Internet cafés. He was being sweet and supportive, and I appreciated him immensely for that.

Even though we had only been there one night, Palolem, our final beach was our favorite. Shielded by forested mountains and nestled behind a sprawling grove of swaying coconut palms lay a crescent of toffee-coloured sand that stretched from the grove into the loden green sea. The sands ran a mile in length with rocky cliffs capping each end. Unlike many of the other beaches, there was barely any development, and only small colonies of wooden shacks lined the threshold of grove and beach.

It was such a devastatingly romantic place, and I dreamed to return one day with Adam.

A rustling in the bushes behind me startled me. I turned towards the coconut grove and spotted a greyish-brown monkey sitting on a fallen tree trunk. Taking slow and careful steps, I approached him, keeping my eyes on the ground but his blurry image in my periphery. Once I was about five feet away, I crouched down and raised my camera. I centered his amber-coloured eyes in the viewfinder, and the instant I pressed the shutter release, he vanished. I checked the playback, and only a brown blur flashed across the emerald leaves.

"Come on! She'll be arriving any moment," Lana called, securing the padlock on the door to our hut.

I turned and padded across the sand towards her. "I'll get you, monkey, one of these days," I said, turning and shaking my fist in his general direction.

Navigating the stretch through the languid beach community of oiled-up sunbathers frying like bacon, peddlers hawking brightly coloured sarongs, and stray dogs managing their turf, we stepped off the sand and into the single road that led into the village.

I had yet to explore the market stalls that lined the road, but when we arrived the previous afternoon, I could see it only as a dizzying blur of colours from the taxi window. Ignoring the calls of, "good price," "come look," and, "looking is free," Lana bought a sizzling beef skewer from a street vendor. Exchanging my rupees for a fresh bottle of water, I pressed it against my chest to sooth my heated skin while trailing behind her. At the road's dead-end, we found an empty bench.

"I can't believe Jade's been holed up in some ashram for like a month," Lana said before blowing on her steaming skewer.

We plopped onto the bench. "I know. What a way to kick off her grand spirit quest."

Flicking through the images on my camera, it struck me how good it felt to be shooting again. As I inhaled the salty breeze peppered with exotic spices, I felt for a fleeting moment at peace with life. Though it wasn't a perfect situation, with a little compromise and humour, I could make my newly edited five-year plan work. While I had my sights set on winning the Awesome Adventures competition, I decided to execute the vision I had presented to Madcap Travels using my Flickr account, and once I had enough images I would build my blog and start my Facebook fan page. You never know who may stumble across them. If I didn't win, I held out hope that magazines and websites would contract my services and work thus getting my creative career back on track, and marrying Adam when I was in a position to hop from Canada to shoot on location. If my plan worked out, I could have it all, and make everyone — Adam, my parents, and me — happy.

"Ohmygodsheshere!" Lana screamed. I yelped in surprise and watched her shoot down the road.

Out of a yellow and green tuk tuk, the three-wheeled motorized vehicle of choice in these parts, flopped a mass of jet-black curls. Jade. I caught up as she hoisted her backpack on. Cerulean parachute pants that complimented her dusky skin billowed in the wind.

"Nice hippy pants," Lana said pulling her into a hug.

"They are *not* hippy pants. They're harem pants and, they're fashionable," Jade replied.

Jade's parents were bona-fide ganja smoking, granola munching, Birkenstock wearing, reggae-loving hippies who had moved from Jamaica to Canada for university, got married and started a very lucrative marijuana farm and cooperative with friends. She practically grew up on a commune but refuses to acknowledge her hippy ancestry.

I threw my arms around her. "I'm so happy to see you. I've been so worried about you."

"I've missed you, too." She smiled and pulled out a self-rolled cigarette. Lighting it up, she said, "I hear we have a lot to talk about."

I nodded.

Lana shoved the skewer in her face. "Wanna bite?"

"No thanks, meat's really bad for you." Jade took another drag as Lana and I exchanged looks, and then she said, "Alright, where are we living?"

As we walked, Jade told us about her weeks in the ashram, meditating, chanting, singing, stretching, and searching for spiritual enlightenment.

"It was purely for research and inspiration for my yogawear collection," she said as we arrived at the little huts we had rented. After a stint as a falafel chef, an organic soap maker, and a very brief and misguided foray into midwifery, fashion design was her latest obsession on her quest to find her life's purpose. My father always said she had Peter Pan Syndrome, but I admired her for refusing to sell out to the corporate world.

Fittingly, our huts reminded me of the house that the lost boys had made for Wendy in *Peter Pan*. Made from plywood and spanning ten by ten feet they were furnished with nothing but a bed and bedside table. Propped up on stilts they had prime waterfront views, and it was all we needed.

"So two huts, three girls. Rock paper scissors?" Jade said.

"But," Lana raised her hand, "if someone, like for example, me, gets lucky, which is what I'm planning on, they get the single hut for the night."

"Okay," Jade said, radiating tranquility, "you take the hut. Harper is taken, and I took a vow of celibacy."

Lana looked at Jade as if she'd grown a second head. "Wha...Why... Wha...But..." she stammered. "For how long?"

"Until the Universe gives me a sign."

Lana was speechless. It was a rare occurrence. I rolled my eyes at Jade's talk of some Great Universal Creator controlling us like some grand puppet-master. I had long stopped believing in such divine tall tales, and knew that Jade was celibate because she threw that wall up after her last boyfriend, an asshat named Cliff, cheated on her and broke her heart.

So it was decided that Jade and I would be roomies. I was glad for the extra time for us to catch up. As she unpacked and feng-shuied the room I filled her in on what happened with my job and Adam. She didn't seem too enthused that I gave him a second chance, and Lana was still mad that I didn't have a ring, but I had to accept that not everyone is going to understand your choices, so you just have to do what feels right for yourself. And Adam felt right to me.

Finding a perfect spot near three sleeping cows, we set our sarongs down on the warm sand and discussed and decided on the travel plans: we will stay in Palolem for two more days then fly to Delhi and spend more time exploring the north.

We then turned our attention back to the vacation at the beginning of the vacation. Lana was spread flat out, greased up, and dreaming of a tan that would make people question her ethnicity, while Jade sat in lotus position in the shade of an oversized hat, eyes firmly shut. I envied their abilities to keep still. The thoughts in my mind swarmed like bees. Since leaving home I fought the feelings of guilt about leaving Adam behind, and the way my parents sobbed through our farewell dinner the night before I left still haunted me. And yes, I was scared of the possibility that I, too, wouldn't make it home like Audrey, but I couldn't live fearing that something bad was going to happen to me. The competition was the queen bee of my worries. If I could nail this, it would make everything I was putting them through worth it.

So there was no time for tanning.

"I'm going for a walk." Though I was already halfway through an eight-gigabyte memory card, I still needed more images. "If I'm not back in thirty, send a search party."

Jade didn't move, and Lana gave me a thumbs up.

I pushed myself to my feet, dusted the sand from my legs and wandered off, stomach tied in knots, running reassuring affirmations in my mind: *It's during the day, and you're not going off into any dark alleys. The girls are near, and there are plenty of people around. There is no danger. I repeat, there is no danger.*

As I calmed myself down, I raised my camera, pretended to be Steve McCurry on location, and lost myself in my art. The scenery was a feast for my lens, and I was a glutton, consuming landscapes and seascapes capturing the beach in its entirety down to macro shots of the details of the sand and seashells, portraits of beach vendors from wild haired children hawking jewelry to women dripping in golden jewelry wearing saris dyed every colour of the rainbow.

Ever since arriving in India I felt like Dorothy who had just landed in Oz. I had left behind the mute monochromatic hues of the Canadian winter for the Technicolour explosion of the tropics. Everywhere I looked it seemed as if the saturation levels had been cranked up. Everything — the saris, the food, the trees, the sky, the sea — dripped with each and every hue of the spectrum. I saw shades of colours I never knew existed.

As thunder rumbled in the distance, I reached the edge of the beach and stepped into a path in the coconut grove. A warm breeze caressed my skin, and an odd feeling washed over me. Perhaps it was the nerves playing tricks, but I felt a pair of eyes on me. I patted my pocket to make sure my mace was there. If anyone tried to mess with me, they'd be in for an eye-burning shock. I slunk down the path scanning the area for friend and foe. Ahead of me was a sea of slender tree trunks, and the occasional one-story wooden house, many advertising yoga classes and massage therapy. I heard a rustle and whipped around. It was then I met eyes with my voyeur.

You fuzzy little bastard. I knew I'd find you again.

I raised my camera and burst the shutter button, but with the first click, he scampered down the path. Hot on his hairy heels I chased after him delirious with heat and visions of National Geographic worthy wildlife shots. But before I could reach him, he darted up a tree. I stood there cursing as he disappeared into the canopy.

I looked down at my camera to see if I had any usable shots, and beyond the screen a piece of paper lay in the sand.

I leaned forward and picked it up, and read verses of poetry. The black words and stanzas were scribbled over, bleeding with red ink. A fluttering blur in the corner of my eye took my attention. Turning, I saw a trail of papers. I snapped three pictures and then picked up each page and scanned them. Heady images of lust, affection, carnal sensations, and human anatomy that would make a porn-star blush frolicked across the pages.

The trail of unwanted words led me onto the porch of the nearest house. Soaking in a small puddle of an aromatic tea flowing from a toppled cup, I found more papers, each scrawled more erratically than the last.

"Looking for something?" a deep voice rumbled behind me.

I whipped around. Heart in throat. Hand on mace.

Now, in an ideal world once I realized I wasn't in any danger, I would retort, "Aren't we all?" But when I met eyes with the owner of that voice, my words abandoned me.

Dark slashes over storm grey eyes knitted in my direction. Those intense eyes were framed by a dripping wet cascade of inky locks that stopped at the square of his stubble jaw.

"I…uh…" I stammered as my eyes drifted south. His tall, taut body spoke of athleticism, neither gym-rat nor couch potato: the perfect balance. A strange curling unfurled in my stomach as I followed the path of a long tattoo of scribbled words down his sun-kissed torso until it disappeared under the towel that was hanging dangerously low from his hips. Heat burst in my cheeks, and I managed to mumble, "....uhhh... I was following a monkey."

Real smooth, Harper.

I snapped my gaze up to find his furrowed brown had been devoured by a wolfish grin. As he strode towards me, I noticed two more tattoos etched on his arms, music notes and sprawling stanzas, but I was unable to make any of it out. I wondered if he had any more, and where they were.

Forcing my eyes back up heat spread from the depths of my stomach to the tips of my fingers and toes. As my vision clouded my mouth felt as if I had swallowed sand and then I realized... Oh, God...

I was having heat stroke.

I froze in place as he stopped in front of me, close enough for me to smell the soap that lingered on his glowing skin. Already off balance from my sun-induced affliction, I craned my neck to look him in the eye hoping I stayed erect.

I mean upright.

He extended his long, slender fingers, and I simply stared at them. Hoping I could figure out what he wanted me to do with his hand I dragged my gaze up past the trail of dark hair leading from the towel to his broad chest and stared into the storm. He leaned in and my lips parted, tasting the spicy chai masala tea on his breath.

I felt something gently pulled from my grip and then the space between our lips grew.

The papers. His papers. He wanted them back. *Of course,* I realized with a mental face-palm.

Pull yourself together!

I shook my head, and some semblance of sense returned to me. "Sorry, I... uh... the heat. Heat stroke."

His smile softened, and he dropped the stack of papers on the table with the others.

"No one was supposed to read these."

Sweet Benedict Cumberbatch, he has an English accent.

"Sorry," I said fidgeting with my camera.

"It's okay. They're going to be burned anyways."

"You're going to destroy them?" I asked finally finding my voice. "What you wrote was..." the words sublime, sensuous, transcendental and spine-tingling came to mind, but I settled on, "beautiful."

"Thank you." His eyes raked down my body, and once he reached my freshly polished toes, he flicked them back up. "Tell me something, have you ever been in love?"

"Love?" *Tell him you're engaged and therefore madly in love. Dammit, a ring would really help right now.* I set my jaw and said, "Yes."

He took a step forward that threw me off balance. "Mad and passionate and all-consuming?"

I thought of my love for Adam.

"All love is different," I replied. The kind of love he spoke of was the stuff of novels and movies.

"So, no then."

There was something about his tone I found condescending. As if the love Adam and I shared was somehow inferior because we didn't have that fictitious type of passion. We had been through more together than any couple should. Our love was deep, built on mutual understanding and respect, but it was love all the same. Then I realized what he was doing.

"Are you hitting on me?"

"No." *No?!* His jaw pulsed before asking, "Do you want me to?"

Of course, I didn't. I was engaged and in love with a respectable soft-bodied non-tattooed, safe and dependable small business owner. Why would I want to be hit on by a dangerously handsome guy who writes of erotic love in such a hedonistic toe-curling manner who probably rotates women on a nightly basis?

Where is a bucket of ice water when you need one?

"I have to go." I darted past him, clutching my camera to my chest and headed in the direction of the beach. It took all of my strength not to turn back for one last look.

Chapter 5

I found the girls exactly where I had left them. Lana had turned over on her back, and Jade had moved into pigeon pose, pencil in hand, and sketchbook pages fluttering in the breeze next to her. I flopped down to the sarong and chugged an entire bottle of water in one go.

"What happened to you?" Lana asked peering out of one eye.

"Nothing. He's just hot." *Shit.* "I'm hot. It's hot."

Jade raised the brim of her hat and an eyebrow. "The energy about you is different."

"Yes, it's called heat." I waved my hand dismissing her words. "You're imagining things."

Her raised eyebrow remained firmly in place. I didn't need her judgment. I was not thinking of that gorgeous…but totally and utterly inappropriate wanton wordsmith. I was delirious from dehydration. We Canadians weren't used to the heat that comes with being so close to the equator. Luckily, I saw a vendor with a basket of fruit balancing on his head padding through the surf towards us. With flailing arms, I flagged him down and bought a coconut while Lana handed over her rupees for a freshly cut pineapple. As I sipped the crisp liquid, I felt my temperature and heart rate begin to return to normal. Pulling my shades over my eyes and feeling more centered, I fished out my book from my bag and lay back on my sarong. I opened it up to the dog-eared page and tried to distract myself...

Tending to her bruised wrists from where he re-strained her with vines during their passionate lovemaking from the night before, she blushed thinking how loud she had screamed only to remember there was no one to hear her except the stars.

She admired his muscular body as he rose from the sea. His spear stacked with fish. His glistening olive skin had turned a delectable shade of burnished caramel. Shaking the excess water from his jet-black hair, he walked toward his love laying naked in the shade of a palm tree. He stuck the spear in the sand before kneeling beside her, a savage look in his eye. Throbbing with desire she took his strong hands and placed them on her —

I slapped the book shut and sat up. It was only making my symptoms worse. Before the girls could notice my heaving breath, I announced, "I'm going in for a dip."

Face first I submerged myself in the cool green water. When I surfaced, I felt relief from the heat, but something within me still buzzed. Turning to face the beach, my eyes drifted towards the grove of the coconut trees raking the flickering leaden clouds. My memory was stuck on playback mode, and I didn't know how to shut it off. As I pushed out each thought of where that tattoo led, another took its place. What did the inked words say? As the images played, the curious curling in my stomach spread south.

What was happening to me?

Maybe it was that meat stick from earlier. *Skewer. I mean meat skewer.* I should have known better than to trust street food.

Then I remembered Jade had said to always focus on what you want, not what you don't want, so I thought of Adam.

You love Adam.

I loved Adam. Adam was sexy. I mean not in a traditional way. But who needs that kind of sexy? That Zac Efron cover of *Men's Health* sexy was so overrated. It can't last. All the superficiality disappears over time. It's best to marry someone who is dependable, punctual, responsible. Tattoos and muscles are the complete opposite of that. Tattoos and mus-cles…writing such graphic words. He was absolutely not my type. At all.

A giggle derailed my train-wreck of thoughts. Looking for its owner, I saw a couple embrace like that stupid perfume bottle. Knees and feet broke the water as the giggler wrapped her legs around her partner's body, kissing with mouths so wide I feared they would inhale each other. Given the pitch of the shark gasp that escaped her mouth I now assumed they were having sex. They were so close. I could reach out and make it a threesome.

How tacky.

When I noticed that her brown eyes were actually hazel I realized that I had been staring at them.

I had to get out of the water.

Marching up the beach I grabbed my sarong. Jade looked up from her sketchbook. "Are you okay?"

"I need to go to bed."

Before anyone could stop me, I ran to the hut, rinsed the salt and sand off with a cold shower, and lay in bed for the afternoon willing myself to nap as the erotic words I had read, the words *he* had written, danced in my mind.

***

"Hey baby, can you hear me?" Adam's voice crackled through the static.

After my attempted nap, I made my down the beach to the Internet café at the threshold of the market and beach for my Skype date with Adam.

"Yeah, just about," I said adjusting the volume on my headset. "How are you?"

"Missing you," he said as his face appeared on the ancient computer screen.

"I miss you too, baby." I reached out and dragged my finger down the cool glass over his cheek. This, I reminded myself, is what love is. This is who I need to fantasize about.

"How's this beach?"

"Yeah, it's an alright place." I wanted to say how much I loved it but the guilty feeling of rubbing my adventure in his face stopped me. "It's a bit of a hippy paradise so Jade's in love. She's at some chanting session right now. How's home?"

"Shit. Freezing, slushy, and miserable. I wish you were here."

His advertising skills left much to be desired. "Me too," I lied.

"So do you feel safe over there? With the men I mean?"

My voice faltered, and I paused to clear my throat. "Yeah, it's a beach town, so everyone is used to seeing women in bathing suits. I don't feel any danger here."

"Good, I'm glad. Your parents have been so worried."

"I know. I try to message them every day."

"They said. I had dinner with them last night. I knew they'd be having a hard time, so I thought I'd check in on them."

My heart nearly burst at his gesture. He was always so thoughtful with my parents. "Thank you. I'm so grateful for you."

"And I you," he said with that adorable lopsided smile. "I've started looking into wedding venues and invites and things."

Then my heart burst. "Oh, baby."

"I know we haven't set a date yet, but I thought I'd get started on planning early so you weren't over-whelmed when you come home."

Home. If I won the competition and joined Awe-some Adventures's photography team I wasn't sure when that would be. I hoped he would be just as supportive if that were to happen. I decided not to ruin the moment with talk of what-ifs, so I said, "How did I get so lucky?"

"I ask myself that every day," he replied. "So when can I see your photos?"

"I haven't had a chance to edit them yet. I'll send you the link as soon as I can." I leaned forward, resting my elbow on the desk and my chin in my palm. I glanced at the time on the computer clock and calculated the time at home. "Have you taken your insulin?"

Before I left, I programmed his phone to remind him every day on the hour he needed to take it.

He nodded and held up his insulin pack to the camera. "Oh, I have so much to tell you about *World of Warcraft*…"

As he went on and on about Eversong Woods, Blood Elves, and spinal dust my eyes turned glassy. Over the years I had found a way to look as if I was paying attention with a practiced smile and uttering, "uh-huh," "wow," and "hmm," occasionally. I thought this whole video game thing was endearing at first, but when he ended up in the hospital after slipping into a diabetic coma from forgetting to take his insulin while bingeing on the game I looked at it as his evil vice I wished he would grow out of. I wanted to be supportive, as I knew he loved it, and it was his escape from grief, but each time he talked about it, I clammed up worrying that one day he'd literally play the game to death. So rather than tell him not to talk about it to me, which would have been unfair, I tuned it out instead.

As his mouth chattered away, I let my eyes wander past the screen and through the window to the beach outside. I watched the people milling about in the lazy afternoon heat, and it hit me that I was really on my adventure. After Jade and Lana and I started talking about it seven years ago in our freshman year of university, and abandoning any hope of going three years ago when Audrey died, I was really doing it.

My eyes narrowed in on a shock of pitch-black hair down the beach. The provocative poet from the coconut grove. Slinking across the sand. In nothing but board shorts. Did this guy even own any clothes?

"Harper?" My eyes shot back to the screen. "Are you listening?"

"Yes, sorry, I just…"

"Baby," he said, cutting me off, "I have to run. Talk soon?"

"Sure. Tomorrow, our anniversary? Same time?"

"Yes. I can't believe it's been two years tomorrow. Best years of my life."

Despite our recent rough path, I believed he was sincere. And because of that rough patch, I needed to hear those words.

"I love you," I said.

I love you," he said blowing a kiss.

I made a gesture as if I were catching the kiss, and when my fingertips touched my lips, the screen flicked to black.

***

That night Lana, Jade and I wandered towards the northern end of the beach near to the entrance to the market road, where restaurants boasting eclectic menus lined the coconut grove in between the huts. Fishermen had returned from the sea, so on the shore of the rising tide wooden boats were beached, and the fresh catch was laid out in ice on tables in front of each restaurant.

"How are things with Adam?" Lana's voice hummed over the live sitar music as we sat down at a table in the more populated open-air restaurants.

"Great, couldn't be more in love," I replied, setting my camera on the white plastic tablecloth. Fearing I might say something I regretted about my meeting in the grove earlier, I changed the topic. "This place is so gorgeous at night."

After the sun set in Goa, the restaurants that lined the coconut grove illuminated with fairy lights that hung from the exteriors, and tables adorned with tea lights spilled out down the beach from the restaurant's main structure to the lapping surf, bathing the beach in a soft ethereal glow. As we ate dinner with our toes in the sand, I played with my exposure setting, hoping I could capture it properly, but I had not been able to master the art of such tricky lighting.

Jade told us about her day finding a great meditation spot on the small island perched at the northern tip of the beach, and Lana chattered on about how she had met a boy earlier while shopping in the market. Naturally, she spent the afternoon at the spa prepping for the prize of the flirtation game. And by spa she meant a shack on the beach that offered manicures, pedicures, and massages. Her bill totaled a whopping twelve dollars.

"Oh my God, Leo's here!" Lana gasped before inspecting her reflection in a spoon. "How do I look?"

Polished and perfect.

"Namaste, ladies." Six feet of swarthy skin, velvet brown eyes, and bee-stung lips bent down and kissed her on the cheek. "How are you tonight?"

"Better now." She batted her eyelashes at him. "Jade, Harper, this is Leo, and, who's your friend?"

I looked up and met eyes with the lewd lyricist from the coconut grove. A dark smile tilted his lips.

"Xavier," he replied.

Without thinking, I gave my hair a quick fluff and immediately hated myself for it.

"Namaste," Jade said as he bent over to give her an air-kiss on each cheek.

He turned to me, and bent down to reach for my hand. The scent of musk and spice enveloped me as his eyes found mine. With my skin pebbling from his touch, he raised my hand to his lips and kissed my knuckles. His lips were soft, and when his stubble brushed my skin a ball of lightning crackled deep within my belly. When he let go I exhaled, our eyes were still locked, and the world around us melted away.

Jade cleared her throat and it sent me crashing back to Earth. I glanced at her, and she stared at me, wide-eyed and brow furrowed. I dropped my gaze to the table, and I gulped the spicy lukewarm liquid of my chai masala tea. I was equally baffled by the moment Xavier and I had just shared.

"What do you have there?" Lana held out her hand, "accidentally" squishing her breasts together in her too small and too tight spandex tank top.

"Flyers for Silent Noise," Leo said handing one to her, as he made no attempt to hide the fact that he was staring at her cleavage. She would have been offended if he didn't look. "It's a silent disco that's happening in a few nights at the bar I work at."

"Silent disco?"

"Loud music isn't allowed in Goa after eleven o'clock," he explained, "so people listen to music through headphones that stream remotely from the DJ booths."

"The opening acts before the DJs start are the best part, though," Xavier said, smirking at Leo.

He was still standing in front of me, close enough for me to touch. I was eye level with where that towel hung, where those tattoos disappeared.

"So, are you organizing the party?" Lana asked, twirling a lock of hair in her index finger.

"Nah, I'm bartending at the venue, so they've put me to work promoting it," Leo said, handing Jade and me a flyer. "And Xavier will be —"

"I just have a keen interest in music," he interrupted-ed.

A salty breeze swept across the table as my mind began to put the pieces of him together. He looked past us towards the sitar player and scrubbed his chin. The ball of lightning in my belly crackled again as I remembered the feeling of it on my skin.

What was happening to me?

I couldn't understand it, but the effect Xavier had on my body scared the hell out of me. It was a feeling I never thought I'd feel. It was a was a feeling I longed to feel with Adam. Leaving Goa couldn't happen soon enough.

"And how you do you know each other?" Jade asked.

"Well, we were flat-mates in England finishing up our degrees for the past few years, but I'm originally from South Africa," Leo said. "And we've just been traveling around."

Okay, so Xavier was around twenty-two. Oddly, it was this fact that forced me to finally dismiss my inappropriate and unwanted thoughts about him. Even if I were single, he was much too young for me to have anything serious with. Adam was the perfect age, established in his career and perfect marriage material — sweet, thoughtful, dependable, loyal. Adam was both perfect on paper, and perfect in practice. And I would not jeopardize that.

Lana bit her lip. "I can hear it now. I like the blended accent," she said with flirtatious promise. I could see her mentally circling 'South Africa' on her international to-do list. "Xavier, are you from South Africa, too?"

"France originally. But I moved to England a very long time ago."

I kept my eyes off of him so I wouldn't feel that curious effect, but his voice sent a chill through me.

"Boys?" A voice shrilled.

I looked up to see a short-haired Indian girl resembling a teapot: short, stout, hand on hip and fuming.

"I need you to finish all of the bars on the beach. Now."

"Ladies," Leo said putting his arm around her. "This is Sarasi, the slave driver." His playful smile was met with a sarcastic one. "Well, it has been a pleasure, and I hope our paths cross again soon."

He bid farewell to Lana with a wink.

"It was great to meet you," Xavier said, looking at the girls. As his gaze turned from Lana to me, he said. "I hope I see you again soon."

They both turned, and Xavier's gaze lingered on me as he walked away.

"Oh my God, I'm in love!" Lana squealed when the boys were out of earshot. "Can we stay for the Silent Disco? And then we fly to Delhi afterwards? Oh please oh please oh please?! It's my birthday that day, and I want him."

As Xavier and Leo made their rounds handing out flyers to the other tables, I could feel his eyes on me. I bit my lip to stop the nervous smile that was tugging at them.

"It's fine with me so long as we fly to Delhi the day after," Jade said before turning to me, "Harper, are you happy to stay?"

I felt a sinking feeling in my stomach. I wanted to say no. I wanted to stick to the plan of leaving Goa and this man who made me feel out of control of myself. But going to Delhi alone was out of the question, and I'd never forgive myself if I spoiled Lana's birthday. She deserved a great day after all of the drama she had been through back home. Though her infamy had done wonders for her bank account, it only seemed to attract low-lifes, users, and moochers into her dating life.

So I said, "Sure, can't wait."

Chapter 6

The sun beat down on me as I plodded through the sand. Two more days, I reminded myself. Only two more days. It was those words that kept me awake last night. Along with thoughts of *him* in that towel. And the poetry *he* had written. When I read *Tahitian Heat* to distract myself that morning, my image of the perpetually naked love interest was replaced by *him*.

I couldn't understand why I stop thinking about a guy I had just met when I loved someone else. I know it was just thoughts, and perhaps a touch of cold feet as I wasn't exactly experienced with men. Or a little harmless curiosity because I had never met anyone like him before. But it still felt as if I were cheating on Adam. I wouldn't stand for Adam thinking about another girl in the way I thought about Xavier. Especially on our anniversary. What was worse, my body responded to those thoughts in a way I never thought it could respond. This was one of those times that called for a talk with your big sis, someone who knew me, someone I knew wouldn't judge me, someone whose advice I trusted. I could speak to the girls, but I know Lana would tell me to go after him and compartmentalize my feelings and Jade would get upset because she's not quite past the pain from being cheated on.

Perhaps I should have stayed in Toronto and eaten the cost of the ticket. But I couldn't go back in time. I had to live with my decision and get my career going. Abandoning my hopes of a monkey shot I stuck to my new plan for the day: to shoot the market, and avoid the coconut grove. I knew I'd have to see him at the silent disco, but I hoped to avoid him until then.

Passing a group of children, I took a better look at the cherubic clan huddling around a boy about seven years old who was holding a guitar in his tiny hands. I had changed the settings back to automatic and raised my camera. Focusing them in the viewfinder, a little girl in a pink sari moved. And engulfed in a deluge of giggles, clapping hands and innocent smiles, I saw him.

Xavier.

His eyes flicked up, and I froze. Lowering my camera, he gave me a nod of recognition.

Damn, he gave good nod.

I had to get far, far away from that nod. Breaking eye contact, I turned and made good my escape, tripping over a sleeping dog with my first step.

"Harper?" he called out.

I sped up, hoping to outrun his voice.

"Hey, stop!" I felt his hand on my arm and electricity surged through it. "Are you running from me?"

"No, I'm…" *Think, girl, think…* "partially deaf?"

Yep. That was the best I could come up with.

His face fell. "Oh, sorry."

And then I felt bad.

"It's okay… It comes and goes."

He raked his fingers through his jet-black hair and said, "So where are you going?"

I suppressed a smile as I noticed the light dusting of freckles across the bridge of his nose. "I'm going to take photographs of the market."

"I'll come with you."

Hell no.

"That's alright, you look busy," I said, glancing at the children before turning and continuing.

"They'll have each other," he said catching up. "Besides, I finished the lesson."

"Lesson?"

"The guy I'm renting the house from dropped my rent in exchange for me teaching his son guitar. The other kids love it, so I teach them all when I'm done with him."

I swore I felt my ovaries explode.

He was dead set on joining me and it would have been rude to talk him out of it, so I decided to keep my thoughts under control, and keep him at arm's length until it was time for my two-year anniversary Skype date with Adam at three-thirty.

***

Xavier was a patient companion as I kept stopping to take pictures as we navigated the market. In the hustle and bustle, I snapped images of the colourful wares for sale, some abstract shots to show the textures of the silks, jewelry, lanterns and kaftans, as well as portraits of the equally interesting characters that make and sell them.

Stopping to buy my third bottle of water for the hour at the stall outside of the Internet café, he asked, "So I never got to ask what brought you traveling. Is this something you always planned on doing?"

As I guzzled half of it, I took the chance to consider my words. "Not exactly. Jade, Lana and I talked about it in university. And then my life took a different path doing the whole marketing career thing, but they still planned the trip. And then about three weeks ago my I lost my job, so I tagged along."

"Sounds like losing your job was a blessing in disguise."

"How so?" The jury was out to lunch on that one.

"Look at your life now. You have no deadlines, no responsibilities, no one to boss you around and tell you what to do."

Lowering my camera, I murmured, "I guess."

"Look at where you are. You're in paradise," he grinned and pulled his Ray Ban aviators off his face, "with a very charming young man, I might add."

I giggled and dropped my eyes to the ground. I didn't think I had giggled since I was a teenager.

"Did you want to do marketing for the rest of your life?"

"I thought I did," I said with a shrug.

"So would you rather waste your youth working a job you're not sure you want or have the most enlightening experience you could ask for?"

"I didn't leave home to *Eat, Pray, Love* and find myself. I booked my ticket because I lost my job and thought…" I caught my words, "I had no other options."

"Well, I'm not one for praying," he leaned in, and my vision tunneled into his leaden eyes, "but eating and loving are two of life's greatest pleasures."

"Oh," I exhaled. Well, who could argue with that?

Pushing his Ray Bans back on he brushed past me, and the air between us crackled. Fixated on him, I spun around and watched him pull a paisley printed guitar from a display and strummed Bob Marley's "Redemption Song" as if he had played it a million times.

"So you *are* a musician." I raised my camera and framed him in the viewfinder.

"I suppose you can say that."

"That explains your tattoos."

"Oh, you noticed them?" His teasing smile knocked me off balance yet again.

He placed the instrument back in place, and my heart drummed as he raised the sleeve of his worn Rolling Stones t-shirt. Pointing out the stanzas of music notes that ran the length of his arm I read the immortal words of Bob Marley.

I began to see stars as I studied the tight lacing of muscle. Then the rapid click of the shutter button rocketed me back to Earth. I had been strangling my camera within an inch of its life.

It was time for a fresh bottle of water.

"So," I cleared my throat and walked into a stall filled with silk garments, "is music what you want to do with your life?"

"Music is my life and will be until I die." His spine straightened, and he leaned against a wooden post. "I'll work somewhere in the industry, but who knows where it will take me. I'm still young."

Too young.

"And your parents support your music?"

"Of course. They're both artists."

I masked a pang of envy and turned away. My parents supported it as a hobby.

"What about your photography?"

My focus fixed on a crimson silk dress, and I rubbed its soft hem between the pads of my fingers. When I started university, I had accepted that it wasn't a viable career option, but I loved it nonetheless. After Audrey died, it was the only thing that would get me out of bed in the morning. But over the years I became too busy with work and Adam to keep it going.

"It's been just a hobby until I came on this trip. I was going through a really bad couple of days after my job let me go, and I lost my mind thinking it could do it as a career."

"Sounds like you had an epiphany."

"A crazy idea during a mental breakdown?" I whipped around and found him a little too close for comfort.

"There's a thin line between crazy and genius," he said, tucking a rogue strand of hair behind my ear, "straddle it."

The devilish glint in his eyes tied a knot in my throat. As I gulped it down, he stepped back.

"Ma'am, would you like to try this dress on?" A speck of a woman in a yellow sari jumped up from a stool. With a soft smile, she said, "Trying is free."

You just had to love the sales strategies.

Behind a brick-coloured curtain, I took a moment to collect my thoughts. I slipped the dress over my head, steadying myself with a hand on the cool mirror. Hoping for some relief after playing with fire all afternoon, I pressed my cheeks against it.

"I love Adam. I love Adam. I love Adam." Circles of fog pulsed on the glass as I repeated the words.

Adam wasn't just any guy. He wasn't even my boyfriend. He was more than that. He was the man I promised to pledge my life to. Even though we hadn't said our vows, to me, our vows of fidelity were in effect the day we used the labels "boyfriend" and "girlfriend". I had always felt cheating was morally reprehensible, and after helping Jade get through her breakup after that asshat Cliff cheated on her, I saw firsthand the immediate and lasting results of infidelity. Seeing her hurting so much broke my heart, and I hoped never to experience it or cause that pain for someone else.

But I had to admit my attraction to Xavier. And it was an attraction unlike anything else I had ever felt. It wasn't like the rational attraction I felt for Adam, but something else, like my body had a mind of its own and was starving my brain of oxygen so I didn't behave how I should. I had hoped that if I denied my attraction enough I could convince myself that I wasn't, and the feelings would go away. That clearly wasn't working, so I decided to acknowledge it and proceed. And this had gone on far enough. I had to tell Xavier that I was engaged, and I was *not* going to cheat on my fiancé.

"Ma'am, I'll give you discount for the dress." The shopkeeper's voice startled me.

I took a quick glance in the mirror and decided that I liked it. It had an empire waistline with elastic ruching that held the bust tight, and a skirt that flowed in a subtle A-line to mid-thigh. Delicate straps in the middle of the bust could be tied in a bow, so it was strapless or around the neck to change it to a halter style. The red popped with my new tan and, dare I say, it was actually kind of sexy. It had been a long time since I felt sexy.

Carefully peeling off the dress, I changed, pulled back the curtain, handed over my rupees and stepped into the road.

"You tried it on already?" His smile faded. "I was hoping to see you in it."

"Well, I bought it so you'll see it at the silent disco," I said, keeping my voice cool and body distant.

He gestured for me to follow him. "I've ordered us a couple of mango lassis from next door. Come, sit."

As I reached to grab the back of my chair, he placed his hand on mine, and insisted that he pulled it out for me. I placed my camera in my bag and set it on the edge of the table as he took the seat across from me.

"Thank you. Who said chivalry was dead?" I joked, trying to deny how special that small gesture made me feel. And how my hand still tingled from the contact.

He laughed. "Force of habit. If I didn't demonstrate proper manners growing up, I was scolded."

"So is that how you charm all the girls?"

I resisted the urge to smack myself in the face for that cheesy line.

His smile faded. "I'm more of a one-woman man."

"Oh," I said, diverting my eyes to stop me from falling into his. I needed to figure out how to steer the conversation. I couldn't outright say, *Hey I'm engaged, by the way, so this can't go anywhere, buddy*, because

71

maybe he wasn't flirting with me, it could have all been in my head, and then I would be left even more embarrassed. "And Leo?"

"Leo plays the field." He quickly added, "But he likes Lana. He hasn't expressed interest in anyone else."

"Don't worry, I doubt Lana's looking for anything serious."

"And you," he said, "do you have someone waiting for you at home?"

Here we go.

I took a big sip of the cool yogurt drink, trying to figure out the best words to use. Once I told him about Adam, everything would change. But part of me didn't want it to change. It had been so long that I had enjoyed someone's company like this. I mean, I loved Adam, but the circumstances under which we met weren't exactly conducive to flirting and sexual tension. We were both depressed and spent much of our time making sure the other was staying afloat emotionally. What I was experiencing with Xavier I had relegated to the realms of fiction, accepting that so long as I could read about it, I was fine with never experiencing it in real life.

"I guess not if you're here with me," he added.

"Well… you see… I…"

Suddenly, in a passing blur, my bag disappeared from the table.

"My bag!" I screamed, bolting up and stumbling between the chairs. "Oh my God, my camera!"

Xavier had already leapt to his feet and was sprinting after the thief. I pushed the table out of the way and trailed behind, weaving throughout the swarming shoppers and cows grazing on garbage, barely able to keep up. Each time I lost sight of the thief, I saw my dreams disappear. All those photos, all that work, poof, gone! And my heart broke at the thought of never seeing that camera again. It had more sentimental value than anything I owned. It was a physical piece of Audrey's memory. As my lungs burned, I wished I had done some real exercise in the past year, but I pushed past it to keep up.

Nearing the end of the stretch of market stalls, the crowd thinned out. Outside of a lantern shop, I saw Xavier tackle the man to the ground twenty feet ahead. As Xavier rose to his feet, he pulled the thief up by the neck of his shirt.

Oh God, he's going to pummel him.

I approached but kept my distance, keeping a quivering hand on my mace.

The thief pressed his hands together, keeping his stance low as he muttered words I couldn't understand, but recognized as begging. Begging for mercy. Xavier softened his posture.

"It's okay. It's okay," he cooed.

He motioned for the thief to follow him to a food stall. Reaching into his pocket he took out some rupees, handed them to the shopkeeper and asked him to give the thief as much food and water as his money would buy.

This guy tries to steal my bag and Xavier rewards him?

I stared down my nemesis. Threadbare rags hung from his skeletal frame. Desperate eyes sunk into hollow cheeks. Only a few teeth were housed behind his ashen lips. He looked as if he hadn't eaten or bathed for weeks. Despite its colourful veneer, India was a country plagued by poverty, and poverty breeds desperate actions. Audrey had paid the ultimate price for it years ago.

Fear gripped me. How could I have been so naïve to think something couldn't happen to me? The world *was* a scary, scary place, and I should never have left home.

Xavier turned and strode towards me, bag in hand, and I felt my face heat. He enveloped me in his strong arms, as tears streamed down my cheeks. As he held me, he stroked my hair and hummed "Three Little Birds", his lips resting on the crown of my head. I melted into him, riding the rise and fall of his ribcage, soothed by the strumming of his heart. And there, on a dirt road in Goa next to a lantern shop, after my first taste of personal violation on the road, I wept on the muscular chest of a guy who made me feel funny feelings I loved and hated in equal measure.

Wrapped in his arms, I found sanctuary. The tears began to stem, and I steadied my breathing. Inhaling his scent, a heady combination of musk and salt, he felt like a perfect summer's day.

He loosened his hold, and I stifled a whimper. I could have lived forever in that moment.

"It's all good," he said with a comforting smile. "I have your bag."

Embarrassment washed over me as I realized our public display. Shoppers and shopkeepers alike were still starting. Wiping my tears, I straightened my back and tried to act as if nothing had happened. Despite my attempts to look like a normal and together person I obviously looked like a mess. I knew so much mascara pooled under my eyes that Marilyn Manson would be jealous and, missing his embrace, I clutched myself as if I was wearing an invisible straight jacket.

"My hero," I joked, forcing a smile through trembling lips.

He peeled my right hand off of my left arm and interlaced our fingers. "Let's go sit down."

In silence, he led me back to where we had been drinking lassis, and we took a different table. He pulled out a chair for me in the corner of the patio and sat across from me so no one could come near the table or me. Placing my bag back on the table, I pulled out my camera, praying that it didn't get damaged.

"Is it alright? I think there's a camera shop in the next town over if it isn't."

I could barely hold it as I flicked the power button. Relief pulsed through me, and a real smile spread across my face as I nodded. It worked.

"My sister gave it to me." I blurted out. I met his eyes, and for someone reason felt the need to explain, "She's dead."

"I'm so sorry." He leaned forward in his chair.

"Thanks." I dropped my eyes back to the camera, cradling it like a newborn kitten. And a story I hadn't told anyone in years tumbled from my lips. "We had this plan. We'd travel the world together, have grand adventures, and blog about it. We were supposed to do it when I graduated university." Her face flashed in my mind, and I smiled as memories of her came flooding back. "She was always doing something amazing with her life and letting me tag along. I was so lucky. People have these high-flying older siblings and resent them, but I never lived in her shadow, she always wanted me to bask in her glory at her side."

He rested his face in his hand. "She sounds like she was an amazing person."

I nodded and swallowed back the knot in my throat. "She was. She always encouraged me to do whatever I dreamed of. That's why she got me this camera. It's why I'm here now."

"Do you mind me asking what happened to her?"

I shook my head. It always upset me to think about what happened to her, but I wanted to tell him. I remembered it as if it happened yesterday. I had just finished my last exam before the Christmas break in my final year, some bullshit elective, and was at my parents' house helping them with dinner.

"She was in La Paz, Bolivia, it was her first time leaving North America, and she went to volunteer for Habitat for Humanity with her new boyfriend. The night before they were supposed to fly home, some men broke into their hotel, robbed the place, and shot them when they put up a fight. She died instantly, and he took a bullet to the spine and will spend the rest of his life in a wheelchair. Just like that. All for some Bolivianos and their passports."

The police caught the guys a week later when they held up another hotel in the city. Thankfully they're locked up for a long time, but since then I felt like there was no way to control the world around me, and I took comfort in control.

"That's awful." His unblinking eyes fixated on me. "I can't even begin to imagine what you went through. What you still go through. You're so brave to come here."

"You think?" I paused to collect my words and said the ones I was never able to express. "I feel like being here is flaunting her death."

"You're honoring her life by being here. It sounds like she'd want you to be here, going after your dreams, putting her gift, and yours, to good use."

"It's not just that," I said, pressing my face into my hands as I pushed through the guilt, "my parents are at home sick with worry that I won't come home like her."

"I can't imagine how difficult it is for them, but you have to live your life for you. At some point, you'll have to show them you can take care of yourself. And you can't live in fear. Despite its faults, the world is a beautiful place."

And his words and my thoughts fought a battle in my consciousness. But with each word I said out loud, I lightened the load on my spirit.

As I wiped away a rogue tear, he rested his hand on mine. Running the lightly callused pad of his index finger over my wrist he frowned. "I'll be right back."

He rose from his seat with a glint in his eye and walked to the stall where I had bought my dress. With my eyes glued to him, I finished my lassi and rested my chin in my hand, studying the dips and curves of his long, lean body as his words rolled in my mind.

With something balled, in his fist he returned to the table. "All travelers have a collection of bracelets. I noticed that you don't have any, so I want to start yours."

He held out a bracelet strung with delicate beads of tiny violet stones. A silver charm hung from the middle. I smiled for a moment at the light dancing through the gems. Then I realized that a man who was not my fiancé was giving me a piece of jewelry.

"I can't accept this."

"It's the Ohm symbol," he said, ignoring my protest. "It's a holy meditation symbol in Eastern religions and has many meanings, including representing the symbolic expressing of the creative spirit, and according to the shopkeeper, amethyst is a protective stone for travelers. I won't be with you for your journey, so I want to make sure you're safe."

Taking my hand, he placed the bracelet on my wrist. "Thank you," I muttered.

I brought my wrist closer to my face for a better look. Then I caught sight of my watch.

"Oh my God, I have to go," I said, scrambling to my feet. It was already past four. "I'm so sorry...I...I... have to call home."

"When can I see you again?" he asked as I grabbed my bag.

I shimmied between my chair and the wall as quickly as I could. "The silent disco," I called back before sprinting down the market.

My feet couldn't move fast enough as I weaved in and out of the throngs of vendors and shoppers to the Internet café near the threshold of the beach. After paying my deposit, I slid into the chair at the first computer and logged in.

"Come on, you piece of crap," I mumbled as the decades-old computer took an eternity to load.

Finally, I logged into Skype, and a message popped up from Adam, piercing me through the heart: "Happy Anniversary."

Chapter 7

Date: January 25, 2010

The next morning, the girls and I rented mopeds and spent the morning driving past waterlogged rice paddies, secret beaches, and murky rivers, exploring the spice farms and beach town of Karwar just outside of Palolem. I tried to focus on my photography, but each image was blurry, poorly composed, over-exposed. I felt so guilty for ruining our anniversary. That Skype chat was the one thing I needed to remember to do. One thing! Sure, having my bag stolen distracted me from my timekeeping, but I shouldn't have been there with Xavier in the first place. If only I could go back in time and tell him to keep his muscles, tattoos, and charms to himself and leave me alone. Even if it meant losing what was perhaps the most fun I'd had in months, perhaps years. I could only now prepare for the groveling apology I would have to give to him in our Skype chat that afternoon.

***

Once we returned the mopeds, I told the girls I was going to hit up the Internet. They decided to join me. I didn't want to tell them what was going on between Adam and me, or even Xavier and me, so I now needed to get through the Skype chat with keeping my emotions in check.

We kicked our flip-flops off outside, and I welcomed the feeling of air-conditioning on my heating skin and cool tile against my bare feet. Taking computers with Lana across from me, and Jade next to her, I logged into Skype.

"Hi." A single word chilled me from across the world as the video kicked in.

"I'm so sorry about yesterday."

"Where were you?"

Telling the truth was the right thing to do, but was it the best? I had been debating all morning.

"I...lost track of time taking photographs. I really am sorry, baby. If I could go back in time and change it, I would."

Xavier would be out of my life in two days. And then everything would be back to normal.

"So your photographs are more important than me? Than us?" he said, pinching the space between his eyes.

"No, of course not." I hated that he thought that, but I understood how he did. "I've just been so focused on getting my photography career going —"

"Harper, be real," he cut me off before I could explain that if I could get it going, it would make leaving worth all of the stress I was putting him and my parents through. "You don't stand a chance in this competition. You're chasing a pipe dream and ruining us in the process."

The air shot from my lungs as his words slugged me in the gut. I barely recognized him. Adam had never been mean to me before.

"I didn't mean to hurt you," I said, steadying my voice, "so don't try and hurt me in return."

"I'm not. That's how I really feel. I think you're being a child with this stupid trip you're doing."

Wow, say how you really feel.

"Yeah, while the rest of us adults are facing up to the real world with jobs and responsibilities you've just run away from it all."

"I did not run away." I struggled to keep my voice calm. I glanced up to the girls, and their eyes were glued to their screens, earphones on, none the wiser to what was going on over this side of the table.

"Yes, you did. You ran away from life. You ran away from responsibility. You ran away from us."

"We were broken up." My face blazed.

"We had a fight." His tone intensified with each word. "In any case, you could have stayed, but you were adamant on going."

"The ticket was non-refundable."

"It's just money." He was now yelling. "I got down on one knee and professed that I wanted to spend the rest of my life with you. You should have stayed. You would have earned the money back eventually. Or is that all I'm worth?"

I pressed my hands against my face to try and dam the tears. "That's not fair."

"You know what's not fair? I'm stuck here all alone while my fiancé is gallivanting across the world with her single friends."

As tears streamed down my face, I tried my best to maintain my composure and discretely wipe my tears away. I knew what he was insinuating. And as insulting as it was, it wasn't unwarranted. But I loved him and wanted for us to work. "I'm so sorry. Please forgive me."

"The only reason I let you go without a fight was because I thought you would have given up and come home."

I blinked at the screen, staring at the man I thought I loved. The man I thought supported me. I opened my mouth to speak, but nothing came out.

"Look, I gotta go," he said, his voice was unnervingly calm and cool.

"Adam, please let's talk about —" before I could finish my sentence, the video screen disappeared. I tried to call him back. But before I could, his Skype ID flicked to offline.

My mouth gaped as I tried to make sense of everything he had said. I felt a flood of tears swelling, and I had to get the hell out of there. Hoping to leave without the girls knowing, I sent them messages on Skype to meet them later. I didn't want to ruin their day with my drama. As I stood I made eye contact with Lana.

Shit.

"Tequila?" she asked.

"Tequila," I replied.

And that afternoon alternating between tequila, lassis, and fried pakoras I told the girls everything that happened with Xavier and Adam, from the coconut grove poetry to the bracelet in the market, Adam's mean words, and my carelessness with the feelings of two guys who didn't deserve it. I was scared Jade would judge me after her experience being on the receiving end of infidelity, but she was supportive and told me to meditate on it.

"Honey, it's okay to change your mind about Adam," Lana said. "Marriage is a big deal that shouldn't be rushed into."

"I made a promise to him," I said, poking at the yogurt that had stuck to the edge of the glass with my straw, "what kind of person would I be if I didn't keep it?

She sighed and replied, "Human."

***

After a very unsatisfying night's sleep, the sound of shuffling woke me from my dreamless slumber. Adam's words kept me awake through the night as I tried to rationalize his feelings towards my choices as some very unwelcome and unhelpful thoughts of Xavier tried to enter the fray. To silence Adam, I played the silent disco in my head like a movie and practiced what I would say to Xavier: the girls and I would turn up and ensure Lana and Leo found each other, then, as he's looking at me with those eyes and using his sexy double-entendres, I would fight his charms with nonchalance and then tell him to stay far, far away from me and find another girl. Then Jade and I would come home at a reasonable hour, leaving Lana with Leo (naturally I had reservations about this). Then, after waking up the next day with no regrets, we would fly north to Delhi where I would be two thousand kilometers away from this messiness and I would repress his memory in the deepest, darkest, dankest dungeon of my mind.

As I heard the door open I peeked through my lashes to catch Jade leaving.

"Morning," I said.

"Morning, I'm just heading to yoga. Wanna come?"

I debated for a second and decided to use the morning to edit images. "Nama'stay in bed," I replied with a wink.

She laughed as the door closed behind her. I sat up and shook off the web of sleep, reached down, and pulled my computer from my daypack. I connected my camera and pressed transfer. Rolling out of bed I took a shower, hoping to wash away the tequila odour oozing from my pores. Then, soapy smelling but still hazy headed, I left the bathroom and saw that the transfer had been completed.

That was quick, I thought.

I disconnected the camera, wiped the memory card, and dressed for the day. Once dressed in my standard work attire — shorts and a tank top — I pulled the curtains back and opened the windows, welcoming the soft morning light and salty breeze. Flopping onto my stomach, I pressed a button to wake my computer from hibernation mode and opened the folder with my images.

"The fuck?" I blurted out.

I hit the refresh button. They had to be there.

"Where are the files?"

I frantically scrolled through the folder, hoping, praying, wishing. I grabbed my camera, turned it on, and pressed the playback button: No Images.

No. No. Nononononononono!

They were gone. Thousands of images. All gone.

Stars danced in my vision as I closed the folder. The stars turned red when I looked at my desktop wallpaper. Adam's smiling face. Mocking me. Telling me that he was right: I didn't stand a shot at the competition. I didn't stand a shot at my dreams.

"No!" I screamed, punching the bed. I would not let him win.

Grabbing my camera, I stormed from the room, locked the door, and tore through all of Palolem filling my memory card with images for as long as the sunlight lasted.

***

As Lana blew out the candles on her slice of birthday cake, I slugged back wine to calm my nerves and to forget that I had erased all of my work. I had beaten myself up all day, but stopped when I realized that it wasn't going to change anything. It was simple human error. Though I took hundreds of new images, I mourned the loss of the amazing images I could never recreate. The images of Mumbai, Karwar, and the other beaches, Anjuna, and Arambol. There were no damn blurred monkeys and no papers full of beautiful words that bled red ink littering a coconut grove. A coconut grove home to a dangerous inhabitant I was going to see soon enough. For the last time. Ever. Thank God.

Eager to get our appearance at the silent disco over with, I asked for the check and tried to shuffle the girls into action.

"I don't think I can make it out," Jade said putting her rupees on the table. "That curry from lunch keeps coming back for revenge."

"Oh no," Lana pouted and pulled a packet of Alka-Seltzer from her purse. It was quite the must-have for India. "Okay, Harper, let's go?" She looked at me with huge saucer eyes.

I wanted to head home with Jade, but I couldn't ruin Lana's birthday. Maybe I could talk Lana out of it. Who needs birthday sex when you could spend it with your two best girlfriends between bathroom breaks?

I'm being ridiculous.

I was perfectly capable of acting like a normal human being who could control herself.

"Okay, but bring him back here to your hut," I said folding my arms. My new plan was to get them together, fend Xavier off until she wanted to leave, walk back with them, get into bed in my own hut, and wake up with no regrets tomorrow. "Please don't go off with him and leave me by myself."

With a nod, it was decided. On shaky legs, I followed her down the beach with the hope that my revised plan would not be edited any further.

Chapter 8

Lana and I followed the map doodled on the flyer down the beach, over fishing boats and through hidden coves being consumed by the rising tide until pulsating music pulled us to a large sign that read, "Silent Noise."

With my heart drumming in time to the music, I handed over my rupees for entry and headphone rental before we were directed into the crowded open-air disco. To our left stood a huge stage with three DJ booths side by side. Each booth was lit up with a different colour: red, blue, and green. On each headset a button toggled between the DJs. On the right stood a thatched-roof gazebo thirty feet in diameter, decorated with white fairy lights and held a circular bar in the center.

"Shots?" she asked.

I forced a smile, and a watery sensation rippled through my arms and legs. We pushed through the sweaty pack of partiers and made our way to the bar. Leo was moving about behind it, taking orders and making drinks. Lana stood patiently, and when his face broke into an unrestrained smile, I knew he had spotted her. She gave him a subtle single eyebrow raise, signature Lana, and I envied her sexual confidence. She always seemed to know what she wanted and made no apologies for it.

"Welcome to Silent Noise, ladies," he shouted over the din of the thirsty crowd. "What can I do you for?"

"Hey, Leo," Lana purred as she leaned over the bar, putting her ample cleavage on display. "Can we get a round of tequila shots and two *screw*drivers?"

Sex hung in the air as they looked at each other like animals in heat.

"It's her birthday," I blurted out, uncomfortable with my unwilling voyeur status.

He broke eye contact and began making the drinks. "Well, these are on the house, birthday girl. I'll have to give you a kiss when I finish work."

Lana's fair cheeks flushed red. "It must be hard…having to work and watch everyone having fun."

Back in my creepy voyeur position, I watched Leo's gaze darken. "Well, good news — I won a bet with my boss so I get to finish work early tonight."

Lana's eyes lit up. "Come find me when you…get off." Lana giggled. "Get off work, that is."

God, this girl should write a book on seduction.

He winked at her and pushed the drinks across the bar. Turning his gaze to me he said, "The opening acts are starting. Don't miss them."

Then we knocked back the tequila and made our way through the crowd, drinks in hand, finding a spot behind the dance floor with a clear view of the stage. It wasn't time to wear the headphones yet, so I hooked mine over my forearm.

"I wonder where Xavier is," I said, looking around and smoothing my dress. The anticipation of getting the initial greeting over with was killing me.

Lana tapped me on the arm and replied, "He's walking onto the stage."

My head whipped around. Illuminated by the spotlight, he walked across the stage with a guitar in his grip. Taking a seat on a stool behind a microphone, he plugged a cord into the instrument.

"Bon soir, good evening and namaste, Silent Noise." His voice thundered through the speakers, and then he began strumming a familiar tune.

As he sang his first words, I had to lean on something. Goosebumps blazed across my skin like wildfire as he sang a stripped-down arrangement of the Kings of Leon hit, "Sex on Fire".

And I thought the original was steamy enough. Boy, was I wrong. His voice rasped softly like lovers' pillow talk. Entranced by his raw emotion, I could barely breathe, feeling, fantasizing that he was singing for me. But, I mean, of course he wasn't. Which was something I shouldn't have been thinking in the first place. I chugged my drink relishing the cool liquid, even though the vodka burned my throat. God, Leo made his drinks strong. I couldn't let Xavier's haunting sex voice and intriguingly dexterous fingers distract me.

Girls crowded in front of the stage and vied for his attention. Which was great, once I tell him that nothing can happen between us, there would be plenty of women for Xavier to choose from.

As he belted out the last words, clearly a metaphor for orgasm (I mean, could he be more obvious?), the crowd cheered.

"I know I'm into Leo," Lana said, breaking the silence between us, "but I think I just came."

I nodded and forced a smile, ignoring the fact that I might have as well.

He then sang a stripped-down arrangement of the Kings of Leon's "Use Somebody", followed by Bob Marley's "Stir it Up", as I clutched my glass and rationed out my ice cubes. Once the next performer took over we went back to the bar, and decided to double-fist a pair of drinks to save us a trip back through the sea of sticky bodies. Back on the outskirts of the dance floor, as the booze of fog clouded my consciousness, his performance replayed in my mind. His soundtrack set to a montage of memories: his eyes, his smell, his fingers, the way his body felt when he held me, the way he looked at me, the way I felt when he looked at me.

Things I should not have been thinking about.

"Let's dance!" Lana turned and yelled at me as the last performer sang his big finale — Journey's extraordinarily catchy "Don't Stop Believing".

Before I could protest, she took me by the arm and dragged me into the middle of the dance floor. I stood as she danced. Then, the music died down and a voice boomed through the speaker announcing it was time to put the headphones on and toggled between the channels. Green was house, blue was trance, and red was pop. Revelers joined us and amongst them, we watched a sea of people dancing to various tempos. It was a little odd, not going to lie.

La Roux's "In For The Kill" pulsed through the headphones, and the tequila and vodka convinced me to move. It began as a two-step, as these things usually do, then my arms joined the party along with my hips. After losing myself in the beats, I felt a tap on my shoulder. My eyes flicked open, and I froze. In front of me stood Lana flanked by Leo and Xavier.

Oh God, how long had he been watching me?

I tore my headphones off, hoping the ground would swallow me whole.

"You look so beautiful." His eyes raked over me. "I've been looking forward to seeing your dress."

I bit my lip to keep control of them. "Thank you," I replied in a casual tone I hoped said, *you're in the friend zone, pal.*

I held my ground with jelly legs as he closed the space between us. "Leo said you were drinking vodka oranges," he said, extending his hand.

I nodded and took the glass from him. I sipped it, hoping that there was more orange than vodka this time. There wasn't.

With drinks in hand, the boys led us to a bamboo booth that straddled the sand and the packed dirt of the venue. Lana fell into Leo's attention, tuning Xavier and me out completely. It was only a matter of time for Lana to decide that she had enough of the opening acts of flirtation and wanted to get straight to the main event.

"So, you're a performing musician?" I said, needing to fill the silence with some form of conversation.

"You're observant," he teased with a cheeky smile. "I began busking on the streets of Marseilles as a child, and I've moved up in the world a bit since then."

"And you're traveling to play in various events?" I asked, feeling a little more at ease with each sip.

"Some performing, some researching, and some good old-fashioned fun. I want to see what music is out there, find musicians I can learn from, but it's not exactly Leo's thing, so planning this trip, he talked of this thing called 'compromise,'" he said, furrowing his brow and feigning confusion with a smile.

Oh God, that smile.

I had to keep the conversation neutral. "I...uh...love Kings of Leon."

"Well, I wasn't sure what to perform tonight, I usually write my own songs, but for some reason after meeting you "Sex on Fire" has been stuck in my head."

My breath held in my throat as his eyes wandered from my eyes to my lips, then my cleavage and back again. I hated myself for liking it. It had been a long time since a man looked at me as if he wanted to devour me.

"How is your photography coming along?"

I shook my head and glanced at the ground. Anger bubbled as I remembered Adam's words. He was just hurt that I missed our anniversary, I told myself. But those words had to have come from somewhere. Before I knew it, the contents of my drink had disappeared. Strange.

"Today I wanted to give up," I admitted. "Pack it all up and go home."

"You've found your passion. It's not easy, but you can never give up," he said, taking my chin between his index finger and thumb and pulling my gaze to meet his. "Believe in yourself. I do."

I sighed as my eyes wandered to the sky and asked the stars why a relative stranger could believe in me, but the man I loved couldn't? They twinkled back at me in response. Unhelpful little bastards.

"Do you want to get a better look?" Xavier said releasing my chin.

I nodded and asked, "How do you say 'star' in French?" Four years living in Montreal and all I had to show for it was swear words.

He held my hand, pulling me to my feet and replied, "Étoile."

Once I was standing, I noticed that Lana and Leo had disappeared. Panic set in. I whipped my head around in all directions and then relief washed over me when he pointed them out, dancing hip-to-hip and lip-to-lip on the dance floor.

"I've been meaning to ask you," I said as we settled into the warm sand. "Why did you reward the guy who took my bag in the market that day?"

He paused taking a handful of sand, letting the grains filter through his fingers. "I grew up very poor, and I guess you could say I know what it's like to be that desperate."

"Oh?"

"I used to have to steal from the markets just to feed myself," he said. "When I was three, my father left my mother, taking his stable salary with him. All my mother knew was her art. She sold what she could, but it was never enough, so I turned to stealing. I was quick and never got caught. When I was nine, a wealthy English aristocrat, Henry, took an interest in my mother's art and became her patron. I was so jealous of him. I wanted to be the man of the house, the provider, the protector, the man my father never was. Even though I no longer needed to steal food, I decided to steal money. I chose a church as my first target. They were there to help those in need, so I could justify it morally.

One day I walked into an empty church, opened the donation box, and began stuffing the coins and bills in my pockets. To a nine-year-old, it was like finding Blackbeard's Treasure. But a booming voice interrupted me, asking, *do you have what you need?* I thought for sure God caught me. I turned and saw the priest towering over me."

He paused and took a sip from his drink as I sat hanging onto every word.

"I was convinced he was going to call the police, but he smiled and offered to help me fill my pockets. I was terrified by him and by how confused I was. When I had thought up the plan, I had a list of the luxuries I wanted to buy, but with the money spilling from my pockets onto the street, I didn't want anything anymore. It didn't feel right as I passed the beggars, struggling to eat, struggling to live. As I made my way home, I threw my money at them."

"You just gave it all away?"

"I had to lighten not just my pockets, but also my conscience. I gave money to people who, if I continued to court bad karma, I believed I would become. I didn't have a single franc left in my pocket when I charged through my doors. I fell into my kitchen in tears at Henry's feet as he was purchasing another piece of my mother's art. She held me and asked what the matter was. I couldn't bring myself to tell her what I had done. I was so ashamed. Then Henry told me he had something that would cheer me up, and he held up a small guitar. Apparently, my mother had told him that I liked to sing. He taught me to play, and I became obsessed. I devoured music theory and poetry classes in school and spent the time I was not at school playing my guitar until I was good enough to start busking on the street and earn honest money. And I haven't stolen anything since. Well…perhaps one or two hearts."

"You scoundrel," I said, unable to restrain a smile. "Is Henry still in your life?"

"I now know that he and my mother were lovers, but his family never approved of her. They thought she was beneath his status. Despite that, shortly after that day, they ran off with me in tow and eloped in her native land of Algeria. He adopted me, and we moved to England, and they've been madly in love ever since."

"Oh wow." I sighed.

He gave a wistful look as he glanced across to the sea. "While we're on the topic of other days, I've wanted to say that I didn't mean to offend you about that question about being in love when we met." He raked his fingers through his hair. "I've been suffering from writer's block and I was hoping to get some insight. It's been a while since I've fallen in love."

The memory of the day in the coconut grove flashed in my mind. Then I forced myself to stop as the image of him in a towel caused some very unwelcome sensations to ripple deep in my stomach.

I nodded and forced a small smile as the word "love" and all of its meanings and manifestations rolled in my mind. I let my eyes turn back to the stars, and we sat bathed in their glow. Back at home it was impossible to see them. I would have needed an occasion to drive to the country, and even then, unless I drove for what seemed like an eternity, the night sky would barely be half as populated with the stars as it was in Goa.

Then one fell and streaked across the night sky.

"Shooting star!" I shouted and pointed. As quickly as I saw it, it burst into sparkling dust and vanished. I turned to Xavier, who was already watching me. "Did you see it? It was so beautiful."

He didn't reply, and I felt his fingertips skimming my bracelet. My breath escaped me as I fell into his gaze. "Dance with me," he commanded, his voice barely louder than a whisper.

Before I could answer, he stood, took my hand, and guided me to my feet and led me to the dance floor. Electricity surged and radiated from his touch to my core. He gently placed my headset on before he put his on, and then toggled his channel to red to match mine. Pitbull's *Calle Ocho* bounced through the earphones. Whatever divinity was in control had one hell of a sense of humour.

It took us a couple of moments to find our groove, and we slowly danced closer and closer. Before I knew what was happening, he splayed his hand against the small of my back, causing me to press my hips into his. As he swept the hair off my shoulders, a chill ran down my spine. My two new frenemies vodka and tequila forced me to cup his biceps with my hands, before running my fingers across his taut chest. It had been a long time since I touched muscle like this. And I liked it.

His eyes darkened and a whisper of a smile escaped his lips. He pulled me closer, his free hand holding the nape of my neck. I didn't stop him. Instead I yielded to him, intoxicated by his scent. As his lips grazed my neck I arched my back, pressing into him and a delicious sensation curled in the pit of my stomach.

He moved his hands down my body leaving a trail of sparks in their wake until they anchored on my hips, pulling me closer. I could taste his warm, bittersweet breath on my parted lips. My breath shuddered and strained with each movement of his hands on my demanding skin. I stifled a moan as his lips grazed mine. I couldn't bear it any longer.

I balled his shirt in my fists and pulled him towards me, relishing his taste as his mouth crashed against mine.

Chapter 9

Light assaulted my eyelids, sending searing pain through my skull. In my stale drunken disorientation, I blindly reached for the water I always left on the bedside table. My mouth was parched. The heat was unbearable. But there was no water. And no table.

I sat straight up and wrenched my eyes open as the light stabbed at them.

Where the hell am I?

I ripped the sheet off, looked down at myself and pulled it back over.

Dear God… I'm naked.

Where was my dress? I frantically scanned the room until I saw a pile of his clothes and my slutty red dress on the floor next to me. I rolled over, reached down, and grabbed it. Sitting upright, I slipped it over my head.

What time is it?

I tried to stand, but my head felt like someone was shanking my brain with an icepick in time to my pulse. Instead, I leaned forward with my elbows on my knees and pressed my face in my palms.

"Morning, mon étoile," Xavier's crackling voice confirmed I just woke up in my worst nightmare. I looked up as he pushed through the door, holding a bottle of water and wearing nothing but navy-blue boxer briefs.

He crawled into bed behind me, and I breathed a deep sigh and turned around to confront the situation. I took the bottle of water from him, swallowed a gulp, and had no idea what to say so I said, "Hi."

"Last night was fun," he said reaching out and placing his hand on my knee. "Come back to bed."

Stay calm. I repeat, stay calm.

I dropped my eyes on a fraying of threads on the corner of the pastel blue pillow and shook my head. "I have to go. We have a flight to catch."

His brow furrowed under his mop of inky black bed head. I would have described it as "just fucked," but I didn't want to face a reality that I couldn't undo. But in the glow of the morning light, he really was the most beautiful thing I had ever seen.

Adam! A voice screamed in my head. *Your fiancé is the most beautiful thing you have ever seen!*

It took all my strength not to run from the room. I found my watch lying on the floor, and as I put it on, I noticed the time.

"I need to find Lana; we're going to miss our flight."

"That wouldn't be such a bad thing," he said as a hopeful smile tugged at his lips.

I stood and slid my feet into my flip-flops that were scattered with one near the head of the bed and the other at the foot. "Please, I need to get Lana. We have to go."

His smile vanished, and he rolled out of bed. His body strong, lean, and perfect. In silence he dressed and led me out of his room, across the common room and kitchen area, and to another door. He knocked on it and called, "Leo, it's me. Open up."

I looked at my watch again. Jade would have a conniption if we missed the flight. Flights were always a considerable part of the budget, and we had to be careful with every penny. I tapped my feet on the ground and bit my nails like a junkie waiting on her dealer until the door swung open. I needed to get out of there. Leo answered, peering around the door, hiding his lower half. He looked at Xavier first, who said nothing, and then me.

"Sorry to interrupt, but we have to go. We need to make this flight."

Leo closed the door, and a moment later Lana floated out from behind the door with her flip-flops dangling from her fingers, and her usually straight hair tousled, and gave him one last kiss to remember her by.

"Don't forget about New Zealand," he said.

"I won't," she replied.

I felt Xavier's eyes drilling into me, but I kept mine on the ground. He sure as hell wasn't getting a goodbye like that.

Once Lana was finished, I grabbed her by the hand said a simple "Bye" to Xavier and ran from the house, through the coconut grove, down the beach, tears streaming from my face.

***

I had sobered up a little by the time we boarded the plane, and the weight of my shame came crashing down on me. For two and a half hours, I was tormented by memories from the night before. Kissing. Caressing. Groping. As I pushed one out, another took its place. Each flashback reminding me of the scum of the Earth I feared and loathed to ever become.

After we settled into a random hotel in Delhi that night, I called down to reception for them to turn the hot water on and undressed. The power of a hot shower was not something to be underestimated. It was the first one I'd had since Mumbai, and it couldn't have come at a more needed time. I stood in the shower and let the near scalding water run through my hair and down my skin. It washed away my tears, the remnants of my makeup, the smell of Xavier that lingered on my skin, in my hair, on my clothes, but not from my mind. As I scrubbed myself more vigorously than Lady Macbeth, I tried in vain to wash away my guilt and my memory of ever meeting Xavier.

But in my dreams, the memory of his lips against mine haunted me.

***

Date: January 30, 2010
Agra, India

There's a famous photograph of Princess Diana sitting in front of the Taj Mahal, perfectly poised on a marble bench with a long rectangular pond running to the white mausoleum gleaming against a cloudless blue sky behind her. It's similar to all of the postcards and stock images you find in coffee-table books and guidebooks, and these consistent representations set the expectations for this world-famous landmark. It is said at different times of the day, the light casts through the translucent marble a different colour ranging from pink to orange and yellow. I had planned to catch it in the perfect afternoon light with fluffy clouds riding the horizon, perhaps a thronging of women in rainbow-coloured saris contrasting against the immaculate white marble. After years of waiting for that moment and envisaging it in the viewfinder of my camera, I stood before the famed wonder of the world, staring out across the garden and thought, *you have got to be kidding me.*

A thick blanket of fog had covered Delhi and its neighboring areas conveniently in time for our visit. The visibility was at best twenty feet. As the girls and I walked down the path next to the famous water installation bundled in all of the clothes we owned, we couldn't see a damn thing. I tugged at the sleeves of my cardigan through the sleeves of my sweatshirt as the damp chill gnawed at my fingers. Despite the poor visibility and flat lighting, I was a woman on a mission to get a good shot of something. Anything!

All I wanted was to distract myself from that night in Goa. How could I have let things get that far? I wished I could wake up one morning in my bed back in Toronto to find out that I had been in a coma for the past few weeks and all of this was just some terrible dream. Well, so long as I didn't have any lasting brain damage. A plot-convenient soap opera type of coma would be great.

"So you see, madams," the tour guide began as the base of the building appeared. "The Taj Mahal is considered the ultimate display of love and affection. The Mughal Emperor Shah Jahan constructed it in memory of his third and most beloved wife, who died in childbirth. The Shah was so grief-stricken, he commissioned the most beautiful and ornate mausoleum built from the finest white marble, painstakingly inlaid with semi-precious stones to house her body, and his when he joined her in death." He stopped and pointed to a box of cloth things that looked like cloth shower caps. "Before we can enter, you must put these over your shoes."

As we settled onto the bench our driver, Hari, dashed over. "Please, allow me, Miss Lana." He dropped to his knees and looked at her with adoring brown eyes.

Lana shrugged and didn't stop him.

When we had arrived in Delhi, we had planned to purchase bus tickets and wing it like proper backpackers, but after falling for the charms of a young man and his dimples in the tourism office, he talked us into hiring a car and a driver for our week and a half in Rajasthan. We paid a negotiable premium for advanced guesthouse bookings and a car and a driver at our beck and call twenty-four-seven. Though it was above budget, it was a sweet deal and worth it to mitigate the hassle of searching for accommodations and purchasing bus and train tickets. Not to mention added safety.

When we checked out of our hotel the day before to begin our road trip, a willowy Indian man in his early thirties, no taller than five feet, sporting bellbottom jeans and a mustache that would make Burt Reynolds jealous greeted us as he leaned against a white sedan. We had to stifle a laugh as the cigarette fell from his gaping mouth, nearly setting his polyester shirt ablaze, the moment he laid his almond eyes on Lana.

"Miss Lana," he said as he rose to his full height, puffing out his chest, "I would build you a mausoleum so grand it would put the Taj Mahal to shame."

Lana giggled and said, "Oh, Hari, you're too silly," before turning her back to him. I looked at Jade, who rolled her eyes with a smile.

Hari leaned against the entrance as if imitating a male model, bedroom eyes never leaving Lana, as the tour guide led us around the paired caskets that lay in the center of the octagonal interior chamber. With the macro setting selected, I photographed the details of the bas-reliefs carved in the marble walls and the polished jasper, jade, and yellow marble inlaid in floral patterns.

"Harper, can we please finally talk about Goa?" Jade said, breaking the silence. "Your aura is worrying me."

Since that horrible night, I had barely spoken. I couldn't face the truth. It was almost as if saying it made it real. But I was bursting at the seams to talk about it. If I didn't get it out, I thought I would explode.

"I cheated on Adam," I said, slinging my camera around my neck. Saying it out loud didn't make me feel any better. In fact, it made me feel like pulling the top off the tombs and crawling in with one of the corpses.

Her mouth dropped, and I heard Lana shuffle towards us. "Well, I figured that much."

"I don't understand. I mean, it must be cold feet, right? That's totally normal."

"Cold feet happens when you're contemplating banging the stripper at your bachelorette party," Lana said. "You've been engaged for a month, your feet aren't cold, honey, your vagina is hungry."

At the word "vagina", two veiled women scurried out of the room muttering what I assumed was some spiritual protection against her blasphemy.

"My *what* is *what*?!" I caught my volume, remembering that we were in a house of God. Or Allah. I wanted to die and she's making jokes. "Jesus, Lana, do you have to be so crass all the time?"

"Vagina isn't crass. If I wanted to be crass, I could have said you have a hungry cu-"

"— I get it!" I cut her off. If it weren't for her and her stupid birthday sex goals none of this would have happened. "Can't you take anything seriously?"

Jade stepped between us. "Why don't we just take a minute to breathe?"

"It's okay, irritability is a sign of a hungry vagina. I hope you feed yours before you get like this," she said to Jade with a smirk.

"See, Lana, this is what I'm talking about," I whisper-shouted, "you don't value love. Or sex. Or anything."

"I resent that," she said, folding her arms. "I happen to value sex rather highly."

That was clear by the way she kept giving us a play-by-play over and over of her night with Leo.

"Yeah and if it weren't for your *high regard* for sex we wouldn't have stayed in Goa and none of this would have happened." Hell, if she didn't encourage me to book my plane ticket, I'd be back in Toronto happily engaged to Adam and planning my wedding.

"Whoa, hold on." She raised a hand. "I never made you do anything you didn't want to do. I didn't push you on Xavier. I didn't make you kiss him. You did all that out of your own free will. You did it because you wanted to."

"I did *not* want to," I said, but I knew deep down I did. And I hated myself for it.

"So why did you do it then?" I stared at her and balled my fists trying to come up with a response. Was it because I felt some strange pull towards Xavier? Or worse, because I wanted to spite Adam for what he said? But before I said anything, she added, "Look, what you did isn't that big of a deal."

Cheating on my fiancé isn't that big a deal?!

I wanted to scream, to yell, to explode into a million pieces, and as I held my breath, I thought I might. Maybe it wasn't a big deal to her, but it was to me. I'd be devastated if Adam did that to me. I could never forgive him for something like that. I really had no one to talk to about this, I read judgment in Jade's eyes and Lana couldn't take it seriously. Before I blew a blood vessel, I turned and marched through the archway welcoming the soothing dampness settling on my burning face as I slumped on the bench outside.

***

February 1, 2010
Ranthambhore, India

By the time we finished our tiger safari two days later in Ranthambhore National Park, Lana and I still hadn't spoken. As we returned to the hotel, a single ray of sunlight pierced through the fog, but I was still fuming mad at her but mostly at myself, and I debated what to tell Adam.

Who I still hadn't heard from.

"Miss Lana, how did you enjoy the safari?" As usual, Hari was hanging around waiting for her. "Did you see any tigers?"

He helped her out of the jeep, leaving Jade and me to help ourselves. We hadn't seen any tigers. Or bears, or hyenas, or leopards, or anything else the website advertised besides some deer and birds. Which wouldn't have been so bad if they all weren't mating like, well, animals in heat, and I could only be reminded of the silent disco. Those storm-grey eyes haunted me, and I hated that I missed the feeling of his callused fingertips dragging across my sensitive skin. I could only imagine what being consumed by him felt like. I hoped I had made better sounds than the deer had. Perhaps it was best that I had blacked out for it.

The tension between us was as thick as the fog as we spent the afternoon organizing our backpacks in our room. Jade and I shared the bed in the middle of the spacious but sparsely furnished room, and Lana slept on a cot in the corner. The building was made of marble, the walls yellowed over time, the floor indented from years of foot traffic, but the high ceiling was carved with subtle yet intricate bas-reliefs. In silence, the girls folded clothes and I loaded the images from my camera onto my laptop, backing them up on a USB storage key I had bought in Delhi. Once everything was saved in multiple places, I emptied my backpack in a corner of the room. Clothes, camera, equipment, and souvenirs tumbled out. As I sorted through the clusterfuck of stuff, I grabbed *Tahitian Heat*. My body tensed as the models on the cover, wrapped in each other with wanton lust and smiles as wide as the heroine's legs, mocked me. Why couldn't Adam and I share this kind of passion? Why did I picture Xavier whenever I read this? If it weren't for that book putting fantasies into my head, all of this could have been avoided. Heat radiated through me and without thinking, I opened the book to the middle, took a half in each hand and began to pull.

KSSSSSSHHHHHHHTTTTT

After the tear was an inch long I stopped, sense smacking me in the face. Since deciding on my five-year plan, I had done all I could to become a respectable adult who stood on her own two feet, but how could I call myself one if I were blaming two fictional characters for bad choices I had made in the real world? I had to take responsibility for my actions. After apologizing to my favourite book, I swaddled it in a tank top and shoved it in the bottom of my backpack.

I stood and made my way to the bathroom to splash water on my face. Padding through the room, I slipped on something and lurched forward catching myself against a wall. I looked for my assailant to find a

Cosmopolitan magazine splayed on the floor. I picked it up and with no words spoken, I handed it over to the only person in the room who would own a monthly sex manual. She dropped it back on the floor, and a thud echoed against the marble walls.

"Guys," Jade said with a sigh as she separated her crystals by colour on the bed, "can you please talk about it and get over it. I refuse to continue to live in this field of negative energy."

Lana's mouth gaped, "Me? I haven't done anything wrong."

She was right. I was acting like a hormonal teenager. Lana had been nothing but supportive since the day I met her, to the worst day of my life, to the present. She didn't deserve this.

Swallowing the lump in my throat along with my pride, I squared my body to Lana, who sat cross-legged folding her freshly laundered panties. "I'm sorry." I crossed my arms to ease my vulnerability. Absolving her meant blame for my actions lay squarely on me. "I'm just so mad that I slept with Xavier. But I shouldn't have blamed you. That wasn't fair."

"Thank you," she said as her face softened. "But you didn't sleep with him."

"What?" I said, steadying myself onto the cot next to her. "But I woke up in his bed. I was naked."

She placed her stack of undies down and looked me in the eye. "The silent disco finished, we started walking back, well, you could barely stand, so Xavier had to carry you. We went back to the boys' house, I changed you for bed in his clothes, you complained about the heat and refused to keep your clothes on and passed out. I made him promise not to touch you, and he said he would never take advantage of a girl. He slept on the couch in the living room."

I collected my memories from that morning. He wasn't in bed with me when I woke up.

"I tried to tell you," she said, "but you refused to talk about it."

And for a moment, just a tiny sliver of time, relief washed over me. But I couldn't deny the simple fact that, "I still cheated on Adam. Kissing counts."

Particularly that kind of kissing. It was the most intense pleasure I had ever felt, and I remembered how my body demanded more. What made it worse was the fact that I couldn't shake Xavier from my memory. I still wanted him. My eyes found Jade, and I knew she could see the guilt that twisted my face.

"You made a mistake. Don't beat yourself up too hard over it," she said.

I breathed out a breath I had been holding. She didn't hate me for what I did.

"Come on, let's take a walk around the gardens."

***

With the sun finally shining, temperatures warmed and as forest turned to desert, we arrived in Jaipur the next evening. The Pink City greeted with whimsical salmon-coloured turreted archways and buildings adorned with rows of windows screened with either sandstone or wooden shutters and shops bursting with puppets, jewelry, parasols, and silks. On our first night, we watched a puppet show fit for the Maharajas at the hotel and spent our first full day avoiding rabies at the Monkey Temple and nearly being trampled by elephants at the Amer Fort. The next day we were still full from stuffing ourselves with a variety of spiced goo of a traditional Thali dinner at the Chocki Dhani cultural village the night before, I still hadn't heard from my fiancé. It had been nine days since he told me he didn't support my dreams, and I had yet to receive an apology. It had also been eight days since I cheated on him, and I had yet to decide what to tell him.

Stuffed and exhausted, we returned to our guest-house, a two-story wooden building that reminded me of a dollhouse I wanted as a little girl and never got (thanks, Santa). We were going to have to speak eventually, and I didn't know if it was best to come clean or sweep it under the proverbial rug. I tossed and turned all night going back and forth, weighing the pros and cons. On one hand, I knew that we had to be honest with each other, honesty is the foundation of a strong relationship, but so is trust, and he might never trust me again. I would give anything to take it back, and I vowed to never put myself in a position like that again. Not for all the tattoos and muscles in the world. And so I decided that I would not have strippers at my bachelorette party.

By the time my eyelids finally closed, I felt in my heart that we had to hold onto each other. There is something special and magical about your first love, and especially with what we had gone through together, what could be more special and magical than your first love being your last and only?

Even through slips of judgment and moments of weakness, love should conquer all. Clichés are cliché for a reason, right?

***

Date: February 4, 2010
Jaipur, India

The next morning as we inhaled the spicy steam of my chai masala tea at breakfast, I asked the girls what they thought I should do. After much debate, Lana said I should definitely, certainly, unequivocally *not* tell him, it wouldn't be worth the drama, and Jade said definitely, certainly, unequivocally *do* tell him, doing the right thing would clear my karma.

After staring at them blankly more conflicted than ever and wishing that I could talk to my big sister, Jade added, "Meditate on it."

***

During the drive to Jaipur, somewhere between a roadside snake charmer and orange stand in a village seemingly inhabited only by men, Lana and Jade decided to go into business together to create an eco-friendly, fashionable yogawear label with the ultimate aim of crushing Lululemon into a spandex pulp. Jade brought the artistic vision, and Lana brought her networking and business savvy. Yin and Yang.

As I flicked through my images, the girls drowned in a deluge of delicate silks in the millionth sari shop they had ransacked in the famed Pink City. When the girls began chatting about strategy, I realized that I needed to take note and step up the business side of my venture. I had enough images to start my Facebook page and upload images to my Flickr and blog. The judges at Awesome Adventures would surely Google search their entrants; it was standard practice in this day and age when screening people from job applicants to potential dates. A rocking social media platform would put me above and beyond the applicants who didn't have one.

So I asked, "Hari, is there Internet nearby?"

Sitting on a couch across from Lana, he told me of an Internet café a few doors down, never once taking his eyes off of her.

The girls pulled out more fabrics for the poor shopkeeper to fold back up and I left the shop, welcoming the warmth on my face for a minute, until I pushed open the door to the Internet café. Logging into Facebook, I grumbled through the new updates, they were always changing the layout, and created a fan page for *Harper Rodrigues Photography* with just the basic information. I could upload photos and really get started when I could get my laptop on Wi-Fi next. Just as I was about to start entering the basic information a new message blinked.

My twisting gut had an idea of who it was. I clicked on it and saw a message from Adam.

> Hey baby, listen I didn't mean to say those things to you the other day. I was just upset, and I shouldn't have gotten so mad at you. It's just been so hard not having you around. Can we Skype to talk about it? Day after tomorrow? You name the time?

My fingers froze on the dirt-smattered keys of the keyboard. Guilt rippled through me as he confirmed that he didn't mean what he said. I thought of what our itinerary held and replied: Sure, eight-thirty p.m. my time, ten-thirty a.m. your time?

I had to tell him. If I could get it off my chest I could put that night behind me. And I hoped he could forgive me and that he could still love me.

***

"Miss Lana," Hari said taking Lana's shopping bag from her hands as we left the shop. "Might I suggest a movie tonight if you are in need of entertainment? There is a very famous cinema nearby I may take you to."

Lana looked at me then Jade, both of us giving a shrug and a nod. "Sure we'll all go, of course," she said.

His smile faltered for a moment. "Of course."

As I towel dried my hair, Jade performed sun salutations and Lana wrote furiously in a notebook. A knock on the door stopped everyone mid-move. Rising to my feet, I padded across the room and pulled the door open. Hari stood in the hallway, shifting his weight nervously, wearing a collared fuchsia shirt and crisp black bellbottoms.

"I have come to escort…" when he paused I knew what he really wanted to say, "… you ladies to the car."

"We'll be out in a minute," I said, closing the door.

"Oh Lana, Hari's looking mighty fine for you tonight," I teased and poked her in the ribs.

She shot me a look and grabbed her purse.

With our VIP balcony movie tickets in hand for the Bollywood blockbuster *3 Idiots,* Hari led us through the crowds into the lobby of the spectacularly Raj Mandir. The lobby looked like a whimsically decorated birthday cake with pink and yellow marzipan walls and blue-sky ceiling speckled with twinkling lights. Finally getting the hang of my exposure settings, I set my camera on the concessions counter hoping for a shot that could do the majestic room justice. Playing with the shutter speed, I pretended not to hear a very awkward exchange of Hari insisting on buying Lana candy and her refusal. Finally, he gave up when she bought popcorn for herself. Then, instructed by ringing bells announcing that the movie was about to begin, we ascended the staircase in the merengue-walled auditorium to our seats.

"So we'll take these three seats and you take the one at the end?" Lana said pointing to the seat furthest away from her.

"Oh, but Miss Lana, my assigned seat is this one next to yours." He pushed past Jade and me, blocked her path, and gripped the back of the seat next to her. "Please," he gestured for her to sit as he lowered into his seat, "the movie is about to begin."

Throwing her hands in the air in defeat, I couldn't help but think how sweet Hari's doting was. As I watched him fawn over her, I missed the way Adam had doted on me at the beginning of our relationship set in, before comfort set in, work deadlines kept us apart, and video games stole our time. But despite it all, I loved him. I missed him. And I missed who we used to be, and I wanted it back.

The movie was a delightful assault on the eyes and ears, alternating between dialogue in English, dialogue in Hindi, and slapstick musical numbers telling a tale of two friends reminiscing about hilarious college antics as they search for their long-lost friend who inspired them to think differently. I smiled thinking of our merry trio of runaways, and how people must have thought we were crazy for what we're doing. One of the songs that inexplicably featured a dance routine in a male dorm bathroom spoke of how to treat life's worries. The movie's take home message was to remember to tell yourself that, "All is well."

And so as I thought of Adam, and what my revelation would bring, I told myself, "All is well."

After nearly four hours it was finally time for the big kiss. As the two main characters finally locked lips, the crowd whistled and hollered like a sexually repressed sitcom laugh track on top volume, and I felt someone nudge my shoulder. Turning my head, I looked at Jade, who was looking down the row. I covered my shock as Lana stiff-armed Hari in the shoulder and wagged a finger in his face. Once she brought her arms back to her own body and folded them in front of her chest, they both looked our way, pleas for very different forms of help etched in their faces.

With my poker face strong, I turned back to the screen and kept my eyes there until the credits rolled.

On the drive back to the hotel, Indian pop music filled the air instead of Hari's usual chattering. After killing the engine in the lot outside of the hotel, he insisted that he walk us to our room, despite the fact that the hotel's security rivaled that of Fort Knox. Jade,

Lana and I bounced off each other as we hurried through the door together, and as Lana turned to close the door, over her shoulder, I saw Hari standing in the threshold, eyes wide like a puppy begging for his new favourite toy.

"Miss Lana?" he said in a pleading voice.

"Goodnight, Hari," she replied flatly before slamming the door in his face.

I could have sworn I heard a pained groan. Either emotional, or the door literally hit him in the face. With a frustrated sigh, Lana flopped onto the bed and covered her face with her hands.

"Can one of you please talk to him? I know it's really high school of me to ask, but I'd really appreciate it."

Seeing a chance to make it up to her for my bitchy attitude, I volunteered.

***

The following afternoon, Hari took us back to the Old City for lunch and more fabric shopping. And, as usual, he was unable to stay more than three feet away from Lana. From the wall of folded fabrics, she pulled out a sari the colour of ripe strawberries accented with a gold paisley trim. As the shopkeeper fumbled with the discarded silks, she told her that it was a wedding sari.

"Miss Lana," he said with wide eyes turning wistful, "that sari would look so wonderful on you. Perhaps you could put it on for just a moment? And then perhaps miss Harper could take a photograph of us together."

Lana shoved it back onto the shelf and glared at me. I tossed my hands in the air. *Fine fine, I'll go ahead and crush this poor man's heart for you.*

"Hey, Hari, would you mind taking me to see some of the sites of the city?" His face flashed with disappointment. "I would really appreciate it."

The girls and I agreed on a place to meet in two hours and, with a sigh, he stood up and I followed behind as he trudged out of the door, turning back to Lana for one last look. We drove in silence through the city until we reached the shores of Man Sagar Lake.

"Miss Harper," he said in his unceasing formal tone, "we have arrived at the Water Palace."

After a couple of beats it came into view. Rising from the glittering waters stood a sand-coloured cube-shaped building, two stories tall from the surface (three more remained below), with elegant domed towers on each corner, arched windows in the walls and the tops of trees that spoke of perfectly pruned gardens fit for the Maharajas of ages past.

Pulling into a parking lot across from the pavement that lined its banks, Hari escorted me across the road. He pulled out a cigarette and began chain-smoking his way through a pack. I adjusted the settings on my camera, stalling. I had no idea how to bring up the topic. I mean, I could have just gone for the jugular: *So Hari, Lana is in no way shape or form attracted to you so just cut it out already.* But that seemed harsh. Or perhaps I could do the roundabout thing and say that she has a boyfriend, or she's a lesbian, or she's asexual, or that she has a rare disorder that leads her to be attracted to inanimate objects. But then I figured he might take it as a challenge and try and convert her.

"So maybe we could come back another time to see this," I said as an idea formed. "I'm sure the girls would love to see this. Especially Lana."

Please take the bait…

I glanced out of the corner of my eye. He dropped the cigarette on the ground, and a smile pulled at his mustache. "I think so, too. I would like to take her here."

Bait taken. It was time to reel him in and club him over the head. "Hari, you know we leave India soon, right?"

His face dropped as he nodded. "I do, that's why I am hurrying to make Lana fall in love with me. She is so beautiful and virtuous. It makes me red with anger to think of another man have her virginity on her wedding night."

I disguised a laugh as a cough. If only he knew that ship had sailed long, long ago. Then I decided it was best to just come right out and say it.

"Hari, it's not going to work." I then proceeded with all of the rational explanations I could think of including, but not limited to, the distance, the cultural differences, the religious differences, she didn't want to live in India, he probably wouldn't like Canada, and finally, "I don't think she likes you in the way you want her to."

And each time all he would say was, "But I love her."

"Hari." I raked my fingers through my hair, struggling to find words that would make him understand.

Heat blazed in my face as I pushed through the guilt I felt for having to break his heart and frustration that he just wasn't getting it. I took a deep breath and out shot, "You don't know what love is."

Hari's eyes bore into me like a wounded animal staring down a hunter. "And you do? You choose to be here, and your fiancé is thousands of miles away."

"My relationship is none of your business," I fired back, steadying myself against the railing.

"And my love for Lana is none of yours."

We stared each other down, and then broke eye contact at exactly the same time. With no more words spoken, he pulled a cigarette from his pocket, and I raised my camera and turned it towards the lake.

Chapter 10

Anxiety twisted in my stomach as Hari drove me to the Internet café for my Skype date with Adam. Since our chat at the lake, things were awkward between us, but he didn't let that get in the way of his job. I had yet to form a plan of how to tell Adam, and without a plan, I felt like a child lost in a crowded fairground.

As I paid my deposit for the computer, the man behind the counter gave me an unnerving look. In India, it is not considered rude to stare, and let's say, he was being a bit too polite. And the fact that it was just he and I in the room made me feel even more uncomfortable. Under the harsh glow of fluorescent lighting, I buttoned up my cardigan as high as it could go, walked past the empty rows of computers, and took the one in the furthest corner away from Creepy McCreeperson, logged into Skype, and pressed call.

I chewed on my lip as the video kicked in. Adam's face wore a solemn look. After a terse exchange of greetings and an awkward silence, he said, "I'm so sorry for what I said."

"It's okay." I forced a smile and bit back an apology of my own.

"At first, I was so upset that you had left," he continued, "and I hoped that you'd change your mind and come home, but now that I've had time to think about it I'm actually really glad you're getting this travel thing out of your system."

"Travel thing?"

"Yeah, babe, I have no desire to go to any third world countries. Not now and not when we're married."

But I wanted to build a career on traveling. I told him on our first date of my dreams of seeing the world.

"Why do you want to marry me?" That question surprised me as much as it did him.

He paused and pressed his fingers into his forehead. "When you told me you were leaving, I couldn't let you go. You know I need you in my life. I love you. You are my happiness."

Suddenly, I felt weighed down. I loved that he loved me, and I brought him happiness, but to *be* his happiness was a huge and unfair responsibility. I was barely managing to maintain my own.

I could feel my own truth kicking and screaming to get out. "I have something I need to tell you." I had to say it. And I had to say it now. "Adam, when I was in Goa, I kissed someone."

His mouth fell, and his face froze on the screen. I clicked the Skype box and moved it around the screen to see if the program had stalled. A sound croaked through the headphones, and he finally moved.

"You did what?"

"I'm so sorry. It was stupid, I was drunk, it meant nothing, and I'll never see the guy again."

"I was scared that you were going to do this, but I actually didn't think you would." I rested my face in my hands, wondering what I could say to make it better. He continued, "Wait. Did you do it to get back at me for what I said?"

"No."

Then I realized I probably should have said yes, we could probably work through me wanting to spite him, but the real truth, I did it because I wanted to, because I felt a strong attraction to someone else that was uncontrollable. Primal. Something I had longed to feel and never could with him was an issue we couldn't work through.

"So why did you do it?"

"I...I... -"

But before I could finish my sentence, I was engulfed in darkness. The only sound I could hear was my speeding pulse. Panic set in as I gripped the edge of the desk unable to see anything, even my hand in front of my face. It wasn't the first blackout we had experienced, but I was never alone in a strange room with a strange man before.

All is well.

Steadying my breathing and forcing myself to stand, I pawed about blindly in the pitch, trying to find my way. Stumbling over rolling chairs as I made my way to the door, it hit me: Creepy McCreeperson had not made a peep. Not even a, "Don't worry, it's just a power outage."

With clammy hands I reached for the mace I kept in my pocket. As my breath began to labour, my mind flashed to a worst-case scenario. Tears pooled in my eyes as I thought of Audrey. But the fear I felt in that moment paled in comparison to how she must have felt staring down the barrel of a gun. Then I bumped into something, and I nearly barfed up my heart. Two hands grabbed me on the ass. I bucked wildly and shoved him, freeing myself from his grip. Pressing on the nozzle in the direction of the clattering sound of a body hitting a desk and chairs, I released the pepper spray into the air.

As it burned my eyes, I fumbled to the door, pushed it open, and ran down the alleyway as fast as my feet could carry me in the direction of the car park. Following the glow of headlights, I found myself drowning in the din of cars honking and men shouting as they thronged in the road, having deserted their pitch-black buildings. Never having felt more vulnerable in my life, I held myself with my left hand and held my mace high in my right hand in case someone else got some ideas about a non-consensual game of Seven Minutes in Heaven.

I called out, "Hari!" but it drew the attention of unfamiliar men. Keeping quiet to draw no more attention to myself, I pushed through them, searching for where he had parked.

A thin frame silhouetted against the headlights of a white sedan caught my eye. Hari. Gulping the muggy air, I walked towards it as if approaching a wild animal, and then past it, so the light would illuminate my face. The last thing I needed was to get in the wrong car with the wrong man. As I recognized those big almond eyes and bushy mustache, relief lapped over me and I nearly, oh so nearly, hugged him.

"Miss Harper, are you alright?"

"Please take me back now," I said, fighting to steady my trembling lips.

On the way back to the hotel, the city lights illuminated again. As I stepped through the door, I walked in on Jade and Lana conducting a business meeting held in child's pose on the bed. When I told them of my time in the Internet café with Rapey McCreeperson, we decided that no one was to be left alone again.

"I told Adam about what happened in Goa..." I said, giving them the events leading up to the blackout.

"So what's next?" Jade asked.

"I don't know."

***

Date: February 6, 2010
Pushkar, India

The drive from Jaipur to Pushkar was one of our shorter trips, and after yet another sleepless night, I stared out of the window as we drove into the endless ocean of rolling sand dunes of the Thar Desert. The Skype conversation with Adam reverberated in my mind. It felt as if he didn't know me anymore, or worse, he wanted me to abandon my dreams. He was neither drunk nor angry and made it clear that he saw what I was doing as a phase when I felt I made it clear that it was what I wanted to do with my life. I really loved him, and I didn't want to lose him, but how could I marry someone who didn't support me?

***

Our new hotel had a shaky Wi-Fi connection in the lobby, and as we were checking in, I looked at my messages. There was a stream of barely coherent angry messages all in caps lock, and I read them in his voice, shouting at me: *How could you do this to me? What kind of person are you? I can't believe I'm over here planning a wedding and you're over there kissing other guys!*

I clenched my jaw, fighting the guilt. Finally the stream of messages calmed down. He said he wanted to talk about it some more after he returned from a work conference in Ottawa in a few days. Something struck me as odd as he had never mentioned this work conference before, but then again we hadn't exactly been talking twenty-four-seven like we used to. I closed the window without replying.

With mango lassis chilling in our hands, we set out to explore Pushkar. Worrying wasn't going to change anything, so I put my focus on my photography. As we walked along the sandy strip towards town, the girls entertained flirtatious young rickshaw drivers inviting us for tours. Still shaken up from the night before, I kept my head down and ignored them completely.

Buildings rose from the desert appearing to have been constructed from the caramel coloured sand, with no building standing taller than three stories. Mangy cows roamed the narrow roads, hand-painted signs plastered to shops begged for our attention, and Indian trance music pulsed through the arid air. Cigarette in hand, Jade popped in an out of Ayurvedic spas while Lana pawed at camel leather handbags. Raising my camera, I captured portraits of elderly women selling fruit and vegetables from burlap sacks, shielding themselves from the blazing afternoon sun under parasols.

Once we had gorged ourselves on freshly fried potato patty burgers, Jade led us to the town's famous ancient Brahma Temple. Reading from the guidebook, she explained that according to Hindu scripture, the god Brahma defeated the demon Vajrayana with a lotus-flower (it seemed to be a much less violent time), and as the petals fell springs emerged, creating lakes. Pushkar was located on the shores of one of these lakes and, as a holy pilgrimage site, many Hindus bathe their sins away in the lake. I toyed with the idea of taking a dip myself. Perhaps it could wash away my Goan sins. Walking through a tall sandstone archway adorned with pillared canopies we entered a courtyard of white marble and stone ghats, or stairs, which led down to the lake.

Taking a look at the holy water, I glanced at Jade. Her serene expression twisted with disgust.

"I'd rather go to hell than go in there," Lana said with a snort.

"Have some respect," Jade snapped. "But yeah, there's no way I'm bathing."

The lake had receded into the sands, but having been prepared for the dry season, the locals constructed a pool to contain some of the water. Along with the feathers and droppings of the millions of pigeons that called the temple their home, the mold-green and stagnant smelling water looked as if you'd come out with a third leg and sepsis.

"Would you like to be blessed?" A string bean of a man said before claiming he was a priest.

Catching me off guard, he shoved a small bouquet of handpicked marigolds into my hand before leading me by the hand down the ghats to the water's edge. Something told me that this man wasn't a priest, and I think it could have been the flared jeans, but rather than fighting what was happening I figured, *when in Rome.* Inviting me to sit with him, he asked my name, where I was from, and how many family members I had. I told him three then realized that there were only two left. Then he asked me to close my eyes. As he held my hands he instructed me to repeat after him as he chanted words in what I presumed to be Hindi. Apparently they were prayers for luck and protection of my loved ones, but he could have been repeating his shopping list for all I knew.

"You may ask God for whatever it is you need. He is listening."

Since that night in Goa, I couldn't shake Audrey from my mind. She has never left my thoughts, but the urge to talk to her grew each day, but I knew she would never answer. I had grown up so thankful to have a big sister to talk to about life issues, jobs, friends, and especially relationships. But I needed to talk to her more than ever, and without her, I felt as if I were flying blind. I asked God if I could talk to her. If only for a moment. I would have given anything in the world just to hear her voice again.

A warm breeze caressed my face, and when I inhaled the scent of my "priest's" Old Spice cologne, I felt very silly.

Peeking through one eye, hoping it would be over soon, I saw him pull a small tin from the breast pocket of his *Saturday Night Fever* shirt. He dipped his finger in the powdery contents. I squeezed my eyelids shut. Then, as I felt pressure in the space between my eyebrows, he branded me.

He told me to open my eyes, and I watched him tie two pieces of red and yellow string to my wrist, fashioning a bracelet next to the one Xavier had given me. Glancing around, I saw Lana rolling her eyes at her "priest" but Jade sat in Lotus position, eyes closed, entirely at peace, chanting away.

When he asked me how much money I was willing to give him to send my family luck, I had enough of my spiritual experience. Everything pointed to tourist scam and requests for money drove it home. But given that we were balancing precariously on the water's edge, I pulled out a few dollars' worth of rupees for insurance that he wouldn't push me into the nasty water. Shoving them in his hand, I carefully backed up and climbed the ghats and waited for the girls.

***

"I see that you have acquired your Pushkar Passports," Hari said, cigarette smoke billowing from his mouth. His gaze still fixed on Lana when we returned from town. Since our little chat at the Water Palace, he had backed off of her. "I am so sorry, I should have said something sooner. I have had trouble concentrating lately." Smiling politely we kept walking through the hotel gate. "Miss Jade, I have spoken to my friend as you requested, and he can take you into the desert tomorrow if you wish."

"Okay, I'll talk to the girls tonight and get back to you soon."

With a nod, he sucked on his cigarette and walked over to the group of men congregating in the road outside the hotel.

Once behind closed doors Jade explained that she wanted to do bhang while we were here.

"Bhang?" Lana and I said in unison.

She explained that it was a drink made from the leaves and buds of female cannabis plants used to achieve transcendental states and aid spiritual ecstasy.

"So you want to go into the desert and trip balls?" Lana replied.

Jade shrugged and said, "Pretty much," before explaining that we would drink it in ritual with a shaman in the desert. Hari had made some calls to friends and found a shaman who was willing to take us, but we had to decide within the hour if we're going to participate. "No pressure to you guys, but I'm going to do it regardless."

By the time Hari dialed the shaman's number, Lana and I decided to join her.

***

After breakfast, Jade spent the morning meditating while Lana and I watched. With my legs cramping in lotus pose, I was trying to get in the right headspace for the day, but I was a bundle of nerves. When her alarm sounded, her eyes flicked open and she stretched her legs, shook them out, and stood up.

Meeting Hari in the same spot where we had left him the day before he straightened his spine as he greeted Lana. All of our attention quickly fixated on the man standing next to him.

"Madams, this is Naresh, he will take you into the desert today."

Encased in saffron robes loomed a thin man with orange and red paint plastered from his forehead to mustache. A long grey beard fell to his chest, and waist-long dreadlocks framed his narrow face. Out of all the "holy men" we had come across, this guy looked legit. With introductions made, he led us down the sandy road where four camels and three teenaged boys waited.

We mounted our desert beasts with our pubescent drivers riding bitch, waved Hari goodbye, and as we set off with our backs to town I hoped that we weren't being led into something that resulted in us becoming a Nancy Grace TV special.

Chapter 11

As I jostled about, squeezing my legs together so tightly I feared I might crush the poor animal, I plotted the demise of the camel saddle's inventor and then wondered why no one had thought to reinvent them. Everything about riding a camel is beyond unnatural, from its lumbering arrhythmic gait to the fact that as a passenger you sit on the front and have nothing to hold onto except a three-inch stub of metal at your crotch. Clutching my camera with my free hand, I tried to distract myself from the pain as my inner thighs and nether regions struck the hard leather over and over and over. For the sake of the ride back, it was a good thing that cannabis was a painkiller.

I quickly gave up on trying to take photos, preferring to focus on balancing and not falling a thousand feet under my camel's plodding hoofs. With our saffron-clad shaman in the lead, we galloped over the crumbling sand for what seemed like an eternity, finally coming to a halt near the base of a rugged mountain range. With groans, our camels lowered to their knees, and we climbed from their backs. Shaking my legs out and rubbing my inner thighs so vigorously I gave my driver impure thoughts, we gathered in the center of the dune and sat in a circle.

Lana stretched her legs while Jade folded hers as our shaman chanted, sang, danced, smattered our faces with orange powder, and finally produced a silver thermos. He poured a creamy milk-coloured liquid in the cap and handed it to Jade. My heart pounded as she held it to hers before chugging it in one go. Lana was next, and when Naresh handed it to me, I nearly passed out as I took the first breath I thought I had taken since he pulled out the thermos.

I had smoked weed a few times after Audrey introduced it to me on a visit to her university, but drinking some weird cannabis cocktail in the middle of the desert where no one can hear you scream was a whole other experience. Hesitating, I looked at Lana, who was still stretching, and then the shaman cupped my hands and forced the cap to my lips. *I guess this is happening.* I opened my mouth and filled it with the cool creamy liquid. *Ooo, vanilla lassi.* He had good taste.

As our designated drivers tended to the camels, we lay on the warm sand, and waited for the THC to kick in. At first everything felt a little fuzzy, like someone was running fur over my skin, and my arms felt a little heavy. When we exploded into a fit of giggles at a camel's snort, I knew it was taking effect. After that, it felt as if I was wandering between worlds of sleep and wakefulness, floating in a lucid dream.

I smiled at the fluffy clouds riding across the blue sky. They reminded me of the cotton candy Audrey and I gorged on at a fair when I was seven. I sighed at the memory of losing my family on the way to the Ferris wheel and subsequently freaking right out. My big sis found me in a bush, clutching the sticky sugar fluff to my chest. Though ants were ravaging me, I had never been so happy when I saw her face.

I sat up and shook out my fuzzy, heavy arms. Picking up my camera, I peered at my newly altered reality through the viewfinder. Snapping pictures of the girls sprawled out in the sun, I turned my camera on our shaman, meditating with the vastness of the desert dunes undulating into the horizon before him. It made me think of my favorite photograph of Audrey and me when we rented ATVs and went off-roading in the Nevada desert when I was twelve. On that trip, we decided we were going to travel the world together one day, live in Sydney, date surfer boys, and never become boring grown-ups.

As I turned and snapped wildly in my dreamlike state, a mountain stopped me in my tracks. Lowering my camera, I stared at the peak raking the clouds. My feet moved independently of the rest of my body as the mountain pulled me towards it. A warm breeze stroked my heated skin as I padded across the dune and over the crest. The moment I was alone, I froze, dwarfed by its immensity.

With my eyes fixated on the craggy crest, I was overcome with a presence and energy so powerful my knees buckled and I sank into the sand. It was kind of like that feeling you get when it's going to rain but magnified to a greatness I could not rationally comprehend. In my heart I knew I was in the presence of something greater than me, greater than all of us, greater than the desert I stood on. I kneeled in the presence of the divine energy that creates, destroys, and animates everything on Earth. Jade called it the Universe with a capital "U," but some may refer to it as God.

That was some good bhang.

I couldn't help but feel like a naughty child, taken aside, as if It was asking, "Is there something you need to say to me?"

I knew what It wanted from me. I knew what I needed to say.

"I'm sorry," I muttered with my eyes fixed on the towering mountain, "I'm so very sorry for taking your gift for granted."

Tears pooled and streamed as I drowned in the emotions I had bottled up over the years since the moment my family received The Call.

It was the worst day of my life, and as I kneeled before the Universe, it flashed in my consciousness. Snow had dusted the city and as my mother pulled out her annual Christmas cake from the oven, I poured myself a glass of Pinot Noir and organized the pastry decorations, while my father fussed over a crossword puzzle in the Sunday newspaper on the couch. My mouth was full of white icing when the phone rang. It rang just like any other time, but when my mother collapsed with the receiver pressed against her face, I knew life would never be the same. Tumbling from the chair I took the receiver from her.

"Mrs. Rodrigues?" A gruff accented voice rolled the "r."

"This is her daughter, what's happened?" I said as my mother clutched at me sobbing.

"My name is Detective Barboza. I'm very sorry to tell you, but we have recovered the body of Audrey Rodrigues."

The body?

I shook my head as I choked on my own breath. It made no sense. She was coming home tomorrow. I had bought her a present. We were supposed to travel together the following year and have wonderful adventures. She was going to grow up. We were going to be the Maids of Honour at each other's weddings. We'd have babies at the same time. We'd grow old with each other.

I refused to accept it. It had to be a mistake.

But, a week later, when we should have been stringing lights on the tree together, I placed my hands on a varnished white casket and reality hit that my world would never be the same.

As my parents unraveled on the pew next to me, I had no choice but to force back the tears. I had to be strong for myself but stronger for them. As they held each other weeping, I vowed that I would give them the future that Audrey never could. They would never see her grow up, celebrate promotions, walk her down the aisle, and cradle her children. But I could give them all of that.

I cried in the bathroom and blaming red eyes on "allergies," perfected a fake smile that would keep a beauty queen stumbling through her final question jealous, and lied to everyone, even myself, about how much pain I felt. But staying strong came with a price.

On the one-year anniversary of her death, my mother didn't bother with her cake, and my father didn't bother with his crossword, and neither bothered to get out of bed until dinner. After we ate take-out and shed tears over stories of her, I returned to my new apartment, before it had any colour, and before I met Adam. Never having felt more alone, I fell to pieces.

Delirious with anger and Pinot Noir, I was desperate to escape the crushing sadness that followed me around every single moment. If every day was going to feel like I was drowning, I wondered why didn't I just slip beneath the water. So I stepped into the bathroom and ran a hot bath. Then, sliding a kitchen drawer open, I drew a large knife from a drawer, went back the bathroom and undressed. Steam rose from the tub and the blade glinted in the artificial light as I set it down on the tile. I lowered myself into the water and turned the faucet off and watched the last drops of water fall. I felt nothing.

Lying back with the water lapping at chin, I stared at the ceiling.

"I can't live without you," I whispered.

When my body was warm and tingling, I sat up and picked up the knife, pressing the cool metal against my wrist. As I applied pressure and began to feel the skin tearing, my phone rang from the pocket of my jeans on top of the toilet, startling me so much I dropped the knife. It hit the edge of the tub, fell onto the tile, and skipped out of reach. It felt as if I had been awaken from a dream. I leaned forward, and with shaky fingers, I fumbled with the jeans and plucked the phone from my pocket.

"Hello?" My voice trembled as I answered.

"It's Mom." Her voice crackled. "I just wanted to tell you I love you. I don't know why but something came over me, and I picked up the phone without thinking."

Guilt knotted in my chest.

"I love you, too," I sputtered out.

"What are you doing?" she asked.

Silence hissed through the receiver, and after a beat, I replied, "Just taking a bath."

"Okay, be careful not to slip. I don't know what I'd do if something happened to you."

When the call disconnected, I set the phone back on top of my jeans, pulled myself from the tub, wrapped myself in a towel, drained the tub, picked up the knife and marched into the kitchen. Feeling horrified at what I had almost done, I slid the knife into the drawer and made an appointment with a grief counselor.

The memory faded and I was staring down the divine force I used to curse that stole her away from me. Over the years that passed since that day I learned to leave my anger behind. And as I felt it simmering and bubbling in my core, I swallowed it and instead practiced the exercise my grief counselor had taught me. Gratitude.

"Thank you. Thank you for blessing me with my loving family and friends. Thank you most of all for bringing Audrey into my life." Then warmth bloomed from my core to my fingers and toes, and I was overwhelmed with a feeling I could only describe as pure, unadulterated love.

The warm breeze caressed my face and a familiar scent I hadn't smelled in years tickled my nose. My breath hitched as I recognized it. Cupping my face in my hands, all the emotions I had been bottling up surged and broke free as a flood of tears of joy.

"Audrey?"

I am here.

Though I heard her voice in my head, I was pretty sure I wasn't going crazy. I know I was higher than Willie Nelson at Woodstock, but it felt as real as the sand beneath me. Enveloped in her scent, a montage of long forgotten memories played in my mind. The summer we spent perfecting our breaststroke when my parents rented a cottage on Lake Ontario, the brightness of her hazel eyes as I draped her in cloth to be my "Afghan Girl", the time I broke my father's golf clubs and she took the blame, the week when I visited her in university and we had a blast playing beer pong. It could have been a minute, but for what felt like an eternity, I lived our lives together again from my earliest memory of her to my last.

But as I saw her waving as she disappeared to start her trip in Bolivia, I felt the energy weaken.

"No," I sobbed, stretching out my hand reaching for her, "don't go."

It's time.

Pain ripped through my chest. The shattered pieces of my heart that had been sewn back together were tearing at their seams.

As I felt her leaving I choked out, "I love you. I miss you."

I am with you always.

And then, as if dropped from the ether, I blinked and landed back on Earth, engulfed in silence. Wiping my eyes I looked up at the mountain, begging for it to let me see her again, but now it was just a mountain, like any other. The air was still and smelled only of dry desert sands.

"Harper?" Jade's voice pierced through the calm. I turned, and through blurred vision I saw her and Lana running over the crest of the dune.

Wrapping me in their arms, they held me until I cried myself empty. And that night, for the first time in weeks, I slept through the night.

***

As I tore my toast, spreading near frozen butter on it the following morning, a welcome feeling of calm lapped over me. Which was promptly interrupted when the hotel manager marched over to our table.

"Miss Harper Rodrigues?" He peered through thick glasses at us.

I raised my hand, like a child in school. "That's me."

"You have a phone call."

I looked at the girls, shrugged as I stuffed the crusty carb in my mouth, and followed him through the lobby to the desk. He passed me the receiver, and my heart stopped as I heard my mother's voice, unnervingly calm.

"It's Adam, he's in the hospital." I steadied myself against the reception counter. "His roommate, Jeff, called me this morning, he's been trying to get in touch with you."

"What happened?"

"Jeff came home and found him unconscious. He slipped into a diabetic coma, but he's awake now. He'll be discharged today."

"Diabetic coma?" The words fell from my mouth before I wondered how Jeff found him. He was supposed to be at a work conference. More than that, how could he forget to take his insulin? I programmed his phone to remind him. "Can you please call Jeff and tell him to tell Adam to get on Skype as soon as he can? I don't care what time it is there."

"I will. And it's the strangest thing, but I had the most vivid dream of you and Audrey last night."

I bit back my words about speaking to Audrey. She was already worried enough about me without having to know I took drugs with total strangers in the desert. Instead, I told her and my father I loved them before hanging up. Feeling the world move in slow motion, I ran up the stairs and grabbed my laptop from my bag. With blood pounding in my ears, I nearly tumbled down the stairs as I ran back to the girls trying to get the damn thing connected to the Internet.

"So Harper, we were thinking about renting bikes today and driving into the desert." Lana's topic of conversation abruptly changed when I crashed into my seat. "Oh shit, what happened?"

"Adam is in the hospital." My voice was frantic as I relayed to them what my mother had told me.

Finally connected to the Internet, messages from Jeff flooded in through Skype, email, and Facebook, telling me to contact him as soon as I could. I replied the same to all: Tell Adam to get in touch as soon as he gets home.

"You guys go ahead," I finally said, glancing up at them, "I need to wait here until he comes online."

After assuring them that I would be fine without them and there was no need for their day to be ruined, they left as I chewed on my lip, staring at my computer waiting for a response. Then I read through Adam's next frantic stream messages: *Can't we go back to how we used to be? I'm not ready to give up on us. Please come home. I can't live without you.*

Then a terrible realization hit me: suicidal depression runs in families. If he did it intentionally because of what I did, I'd never be able to forgive myself.

I pushed the thought out of my mind for no other reason than the preservation of my sanity. Through three more cups of chai masala tea, I still hadn't heard anything so I popped upstairs, grabbed my camera, and sat cramped in a corner next to the one outlet in the room, keeping myself occupied by editing images and updating my Facebook and Flickr and blog through the morning and afternoon, as the wait staff tidied around me.

Rising to relieve myself from all the tea, a message blinked. It was Jeff: Hey, we're taking him home in a few hours. He'll be online at twelve-thirty our time, so ten p.m. your time.

With my pulse normalizing, I blew out a sigh of relief that he was well enough to go home.

Chapter 12

Standing in the room after locking away my computer and camera, claustrophobia clawed at me. Why was he in Toronto and not Ottawa like he said he was? I told myself that maybe his plans changed and it slipped his mind to tell me. Or he was so mad at me, he decided not to. Either way, it still felt like he was lying to me.

There was a time where we would burst to tell each other even the most mundane detail of our day.

I squeezed my fists so tight I could feel my skin tearing under my nails. I had to get out of there. I needed fresh air. As I walked past the hotel gate and into the sandy road, Hari called out to me. Stomping out his cigarette, he asked me how we enjoyed our time in the desert and if we needed to be taken anywhere. Despite our little tiff at the water palace in Jaipur, we didn't hold a grudge towards each other. After I declined, he shifted nervously and then said, "As it is your last night in Pushkar and..." he cleared his throat... "last night with me, I would like to take you ladies somewhere tonight for dinner. It is nearby and I think you will like it."

I nodded and told him that I would speak to the girls about it. Lifting my face to the sun as I walked away, I focused on my breath as I let its rays beat down on me. Even with just that I felt myself returning to my body. After shaking the nerves out of my arms and legs, I checked my watch. It was four-thirty. The girls should be back soon. To stretch my legs I wandered down the road towards town and bumped into my two best friends, smattered in sand, telling me of how their bike broke down in the middle of the desert and their ordeal making it back to civilization.

After taking Hari up on his offer, (he knew this place better than us), we returned to the room. While the girls were taking turns showering and napping, I took Lana's *Cosmopolitan* magazine and caught the last of the sun's rays lying on a lounge next to the kidney-shaped pool. I opened it up and flicked through the sex advice, glossy ads, airbrushed models stopping when I reached an article titled: Are You Ready To Break Up?

The first line read: if you need an article to help you decide, the answer is yes. I slapped the magazine shut and dropped it on the floor.

As the cool evening breeze swept over me goose bumps spread across my arms. Glancing to the sky, the sun began to tuck itself behind a mountain range, and I thought of the day before. I thought of Audrey's last words to me: *I am with you always.*

I whispered to her, "I don't know what to do. I need you."

A voice inside my head, this time sounding more like my own, echoed back, *You'll know what to do.*

***

At six o'clock on the dot, a gentle knocking rattled the door. I turned the handle and peered beyond the chain lock, meeting a pair of familiar brown eyes under a mop of black, slicked back hair. Hari had really outdone himself tonight. I struggled to maintain my poker face as my eyes fell upon the yellow and orange bouquet in his hands.

This won't end well.

"Lana, I think you should come here a second," I called as I closed the door and undid the chain.

After taking his flowers and throwing them on the bed, we followed him to the car. He opened the passenger door for Lana, who instead opened the door to the backseat, climbed in, and slammed it shut. With Jade taking shotgun, I slid into the backseat next to Lana. A cooler was strapped into the middle seat.

"What's this?" I asked Hari.

He turned the key, and the engine rumbled. "I have a connection to a very special vineyard in India. I have brought some bottles for you to try."

So, India had vineyards — you learn something new every day.

We drove only a few hotels over before Hari parked and scampered to open Lana's door. With a huff, she stepped out, ignoring his outstretched hand. He then grabbed the cooler and locked the car. In the evening glow of streetlamps, we followed him through a stone archway into the grassy courtyard of the hotel. Empty tables dotted the space around the base of a tree with a trunk so wide it would take all four of us linking arms to hug it. Beneath the branches adorned with whimsical white fairy lights, Hari waved at a waiter and chose a table close to the trunk. Pulling out a chair for Lana, he then took the seat across from her. As Jade and I sat down exchanging confused expressions across the table, a waitress came over with the menus and wine glasses.

"Please, order whatever you like. It is my treat," he said as he placed the cooler on the table, his eyes fixated on a very uncomfortable looking Lana.

"Hari, we can't stay long, we have dinner reservations," she said before looking at us with wide eyes.

Dinner reservations? What was she talking abou—" Oh yes," I realized what was going on, "I forgot...yes, we do. At...that restaurant in town," I said, fumbling through my lie.

He looked down at the table and disappointment flashed in his face nearly imperceptibly. Then he nodded, and then pulled out two wine bottles from the cooler. One red, one white. Both cold. Horror carved Lana's face as she stared at the bottle of red sweating with condensation. To a hedonist, defiling red wine was a sin punishable by social exile. When he asked which wine we would prefer, we all chose white.

I read the label as I sipped. As "notes of apricot and lemon ambled like the spring that feeds the Ganges" on my palate, I admired the marketing of wine. The top, base, and bottom notes were listed on the bottle, but it just tasted like any old white wine to me. And as we drank our surprisingly tasty wine in awkward silence, a look of satisfaction danced on Hari's bronzed face, winking at his waiter friends as they walked by. When the waitress returned, he spoke to her in Hindi and pointed at the menu. Our protests against food were ignored, but the waitress quirked an eyebrow at us anyways as she jotted down the order. We all seemed to be well aware of the inappropriateness of the situation. Well, except for Hari.

"So Miss Lana, how have you enjoyed your time in India?" He purred. "I hope I have been a satisfactory host."

"Yah, it's been good," she said gruffly with her eyes glued to her glass.

"So good you might want to remain here?"

Lana shot daggers at me through her eyes. I pulled my gaze to him and jumped in, "Hari, remember what we talked about the other day?"

He ignored me and kept his attention on Lana. "India is a very wonderful place to live."

Lana gulped her wine and then emptied the rest of the bottle in her glass. An uncomfortable silence filled the space around us. Anxious about my call with Adam, I checked my watch, thinking that at least half an hour had passed. Nope, not even fifteen. "Awkward" has this very annoying ability to slow down time. And the fact that no one was talking kept time at a near standstill. I had nothing to distract me from thinking about Adam. I was scared to talk to him, but I needed to see for myself that he was okay. I wanted to know why he wasn't where he said he was, why he didn't take his insulin, and what he wanted to do about us. I was torn about us. I loved him, but I wasn't sure that we were meant to be together anymore.

When the waitress finally appeared, I had never been so relieved to see a total stranger, but as she placed two medieval feast sized platters of pakoras on the table, I wished she had never come at all.

"Please, enjoy," he said, taking a slow bite of one of the golden fried vegetable nuggets.

I plucked one from the pile and juggled it as it burned my skin. As I blew on it, the delicious deep-fry smell tickled my nose, and when I bit into one, I realized just how hungry I was. As we ate, Hari continued to try and sell Lana on the benefits of living in India. When Jade tried to intervene, he pulled out a foil ball from his breast pocket containing a nugget of hash and suggested that she and I take it to the corner of the courtyard. Refusing it, we tried to eat the pakoras as fast as possible and keep the conversation neutral, but when Hari brought up child rearing and how his mother would help her out with their children, Lana's patience had been exhausted.

"Alright, it's time to go," she said, looking at her bare wrist.

"Yes," Jade said, rising to her feet. "This has been great, thank you for taking us here but it's time for us to get to our dinner reservation."

He fought back a scowl then sighed. "As you wish, Miss Lana."

Gently placing the wine bottle back in the cooler with the other two bottles, he left a pile of rupees on the table and began walking towards the archway. As he passed the tree, he slowed down and called Lana's name. She groaned and halted. Jade and I pressed forward and hid in the shadows in the archway. She had to finally tell him herself that he had to stop.

"Oh no," Lana gasped.

I turned, and my mouth hung agape.

In a grassy patch in the ethereal glow of the fairy lights, Hari had dropped to one knee. Under other circumstances, this setting would be incredibly romantic. Watching this made me terrified of being single. Good men were hard to find, but the crazy ones grew like weeds. Despite being deaf to the conversation, it was pretty obvious what was being said. Hari begged, reaching for her hand as Lana waved them in the air wildly stomping her feet as her head bobbed, whipping her hair. Turning on her heels, she marched towards us, through the alleyway, and back towards the hotel as Hari buried his face in his hands.

As we followed her down the road, he called out, "Please, I'm sorry. I must drive you to town." Lana sped up. "It is dangerous at night and it is my duty to keep you safe."

Hearing his very rational argument, we stopped. Keeping our backs to him, we heard the engine rumble towards us. We climbed in the car, and he drove us in silence. He parked in one of the bays at the entrance to the town center.

"I will be here when you are finished," he said, still gripping the steering wheel and staring straight ahead through the windshield.

Before he could finish his sentence, Lana had bolted from the car and down the road. After receiving a stern warning that she was in no mood to be teased about Hari, we found a quirky café in a garden and ordered falafel sandwiches. As we ate, I checked the time every five minutes, and Lana filled us in on what she had told Hari. Long story short, she told him to, "Fuck off." No surprise there.

"I think we need to come up with a codeword," Jade suggested. "A word if we feel we need to leave a situation."

"It would have been useful tonight," Lana said with a snort.

"I like this idea," I said, nodding. "It needs to be something that isn't going to sound weird in regular conversation."

Jade pulled a cigarette from her pocket and popped it between her lips. "Damn, I need to grab a lighter."

"What about matches?" Lana said.

"Well, if you have any that would work, too."

"No no, *matches* could be the codeword," Lana said, smoothing her poker straight locks. "Usually you carry a lighter, not matches, so saying something like, 'Hey, I need to get some matches' sounds normal in conversation but isn't something any of us would say."

And with that, our code word was born.

After stuffing ourselves with chickpeas and cabbage, we hurried back to the car so I wouldn't be late for the big talk I was about to have with Adam. As the anxiety twisted in my chest, I began to see stars. I still didn't know what I wanted the outcome to be.

Crossing the traffic barrier just past the center of town, we found the car exactly where it had been before, but with Hari sleeping peacefully in the fully reclined driver's seat with the doors locked. Jade knocked on the window, softly at first but once she began to bang Hari shot straight up. With glassy eyes he looked in our general direction and unlocked the car.

"Hi Hari," I said, sliding into the passenger's seat, filling the space with the smell of my leftover falafel.

He grunted back and turned the key, keeping his eyes forward. As he struggled to complete the three-point turn, it struck me how washed out his skin looked. I could understand his miserable expression, but he looked as if he were going to be sick. What the hell happened to him in the past two hours?

He drove slower than usual, swerving in the barely lit road from side to side, and I noticed that something was off. Something was missing. The bottles had stopped clanking. They stopped clanking because they weren't there anymore. Someone had drunk them all.

Our designated driver was shit-faced drunk.

Whipping around, I read the girls' alarmed expressions as they inspected the empty cooler. I mouthed the words, "he's drunk," before turning back, trying some conversation topics to keep him lucid. But he was in no mood for chitchat. Finding myself at a loss for words I said the only thing that popped into mind, "Want some falafel?"

With the foil unwrapped around the soggy remains of my sandwich, I held it out. Without a glance, he took the foil in his hand and devoured the sandwich in one bite, then tossed the foil out of the window. Letting out a loud belch with a smell that made me worry for his digestive health, he kept driving in wide zig-zags, and I kept my hands ready to grab the wheel if need be. A wave of relief washed over me as I spotted our hotel down the road. But the wave broke when he began retching and swerving uncontrollably as he tried to pull over to the side of the road. I reached for the wheel but before I could get a grip on it, the car lurched to a stop with a loud *WHUMP*.

Sliding off my seat, I collided with the dashboard. I yanked up the hand break, rubbed my sore elbow, and opened the door, joining the girls outside to inspect the damage. Hari remained in his seat doubled over with one foot out of the door. The car had crashed into a shallow ditch, narrowly missing a cow that was now hightailing it into the darkness.

"There will probably be a bit of a dent," I said.

"Perhaps a few scratches. I hope Hari's okay," Jade added.

"It was nothing major, he and the car will be fine," Lana said, waving her hand dismissively. "He'll just have to deal with his boss back in Delhi. Let's just get back to the hotel."

I glanced at my watch. It was nine forty-seven. If we left now, I'd have time to prepare myself.

"What's going on here?" An unfamiliar male voice startled us.

We turned around to see two figures approaching us. As they strode through the light of a street lamp my stomach flipped. Fuck. The. Police. I glanced back at Hari, who was still slumped in his seat. There was no way we could pass him off as sober.

"Nothing, officers, we're fine," Lana said, her voice dripping sugary sweet.

Ignoring her, they marched towards the car. I grabbed the girls to form a human wall in front of Hari. "Now would be a great time to get some matches," Lana said.

No kidding.

"Please step away from the car," the taller officer barked.

Slowly, we stepped back. *Please, Hari, pull yourself together.*

With possibly the worst timing ever, Hari pushed the door open and vomited into the sand. The taller officer raised his foot and inspected the drops of red-wine sick that had splashed onto his toes. He then grabbed Hari by the right arm, and the shorter officer took the left. His knees buckled, and they struggled to keep him upright as they yelled at him in what we presumed to be Hindi.

"Please let him go," Jade said, mustering as much conviction in her voice, but it was as intimidating as a hungry kitten's mew.

"Your driver is clearly intoxicated. We will not tolerate this." The shorter officer snapped.

As Hari struggled to stand the foil ball fell from his shirt pocket. Then *I* thought I was going to vomit.

The hash.

The taller officer restrained Hari as the shorter one picked it up and opened it up. With bulging eyes, he sputtered, "Drunk driving and possession of an illegal substance?" Then he grabbed one of Hari's arms.

Turning, they dragged Hari down the road. I looked at my watch. I had to get to the hotel. But we couldn't just let Hari get arrested. Despite his faults, he was one of us, and no one gets left behind. *Think, Harper, think!* Then an idea hit me. "How much US cash do you guys have on you right now?" I said to the girls.

They pulled some green bills out of their purses and adding mine, I counted it. Traveler's tip: always keep some US money on you, you never know when you might need it.

"We'll give you fifty American dollars if you let him go right now."

The officers stopped, turned, and mumbled something to each other. "Make it one hundred for each of us and you have a deal."

"No way," Lana said, throwing up her hands.

"Well, we will have to arrest all of you for attempting to bribe officers of the law," the taller one said with a shit-eating grin.

Piling into the car with Lana at the wheel we headed back to the hotel. Jade waited with the officers outside the hotel while we dug out our emergency money. In the lobby with my laptop clutched to my chest, I shoved my cash in Lana's hand and settled into the table from earlier next to the last diners paying their checks for the night. As it powered up, my stomach roiled, adrenaline surged, and irritation of having just been extorted of money I couldn't afford gnawed at me.

Once logged in I clicked the dial button. The video kicked in. His face was pale and bags hung from his eyes.

"Hey, baby," he said, his crackling voice barely above a whisper.

I drew a deep breath before I spoke, trying to figure out what to ask first. "What happened? Why weren't you in Ottawa?"

"I wasn't totally honest with you about the work conference." He rubbed his chin and heat blazed through me when I saw the hospital bracelet. "I needed some time to think about us, and then when I started, I didn't want to think about us, so I started playing World of Warcraft."

"And you forgot to take your insulin?" I said. He nodded. "You had phone reminders."

"I just sort of ignored them telling myself I'd take it later and then I forgot."

"You nearly died because of a stupid video game." I clutched at the edge of the table until my knuckles turned white. "Again?"

"I wouldn't have done it if you hadn't gone slutting it up in Goa."

Red veiled my vision. He was an adult and responsible for his own actions. I owned up to mine. He couldn't blame me for his. But what upset me the most was that he had never before said such disrespectful things to me. Maybe it was always there, but I never saw it because we had never really tested our relationship.

I felt like I no longer knew who he was. This wasn't the man I fell in love with.

"I can't do this," I said. I was barely able to keep myself together. I couldn't bear the responsibility of keeping him together, too. "You have an addiction, and you need help. I'm not going to marry someone who I'm scared I'll have to bury because of a video game overdose."

He had to find a healthier way to deal with his grief than escaping into that fantasy world.

"You can't be done with us." His voice became desperate. "I love you."

"Adam," I paused as all of the emotions I had been holding back, all of the thoughts I had been fighting not to think about, burst forward. "I love you, too. But I can't marry you."

Tears pooled in my eyes, as I knew I couldn't stay in this relationship any longer. As much as it broke my heart, we had become different people and wanted very different things out of life.

With his pained sobs pulsing through the earphones, I pressed my hands to my heated face, and the moment I stemmed the tears with my fingertips, the cartoon-like *bloop* of the call disconnecting sounded. As I opened my eyes and stared at the blank screen, an odd feeling washed over me. More of a lack of feeling, total and complete numbness. Perhaps it was because I had used up all of my allotted emotions for the week, or perhaps it was because I had finally made a good decision.

The latter would really be a welcome change.

I turned the key into the doorknob as quietly as I could, but the girls were awake. The moment I set foot in the door, the inquisition began. After confirming that I was, in fact, emotionally stable and not in some bhang-induced delirium, Lana, always seeing the silver lining, clapped and beamed, "So you've come to the single side, just in time for Southeast Asia."

Chapter 13

Date: February 18, 2010
Chiang Mai, Thailand

It is a truth universally acknowledged by travelers that when you set off into exotic locations, you will get sick. It's not *if,* but *when.* No matter how careful you are, your body will be introduced to new microbes in a variety of manners: touching strangers, touching things strangers with unwashed hands have touched, improperly cooked food, animals, insects, contaminated ice, tap water. Given that I had made it through India physically unscathed, save for the odd upset stomach here and there, I was lucky. But two days into our stay in the city of Chiang Mai, tucked away in the jungles of Thailand, my luck ran out.

After a few nights in the hot and sticky capital of Bangkok, we flew north and settled into a basic guesthouse across the street from the Tha Phae Gate, a relic of ancient Thailand that separated the old city of Chiang Mai from the new. Chiang Mai was a charming little city with cute boutiques, cosmopolitan cafés, and friendly people who proved why Thailand was called the Land of Smiles. Our days were spent wandering through the pagodas and temples, hunting down the city's best Nutella crepes, buying handicrafts at the night market and getting massages each day. No, no happy endings for us. But on our third day, I woke up wracked with nausea, a raging headache, aching joints, fatigue, and fever. My next three days were spent bedridden on a thin, lumpy mattress on a creaky frame, alternating between chills and sweats, convinced that I was going to die of malaria. As I lay in our basic little room that had no other furniture than a double bed and cot, listening to the hum of voices from the street two stories below, I watched the ceiling fan turn. And I had nothing but time to feel sorry for myself and debate whether I had made the best decision of my life or worst.

I checked my messages in Bangkok, and Adam had progressed from the shock and denial stage to the bargaining stage of grief and loss. I imagined him at his computer, tears flooding his cheeks as he pled with me through message after message to give him another chance. It took all of my strength not to reply. I didn't trust myself enough not to balk and say yes. I had to stick to my decision. I could no longer feel the same kind of love I used to feel for him. Even though I was scared that I would never find love again.

This was my first break up, and I had no idea what to do. It was yet another moment in my life where I needed the guidance of my big sister, and I thought back to the desert, wishing there was a way I could find her again.

As I sat up and blew my nose, finishing off my fourth roll of toilet paper, I thought of the first time I got sick after Adam and I officially labeled ourselves a couple, and he insisted on taking care of me. I was stricken with the cold to end all colds. My eyes were puffy and red, my skin was the pallor of a zombie, and my hair had been hair uncombed for days. I scared myself each time I passed a mirror. Seriously, I kept thinking the ghost from The Ring was haunting my apartment. At first, I refused to open the door to Adam, terrified that he wouldn't be attracted to me anymore, and that every time he saw me after I recovered, the image of how I looked while sick would be burned into his memory.

"Open up, you know I'll always see you as the most beautiful girl in existence," he said through the door as I leaned against the cool wood.

He had come all the way to my apartment in the middle of a blizzard to see me and, given the city had practically been shut down, he had to walk over fifteen blocks to get to me. I sighed and opened the door.

"You," he stepped in, dusted with snow, and kissed me, "have never been so lovely."

"I don't know whether to take that as a compliment or an insult," I said, wrapping my arms around him and sneezing into his warm chest.

He shrugged off his coat, and when he pulled off his beanie he replaced it with a Halloween costume nurse's cap and in a silly accent said, "Nurse Adam at your service, m'lady." Then he pulled out a container of chicken soup and a stack of DVDs from a canvas bag.

That was the moment I fell in love with him.

The rattling of the door pulled me back to the present. As the door swung open part of me hoped that Adam was about to stride in with that nurse's cap and cradle me until I felt better. Instead, Jade appeared, then Lana, both carrying plastic shopping bags.

"How did things go with the tailors?" I asked, pulling the sheet up to my chin as a chilly spell shuddered through me.

Jade dropped the shopping bags on the floor and nodded. "Good, but I think we'll wait until Hoi An in Vietnam to get the pieces made."

"We brought you some noodle soup from downstairs if you're feeling up for it," Lana said, placing a container on the foot of the bed.

I was beyond grateful for my girls, and I had to accept that Adam would never nurse me back to health again.

***

Date: February 19, 2010

The next day, I felt more human, more like myself again, and good enough to get back out into the world, but all I wanted to do was go back to bed. I missed Adam. I missed him so much, and I was so very sorry for hurting him. But I knew deep down that we couldn't go on. The painful realization had set in that we weren't supposed to be together. Adam helped me to sew up the hole in my heart that was left after Audrey's death, and the thought of being without him tore another hole. But I he was still alive, and in time, I would stitch this new hole up on my own.

To help me feel better, Jade offered to perform Reiki on me. After her break-up with that asshat Cliff, she was convinced that she was supposed to be a Reiki healer, so she took a course but never brought it up again after I joked that she was finally giving into being a hippy. Truthfully, I didn't really believe in Reiki. I mean, people paid actual money to lie down and have someone hover their hands over different body parts and "balance their energy", but I said yes, mostly so I could lie in bed some more, and she looked excited to put her skills to use.

While Lana popped out for her daily Thai massage, I cleared my mind and let Jade believe she was actually doing something beneficial to my body. An hour later, I sat up feeling almost as if I were in a lucid dream, and Jade wore an odd expression.

"What?" I asked, shaking the sleepy feeling from my body.

She paused with a weird combination of a frown and a smile. "Nothing, it's just…"

Before she could finish her sentence, Lana strode into the room glowing.

"Alright, sickling," Lana said, looking at me, "you're looking much better. Let's go get you over this break up the normal and healthy way: eating comfort food until we burst."

To Canadian gals like us, no food could be more comforting than waffles and bacon, and thankfully there was an all-day breakfast joint around the corner ran by a fellow Canadian who served his waffles with thick, juicy Canadian bacon and good old-fashioned syrup tapped from the maple trees of Quebec.

"So how did Reiki go?" Lana asked as gobs of waffle rolled in her mouth. "Is she all balanced and back to normal?"

"Well," Jade said with the smile-frown returning. "I noticed that her energy was all off on her second chakra."

"Give it to me straight, doc, am I going to live?" I held my hand over my heart and feigned concern.

"What was your sex life with Adam like?"

I stopped chewing. Bacon hung from my lips. I did not want to have this talk.

"It was fine," I said. "So we should go check out jungle zip-lining."

"Just *fine*?" Lana asked, getting excited. "Not earth-shatter-scream-his-name-until-you-black-out-from-sheer-pleasure."

I was never into the whole screaming his name thing.

"It was fine, yes fine. Beautiful, sweet, connecting, loving. Our relationship wasn't defined by sex." It was based on something deeper. Mutual respect, love, and understanding for the trauma we both had gone through. We had been each other's lifelines, and that meant more than just some primal act. "We loved each other and that was more important."

Lana narrowed her eyes seeming to search for the next question in her sexual inquisition. "Did you do it often?"

"Everyone's definition of 'often' is different," I said, straightening my back.

"That's a no." Lana swept her glossy locks from her shoulders as she gave some cute guy passing by a smile.

It was so easy for her.

Hot tears began to pool in my eyes. It didn't happen often because I didn't want to do it. Since my hormones had set in at puberty, and through my teen years, I did have lusty feelings, just no one to act on them with. Then one night at the end of my first year in university, I let them get the best of me. I made a regretful decision with a crush when I was nineteen, and afterward I was so put off by men, I never bothered with anyone else. And then when Audrey died, my depression broke me and took everything from me. My joy, my spark, my mojo. It was my fault that we used the bed for sleeping more than sex. And he suffered for it.

"No, we didn't. And it's my fault," I sputtered dropping my cutlery on the ceramic plate. "Because I'm broken."

Jade rubbed my shoulder as I pressed my napkin to my eyes. "No. No, you're not broken, Harper. Everyone is different. We can't be all hot and wet at the flick of a switch like this one over here. Perhaps you're more of an energy reader like me, and as much as you loved Adam, maybe you just didn't have any chemistry, but you and Xavier did. Besides, sex only matters if it matters to you. It's okay if it doesn't."

Since Goa, I questioned my belief about being broken, and about how much the primal act meant to me. Before it didn't matter so much, mostly because I had believed that I lost my mojo forever, but after my mojo seemed to make a comeback with the chemistry I felt with Xavier, it felt as if my eyes had been opened, and I could never close them again.

"Wait," Lana said. "Was Adam your first?"

I took a sip of coffee and kept my eyes on the table. "Yes."

"Uhh, Harper?" Jade said.

I glared at her. "Yes," before giving a quick forced smile to Lana. "He was my first. So how about we check out the jungle zip-line tours?"

"That explains this. I know what you need." Lana narrowed her eyes at me and clutched her knife as syrup dripped from the shiny metal. She leaned over and whispered something in Jade's ear. Jade's eyes shot open and her mouth stretched into a huge smile. Turning back to me Lana said, "We're going out tonight. I won't tell you where, but you have to trust me. Do you trust me?"

"Put the knife down, and I'll consider it," I said, equally intrigued and terrified.

***

We dressed for the evening and Lana and Jade couldn't stop giggling every time they looked at me. As we prepared ourselves for the night, both of them were smug and smugger, giving me knowing smirks as I fingered through my wet hair and dabbed some lip-gloss on. It was too hot to bother with any more makeup than that. After closing the padlock on the door behind us I followed Lana and Jade as they pranced down the stairs and onto the sidewalk. Twilight had fallen, and the street lamps were warming from orange to yellow. Across the street locals and foreigners alike gathered in the paved area closed to traffic that ran from the sidewalk one hundred feet to the turreted red brick wall than enclosed the Old City. The ancient wall was broken by the open doors of the wooden Tha Phae Gate, letting pedestrian traffic flow from the Old City to the New.

Lana flagged down a tuk tuk, similar to those in India except these were blue and yellow, and as Jade and I slid across the worn blue leather of the backseat, Lana whispered something in the driver's ear with a mischievous glint in her eye. My worries about where I was being taken to were made worse when he threw back his head and laughed in a way that I could only describe as an "unbridled guffaw".

With the breeze tangling our hair, we weaved through the quiet city roads past tire shops and furniture stores, markets and restaurants away from the touristy side of the town until he stopped outside of a modern three-story building with the words "Adam's Apple" glowing in neon lights. We slid out of the tuk tuk and handed over our Thai *baht* to pay.

"Have fun, girls!" The tuk tuk driver yelled with yet another guffaw before he puttered down the road.

"Where are you taking me?" I said with a nervous smile pulling at my lips.

Lana's eyes glowed. "We're going to see a show."

Most of the shows I had heard of in Thailand involved Ping-Pong balls and impossibly controlled pelvic floor muscles, but I had a feeling that this wasn't one of those shows.

The interior of the building was just as modern as the exterior. I ran my fingers along the cool gunmetal granite walls as we climbed the black tile stairs. When a firm-bodied Thai guy in his early thirties greeted us wearing nothing but dress pants and a bow tie, I figured out just what kind of show the girls had taken me to. I was relieved to realize that there would be no Ping-Pong balls involved in the night.

Everything in the room was black: the walls, the floor, the stage, the runway, the booths that lined the walls, and the bar on the opposite side of the stage. Male couples occupied three booths on the wall closest to the door, and six Asian tourists sipped highballs at the bar perched on black leather stools. We were seated in a booth on the wall opposite to the door, ordered cocktails, and were given a complimentary container of popcorn, which was quite nice of them. There's nothing that adds to a performance quite like freshly popped and salted popcorn.

"To commemorate your new life in singledom," Lana said, raising her glass.

As we clinked glasses, the lights dimmed, Ginuwine's classic sex hit "Pony" pulsed through the speakers, and five men wearing nothing but tighty-whiteys and smiles walked on stage. Jade giggled, Lana whooped, and I knocked my drink back.

At the climax of the song, Lana yelled, "Take it off!"

At her request, the tighty-whiteys came off, and the hip gyrations increased. In less than five minutes I had seen over double the number of penises I had ever seen in real life. And it was something I could not unsee.

"Matches! Matches!" I called out our code word and laughed.

"Nice try! This is to warm you up for the new men to come," Lana squealed in my ear.

We giggled, whooped and covered our eyes, peeking through our fingers as we watched such erotic tales including: the naked construction worker, the naked pharaoh who like to shower with his page boy, and a naked Count Dracula looking for a mate. Shakespearean stuff, really. Even though I was in no way shape or form aroused, I did laugh. I laughed a laugh, deep from my belly, a laugh I had long since forgotten I had, a laugh that made me remember that I had so many good times to come.

***

Still giggling, a little tipsy, and high on the ridiculousness we had just experienced, we slid into a tuk tuk and cut back to the Tha Phae Gate through the Old City. Spilling out of the tuk tuk, we crossed through the gate into the New City.

"I think I need a cigarette after tha...look up there," Jade said, pointing up.

My eyes darted to the sky. Hundreds of flying lanterns glowed cool gold, floating in the sky like stars sent from Earth to find their place in the heavens. In front of us hundreds of people were lighting the little candles at the base and raising the paper balloons over their heads. Each one had writing scrawled into them. I had read that entire festivals were dedicated to sending them off with wishes written on them.

I knew I had to let go of Adam at some point, and I knew it had to be sooner rather than later so we could both begin to heal and move on with our lives. The girls and I bought each one from a vendor, a Thai girl no more than fifteen years old, and I borrowed a pen from her and wrote on the thin paper:

Adam,

I have loved you, and I always will love you. I'm sorry I hurt you. I accept that we are not meant to be together, and I have to let you go. I wish you all the happiness in the world.

Eternally grateful for you,
Harper

Then I carefully pulled the paper apart, and the lantern took shape. Jade held the wire at the base, and I took her lighter and lit the fuel cell. Once it sparked and ignited, I held the wire base as it lifted from my fingertips. And as it ascended into the sky with a hundred other wishes, I exhaled the breath that I had been holding and listened to a little voice in my heart saying, *all is well.*

***

The next day, I felt one-hundred percent better. After indulging in another waffle and bacon breakfast with the girls, we wandered the silver boutiques where I bought a necklace for my mother. As the sun rose to high noon, we ducked into an air-conditioned Internet café, ordered iced lemongrass teas, and sank back into the cushioned chairs, and fingers on modern keyboards.

Excitement bubbled as I read the email from my mother.

> Hello darling,
>
> Your father and I are booking our flights to Sydney this week. Please let us know as soon as you can what you want to do in Australia so we can sort our dates. We can't wait to see you!
>
> Love,
>
> Mom and Dad

They hadn't left Toronto since Audrey died. Like me, they had been held captive not only by their crushing depression but also by their fear of traveling, and I was ecstatic to see them overcoming it. With my guilt for leaving them lifting, I began researching things for us to do: the Zoo, the Sydney Harbour Bridge, of course the Opera House and since they will have flown around the world, we should go up to see the Great Barrier Reef.

After my research, I logged into Facebook and scrolled through my notifications. A message stopped my fingers. A message from the crush I had made *that* regretful decision with when I was nineteen. *Hey, Harper, I trust you are doing well. I heard that you are in Southeast Asia. How long are you going to be there? Where are you going to be? — Miles*

My face froze as my nails dug into the keyboard.

"Everything okay?" Jade asked, peering over her monitor across from me.

"Yah, yah, fine. Just breakup stuff blah blah blah," I lied.

If she knew Miles had messaged me she would have thrown the computer across the room. Hell hath no fury like the best friend of a woman scorned.

I had heard this from Lana before and didn't know if there was any truth to it, but it seemed that the moment you became single and happy with life, a pulse is sent out across the universe alerting all ex-flames to reach out to you, and try to ruin your happiness.

At first, I was intrigued to hear from him. Even after all these years, he could still make my heart flutter. But then I remembered why I hated him. It took all my might not to respond, *what's it to you, asshole?* But no, I was in a good mood that day and I wasn't about to let him ruin it, so I closed his message instead.

I still hadn't responded to Adam, but I couldn't tell him that it was over for good in such an impersonal manner as Facebook. So I logged out, paid for my Internet time and tea, and left the girls to go to the boutique across the street we had fallen in love with. Browsing the gift items, I picked up a stationery set crafted from mango leaves. Back in the Internet café, I took a table near the window and drafted a letter that included the words I had sent into the sky the night before, along with my explanation of why I couldn't marry him. I owed him that much. And before we left Chiang Mai the next day I dropped it into the postbox.

It was the final act of letting go of my first love.

As I stared into the dark abyss through the slit in the post office, I decided that it was time to focus on myself. Focus on my work and focus on winning the photography competition.

Chapter 14

After our time in Chiang Mai, we headed northeast to the Thai border. As we left civilization, we were subjected to the worst music on Earth from an obnoxious Eastern European eighteen year old riding shotgun who insisted on controlling the minivan's stereo. Lana proposed a coup, and all of the passengers in the back, myself and Jade included, plotted to overthrow the tone-deaf tyrant. But before we could hatch our plan we arrived at Chiang Khong on the eastern banks of the Mekong River. It featured little more than a hostel, a few roadside noodle stalls, and two passport photo "studios." There really was no reason to go to the remote jungle town except to cross the border into Laos.

We crossed the river, which served as the border, and even as we were herded like cattle through the immigration line on the muddy banks, I still knew nothing about the country I was standing in. Lana only said something about "tubing," whatever that meant. But there's something to be said about going somewhere with no expectations whatsoever. Even while stuffed in a very uncomfortable minivan for eleven million hours straight, thankfully sans the insufferable stereo hog, I was completely taken by surprise. It turned out Laos is one of the least known countries in the continent, so it was delightfully undeveloped and under-populated with tourists. For the eleven million hours I had my face pressed against the glass I could count the number of buildings we passed on one hand. However, as we approached Luang Prabang in the falling dusk, the number of man-made structures increased. Once night had fallen we were dropped off in the town with little to orient us besides the driver pointing us in the directions of guesthouses, leaving our new surroundings to be a surprise. We found a spacious loft that resembled a dollhouse with dark wood floors, antique furniture, and gossamer mosquito nets at a steal of a price.

***

Date: February 23, 2010
Luang Prabang, Laos

We slept in as much as we could but were pulled from our beds by the aroma of freshly baking bread. It turned out that our loft sat above a bakery. Luang Prabang was a ghost of French Indochina, and as such, much of the French culture and influence still permeated every day life. As we ate breakfast al fresco on the sidewalk table downstairs, I drank in the easygoing energy of the town where East and West fused in its energy, colonial architecture, and food. Vintage cars that suggested summers on the Riviera puttered down the road while local girls whizzed by on motorcycles, accelerators in one hand and parasols in the other. I wondered if the part of France Xavier was from looked like this.

"So what's there to do here?" Lana asked before stuffing a flakey piece of chocolate croissant into her mouth.

"Well, we can do the Buddha Caves or the Kung Si Waterfalls," Jade replied, slathering strawberry jam onto her toast. "Keep in mind we'll only have one full day here."

"I vote waterfalls," Lana said. "It may be our only chance to bathe."

When Lana tried to shower earlier, we learned why the gorgeous room was available at such a low price: we were robbed of running water.

With the decadent aftertaste of croissants and bittersweet coffee lingering in my mouth we wandered the main street, which stretched barely a Toronto city block, popping into jewelry and art boutiques. Stopping in at one of the few tour counters, we booked our minivan to Vang Vieng for the following day, and as the girls asked about getting to the waterfall, I snapped away at the Technicolour orchids that adorned the building.

"Harper?" Jade called out as I turned my lens on a tangerine-robed monk. "Want to cycle to the waterfall with me?"

Checking the playback, I called back, "Sure," before looking up to find his baldhead disappearing through a temple door across the street. I would definitely be able to capture more of the countryside taking our own time rather than shooting out of the back of a speeding tuk tuk.

As Jade and I mounted our black and yellow bikes, seemingly built for the roughest terrain imaginable, Lana bid us farewell as she headed off for a massage. It only took ten minutes to leave our charming urban oasis behind as we peddled towards the lush green countryside. It also didn't take long for me to ask the question I should have asked from the start. "How long is this going to take?"

"Well, we're cycling thirty-five kilometers."

"Are you trying to kill me?" I wheezed.

"It'll go by quickly," she said, but the tremble in her voice made me suspicious.

The first several kilometers weren't actually so bad. The emerald green hills rolling into the horizon like enormous sea swells provided a welcome distraction from my seriously under-exercised legs. Stopping periodically, I was able to put my panoramic setting to good use.

But about an hour in at the ten-kilometer mark, I was choking on those words. Half way up a ceaseless incline I affectionately called Death Mountain, I began to see stars. The sun beat down on us from its zenith in a cloudless sky. Despite the forested hills surrounding us in every direction, the trees sat beyond the deep ditches that flanked the road. Setting my bike down, I stumbled for shade as Jade followed my lead.

"Are you okay?"

Collapsing into the meager shade of a scraggly bush, I pulled my water bottle from my bag and sucked on the few drops I had left. "I'm just trying to remember why I thought this was a good idea."

Jade flopped to the ground next to me and offered her water bottle to me. Though my tongue scratched at the roof of my mouth like sandpaper, I refused it as she barely had any left. I figured I'd take one for the team and die of dehydration first. The world needed her ethically conscious yogawear. After leading a breathing exercise, she pulled me to my feet and showed me how to stretch my leg and ass muscles. Even with just that little break the stars retreated, and I began to feel more like myself again.

As she began to fold forward to stretch the back of her legs, she stopped mid bend. "Do you hear that?"

I shook my head. The only thing I could hear was my pulse pounding against my eardrums. She turned and looked down the road in the direction we had come. Hearing the faintest sputtering sound, I stared down the crumbling tarmac, and then I saw it. Over the crest of one of Death Mountain's mini-hills the top of a jumbo-sized tuk tuk puttered into view.

"We can flag it down," Jade turned to me with an unreadable expression carved in her face. Disappointment? Concern? "I mean, if you want."

Dear God, I wanted to give up. And salvation was approaching. My legs were on fire, my nether regions were beginning to bruise, and I was acutely aware of how out of shape I was, but as the tuk tuk approached, I couldn't find it within me to raise my hand. Maybe I was more exhausted than I thought. As it passed us I saw Lana waving out of the back as she and a few other passengers laughed. No doubt laughing at our dumb decision to cycle.

In my dehydrated delirium, those faces and voices melted and transformed. Lana's face morphed into Adam's, mocking me, "You don't stand a chance in the competition!" Ms. Hatching appeared next to him. "I always knew you were dead weight." Even my tenth-grade teacher who failed me in art peered out of the window. "Ms. Rodrigues, I'm afraid to inform you that you have little to no artistic vision, and no sense of humour."

Their faces faded into the ether as the tuk tuk disappeared over the crest of Death Mountain and my blood boiled over.

I'll show them all.

"We could get the next one." Jade's small voice was even quieter.

"No," I said, balling my hands into fists and marching towards my bike. "I can do this. We're finishing this ride."

Pushing through the burn flaring in muscles I never knew existed, we came over the crest of Death Mountain and as I gently braked on the long decline, I relished the cool breeze licking my sweaty skin. A new energy filled me as I caught my breath — at the same time I saw two young local girls selling bottles of water on the side of the road in the shade of an oversized umbrella at the base. I braked and pulled over in front of them with Jade following suit.

"The Universe delivers," Jade said setting her bike on the ground next to them.

As we drank, we chatted with them. In broken English they told us they were thirteen and eleven years old, they spend the time they weren't at school selling water, and they were sisters. They reminded me so much of Audrey and me. Swallowing the lump in my throat I thought of how theirs was a love I once had and will never have again. I asked if I could take their picture, and the older one gave an enthusiastic yes, while the younger hid behind her hands. My heart nearly burst as the older one grabbed the younger one, pulled her hands down, and rained kisses on her cheeks. I captured the entire scene like a comic book, and they laughed with delight as I showed the series of photos to them.

"Let's get moving?" Jade said.

I nodded, finding it difficult to tear myself away from them. Freshly hydrated, we stocked up on as much water as we could carry, bid them farewell and set off for the remaining twenty-five kilometers.

Five hours after setting out, just as my legs were about to give out on me again, we saw the sign just past a grassy field for the waterfall. We pushed through those last few kilometers. After locking our bikes together to a tree in the parking lot, we high-fived each other, bought fresh mango fruit shakes, and followed a dirt path in the welcome shade of tall jungle trees. My breath caught in my throat as we followed a series of waterfalls, some narrow, some wide, feeding crystal blue water to lagoons surrounded by an overgrown forest.

My shutter stopped when a tuft of sandy blond hair in the distance caught my eye. He looked so familiar.

"Are you okay?" Jade asked. "You look like you've seen a ghost."

"I thought I saw...someone. But it couldn't be," I said, shrugging off the thought.

Following the path upstream we found what appeared to be a jungle watering hole for backpackers. Bandana-clad wanderers hung out on picnic tables chatting and mingling while others waiting for a turn on the rope-swing queued up on the fat branch of a huge tree overhanging a lagoon slightly larger than the first.

"Took you guys long enough," a dripping wet Lana called from a picnic bench. "Go get in the water!"

Jade and I stripped to our bikinis, leaving our things with Lana, who was deep in flirtation mode with a pair of guys with muscle shirts and strange accents. Climbing the tree we waited for our turn on the rope-swing. As I watched the macho males try everything from dives to backflips, many ending in belly flops and face-plants, we decided to keep it simple and just swing and let go. Once Jade splashed into the water, I took the rope and stepped from the branch, full of my newfound confidence. As I broke the surface, the cold water punched the breath from my lungs. Ignoring the chill biting at my skin I ran my trembling fingers through my greasy hair as Jade floated on her back enjoying the serenity. I had seen pictures of waterfalls from all over the world, but none quite looked like this one.

I swam around, taking a closer look at the rocks, and the delicate leaves of the ferns hanging over the water. Leaning over the waterfall, I stood in the current, watching the water cascade to the next pool a few feet below, watching a tiny rainbow hovering in the mist, proud of myself for finishing the cycle trip. Jade and I already decided that we would take a tuk tuk back with Lana instead of riding. Doing that trip once was enough.

"Help!" A voice shattered the quiet. "Someone please help!"

I turned towards the direction of the voice to see a woman standing at the water's edge pointing frantically at the water. "He jumped but didn't come back up!"

Jade turned and dove beneath the water. I held my breath, staring at the water as I waited for my best friend to reemerge. I looked up to see people gathering around the woman who had collapsed to her knees in the dirt.

Where are you, Jade?

Then she broke the water's surface clutching the lifeless body of a man around his torso. I swam across the pool as fast as I could and helped her lay him flat on his back in the mud. The crowd that gathered had multiplied, each closing in for a better look.

"His pulse is weak," Jade said holding two fingers to his throat.

"Mark, no, no, no!" she wailed.

"Lana," I called, recognizing her flip-flops and summoning my relevant knowledge from Baywatch reruns, I yelled, "Move everyone back, please." I turned to the wailing girl. "What's your name?"

"Veronica."

"Veronica, I'm going to need you to remain calm," I said looking her in her dinner-plate eyes. She nodded, and for some reason listened to me.

As I stretched my arms out trying to keep the crowd at bay, Jade began chest compressions. Nothing happened. Veronica was now crying hysterically as Jade pinched Mark's nose and covered his mouth with hers. His chest rose and fell but still nothing happened. The moment she pressed her hands to his chest once more a low, yet strangely familiar voice thundered from above me, "Let me do it."

It couldn't be.

Moving to the side he crouched next to me, and I looked at his face.

Holy shit, it is.

My gaze never left him as he performed a set of forceful chest compressions. After two rescue breaths the lifeless vagabond was reanimated, gasping and vomiting out water.

"Oh my God, Mark, I thought you died," Veronica said, pushing me out of the way. Sprawling in the mud and not sure if I was actually awake I watched her throw herself on my apparition. "Thank you for saving him."

I suppressed a smile as his eyes scanned her half naked body.

"You're welcome," he said, as he stood and pulled Mark to his feet. "Let him catch his breath. He should be fine, but if he's still not feeling well within thirty minutes find a doctor."

Jade and Veronica slung Mark's arms over their shoulders and led him to the picnic bench.

"Miles?" His name tumbled from my lips as I turned my gaze to him.

"Harper?" A smile crept across his face. "Well, aren't you a sight for sore eyes."

My mind drowned in a flood of memories as I stared into his dark eyes, trying to put it all together. For years, I had practiced over and over in my head what I would say to him if I ever saw him again. It was filled with four letter words but as my consciousness struggled to stay afloat, it could only send a few words to my mouth. "It's been a long time."

"Too long," he said in his affected transatlantic accent before wrapping his arms around me. I closed my eyes and inhaled his scent, DEET and fresh laundry.

As his grip loosened, I took a step back to get a better look at him. It was like looking back in time. He had the same sandy blond hair cropped close to his scalp and country club prep. Navy polo shirt, khaki Bermuda shorts, boat shoes, and despite the hot weather, he had a red sweater tied at his neck hanging down his back like a cape. A smile pulled at my lips when I noticed the Lacoste alligator embroidered on each piece of clothing. Only he would go traveling and bring designer brands.

"Hi, I'm Lana." She bounced over and stopped dead in her tracks. "Miles?"

"Lana, you are looking well." He leaned in and kissed her on the cheek.

A mass of oil-black curls jumped in between him and me. "Miles Cooper," Jade roared, "what the hell are you doing here?"

Keeping his demeanor stoic, he replied, "Jade, it's so lovely to see you, too."

"Stand down," I whispered to Jade. She turned and glared at me before stepping aside.

"Mr. Cooper, we are leaving." Behind him a thin woman in her forties holding up an unopened umbrella stood with a group of older, more well-to-do tourists like a shepherd and her flock.

"Shit," he said, scrubbing his freshly shaven chin. "My tour group is leaving." He reached into his pocket and stretched out his hand holding a shiny black pair of matches with the words *Bamboo Club* etched in silver across it. "Meet me here tonight at nine o'clock for a drink. It's by the night market."

I took it and pressed my fingers into the smooth card of the pack as he kissed me on the cheek, turned and merged with the crowd of polo shirts and Bermuda shorts, and disappeared down the path.

Chapter 15

"I can't believe you're going to have drinks with him," Jade said as she pushed the door to our dollhouse loft open.

"What was I supposed to say? No?"

"Yes!" She flopped onto the stack of floor pillows strewn on the intricate oriental carpet in the middle of the room and huffed in exasperation. "The last time you saw him, I helped you put the pieces of your broken heart back together."

"Okay, you need to fill me in on what the deal is with you and Mr. Big Shot on Campus," Lana said as I took my brush from the antique vanity.

I kept forgetting that Lana had left university at the end of the first semester of freshmen year after she was discovered by a news producer. And so, as I brushed my hair, painted my face with makeup, and dressed, I told Lana the history while Jade rolled her eyes and sucked her teeth. I began with, "So you know how I said Adam was my first? Well, that isn't entirely true…"

I had first met the infamous Miles Cooper when I was seventeen, and my parents took me to visit Audrey in university. She had taken me to a party, much to my parents' objection. However, given that I still had the figure of a prepubescent boy and train-track braces so big the Trans-Canada Railway could run on, they didn't have much to worry about by way of college-aged boys thinking I was older than I was. It was a kegger, my first real kegger, with solo cups, frat boys, drinking games, and people passing out in the toilet — everything they always had in the movies. Of course, I was making my rounds at the party tied to Audrey's hip, known simply as, "Audrey's Little Sister", but once she asked me to be her beer pong partner, it all changed. Sports may have worked against my desirability with boys, in high school, but if you can emasculate a college boy by repeatedly landing a Ping-Pong ball into a red plastic cup, well, they rather like it. As the crowd gathered to watch Audrey and I take down the frat boys, a guy who I later learned to be Miles Cooper stepped to the table for a better look.

You know those teen movies where the hot girl is revealed, steps into frame and time slows down, a cheesy saxophone track plays and an inexplicable breeze blows through the room billowing through her hair as she glows like an Oscar statue? Well, that was how he looked to me. And we were winning by four cups and had only one more to make. I had been carrying the team, but now I rimmed out every time, folding under the weight of the gaze of my Adonis. And then it was one cup each.

"Who's your partner?" Miles said.

I could barely look at him, almost as if I deemed myself unworthy to.

"This is my sister, Harper," she said.

I allowed myself to make eye contact, and he stood with his arms folding, his gaze lingering on me. "More like your badass sister."

I nearly melted. No boys in high school gave me a second look, but a college boy noticed me. An impossibly beautiful college boy noticed me *and* called me badass.

But I had to focus on the game. I had to impress him by winning.

When the other team, a pair of unkempt and overexcited bros from Phi-Alpha-something-or-other made both throws in the final cup, we met defeat. Audrey hugged me, proud of how well we had done, but when she released me, I looked up and Miles was gone.

Audrey gave me the rundown on him: his parents were two of the most high-profile lawyers in the country, he was captain of the swim team, once modeled for Ralph Lauren, and almost needless to say, he was the most desirable junior on campus.

And he noticed me.

When I sat with acceptance letters to five universities many months later, weighing my options, I was still haunted by the glowing boy, the most beautiful man I had ever seen in real life. The boy Audrey had said was a third year, and so would still be there during my first. And being the horny and delusional teenager, I said yes to McGill, dreaming that he would see me as my own person now that I had my braces removed, and I could fill out my bra without the help of tissues and socks. Within two weeks of first semester, I learned that he ate lunch in the Shatner Building's student center cafeteria every Monday, and so on the third Monday, Lana helped me dress like a woman and I strutted in wedge boots to the Shatner Building to "accidentally" bump into him.

By the time I got there, he was leaving, and so I waited around the corner of a pillar, and then came around the corner and literally bumped into him. I was so nervous, I didn't know what to do next.

"Oh, hi, Miles," I said, twirling my hair as Lana had taught me.

He furrowed his brow. "Have we met?"

Not the response I was hoping for.

"Sort of, not exactly..." I fumbled. "I was at that kegger last year." He gave me a pitied look as he failed to recognize me. "I'm Audrey Rodrigues's sister, Harper."

"Oh right, Audrey's badass sister," he said with a big smile. "How is she doing?"

He remembered me.

"She's great," I said, trying my best to act nonchalant.

"My, Harper, you have blossomed beautifully." His eyes scanned my body, and I nearly fainted. Miles Cooper was checking me out. Every girl within sight gawked at me, no doubt plotting my death. "Well, it was good to see you. Please tell Audrey I say, hi."

"Okay," I mumbled, steadying myself against the wall. And then he disappeared. *Miles Cooper just called me beautiful.* My teenage fantasies came true, and I believed it was meant to be. But then a week later I learned that he had a girlfriend, Celia Butterfield. However, that didn't stop me from spending freshman year chasing him around from classes too advanced for me and dragging Jade and Lana to parties to see him. He would always give me a nod and wave of recognition. He noticed *and* remembered me. I bided my time and by second-semester finals, he and Celia had broken up.

After finals were done, sat I dragged Jade once more to the big end-of-year kegger. It felt like everything was coming full circle. He spent most of the party with his guy friends but as the party wound down I found him alone in one of the frat boys' bedrooms (I was just checking out the house!) and on a beanbag on the floor, I held him as he cried in my arms about getting dumped. When I asked him if there was anything I could do to make it better, well, I don't think I need to tell you the rest.

"The old hit and quit," Lana said, shaking her head.

"I didn't count him because I freaked out by thrust ten and made him stop, and that's not exactly how a girl wants to remember her first time. I was so ashamed I didn't even tell Audrey," I said, laying my brush on the vanity. And if Adam and I ended up together I could say that I had only been with one man my entire life. That was a little fantasy I liked to keep to myself. "And yeah, I never heard from him again. Well, until he messaged me a week ago."

"You never told me that," Jade said, pushing to sit upright.

"I wasn't expecting to actually see him," I said pulling a silk kaftan over my head. "And I didn't reply anyways."

Once the girls were ready, we set off for dinner across the street. And afterwards we walked off our stir-fried veggie dinner, checking out the handicrafts at the night market. Then at eight fifty-five, I hugged the girls and set off for Bamboo Club as a ball of nerves. I was still angry with Miles for never contacting me after that night, but there was something inexplicable about my attraction for him. He was still as gorgeous as he was the moment I saw him and an insecure part of me felt like he was too good for me but wanted to prove that I was good enough.

Jade pointed her finger in my face. "You better come back home before midnight."

"Yes mom," I said, swatting her finger away. "I'm only meeting him to be polite."

***

"Miss Harper Rodrigues," Miles purred as I approached him at the bar. "How the hell are you?"

To be honest, I was wonderstruck by the unusually classy surroundings. "A little sore from cycling to the waterfall today, but fine otherwise," I said with a smile as he pulled out a lacquered barstool.

"It really is good to see you again," he said, his wandering eyes setting my cheeks ablaze. "Beautiful as always."

I squirmed, feeling self-conscious as I settled into the stool. He looked so put together, as if he fell out of a magazine ad. Baby blue collared shirt, smart-causal navy slacks with a subtle detailing that suggested Ted Baker, with that red sweater firmly tied in place. And

189

then there was me wearing the fanciest thing I owned — a simple silk kaftan I had bought from a man with a pet monkey on the roadside in Jaipur.

"Thanks," I muttered.

The bartender, a slightly built Laotian man, placed two martini glasses on the bar. One dirty with two olives, still his favourite, the other a fuchsia-coloured concoction featuring a purple orchid speared with a colourless plastic sword.

"Cheers," he said, raising his glass before whispering, "Sorry they didn't have any Grey Goose, we're not exactly in civilization."

I was tempted to tell him that I would have been happy with the local beer. After a sip he placed the glass back on the lacquered bar and took me by surprise by placing his hand on mine. "I'm so sorry to hear about Audrey. I can't imagine what it's been like for you."

"Thank you," I said, not meeting his eyes and pulling my hand back gently. This was a platonic meeting and the less touching the better. "I miss her so much. But last month when we were in India, I got to talk to her."

It was one of those things that sounded better in your head. And I wished I could take it back. I just wanted to tell someone who knew her that she was out there, somewhere.

"What were you smoking?" he said with a laugh. I met his gaze and didn't blink. After a beat, his face contorted. "Are you crazy? That's not safe."

I had forgotten how sheltered and straight-laced he was. I'd thought maybe age, life experience, and some travel may have opened his eyes and his mind, but I was wrong. He had a sheltered upbringing and judging by the kind of tour he was traveling with, he had kept adventure and authenticity at an arm's length. But I wanted to tell him that ever since talking to her in the desert, I felt as if, even though I was completely stoned, the feeling that she was out there somewhere plugged the hole in my heart. And then an idea blossomed — perhaps I could speak with her again. I stored it and changed topic. "Yeah, I know, it was crazy. So what are you doing here?"

"I'm on a bit of a sabbatical from work…" As the empty glasses of too small and too easy to drink cocktails piled up, he told me how he had been working his way up the ranks of the family law firm, most recently in the Vancouver office, and had been tasked with opening a branch in Singapore. "I told Piers and Isabelle I would need some time off before taking that responsibility on. They acquiesced, and I booked a tour of Southeast Asia."

His calling his parents by their first name never failed to amuse me.

He continued, "My mother heard through the Toronto grapevine that you were traveling the area, so I reached out to you on Facebook, but you never replied."

"The Internet is really bad around here," I lied.

"And you? What's a nice girl like you doing in a place like this?"

I snorted a laugh.

"I guess you could say I'm on a bit of a sabbatical myself," I said before giving him a heavily edited version of the events between me leaving university and my unjust dismissal from my first attempt at adult employment. "So I thought, you know, I'm young, and I should give my dreams a shot before I'm bogged down with children and mortgages and what not."

I pulled out my camera and showed him a couple of the unedited shots I had taken at the waterfall that day.

"So let me get this straight," he said before pulling an olive from a plastic sword into his mouth with his teeth, "you're spending your whole life savings on this?"

With a smile, I nodded, ignoring the explosion of nerves in my stomach. When he put it like that that it hit me how insane my decision was. But I was in too deep to pull out.

"I have to say I'm not sure if you're ballsy or crazy."

"There's a thin line between crazy and genius, I've been told to straddle it," I said straightening my posture.

As he took a sip his eyebrow quirked, and I realized that he may have taken my attempt at being witty as flirtation. "So, where's your boyfriend?"

"What boyfriend?" I said without thinking, immediately wanting to slap myself in the face.

His too-white teeth appeared behind a smile. "A while back I tried to friend you on Facebook. Finally signed up after being inundated with invites in my email. But you were with what appeared to be your boyfriend in your profile picture. I supposed I chickened out on ever trying to get you back. I figured it wasn't meant to be."

My stomach turned inside out. This was not how it was supposed to go. I thought the next time I saw Miles Cooper, I would punch his perfect little nose into his perfectly manicured face, but the way he looked at me only brought me back to another time, a good time before life got so damn complicated.

Don't tell him you're single.

"Well, that's no longer the case."

His face lit up.

Shit.

Before I could explain that I was emotionally unavailable and still wanting to punch him in the throat, he raised his glass. "Cheers to moving onto bigger and better."

After the conversation had moved to the more neutral topic of travel stories, I realized the time, and hugged him farewell, declining his offer to walk me down the street to my guesthouse. Our farewell was more of a see you later, as our itinerary dates overlapped in Vang Vieng. Given the conflicting tides of feelings towards him, I decided it was best to keep him at arm's length.

Chapter 16

Date: February 23, 2010
Vang Vieng, Laos

After eight hours stuffed yet again in another minivan, rattling over unpaved roads snaking through the mountains (a recipe for motion sickness especially for me after a night consuming a regrettable number of sugary cocktails), we made it to Vang Vieng. It turned out that over the years Vang Vieng became a mainstay on the Southeast Asian backpacker trail and so brought development to this formerly sleepy village perched on the shores of the Nam Song River. Concrete buildings standing no taller than two stories lined crudely paved roads housed tour centers, restaurants, and guesthouses. It stood in stark contrast to the colonial charm of Luang Prabang.

Jade kept her nose in the guidebook, and Lana and I followed her dutifully through throngs of soaking wet westerners who carried black inner tubes towards the river. We were in search of a colony of thatched huts Lana had been told about while waiting for us at the Kung Si Waterfall the day before.

Crossing a narrow bamboo bridge that spanned the river, we continued following a narrow trail towards a grassy field. The field fronted massive limestone cliffs, and the sun hovered just above the crest. And in the shade of the cliffs, we found the colony of thatched huts. After we had paid for two huts, we settled in with Lana as my roommate. Each was just big enough for two feet of space around a double bed. Eager to catch the images of the children playing in the shallows of the river in the soft early evening glow, I reached into the cloth handbag I had brought with me to the bar the night before.

The blood drained from my face.

"Oh my God," I muttered as I emptied the contents onto the bed. "Oh my God, oh my God, oh my God."

"What's wrong?" Jade called from the hammock outside.

"My camera. It's not here."

I heard the creaking of rope and footsteps on the dusty wooden floorboards. "Just breathe, I'm sure it's there."

With neurosis in overdrive, I laid out the contents of my daypack and my backpack on the bed, touching and accounting for every single item except the one that really mattered. I knew I had it last night at the bar with Miles, but I was too hung-over to bother with it on the drive that day, so there was only one place it could have been. "I left it in Luang Prabang. It must be in the room."

Tears streamed down my face. I had no way of contacting the guesthouse. It had no name and no number. Perhaps I could leave on the next bus back to Luang Prabang in the morning and see if I could track it down? And then meet the girls back up the day after. Then a realistic and depressing realization struck: someone would have taken it by now.

"We can get you a new one in Hanoi," Jade said, rubbing my back.

I sobbed and nodded my head. Rationally I knew it was just a camera, a thing, and object, but it was the last gift Audrey had given me. How could I have been so careless?

The girls decided that food would do me good, so I pulled myself together and followed them through the field, across the bridge and back into town. The street lamps flickered as we wandered around wondering if we should go to the restaurant with the hung-over backpackers splayed out watching reruns of The Simpsons, or the restaurant with the hungover backpackers splayed out watching reruns of Family Guy when someone called out, "Hey, Canada!"

Turning back towards the river, we saw three guys who were part of our musical uprising on the bus from Chiang Mai to Chiang Khong. Lana called back, "Hawaii!"

Chad, Kelly and Felix were fresh off a bus from Luang Prabang and also in search of sustenance. As we stood debating food options, Chad's brown eyes raked over Lana, who had taken the time to brush her hair and slap a bit of makeup on. "Lana, are you Lana Brooks, the TV weathergirl?"

"Former weathergirl," she said, batting her thick eyelashes.

"I thought it was you!" he said, stepping closer. "Guys, remember when I showed you that *Chive* article of the world's hottest weather girls? This is the one from Canada."

I smiled as Lana basked in the attention the guys were giving her. Some people collected souvenirs along their travels, but Lana collected admirers. Felix's green cat-like eyes glittered as he realized he was standing in the presence of a *Chive*-worthy hottie.

"Dude," Kelly said, smoothing his shaggy, dirty-blond hair before shaking her hand. "It is a privilege and an honour to make your acquaintance."

"Alright, alright, can we please choose somewhere to eat, please?" Jade huffed crossing her arms.

And, with that the boys led us to a restaurant perched over the waters of the river that featured neither animated sitcoms nor hung-over backpackers and began our first night out in Vang Vieng.

***

I rifled through my things twice more the following morning in the vain hope that my camera would magically appear. After giving up, I let the girls pull me from wallowing in my misery and we set off to do the one thing we had come to Laos for: tubing. In town we followed the swarm of swimsuit-clad westerners to a small storefront where we had been dropped off the day before. It was a scene of organized chaos spilling into the street. Tiny Laotian women darted about writing guesthouse names in notebooks and writing identification numbers on arms while others handed out black inner-tubes and collected money. After we were branded with a black sharpie and received an inner tube, the women herded us into jumbo tuk tuks and we were whisked up river.

Ten minutes later, the tuk tuk dumped us in a dusty patch of land where we were accosted by a flurry of westerners working as bar promoters. By the time we made it to the river's edge, each of our wrists were wrapped with an assortment of brightly coloured string bracelets, each representing a free booze bucket at each of the bars scrawled in permanent marker on our arms. We froze as we took our first glance at the madness that was Laos tubing.

"This isn't what I expected," Jade said, "What have they done to this beautiful Buddhist community? I thought it would be more of a lazy river ride."

Laos tubing had obviously evolved over time. Ramshackle wooden bars built on platforms balancing on bamboo stilts lined the river's banks. Revelers were flinging themselves off zip-lines, high dives, rope-swings, and trapeze swings into the green water, narrowly missing rocks, tubers, kayakers, longboats and each other (we heard last night that there were already eight deaths on the river that year). The tubes served merely as transport between the bars.

"This is *so* much better!" Lana squealed as she pushed past us towards the bar at the starting point.

With beers condensing in hand, we hopped into our tubes and floated towards the next bar. Laotian boys no older than thirteen stood on the bar's lower platform that hovered at water level and tossed out empty water bottles tied to ropes. I grabbed one and was pulled from the water's current to the bar with Jade and Lana hanging onto my tube. Stashing our tubes under the upper platform with countless others, we climbed the ladder and joined the party.

"Welcome, ladies, come to Bucket Bar tonight and get a free bucket at nine," said a short guy who seemed far too old to be working in a bar on his gap year. He delivered his invitation in a coarse English accent as he wrapped yet another string bracelet around our wrists. "The name's Kush, and I'll be happy to serve you free buckets all night."

Pulling my hands from his lingering grip, I followed the girls across the splintered wooden platform. We made our way past dozens of westerners sitting with their feet dangling above the water, watching daredevils attempting backflips off the trapeze swing. Next we navigated through more westerners writhing to house beats before we found our Hawaiian friends gathered around tables strewn with red plastic cups and drenched in stale beer. Though thirteen thousand miles away from Toronto I felt comfortingly at home.

"What up, Canada?" Chad said, enveloping Lana in his bronzed arms before greeting us with a wave.

Felix and Kelly both had red cups tilted back, Adam's apples bobbing furiously, engaged in a one-on-one chug off. Slamming their cups on the table at the same time Kelly burped and Felix turned and said, "You girls want to get on our team for flip cup?"

"Sure," Lana said, twirling a strand of hair in her finger.

Jade looked at the ground. "I think I'm going to sit this one out."

Before we could stop her, she turned and nestled herself in the crowd sunning themselves at the platform edge. I watched her bum a cigarette off a random guy and waited for her to look back our way. When she glanced back, I mouthed, "You okay?"

She shot me the "OK" sign with her fingers, blew out a long stream of smoke, and folded her legs into lotus pose, watching the water.

With beer bloat setting in after four rounds of flip cup (three wins, one loss), the boys suggested beer pong. As we arranged ten cups per side, the boys hurried to the bar for more beers.

"Hello, Petal," Kush, A.K.A. Baldy McCreepy, was back. "If you're playing beer pong, you're going to need balls. Fortunately, I have two just for you."

With my eyes on the little white spheres suspended on the tips of his stubby fingers I forced an unconvincing polite smile on my face. "Thank you," I said, reaching for them.

"Need a partner?" he asked pulling them away from me playing that stupid sandbox game.

I shook my head and stared in his beady blue eyes, one hand on hip, the other hand outstretched. With a wink that made my skin crawl, he dropped the balls in my hand.

"Hey dude, thanks for the balls," Kelly said placing one hand on Kush's shoulder and placing an oversized can of Lao beer on the table with the other.

Saved by the Kell.

Instead of crawling back under whatever rock he came from, Kush crossed his arms and hung around to watch the game. With Lana and Chad on the other side of the tables, backs to the water, Lana began the game by maintaining eye contact as we threw a ball at the same time. Her ball hit the table, mine hit the cup at the top of the triangle. And thus began our domination of beer pong on the Nam Song River. After countless games against unworthy opponents, we faced our toughest challengers yet, Kush and some guy who made it to quarterfinals of the World Beer Pong Championships. Apparently it's a thing.

During this game, much shit was talked and beer was drunk. Assisted by Lana's distracting assets spilling from her string bikini, a crowd gathered and we whittled down cups to one cup each.

"You're going down," I said, pointing at Kush across the beer-puddled table.

Kush's lips curled into a smile. "Is that a threat or a promise, Petal?"

And with those words, I had to win. I refused to let Baldy McCreepy wear a shit-eating grin on his face from beating me. But he made the cup. The infuriating grin would remain firmly in place. If his partner made this cup, it was all over. No chance for rebuttal. Keeping my eye on the little white sphere, I watched it sail through the air and bounce on the rim of the cup. I swatted the ball into a bystander's face with the fierceness of Serena Williams in a Wimbledon final.

As he handed the ball to Kelly, I prayed for him to make the cup. He threw, but it missed the table by nearly a foot. It was all up to me. I knew I could make it. I was in my groove. I had barely missed a cup all day. As I drew my hand back, a tall, lean body topped with a head of sandy blond hair stepped to the table. It was like stepping back in time. My breath caught in my throat as he turned his head.

But beneath the sandy blond crop was a face I had never seen before.

"Show me what you've got, Petal." That grating voice pulled me back to the little red cup.

After shaking off the nervous tingles radiating through me, I took a deep breath, angled my body, cocked my wrist, and released the ball. It floated over the table, began its descent, and landed in an empty cup on the corner of the table. I folded forward in defeat.

"Sorry, man." I turned to Kelly.

He grabbed my hand and shook it. "Dude, that was an awesome game."

"Good game, Petal," Kush said walking over before taking my hand and kissing it.

Once all hands were shook and sportsmanlike expectations were upheld, I suggested to Lana that we check in with Jade. The Hawaiians joined us as we waded through the bodies to sit next to her.

"Do you guys want to get in the tubes and float down the river?" She rolled an unlit cigarette in her fingers. "I mean, unless you want to keep partying."

I knew she was over the party scene, and I didn't mind getting away from Kush's beady stare. Lana agreed, doing a terrible job at masking her disappointment at leaving a party early, but with the Hawaiians in tow, we grabbed tubes from under the bar, dropped them into the water, climbed in and pushed off from the platform.

We surrendered to the current, floating past bar after bar, each less busy than the last, until they became nothing more than wooden carcasses. The sun had passed its zenith, lazily making its way west toward the forested limestone karst cliffs. The towering cliffs ran north to south as far as the eye could see. Their immensity reminded me of the mountain from Pushkar. I scanned them, hoping that perhaps, one of them might call to me. Hoping that I might hear her voice. Hoping to know that she still existed. Hoping that I didn't have to live without her.

But the cliffs were silent.

As I leaned back, dipping my overheating scalp in the cool water, a familiar voice called my name. I turned to see Miles paddling towards me in the middle of a flock of bright yellow kayaks. My stomach tightened with surprise.

Gliding alongside me, he said, "Hey, I have your camera."

I shot up as my heart thumped against my chest. "But how?"

"You left it in the bar in Luang Prabang." He glanced ahead at his tour leaving him behind. "I'll give it to you tonight, after dinner sometime."

I could have sworn I had put it in my bag when I had finished showing him the pictures, but in that moment I was too happy to care about how I lost it.

"Meet me in Bucket Bar tonight at nine," I said. "It's the first bar down river on the island."

He nodded and paddled ahead to join his group. But as he faded from sight I threw my head back against the warm rubber and watched the clouds sail across the skies, thanking whoever was listening for the return of my camera.

***

Just before nine o'clock, Lana and I kissed a meditating Jade goodnight and followed the pulsating house music across a small bridge onto an island in the river and down a dirt path through the jungle to Bucket Bar. We had passed through the night before but only stayed about half an hour before nearly passing out from exhaustion. It was a crudely built structure of wooden columns no more than fifty feet in diameter, with no ceiling, no walls, and a packed dirt floor. One large elevated wooden platform stood in the center, and four more lined the perimeter. Bartenders slid buckets and shots across the bar to the right of the entrance. A dozen or so partygoers danced under multi-coloured strobe lights on the middle platform and two dozen more lazed about on oversized cushions on the elevated perimeter lounges. As we stepped over the threshold, we ran into our Hawaiian friends and made the way to the bar for our free buckets.

Southeast Asia took drinking to a whole new level — serving mixed drinks in buckets. Actual buckets with handles and everything. Perfect for sharing or getting smashed all on your own.

"Hello, Petal," Kush greeted me with a Cheshire cat grin. "Come to see me or your free bucket?"

"Bucket," I snapped with a terse flash of a smile.

"Now now, don't be mad because I beat you," he said, taking a bottle from beneath the counter. It contained amber liquid and a pickled snake curled up inside. I grimaced as he poured it into two buckets and then emptied a can of cola in both. "You were rather impressive earlier."

"Thanks," I mumbled, dropped my gaze, and found the bar menu.

This menu, however, didn't have drinks on it. Weed garlic bread, opium joints, mushroom tea. And then I thought, maybe one of these could open the portal back up, and I could speak to Audrey again. I nudged Lana, who stood with her back to the bar, no doubt keeping an eye on the Hawaiians. She took the laminated sheet in her manicured hands, and after giving it a once over, she turned her eyes to me with a mischievous smile.

"I see you've found our happy menu," Kush said, sliding the blue buckets across the bar.

Lana took her bucket and stepped away from the bar.

As I placed my hand on the rim of the bucket, he took the other side, his eyes lingering on my neckline. "You know Petal, you really have a beautiful tan. And you know what they say, tan lines are like chicken, the white bits are the best bits."

Ew.

Before I could think of an appropriate response for his inappropriate comment, a voice thundered from behind me. "Harper, you really must be cautious of the company you keep."

Miles.

I turned to see his blazing eyes fixated on Kush.

"It was just a joke, mate," he said, folding his arms.

Miles stepped forward between the counter and me. "Jokes are funny, that was not. I think you should apologize to her."

Kush glared at Miles before looking at me. "Sorry, Petal, I didn't mean to offend you."

I pressed my lips together in a faint smile, grateful for the apology and for Miles defending my honour.

"Miles," I said placing my hand on his forearm hoping to get away from the bar before a pissing contest could ensue. "Why don't you get a bucket and we'll find somewhere to sit?"

He nodded, and his face softened as he looked down at me. "Fine. I'll have whatever she has."

"Forgot your manners, mate?" Kush said puffing out his chest.

Miles clenched his jaw, and through a fake smile he hissed, "Please."

"Sorry, mate, fresh out of free buckets."

Miles splayed his large hands on the bar and looked down at Kush. "How much for one then?"

"Fifteen thousand kip," Kush said, slamming a bucket on the bar, its amber contents splashing onto Miles's formerly spotless white button-down.

"That's what, less than two bucks?" he said, pulling out a white and beige Louis Vuitton wallet before throwing his money on the bar. "What's your salary like working in a place like this?"

"Miles!" Though I had little sympathy for Kush, his vulgar humour was no excuse for Miles being plain disrespectful. He was only bringing himself down to Kush's level. "That's enough. Let's take buckets over there."

He hooked his arm around my neck, and I led him away. I scanned the scene and caught sight of Lana's strawberry-blond locks. She was lounging on a purple cushion on the elevated platform on the other side of the dance-floor with the Hawaiians. Stepping onto the wooden platform I lowered onto a cushion and introduced Miles to the boys. Chad couldn't stop staring in the same way Lana stared at Ryan Gosling when he sat next to us in Starbucks years ago. It was the only time she was too afraid to talk to a guy.

"So Felix," Lana said, "I forgot to ask, how did things go with the Swedish girls last night?"

I turned to Miles and whispered, "Last night we came here, and Felix disappeared with two very friendly Scandinavian girls."

Felix pressed his hand against his chest and looked into the distance with nostalgia glistening in his eyes. "It was the best night of my life. If I died tonight, I would die a happy man."

Kelly raised his hand to his forehead. "I salute you, sir."

As we lay out in the cool night breeze, we watched the stars and swapped stories of interesting eats, disgusting accommodations, and quirky characters we had met along the way. Miles didn't have much to add, his luxury tour consisted of weeks of scheduled "fun" with snobby middle-aged couples.

After staying silent for much of the conversation, he finally spoke. "Do you want to come get your camera? I thought it was best to keep it locked away in my safe."

"Yes, please," I said, jumping to my feet. Once it was in my hands, I could breathe easily again.

Bidding the crew farewell, Miles and I walked side by side back across the bridge. We followed the road down river, past the street vendors ladling pancake batter onto griddles, and away from crowds of rowdy revelers with buckets in hand. In silence, we strode down a neat brick path lined with tall bushes and fire-lit lamps. My heart drummed as he led me through a cherry wood hotel foyer adorned with orchids. After passing two women who greeted us by bowing with their hands in prayer position, we followed the same brick path to a dark wood bungalow triple the size of mine. As he fished the keys out of his pocket, I contemplated waiting outside. But as he turned the key in the golden door handle and swung it open, my mouth dropped as I peeked inside. I had to see more.

In awe, I slipped out of my flip-flops and padded across the varnished floorboards. On each wall hung a landscape painting in a gilded frame. In the middle of the room lay a king-sized bed, its white cotton sheets freshly turned down.

"I know it's rather basic and within earshot of that infernal racquet from Bucket Bar, but it's where our tour stays," he said, removing his Rolex and placing it on the bedside table.

"Are you kidding me? This is a castle compared to what I'm staying in."

He moved towards the curtains and pulled them back to reveal glass doors. "It does have a nice view."

I followed him, and when he slid one back and stepped onto the balcony suspended above the river.

"That's where I'm staying," I said, pointing past the bamboo bridge. "There are like a million bugs living in the thatching."

"You should be staying in a place like this," he said, before clearing his throat. "With me."

"The crappy places aren't that bad," I said, ignoring his last two words. "They make for good stories."

"I suppose that's one way of looking at it." He took a step towards the door. "Can I get you a nightcap?"

"No, thanks." I shook my head. I just needed to get my camera and get out of there before he got the wrong idea. "I should get back to Lana."

"Lana Brooks is a big girl," he said, scraping two wooden deck chairs across the floor. "Come sit, the moon is about to rise."

I had never seen a moonrise before. I didn't even know it was a thing. But I couldn't get comfortable: just see it and get out of there. "Okay, but I'll stand."

As I leaned against the lacquered railing, he stood next to me. He was a little too close for comfort, but before I could step away, the moon peeked over the top of the limestone cliffs. Had LMFAO's "I'm In Miami Bitch" not been playing quite so loudly, and had I not been there with such an immense asshole, as gorgeous and charming and witty as he may be, one could say it was quite romantic.

"It's beautiful."

"You're beautiful," he whispered.

I didn't know what it was about Miles Cooper. As much as I could hate him in any given moment, he always made me feel that teenaged puppy love.

"Harper?" His warm breath surged against my ear.

As I looked up at him, he pinned me against the railing and as his lips zeroed in on mine I turned my head and gave him nothing but cheek.

He had started my very awkward sexual awakening, and for over two years, an eternity in teenage years, I wanted nothing but this, nothing but him.

But I wasn't a teenager anymore.

"Stop." Pressing my hands to his chest, I pushed him off me and pulled a chair between us. "This is *not* going to happen. This is *not* why I came here."

"I'm so sorry," he said, raking his hands furiously through his hair. "I don't know what came over me. I've been so stressed out about moving, and I've been so alone, and then I saw you, and it brought back so many feelings. And I thought, I just thought..."

"You broke my heart the last time I saw you. Do you remember that night?"

He slumped into the chair behind him and rested his face in his hands for a moment. "I'm so sorry about that. I really am. I've always felt dreadful about it, and I've thought of you constantly since." He tilted his eyes up. "That was the biggest mistake I've ever made, and I want to make it up to you."

I gave serious consideration to slapping him across his face. But as he sat wiping away tears streaming down his perfectly shaven face, I felt story for him. Miles Cooper, sheltered country club boy, sent off to the other side of the world, alone and afraid. Not everyone can take such radical change. I pulled the chair back and sat across from him, knees touching.

"You can start by giving me my camera and we can go from there."

Chapter 17

The following morning, Jade, Lana and I rented mopeds in search of Vang Vieng's famous Poukham Cave and Blue Lagoon. We set off from town driving through grassy fields passing farmers leading lumbering water buffalo through waterlogged rice paddies and across rickety bamboo bridges above fishermen casting nets into the river. Gripping Lana around the waist as the moped sputtered and clattered over the rugged terrain, I tried to push what happened the night before out of my head. Though I left Miles as soon as my camera was in my hands, I shouldn't have gone into his room in the first place. I should have known that he would try something. But I couldn't deny that his wanting to kiss me brought back some very unwelcome feelings.

After finding cave after cave with some alternate spelling of the word "Poukham" (none were clearly *the* Poukham Cave), we stopped on the dirt path under the shade of a flowering tree. I slid off the seat behind Lana as she pulled the bike onto its stand, and I carefully cleaned the dust off my camera lens. I flicked through my images I had taken and was pleasantly surprised with the landscape shots, but my attention lingered over a shot of a fisherman teaching his young son how to cast a net properly. The child, no older than ten, looked up at his father with such respect and adoration, and the father looked at his son with love and a hint of frustration as the child kept getting tangled in the net. Though I was happy with my shots, I felt frustrated looking through my images. I didn't know what Awesome Adventures was looking for in the competition. Were they looking for perfectly composed landscapes or candid portraits? Did they want a commentary on social issues of locations or impeccably framed architecture?

"Can we go back to the river today?" Lana asked as Jade pulled out a map of the cycle livery drew for us.

"We did that yesterday," Jade said, crumpling the paper in her grip. "I didn't come all this way to drink and party and talk to boys. I want to see the country, do things we can't do at home."

Lana crossed her arms. "We can't party in rivers in Toronto."

They glared at each other as they sat on their bikes, front tires a foot apart, like a freeze frame from a game of chicken.

They both turned to stare at me.

"Harper, what do you want to do?" Jade said.

"Well, I mean," I started, rocking back on my heels. No matter what I chose, someone was going to be pissed at me. But sometimes you have to think of yourself and your needs. "I don't have any pictures of tubing."

"Fine. I'm going to find the real Poukham Cave," Jade said, pushing the bike off the stand.

"Jade, don't be like that," I said, throwing my hands in the air. But she ignored me as the engine roared, pushed the bike off the stand, and flew past us, vanishing in a cloud of dust.

"Yup…hungry vagina…I knew it would happen," Lana said shaking her head and turning the key in the ignition. "To the river?"

"Should we go after her?" I asked. We had made a pact in India that no one gets left alone again.

Lana shook her head. "If she wanted us to go with her she would have insisted. The only danger in this town seems to be the rocks in the river."

I paused and reassured myself that Jade would be fine. We had never felt uncomfortable in Laos, nor had we heard of crimes against tourists. I had to trust that she would be okay. Lana pushed the bike off the stand and I slid back onto the seat behind her, and then we crossed the field and crossed the river over a toll bridge. Following a jumbo tuk tuk stuffed with backpackers and topped with tubes up river through the town, we parked in the dusty lot and walked over the riverbank and into the bar we had been in yesterday. I followed Lana to the bar and saw Kush behind it, pouring drinks.

"Hello Petal," he said with a wink, "what can I get for you lovely ladies?"

"Two Lao beers," Lana replied.

He plucked out two cans from a cooler of ice and placed them on the bar. "Come see me tonight, for my magical mushroom concoction. I make the best in all of Vang Vieng."

Lana's face lit up as she took one of the cans.

"Funny, I don't remember reading that in the guidebook," I said, wrapping my fingers around the chilled metal.

"Just leave your boyfriend at home."

The memory of Miles's attempted mouth invasion lit a fire in me and I blurted out, "He is not my boyfriend."

"Good, I hoped a pretty girl like you had better taste in men," he said with yet another wink. As I regretted my words, I wondered if he had an eye condition. "Drinks are on the house."

I threw some *kip* on the bar to let him know that I didn't owe him anything, took Lana by the elbow, and led her to the edge of the platform to join the lazy sunbathers watching the rope-swingers.

"Miles made a move on you last night, didn't he?" she said raising her beer to her lips.

I lowered my camera. "Yes."

"Okay, I have to ask, he's freaky right?" She poked me in the ribs. "The uptight ones are always the worst."

I laughed. That boy was vanilla to the core. "No, and nothing happened last night. I don't know if I can ever forgive him."

"You don't think he's changed after all these years?"

I smiled at her. No matter how many undesirable low-lifes had passed through into Lana's heart and loins, she never became jaded.

I wanted to believe that people could learn and grow and change. And perhaps on some level I was open to it, I mean, if it worked out with Miles, it would be a hell of a story for the grandkids, but I decided that I wasn't going to rush into anything. If it happens, it happens, but it was much too early to determine if he had left his old ways behind.

But after Adam, at that moment, I felt both emotionally and physically "closed for business".

So I replied, "Maybe."

***

When we returned to the huts, Jade was swinging in the hammock on the patio. As I took a step to our hut and Lana headed to hers, Jade's face popped up over the brick-red canvas.

"Guys? I'm really sorry about today," she said as we slowed to a halt next to her. "I don't know what got into me."

Lana took hold of the top of the hammock and gave it a gentle push. "How about we go trip on mushrooms tonight and forget all about it?"

Jade smiled and nodded.

After a nap, shower, dinner, and dousing of bug repellant we headed to Bucket Bar. As we crossed the bridge, I was a bundle of nerves. I had never done mushrooms before, but I figured it couldn't have been that much different to the bhang. I hoped beyond hope that whatever portal had been opened in the desert could be opened again.

As Dizzy Rascal's "Bonkers" blared through the speakers, and the lights flashed like an epileptic's nightmare, we weaved through the writhing bodies to the bar.

"I've been waiting all night for you, Petal," Kush said giving his signature sleazy smile.

I grabbed the bar menu and kept my eyes glued to it. "I'll take you up on your offer."

"Which one?" he said, plucking it from my fingers. "I have many on the table."

"Mushrooms," I replied, meeting his eyes with a look that channeled Lorena Bobbitt.

"Tea or shake?"

I nudged the girls, who had their backs turned to the bar, and asked them what they wanted. Lana shrugged.

"Tea," Jade said, "Just one to start."

With the order placed, he disappeared into a hut behind the bar. Before long he returned, placing a steaming mug full of indigo-coloured liquid on the bar. Throwing our money on the bar, Jade took the mug in her hands, and we made our way to the cushions we sat on the night before. As we kneeled in a circle facing each other, Jade held the mug in the air like Rafiki showing off Simba, closed her eyes, and muttered something. Even in a club, she drank her hallucinogenic in ceremony to the gods. Then she took it to her lips and when she opened her eyes, her pupils had dilated, consuming her iris, leaving just a sliver of colour. Lana took the mug next, knocking it back, not bothering with ceremonial formalities, and then passed it to me. As the compost-smelling steam condensed on my face I held the mug to my chest just as we had in the desert, drew in a deep breath and whispered to Audrey, "Speak to me."

The moment the hot liquid hit the back of my throat, the effect was like a bullet to the brain. In an instant, my senses were assaulted with a symphony of rainbow-coloured lights and sounds as my mind failed to group musical notes together. I looked around noticing every detail of everything going on around me. Time seemed to slow down and speed up at the same time. I took the cup to my lips once more and drained it until all that was left was a heap of translucent mushrooms, each one no longer than my thumb.

I put the mug down and looked at the girls, and a goofy grin spread across my face to match theirs. Suddenly a beetle fell from the sky and landed on the bamboo mat between us, sending us into a laughing fit. In stitches, we flopped down on the cushions and took turns poking at it until it flew off. Rolling onto my back, I stared at the constellations in the night sky and waited for Audrey to turn up. But as the lights pulsated and moved to the music, stars fell, and beetles fluttered past, she was nowhere to be found. I sat up and looked west towards the karst cliffs, hoping perhaps God was waiting in another looming structure, figuring It had a flair for drama, but even as the moon hovered above the crest bathing the craggy cliffs in a soft glow, like earlier in the day, they were nothing but limestone.

As my eyes followed a piece of fluff across the lounge, a head of sandy hair at the other side of the dance floor caught my attention. Miles made his way around the perimeter of the club in our direction. The memory of his reaction to my story in the desert flashed. If he couldn't handle the thought of me high, he certainly couldn't handle me while I was high.

I had to escape.

I opened my mouth to say our code word, but the words stuck in my throat. Instead I pawed at the girls, Jade lying on her stomach watching an ant trail while Lana stared at the palms of her hands. I was met with lopsided grins. I pressed my index finger against my lips, pointed in Miles's direction, and then to the exit. The girls nodded and pushed to their feet. Focusing on limb control, I carefully placed one foot in front of the other, getting the hang of walking again as I made my way through the strobe lights.

And just as I made it to the exit, a hand landed on my shoulder. "Leaving so soon, Petal?"

I had no time for his shit, and my brain had no sense to form a response, so I shook off his hand and kept moving before my trip turned sour. The girls must have lagged behind, as about twenty seconds later, they caught up to me. Or it could have been two seconds or an hour, time made no sense anymore.

"Miles saw us," Jade said, vacant eyes staring past me.

I stopped at a fork in the road, we could go back over the bridge or head down a path to the left with a sign advertising another club, Smile Bar. I glanced over my shoulder down the path, but no one was following us. Lana walked ahead, turning left, and Jade and I followed her. In a clearing of trees, we found another bar, just like Bucket Bar except no strobe lights and no people.

Perfect.

Hammocks hung from wooden gazebos nestled against the trees, tucked away from view. We floated down to them, but the girls wanted to find water, so I cocooned myself in one, the rocking soothing me back to enjoy the moment. Until…

"Petal?"

Oh God, he couldn't take a hint. Baldy McCreepy earned himself a new nickname: Douchey McTripshitter.

I stayed still, hoping to melt into the fabric, but I knew he would spot me eventually. I squeezed my eyes shut, hoping if I couldn't see him, then he couldn't see me.

All is well. All is well.

"Petal?" he repeated, his voice louder, closer.

All is well. All is well.

"There you are, Petal." I opened my eyes, and he loomed above me. "I wanted to see how you were feeling."

I forced myself upright, feeling too vulnerable horizontal and held the rope that connected the hammock to the wooden column. "I'm fine," I managed to eek out with a thumbs up.

"Listen, I've got some mates at a bar a little way down the island. You and your girls should come, it'll be fun."

I shook my head. Scanning the scene for any sign of the girls, or anyone. I could see silhouettes of what I hoped to be the girls near the entrance.

"I've got some great opium we can smoke in the jungle along the way. Best in all of Laos," he said with a smile ever so south of sane.

I shook my head screaming on the inside, *leave me alone!* But my tongue stopped working.

He gave a sigh of defeat. "Alright, Petal, well, I'll just wait with you until your friends return. Wouldn't forgive myself if I left you alone and something happened to you."

I appreciated the sentiment. As creepy as he was, he really was harmless, but I still wanted him to go away. I shook my head again and managed to say, "No."

"Oh, come on, Petal," he said taking a step forward, wrapping his fingers on the hammocks rope, his hand barely touching mine. "I know I'm a little crass, but I'm not a bad guy."

"I believe she said no," a male voice boomed from behind him. A hand gripped him by the shoulder and pulled him backwards with such force, he tumbled to the ground. I tried to get out of the hammock. My wobbly legs gave way, and I fell. The girls appeared, and they dropped the bottles of water and helped me to my feet. Steadying myself I saw Miles and Chad towering above Kush, fists cocked.

"Listen, mate, I was just trying to watch out for her," Kush said cowering on the dirty floorboards. "Petal, tell him —"

Before I could say anything, Miles laid two solid punches to his face. "I swear to God if you so much as look at her again, I'll beat you until you can't remember your own sorry name." As Chad yanked Kush to his feet and shoved him down the gazebo step, Miles turned his attention to me. "Are you okay?"

My thoughts spiraled out of control. With each happy thought I tried to force into my head, it was countered with a replay of what just happened. I should have been smarter, I should have gone with the girls to get water. I should have been clearer with Kush. Perhaps he took my non-rejection as flirtation? I hated the sight of violence. Audrey lost her life in a senseless act of violence. There were other ways to handle things. And as creepy as Kush was, he didn't deserve to get punched in the face.

As pain throbbed through my knees from the fall, everything was now too much, the eyes on me, the frantic music, my dry-ass mouth. I had to get out of there and away from everyone who wasn't Jade and Lana. So I opened my mouth and called out our code word, "Matches!"

Chapter 18

Date: March 3, 2010
Hanoi, Vietnam

Five days and five hundred and thirteen kilometers later, after traveling by tuk tuk, kayak, minivan and Boeing 737, I stood in the hostel common room between Jade and Lana. Their claws were bared during their first fight as business partners. The day had started well enough. We had awakened bright-eyed and bushytailed and spent the morning exploring Hanoi's Hoan Kiem Lake, the markets in the Old Quarter, and the "Hanoi Hilton" (it's not a hotel). By lunchtime, my camera battery was dead, and our legs were worn out. So, after nearly two months of continuous sightseeing, watching movies and hanging in the common room seemed like it would be a relaxing time.

I lazed on the couch, editing images as *Ever After* played on the television, and Drew Barrymore and the prince bantered. The girls sat at a table by the window, going over their strategy to tackle getting the collection made. Their business meeting began with the conceptualization and designs, but things went south when Lana produced a profit and loss sheet.

"Why does everything have to be about money and consumerism?" Jade said as paper crumpled.

"Are you kidding me?" Lana raised her voice. "You're trying to enter a consumer industry!"

"I want this to be about spirituality and ethical consciousness, not simply profits."

"This is a business, you damn hippy!"

A chair scraped back, and I turned to see Jade leaning over the table, finger in Lana's face. "I am *not* a hippy you…you…slut!"

Before Lana could get another word out, Jade stomped through the room and out of the door. Lana shook her head, gathering sheets of paper, and flopped onto the couch with the longest sigh I think I had ever heard. The girl had some big lungs.

"Is there anything I can do to help?" I asked placing my hand on her knee, but she shook it off.

"I think we could all do with a little space from each other."

Ouch.

The day after our little shroom escapade in Vang Vieng, we ended up sprawled out with the other hungover travelers at the restaurant that played reruns of *Family Guy,* mindlessly pushing stir-fried vegetables and rice in our mouths as morning turned to afternoon, and afternoon turned to dusk. I had neither seen nor heard from Miles since that night as his tour had left. Though I had little sympathy for Kush, I couldn't condone the sheer brutality that Miles inflicted on him, and I had let him know. I spent the next day and a half after that incident laying low and avoiding Kush. As we boarded a minivan heading to the capital of Vientiane, I saw Kush one last time, his face decorated with a shiner of a black eye, and I couldn't help but feel a little guilty. Had I told him to fuck off point blank, perhaps it all could have been avoided.

Lana and I sat in silence alone in the common room, and I played with my pictures until the credits rolled and she left without a word. Taking a break from editing I pulled up Facebook. Though it was banned in Vietnam, Facebook has prepared for the communist exile. Our hostel had posted a sign for an alternative URL directing me to a stripped-down version of the social media giant. Upon logging in, I was greeted by a million notifications.

Most of them I could ignore, but there was one I didn't. Among friend requests from our Hawaiian boys blinked a friend request from Miles. I accepted all. Within a minute of scrolling through the newsfeed, a new message appeared in my inbox.

Miles Cooper: *Are you in Hanoi?*

I ignored it and kept scrolling. Then more new message notifications blinked: *I'm so sorry for my behaviour in Vang Vieng. Where are you? Are you safe? Please message me.*

I sighed and responded: *Yes, I'm at the Drift Back-packers in Hanoi.*

He wrote back instantly: *Please wait there. I'd really like the chance to apologize in person. I'm on my way.*

Why did I tell him where I was? I had so many images to edit. Before I closed the browser, I noticed something in my newsfeed. Adam had changed his relationship status to single. Even though I deleted him, Facebook thought it would be lovely to share that a mutual friend liked that he was advertising his availability to the world.

I closed the browser, and his face met me once more, smiling at me from my desktop background. I changed the image to the image I had taken of my lantern in Chiang Mai, floating to the heavens with a hundred others, on the night I decided to let him go. Then I turned my attention back to my images and tried to get as much work done as I could before Miles turned up. But the thought of his status wouldn't leave my mind. Alone in the common room, the sterile white walls closed in on me. I stood and walked to the window, pressing my face against the glass. I knew I had let Adam go, and it was for the best, but for some reason, it still bothered me. Perhaps because I had let him into my heart, he left footprints that would remain forever. Or perhaps it was the fact that he seemed ready for love, ready for the next girl, ready to replace me, even though it had barely been a month since I left his life. I turned and forced my attention back to my images.

"Harper?" Miles's voice broke my concentration as I was playing with the dodge and burn tool on my favorite image of the sisters from Death Mountain. He stood in the middle of the room looking at me like a puppy that peed in my shoes. "Please come for a walk with me?"

I nodded. Though I had images to work on, I needed to get out of that room and get some fresh air. After running my laptop back to the room and locking it away, I led him downstairs and out the door. I met eyes with Jade, who leaned against the building sharing a cigarette with one of our roommates, a cute and scruffy Argentinian yoga instructor. As we walked past, I gave her a slight smile, but instead of returning the smile, she glared at Miles.

Crossing the road in Hanoi was like walking through a swarm of bees around a knocked over a hive, and confronting the two-wheeled traffic was a real test of mettle. The scooters didn't stop for pedestrians. Instead, you walk steadily across the road, trusting that they drive around you. You stop, or you run and get hit. We stepped into a one-way street, and Miles walked on the side of incoming traffic until we made it to the sidewalk. Just a few beats later, we were walking past the murky Hoan Kiem Lake, an urban oasis surrounded by cafés and shops.

"So the hostel didn't look half as bad as I had thought it would," he said after ordering a cone of vanilla ice cream from a street vendor.

"It's actually the cleanest place we've stayed in. We do have to share it with seven strangers, though."

With ice cream in hand, I followed him to an empty bench in the shade of an ancient weeping willow on the edge of the water. A moment after we sat, he blew out a deep breath and said, "I'm so sorry."

"It's okay," I said, licking the chilly confection.

"No, it's not. I let my temper get the better of me. I just lost it when I saw that creep get too close to you."

"After you put your hands on me?"

He scrubbed his hairless chin with his hands. "I'm so sorry for that, also. I haven't quite been myself lately. And I still want to make amends for it, for all of it."

"Well." I held up my ice cream before licking it. "This is a good start."

I had waited years for an apology from him, and now it seemed I was getting one on a weekly basis. Memory is a funny thing; the more time I spent with him, the harder it was to remember why exactly I hated him. As I finished my cone, clouds blanketed the blue skies. A breeze nipped at my skin, and I shuddered and wrapped my hands around my bare arms.

"Here, take this," he said untying the red cashmere sweater from around his neck before handing it to me.

I smiled as I pulled the oversized garment over my head, inhaling the lingering scent of laundry detergent. "You know I always made fun of you for the pointless sweater tied around your neck."

"Well, it seems you've finally realized the method of my fashion madness," he said nudging my shoulder with his.

"So things seemed kind of tense between you and Jade."

It was then I realized that he had stretched out his arm along the top of the bench behind my neck. And I don't know what came over me, perhaps it was because I was a little homesick and he reminded me of home, but I snuggled into the warm nook under his arm and unloaded everything I had been bottling up. I told him of Jade and Lana's bickering over the business and how we should spend our days, an abridged version of my story with Adam (omitting Xavier), and my guilt for

227

making my parents worry when I couldn't message them every day. And how much I missed Audrey. I felt so guilty that she would never get to experience traveling the world. His arm curled around me and he wiped the tears away, and once I had drained myself of all the words and emotions that had been overflowing within me, we cuddled in comfortable silence, watching the gentle lapping of the water.

A stroll through the Old Quarter, two pho soups, a water puppet show and several martinis later, he walked me back to The Drift.

"Welcome to my humble abode," I said, as we stood in front of the reception desk, wondering who put those words in my mouth.

"Yes, humble it is," he said, with a smirk as he strolled past the row of computers next towards the elevator.

I swatted his shoulder. "It's not that bad. Seriously, come upstairs and take a look. It's only eight, everyone should still be up."

He hesitated before joining me on the staircase that twirled through the center of the building. It would be innocent enough, I could prove to him that I wasn't living in squalor in a very non-romantic room of multiple occupants. I slid my keycard into the slot and pushed the door open, but no one was in sight. Miles stepped in behind me and browsed the room. I pointed out the lockers to the right of the hallway, the bathroom on the left, and the four bunk beds pushed against the light blue walls.

"It's much cleaner than I expected," he said running his fingertip along a metal bedframe and inspecting it. "And what about your roommates?"

"They seem normal, though I haven't met them all." I pointed at the bunks that weren't ours. "This one comes in when we've all gone to bed and leaves before we're up. We went out last night with these two girls from Ghana, they're really cool and coming with us to Ha Long Bay tomorrow. This one is empty, and that one is the Argentinian guy, Arturo, you saw earlier with the pajama pants and man-bun with Jade. I think he as a crush on her."

When I turned around, he looked as if he hadn't heard a word I said. "I like that we're friends again," he said, taking a step towards me.

Relief washed over me when he said *friends*, as if he drew a line in the sand, a boundary for expectations. But as I looked into his eyes, I saw that spark I remembered too well, and a smile curled my lips as I remember doodling "Harper Cooper" over and over again in my notebook as I studied for my final exams in high school. He took a step forward and raised his hand, brushing the back of his hand against my cheek. Then I remembered that I needed to be the one to enforce the boundaries. I gently pushed his hand away.

"Miles, we're friends again. Just friends. So let's not ruin this."

Then the door handle clicked, and the door swung open.

"— and Harper is always such an idiot when it comes to that sack of bad energy, Miles. She just keeps going back for —" Jade stopped mid-sentence when she saw us, Argentinian man-bun towering over her from behind.

Heat spread across my skin like wildfire as she slapped me with her words.

"I should go," Miles said, stiffening his posture.

Before I could protest, he turned and strode past Jade and out of the door. I glared at her as she skirted around me and into her bunk with Arturo. I bit my tongue, grabbed my towel, and headed for the shower and lathered up. I knew she was just stressed out, but she had no right to act the way she was. And I was not an idiot. I was in full control of the situation. She had no idea what it felt like for me to run into him again, to be able to patch things up, make peace with my past and maybe, just maybe, hang onto a piece of the past where Audrey still lived. I knew she hated Miles, but there was no excuse for bitching about him and me behind my back. I decided to say something to her and stand up for myself. I yanked my pajama bottoms on and ripped a t-shirt over my head as I placed my hand on the bathroom door handle I heard the room fill with people.

Lana and the Ghanaian girls had come back, and I was not about to make a scene and bring our roommates into our squabble. With the air-conditioning chilling my damp skin I padded through the room giving a polite but terse greeting, climbed to my bunk, stuck my earphones in, and decided that a good night's sleep would be the best course of action.

***

In the morning the air was still tense, and we kept our space from each other as we gathered our things and boarded the bus for our day excursion to Ha Long Bay. Lana sat with the Ghanaian girls taking up the three seats at the back, and Jade and Arturo found seats in the middle, leaving me to take a seat by myself at the front. I rested my head against the glass and fought with my eyes to stay open as we made our way through the city picking up passengers from other hotels and hostels. The bus was almost full when we approached a five-star colonial style hotel far fancier than all of the other hotels combined. The words "Hotel Metropole Hanoi" were splashed across the covered entranceway. I turned as green as the shutters with envy as I stared though the doors into the marble-lined foyer. As fun as hostels could be, there really was no comparison to traveling in style. A figure I swore was a mirage pushed through the doors and approached the bus.

"Good morning," Miles greeted the bus as he boarded. He looked at me and I thought I was still asleep. "Is this seat taken?"

"What are you doing here? Aren't you on a tour?"

I glanced back to the girls. Lana was too caught up chatting with her new friends to notice, and Jade scowled at him.

"I'll take that as a no," he said gliding into the seat, enveloping me with subtle musk cologne. "My tour was planning on going to Ha Long Bay today anyways, so when I left last night I booked the last spot on your excursion at the hostel's front desk. I'd rather go with you, I hear slumming it is in fashion."

I rolled my eyes with a smile. I was glad that we could put the past behind us and become friends again, particularly on a day where I felt so alone. After we picked up the last people and the bus was full, we set off onto the highway. As we left the city behind, we passed suburbs leading into rural areas, and I lost my battle with my eyelids when we drove through rice paddies rambling into the horizon.

"Harper? Harper? We're here."

My eyes flicked open. To my horror, I had fallen asleep on Mile's baby blue Lacoste polo-shirt clad shoulder. My cheeks seared and I checked for signs of drool. All dry, thank God.

"Sorry."

He gave me a shy smile and rose to his feet before helping me to mine. Miles and I were the first to step off the bus, and then everyone else disembarked and congregated in the parking lot. Again Lana and Jade stood at opposite ends of the crowd. A warm breeze swept across my face as gravel crunched beneath my flip-flops as our tour guide, Lucky, led us across the lot and towards a sprawling bay of emerald green waters. According to Lucky, as legend would have it, the gods sent dragons to defend the infant nation of Vietnam against invaders and the dragons spat out jewels and jade, which formed the series of limestone isles and islets topped with rainforests dotting the waters as far as I could see.

Lucky herded us down a gangplank and onto a pier on the edge of the bay, through the throngs of tourists, and onto one of the countless wooden Vietnamese "junk boats." Each spectacularly crafted ship ran over fifty feet in length and had two or three decks. The upper-most deck was open to the elements. Many of the ships were topped with orange sails coiled around tall masts. With Miles escorting me onto the lower deck, we were seated at tables draped with crisp linens with cutlery set for lunch. The lacquered cherry wood benches matched the rest of the wood paneling on the hull. Jade sat with Arturo near the bow, Lana sat nearest the stern and Miles and I took a table in the middle.

"Hello, and welcome to UNESCO World Heritage site Ha Long Bay!" Lucky announced once we were all seated. He then proceeded to walk us through a safety briefing. Once the engines rumbled, we set off and soon dining on a lunch of spring rolls, steamed fish in lemongrass broth, rice, and vegetables were laid out on the tables family style.

Since the moment I first laid eyes on Miles Cooper, I had always wondered what it would be like to date the most in-demand man in university. Had someone told my eighteen-year-old self that we would be eating lunch on a junk boat in Vietnam one day, I would have laughed, fainted with delight, and then asked what a junk boat was when I awoke. But as we dined, I felt less like the awkward and self-conscious teenager I used to be, and more like a confident woman in control of her emotions. I smiled as he fiddled with his chopsticks, eventually ditching them in favour of the fork and spoon. And though I enjoyed our newfound friendship, there was the faintest whisper at the back of my mind wondering if perhaps, just perhaps, he was sent back into my life to be something more.

As we were finishing our last bites, Lucky announced that we were approaching the floating village. I pulled out my camera and followed the crowd up a lacquered ladder to the top deck. The sheer magnificence of the landscape of limestone karst cliffs rising from the waters blew me away, but when I raised my camera to capture it, through my viewfinder I found the beauty in the details.

At the base of the nearest cliff-face sat a network of small floating huts docks and pathways. Vietnam flags waved proudly from each hut. Children dove from the platforms into the water. It looked like a wonderful place to grow up. Women rowed rowboats filled with sodas and fruit between the junk boats. One of the boats caught my attention, as a tiny speck of a girl sat in her wares handling the money, her mother beaming proudly at her. I was so caught up with capturing a moment between the mother and daughter, I barely noticed that Miles was no longer there. Nothing else mattered to me, until something ice cold was pressed into my back.

I squealed and whipped around to see Miles holding up a can of Coke. After swatting his forearm, I took it from him. Hanging the camera around my neck I thanked him, cracked open the can and sucked down the cold sugary goodness. Taking a glance around the boat, Jade and Lana were off in their own little worlds, but they seemed happy and I just wanted us all to talk and clear the air so we could go back to being friends already. As Miles and I finished our sodas, the junk boat puttered through the islets before slowing to a stop outside of the largest of three limestone isles. Lucky told us that this was a large circular cavern accessible only by kayak through a small cave.

"Want to go with me?" Miles asked, giving my hand a squeeze that made my stomach skitter.

"Sure."

Back on the lower deck, I debated whether or not to take my camera with me. I didn't have a waterproof housing, but I toyed with the idea of taking the chance. Ultimately I decided that losing it, along with the images I took that day, wasn't worth the risk so I packed it away. As Miles peeled off his shirt, exposing his pale unblemished skin, some old feelings stirred. He still had that strong, broad-shouldered swimmer's body. And though he had seen me in a bathing suit in Vang Vieng, as I undressed I felt shy under the weight of his gaze.

Lucky and a deckhand passed him a kayak on the swim platform, and he dropped it into the water. He got in first at the front seat and held the platform, steadying the kayak as I lowered myself into it behind him. Along with four other kayaks, one containing Jade and Arturo, we paddled away from the boat and towards a looming karst cliff-face.

The tide was low, so we didn't need to duck as we glided under the entranceway that narrowed from twenty feet to ten feet wide into a ceiling-less circular cavern. It was like being in the middle of a limestone donut topped with a glazing of forest. Sounds echoed off of the limestone, reverberating in all directions until dying out. Soon the other kayaks left, and with no voices to bounce around the cavern, it was almost too quiet.

And as I dropped my gaze from the cloudless blue sky, my eyes glued to Miles's back, watching his muscles flex as he paddled. On paper, he was a perfect catch: good-looking, great family, well connected, established in his career. If I got my five-year career plan on track, he would make the perfect partner. Though I knew I had decided to put boys on hold, I still wanted to get married one day, to love and be loved, and birth adorable babies. And in reality, he was sweet, caring, charming and he gave me butterflies, and...

Oh God, I think I like Miles Cooper again. As in, like-like him.

And that thought terrified me.

I really am over Adam.

After returning to the boat we continued cruising through the bay until we made berth at a long pier at one of the larger islets to explore "Paradise Cave." With a new set of nerves balling in my stomach, I let Miles take my hand as we navigated through the tourists down a slippery path past dripping stalactites and towering stalagmites and columns ages old and bathed in coloured lights, pausing to capture its beauty. I was finally getting the hang of my exposure setting.

After exiting through the gift shop, we found a bench away from the crowds and as we waited for our tour to head back to the boat, we stared across the bay and I reeled from my revelation.

"Travel with me," he said, finally breaking the silence.

"You can't be serious," I blurted out in surprise.

"Why not?"

My stomach tied in a knot as I turned to meet his eyes. How could he be serious? We had only run into each other days ago. What would that make us? What would he expect from us? From me? Amongst the many reasons I could think of, I said the most important one: "I can't leave my girls."

"They have each other. Whatever they're going through, they'll work it out." He placed his hand on my knee. "Come with me on my tour. We'll travel properly, stay in nice hotels, eat amazing food, see each country in style."

"Miles, I can't afford that."

"I'll take care of it," he said, leaning in. "Haven't we had fun today? I've missed you so much over these years, and I don't want this to end. Not yet."

He caught me so off guard, I couldn't think or move. I blew out a deep breath and tried to rationalize what he was saying. "This is happening so fast, don't you —"

"Before you know it, your trip will be over."

He did have a point. Time was slipping away faster than I cared to admit. It felt like only yesterday that Lana and I landed in Mumbai. To travel in style did sound awfully appealing, but my latest realization about my feelings about him scared me. But I had to know. "What would that mean for us? For you and me?"

"Whatever you want. Friends and we'll see what happens? I just know I'd regret it forever if I didn't ask."

I stared at the horizon as my mind spun with so many questions — could we travel as just friends? What if more happened? Was that what I wanted?

"Don't answer now." His words cut off my train of thought. "Please think about it, but I do need to know by noon tomorrow. My tour leaves for Sapa tomorrow evening."

I nodded, took a deep breath, and decided to do just that: think about it on the drive back to Hanoi. But I felt more conflicted than ever.

***

Back in the crowded hostel room, tensions continued to flare between Jade and Lana. I had always wondered about the origins of the word *hostel*, but when you cram together a group of sleep-deprived, malnourished vagrants where women's hormones cycle together, it ends up creating a rather *hostile* environment. For the sake of their business I hoped they could hash it out before we arrived in our next stop, Hoi An. They would need to communicate effectively as partners with each other and the tailors so the pieces can be made properly.

As the girls organized their lockers and got in each other's way, I sat on my top bunk uploading images to my computer, weighing the pros and cons of Miles's proposal. He and I had been getting along great, and the same could not be said for the girls and me. If I went with him, I wouldn't have to put up with anyone else's PMS. I would have more living space, *better* living space. I would eat the kind of food you savour rather than eating to survive. I would be giving up on the social aspect of backpacking, we have met some really fun people along the way, but then it would be a matter of quality over quantity of social interaction —

investing in one friendship with Miles rather than the fleeting friendships we made. And the romantic in me allowed myself to dream the dream I had when I first laid eyes on him when I was seventeen.

But a little voice kept saying, *Miles Cooper will always be Miles Cooper.* He would always be the guy who took my virginity and broke my heart.

Suddenly a foul smell permeated the air. Like rotten eggs and blue cheese that had been left to sit in the sun for a day. Then the random roommate who we had never seen before emerged from the bathroom. "Sorry, guys, you do *not* want to go in there for at least an hour."

And then I decided: I was going with Miles.

Chapter 19

I awoke with my body shaking violently. My eyes flicked open. Lana was straddling me on the bed.

"What? What's going on?" I yelled.

She shoved a piece of paper in my face. "She's gone!"

I grabbed the piece of paper and waited for my eyes to focus in the dim light, turning black squiggles into letters and words.

> *The Universe has spoken to me. I've left with Arturo. I'll meet you in Phnom Penh.*
> *- Jade*

As her words registered, I realized that traveling with Miles was circling the toilet.

"What do you want to do?" I asked, still pinned to the bed by Lana's womanly hips.

"I'm not giving up on the business. I'm going to Hoi An as planned," she said, finally releasing me.

Sapa was due north of Hanoi, Hoi An was due south, and I wasn't about to let Lana go alone. So there it was, my teenage fantasy being sucked into the sewers. But when I saw Lana's face scrunched up and wet with tears of frustration, I put my disappointment aside.

We got dressed and ate breakfast in the café on the first floor of the hostel. Lana rammed spoonful after spoonful of oatmeal into her mouth while I pushed mine around in the bowl. Barely a word was spoken, but anger was written all over her face. Once we were finished, she distracted the receptionist, and I stole a wad of paper from the hostel printer and we ran up to the common room. I worked on my images while Lana spent the rest of the day trying to recreate Jade's drawings. I admired her resolve and determination, especially for the fact that she had the artistic skills of a colour-blind second grader.

As she scribbled, I sat next to her, wondering how to phrase my message to Miles. Should I tell him that I was going to say yes, or should I leave it as, "I can't"? For some reason, I balked at telling him outright that I planned to come with him as if it was a definitive proclamation that I was open to the prospect of our relationship progressing beyond friendship. In the end, I decided to tell him about Jade's disappearance and that I could not leave Lana by herself.

Opening a new message for Jade, I restrained myself from spewing out all of the angry things I wanted to say to her. For letting Lana down, for putting a kink in my plans, and for making me worry about her every moment she'll be God knows where with some guy we know nothing about. I was once told never to write letters, emails, or Facebook messages while angry. So I asked her to check in with me every day so I knew she was safe. But the next night as we crammed ourselves into brick hard beds no wider than out bodies on a sleeper bus headed for Hoi An, I rehearsed the choice words I had for Jade for the twenty-two hours we were stuck on that bus.

***

Date: March 7, 2010
Hoi An, Vietnam

We arrived in Hoi An at dusk too tired to be angry. Instead, we focused our energy on finding a place to stay, and then food. After checking into a guesthouse, we wandered the banks of the Mekong River into the Old Town and were too wonderstruck to be mad. Except for the temples and pagodas, shops and dressmakers filled the buildings, none standing taller than two stories, each painted a soft yellow and adorned with dark wooden shutters. Light poured from the open storefronts into the streets and strings of Chinese Lanterns zigzagging between the scalloped roofs gave the town a magical feel. On the bus I had plenty of time to read the guidebook and get the fast facts on this place. Hoi An was another UNESCO World Heritage site that was a restored relic of old Vietnam preserved in time. As a trading port, it experienced a constant influx of foreign ideas and cultures, which explained the beautiful muddle of architectural styles and cuisine. We walked off our dinner of spring rolls and risotto with passion fruit ice cream cones in hand, and Lana planned her attack of the dressmakers for tomorrow.

In between eating our way through all the Old Town's restaurants, we lugged around silk saris, struggling to choose from the six hundred dressmakers in town. The colourful silks would serve as trim to accent the stretchy and hard to find bamboo cotton. The pricier dressmakers had the bamboo cotton Lana wanted, but with the language barrier, Lana struggled to explain her rudimentary drawings to the tailors who only spoke rudimentary English. The first day began in high spirits, with us zipping from shop to shop through the narrow streets on bicycles, but after two days of fighting the language barrier I could see the fire in her soul slowly extinguishing. And on the third it was time to pick up the final pieces. When she unraveled the garments, she was near catatonic with disappointment. While I could appreciate the craftsmanship of the seamstresses, the garments looked as if they were based off the drawings of a colour-blind second grader.

As she stood in the middle of the road holding up a piece that vaguely resembled yoga pants, I took her by the hand, pulled her out of the way of the rickshaws, and into our favourite restaurant, The Mermaid. With elbows propped up on the table, she rested her face in her hands, unable to respond to anything I, or the waitress, said. I ordered her a green mango salad, and as I pushed food through her partly opened lips, the life began to return to her.

"I don't know why I thought I could do this," she spoke her first words in nearly three hours. In Lana time, that was like a week.

"You're great with the business side of things, but you needed Jade here to explain the designs. It's not your fault. She shouldn't have left you," I said before stuffing a deliciously crispy crab wanton into my mouth.

"To be honest, I thought I'd be the flakey one running off with some guy. I can't be mad that she ran off to have sex with some bendy tantric hottie who can probably go for days at a time." She finally picked up her fork and pushed around the salad around her plate. "I just thought with this business that I found my place, my purpose."

I knew how she felt. We were all looking for our callings, and I was grateful that I believed I had found mine in my photography.

"You don't want to get back into broadcasting?"

She shook her head. "I've burned all my bridges there."

"There's always porn," I joked, poking her hand with a fork.

She sank into her chair and rested her chin on the heel of her hand. "The sad thing is, I don't think that's the worst idea in the world. Maybe that is all I'm good for."

"No, Lana, that's a terrible idea." And as she descended back into her catatonic state, I didn't know what to do. I took a sip of my iced lemongrass tea and checked my watch. It was time for me to pick up a dress I ordered for myself. "I'm popping across the street. I'll be right back."

She gave a nearly imperceptible nod as I stood. After stepping through the bougainvillea-draped doorway, I walked across the street, through the bike parking lot, and into the hectic cloth market. Under a corrugated tin roof, reams of folded fabric were stacked in bookcases blocking off each vendor's space. Rows of sewing machines stood side by side waiting for something to sew, and the windowless walls echoed the chattering of the day's business. Threading my way through people shopping, and dressmakers promising me "best price," I found my lady: an aggressive saleswoman who had sized me up with a tape measure and said I would make a perfect wife for her son as I stepped into the market the day before. She handed me the garment and pushed me into the changing room.

In his last message, Miles invited me to dinner on the evening when our upcoming nights in Phnom Penh would overlap. Everything I owned was pretty ragged and stained at this point, so I figured I might as well get something personal made. I slipped the fabric over my head and breathed a sigh of relief that the simple purple cotton sundress fit perfectly. It had a fitted bodice that pushed up my boobs, and the A-line skirt and cinched waist gave me curves. In that dress, rather than feeling like a dirty backpacker, I felt like a classy woman. I wished Audrey could have seen me. She had only seen me in a dress on perhaps less than ten occasions since I was old enough to dress myself.

I wondered what Audrey would have thought about me reconnecting with Miles. Part of me couldn't believe that I almost went traveling with him. Would she think I was naïve to think that we could travel as just friends? I never told her what happened between us, but she was well aware of his reputation in university. Though the thought crossed my mind more times than I could count, he seemed truly intent on building things back with me. And he was a different person than he used to be. Sure, the old Miles was there, charming, a little brash, and spoiled but he had grown up. He was a man now. And he was a man who wanted to take things slow with me. And as much as I did love the idea of traveling in style, I loved more the thought that maybe there could be something between us.

After spinning and twirling in my purple frock like a little girl, I changed back into my tank top and leggings. I handed over my money, the hilariously named *dong*, and as she folded my dress, and slipped it into a bag, she insisted again to introduce me to her son. With a laugh, I declined the offer, thanked her for my dress, and navigated my way back through the cloth market and inhaled the fresh air, happy to leave the frenetic energy behind as I stepped back into the street.

"Canada!"

I stopped mid-step, turned in the direction of the voice, and saw a face I would have paid my last *dong* to see.

"Hawaii!"

Chad was sitting on a blue motorcycle in the parking lot of the cloth market. I walked over, grabbed him by the hand, told him to, "Come with me," and marched him into the restaurant.

I called her name as we stepped back under the bougainvillea, and as she looked up, for the first time since Ha Long Bay, a smile blossomed.

Thank God.

He took a seat next to me and across from her.

"Hi," he said with a goofy grin, staring at her with that star-struck look in his eyes.

"Hey." She batted her eyelashes back at him.

I stuffed another wanton into my mouth and asked, "Where's Felix and Kelly?"

"They went on a boat trip to some nearby island to go diving." He paused to pull his sleeves back to his elbows. "I get seasick, so I rented a motorcycle for the day. Do you girls feel like riding up the coast to Danang?"

Lana nodded and smoothed her hair.

"Can we all fit on your bike?" I asked. I would have gladly stayed behind if it meant Lana was happy. "I can stay."

"Have you seen how many people can fit on a motorbike over here? We'd still have space for two more people, a dog, and a tree," he said, making Lana laugh.

"Come with us," Lana said, reaching across the table for my hand.

I raised my eyebrows and mouthed, "Are you sure?"

She nodded back and mouthed, "Yes."

Once we paid our bill, we piled onto the motorcycle and left the Old Town. As we rode along a sandy road next to flooded rice fields into the surrounding lush green countryside, I looked up at the blue sky and told whoever was listening, "Thank you."

**

After one more day in Hoi An, we took yet another sleeper bus to Ho Chi Minh City, and this time the journey lasted a delightful twenty-six hours. We wandered in the sweltering heat of "The Paris of the Orient," nibbling on flakey pastries, and Lana decided that perhaps jumping into such a large-scope business wasn't the best of ideas, particularly given that she had little experience and no formal business education. She was still mad at Jade for leaving with barely any communication. And once we received word from Jade to meet us at the guesthouse she was staying at in Phnom Penh the following day, we booked our bus. As I stared out the window of the bus, the air and terrain became arid, the bushes and trees brittle and brown, and I debated whether to tell Jade about my plans to travel with Miles. It would probably make her defend her decision to leave even stronger, anything to keep me away from him.

Chapter 20

Date: March 14, 2010
Phnom Penh, Cambodia

As the sun hung low above the horizon, the bus deposited Lana and me in a parking lot in Phnom Penh into a hoard of aggressive tuk tuk drivers desperate for business. After one pushed us into his tuk tuk, we handed him a piece of paper with the guesthouse address and a crudely drawn map, and we set off into the stifling and overcrowded city. The wind licked through our hair as we puttered down the boulevard next to the Tonle Sap River. We passed palaces, pagodas, and manicured gardens until the water disappeared, and the ornate buildings turned to rows of crumbling apartment blocks. Under a tangle of sparking electrical wires running the length of the block, our tuk tuk driver parked and pointed to an entranceway between two street vendors turning smoking sticks of organ meat on small grills.

The slapping of our flip-flops echoed on the stained walls as we climbed the tile staircase and found Jade's room number. We knocked, having prepared ourselves for "the talk", but when the door swung open, an oddly familiar face I couldn't place greeted us.

"Hi, you guys must be Harper and Lana," the voice came from a tall girl with white-blond hair. "I'm Mira. Come in."

She stepped aside, and I followed behind Lana into the room. It was a large room with a discoloured tan tile floor and bare, windowless white walls that had all the charm of a mental institution. Two double beds and a slender cot with threadbare sheets were pushed against one of the walls with little more than a foot between them. At the wall nearest the foot of the beds sat three backpacks overflowing with clothes. A petite brunette with golden skin and rectangular glasses sat on one of the beds and introduced herself as Elin.

"We sort of met the other week in Vang Vieng," Elin said, peering over her glasses.

Then I recognized them. These were the Swedish girls Felix had gone home with on our first night at Bucket Bar. I glanced at Lana, who was suppressing a smile. Hoping my poker face didn't crack, I said, "Ah yes, I remember."

As we set our bags down, the toilet flushed, and Jade emerged from behind the plywood door. Lana crossed her arms, and I gave her a terse smile.

"Girls," she said, looking at Elin and Mira, "could you give us a moment?"

Elin rolled off the bed and Mira grabbed a purse from the floor. "Sure, we were just going to get a snack. We'll meet back up for dinner?"

Jade nodded, and when the door closed behind them, Lana and I stood with our feet apart, arms crossed, waiting for Jade to explain herself.

"I'm really sorry for ditching you guys," she said, taking a seat on the foot of the cot. "It's just Arturo and I were connecting in a way I had never felt before. His aura was so spectacular."

"Jade, we had a plan. We were business partners. You couldn't have communicated with me in advance?"

"I didn't think the business meant that much to you," she said, her eyes wide.

"Yeah, well it did. Here, look at what happened to the vision." Lana pulled at the strings of her backpack. She pulled out a cloth bag and dropped it on Jade's lap. Jade pulled out the garment that vaguely resembled yoga pants and inspected it. "There are plenty more pieces of butchered saris in there."

Biting her lip, Jade looked back up at Lana. "I'm so sorry. I thought all this time you were just trying to help me with my crazy idea. And…and, to be honest, I was jealous of you girls. Xavier and Harper, Chad and you, I just wanted a love affair of my own."

Lana lowered onto the cot next to her, and Jade threw her arms around her neck, apologizing over and over again. Then, as if someone flicked a switch, Lana's face turned from irritated to intrigued. "So spill. You better not still be celibate."

A dirty little smile crept across Jade's face as she shook her head. I was happy for her, too. Happy that she let someone break through the wall she had put up after that asshat Cliff's infidelity. She was healing and learning to trust again.

"Well, then," Lana said with a wink, "so long as someone got laid, I guess it wasn't for nothing."

Then with a hug, Lana rose to her feet and disappeared into the bathroom. Even though I was happy that they had patched things up, a coal of irritation burned for what Jade had said about Miles and me. She looked up with a smile that hadn't quite made its way to her eyes. "How did you like Hoi An?"

"Jade," I said in a strong yet measured tone. I was tired, hungry, bursting to pee and in no mood for her to ignore the issue.

She sighed and threw up her hands. "I'm sorry that you heard what I said."

"But you're not sorry you said it?" I crossed my arms.

"Harper, remember how you helped me get through getting my heart smashed? If I said I was getting back together with Cliff, how would you feel about it?"

"That's different. And a lot of time has passed since that party."

"Answer my question."

As I leaned against the cold wall, I thought of myself in her shoes. I would do whatever I could to talk her out of it. "Not happy."

"I only feel so strongly because I love you. Same goes for that beautiful spirit in there," she said, pointing to the bathroom.

I sighed and took the seat next to her. I understood where she was coming from, but I had to do whatever I felt was best for me. "I love you both, too."

Once Lana and I showered, we joined the Swedish girls for dinner at one of the many colonial-style restaurants on the river boulevard and spent the night eating, drinking, and swapping stories. The stories continued through the next day as we braved the oppressive heat, riffling through knockoff designer goods at the Russian market and admiring the cultural artifacts that had survived the brutal genocide of the Khmer Rouge at the National Museum. After a tour of the magnificent gold-adorned Royal Palace, we crossed the boulevard and sat on a panel of grass in the sidewalk next to the riverbank. Catching the warm afternoon sun, we munched on lightly sweetened popcorn from a roadside vendor and I thought about my upcoming date with Miles that night, and wondered what it meant for us.

I took a look at my watch and realized that I only had an hour to get myself ready. I shot to my feet. "I'm going to head back to the room."

"Oh right, your date," Lana said, picking grass off of her legs.

Jade shielded her eyes from the warm light as she looked up at me. "You have a date? With Miles?"

I glanced at my toes before straightening my back wondering why I felt embarrassed. I was an adult. I could make my own decision. "Yes."

"Miles Cooper?" Mira said.

My eyes shot to her., "How do you know him?"

"We met in Krabi the week before we were in Vang Vieng," she said, turning to Elin. "Remember the uptight guy with the polo shirts?"

I smiled at the description as Elin nodded and stuffed another handful of popcorn in her mouth.

"So I'll see you girls later then?" I ignored Jade's death stare and waved down a tuk tuk.

With barely an hour until I was to be picked up, I washed and towel-dried my hair, attempted an up-do, and then abandoned said up-do. After slapping on some eye shadow, mascara, and blush, I reattempted the up-do only for it to be abandoned again. Then I had to reapply the makeup that sweated off during the reattempted up-do that was a bad decision to begin with. Slipping into my purple cotton dress and sliding on a fresh pair of silver knockoff Havaiana flip-flops from the Russian market, I grabbed my purse and fanned myself as I made my way down the stairs. With nerves tangling in my stomach, I stood on the curb swatting hungry mosquitoes from my legs until a slick black sedan pulled over in front of me.

The door opened, and Miles stepped into the street, his movements as fluid as water, and reached for my hand. He wore khaki slacks and a crisp white button-down shirt, the sleeves rolled to the elbow. Nerves took over when he leaned in and kissed me on the cheek.

"Your chariot, my lady," he said as he pulled his face back from mine with a smile.

I slid across the cool black leather as he closed the door. I greeted the driver, only able to see his spotless gloves on the steering wheel. A moment later, Miles opened the door on the other side and joined me in the back seat. He took my chin between his thumb and forefinger, and I lost myself in his eyes.

254

"I'm the luckiest man in the world, to dine with you tonight."

Heat spread across my skin as I muttered, "Thank you."

The engine purred, and I fiddled with my fingers looking ahead, neither one of us speaking a word in the five minutes it took to reach the hotel. We made eye contact, and the air between us seemed to crackle. As I noticed the trail of freckling on his forearm, I remembered a birthmark that kissed his pale skin just below his hipbone. We were now both grown adults, I wanted to feel those greedy feelings I had felt with Xavier again, and I could only imagine that if we took the chance to be intimate he could make me feel that way.

The car turned off the main road and rolled down a path towards a towering cream-coloured building ten stories tall topped with a red-brick roof. As the car stopped under a covered archway, I reached for the door handle.

"Allow me," Miles said as the bellhop opened his door.

I sat with nothing but my butterflies to accompany me as he dashed around the back of the car and opened my door. Gently pulling me out by the hand into the dry evening heat, he offered me the crook of his elbow. I linked my arm in his, and he led me through the doors into the elegant marble foyer. A soft pink glow from the setting sun spilled through the windows onto the rich gold and brown hues that were splashed onto the walls and embedded in the intricate designs on the reception desk. After walking down a long hallway, we arrived at the restaurant, Do Forni, and I was not in the least bit surprised that he came all the way to Southeast Asia for Italian food.

The room was semi-oblong shaped with a concave dark-wood paneled ceiling, a brick pizza oven at one end, and white, windowed walls curling around the other. We were greeted by a beautiful Cambodian woman and shown to our table. As I sank into the red-cushioned chairs, I splayed my fingers across the soft white tablecloths, grateful to be there, but somehow feeling a little like an imposter.

"This place is really nice," I said, noticing the elaborate detail on the walls where the curved windows ended.

"Yes, and they bring the food and drinks in the proper order. I've had too many experiences at these provincial restaurants where they don't bring everyone's food out at once. One time, half of the meals came out before the drinks."

"Well, it's because of the communal culture here. Food is meant to be shared, so they just bring it out when it's ready," I said, remembering picking that piece of information up in Vientiane. "In fact, in Laos they don't even have a word for my or mine."

His lips spread as he leaned in. "What would I do without you?"

"Offend everyone?" I teased.

As we fell into each other's gaze, the waiter appeared next to the table. Miles ordered a bottle of wine with a name no normal person could ever hope to pronounce.

"So Jade ran off with that unwashed Argentinian in pajama pants?" he said, offering me the breadbasket across the table.

I took a roll, tore it in half, and proceeded to tell him the story of the implosion of her and Lana's business venture. By the time I told him about our Hawaiian savior in Hoi An, the waiter brought our wine.

"You ladies must have had your fair share of admirers along the way."

I shot him a smirk. "Mostly untouchables."

"I hope that doesn't mean me."

I raised my glass with a wink. "To untouchables."

"Hopefully changing their caste." He tipped his glass forward to touch mine.

With the first sip of wine. I felt more relaxed with him, and more at ease in our plush surroundings. As the wine flowed and decadent food was ordered, laid out on the table, and eaten with no shame at the calorie count, he told me of his time in the north touring pristine waterfalls, undulating rice paddy terraces, hill tribe markets, and witnessing the most spectacular sunsets imaginable.

"It sounds amazing. I wish I could have seen it." I blew out a breath and thought of the possibilities.

"Me too," he said, reaching across the table. As he took my hand, a ghost of a smile curled his lips as the realization hit. "You would have said yes to come with me?"

I bit my lip and the word "Yes," tumbled out. And without having to say it, I told Miles Cooper that I liked him. Unspoken words hung in the air as it shifted between us. Feeling self-conscious in his hooded gaze, I had to change topic. "So, Singapore. Are you excited?"

He drew in a deep breath and dropped his gaze. "New beginnings can be exciting, but I don't know anyone. I'm a little scared to be honest."

His vulnerability tugged at me. I knew how hard it was to be alone, but I couldn't imagine setting up a new life fifteen thousand miles away from home by myself. And I knew his parents were hard-assed, ruthless lawyers who were two of the most respected legal minds in all of Canada. The bar for him had been set high.

As the waiter opened a new bottle of wine, he sipped the dark red liquid, and as he swirled it around in his glass, inspecting the "legs" dripping down the sides, his eyes darted to mine. "You should come to Singapore with me."

"It's a nice thought, but I can't fit it in. I have to fly to Sydney in less than two weeks to meet my parents."

"What about after that?" He paused to take another sip. "I don't mean just to visit."

Was he saying what I thought he was saying? If he was, this date just escalated really quickly.

"What do you mean?"

"Harper, seeing you again turned my world upside down. I don't think us running into each other is just a coincidence."

Yes, yes, he was saying what I thought he was saying. And then all of the questions crowded in my mind.

"Where would I live? What would I do in Singapore?"

"Be with me. I can help you find a job."

Why do boys never listen? "I want to do my photography."

"You can do that, too," he said, reaching across the table for my hand.

His eyes pleaded with mine. If he paid for my change of ticket, I could fly back from Sydney when my parents left. I had fallen in love with Southeast Asia. I liked Miles. It all certainly fit with my five-year plan, but for some reason, I couldn't say yes. Instead, I stated the obvious. "Miles, this is crazy."

"Isn't it?" he said before throwing his head back, laughing. I covered my face as the other diners glared our way. "Harper, look at what you've done to me. What you do to me. I barely recognize myself. You want to know what is crazy? In Luang Prabang, I took your camera."

My body flushed red-hot.

"You what?!" My voice now drew stares from the other diners. "I can't believe you —"

"I know, it was stupid and reckless and I'm sorry. But don't you see? I had to see you again."

I paused. What he did was thoughtless and infuriating, but his reasons were, dare I say it, romantic.

"You just keep digging your hole deeper."

"I know. But look at what I was willing to do to keep you in my life. That is what you mean to me."

I glared at him as I clutched the stem of my wine glass. I opened my mouth to tell him off for giving me the fright of my life by taking my camera, but before I could say anything, he spoke again.

"And I have to tell you some things about my life before I came here, please try to understand me. I was in a serious relationship, you remember Celia Butterfield?"

Of course I did. She was the bitch who broke his heart days before our night together. After all these years, I never knew they got back together.

"We were heading towards marriage but when my father gave the orders for me to open the Singapore office, she left me. I was heartbroken. But when I saw you at the waterfall, it was like the sun rising on my soul again. And an epiphany hit me that night when we had drinks: this awfulness happened to bring me closer to you. And I will spend as long as it takes to dig myself out of my hole, fill it in and build a pedestal to put you on."

As much as the thought of her name stung me at first, I had to appreciate his honesty. Maybe all of this — Celia, Adam, losing my job — happened to bring us together.

"Well, if you promise to put down your shovel and act reasonably, we can entertain the possibility."

"I promise." Miles held up three fingers like a Boy Scout. "Is that a yes?"

"It's a definite maybe," I said. It was a huge step that caught me by surprise and a decision not to be made on a whim.

"Good, because I think I might be in love with you." My breath caught in my throat. Did he love me, or did he only think so? As much as I wanted him to outright say he loved me, I could understand his emotional vulnerability after the traumatic ending of such a serious relationship. I wanted to take it slow, and I was happy he wanted to, also. He raised a glass and said, "To us. To new beginnings."

I raised mine, and after we clinked, we drained our glasses, and over dessert we finished the bottle. After charging the bill to his room, he took me by the arm and led me out onto the terrace. Enveloped by a warm evening breeze, I leaned over the railing, watching the reflections of street lamps shimmer on the rippling river surface, his words still racing in my head. I felt the energy shift as Miles's footsteps stopped behind me. He gently dragged his finger down the back of my arm, causing my skin to pebble. When he whispered my name, I turned to face him, and he stepped forward, pressing me against the railing, his lips planting firmly on mine. He pried my lips open with his tongue as his hands grabbed at my thighs under my dress. His touch felt foreign and familiar all at the same time.

"Come upstairs with me." His fingers dug into my hips, his breath hot in my ear.

It was the most perfect of nights and the most perfect of dates. But as his lips skated down my neck, instead of the way my body demanded his like it did with Xavier, I bristled to his touch. It felt more irritating than erotic. My mind was consumed by thoughts of his life-changing proposal. It was all happening so quickly. Less than two weeks ago, I wanted nothing to do with him, and now we were talking about love and moving to Singapore together. It was all too much.

I pushed him back. "This is moving too fast."

He dropped his hands and stepped back.

"Fast? You were going to come traveling with me, did you think we were going to sleep in separate beds?"

Perhaps I had been naïve.

"You said we'd travel as friends... I thought..."

"What's the problem? You're not a virgin anymore." His words knocked the wind out of me. He behaved exactly the same way he did on our last night together eight years ago: drunk and pushy. The difference now was that I had the strength to say no to him. As I steadied myself against the railing, his face flashed from angry to embarrassed. "I'm so sorry, I didn't mean it like that."

Overcome by anger, I slapped him across his cheek.

Shocked by my actions and still fuming, I strode across the terrace, through the door and down the long hallway, wondering how the best date of my life turned into the worst. I expected him to stop me, but he said nothing as I strode down the hallway to reception. I stopped in the center of the foyer, between two light brown leather seats and looked around. Reception clerks and bellhops smiled and bowed, but Miles was nowhere to be found.

He didn't come after me.

Chapter 21

Date: March 22, 2010
Siem Reap, Cambodia

I nestled into the crowd of photographers on the muddy banks of the moat, waiting for the sun to rise over Angkor Wat. As the darkness lifted, salmon pink light reflected off the wisps of clouds silhouetting the swaying palm trees and the five redented towers that gave the temple its iconic shape. I had less than two weeks until the competition deadline, and while I had tons of images, I struggled to silence that little voice that said, *none was a winner.* And though I wanted to be able to shoot sprawling landscapes like Steve McCurry, I realized that after my experience at the Taj Mahal, these famous images had been done spectacularly once and recreated by every other professional, wannabe professional, and amateur alike. If I were going to make my mark in this world, I had to listen to my creative instincts and find my artistic voice. I had to show them who *I* was. So I turned my camera on the hundreds of hopeful photographers pushing each other for a clear shot and captured the temple through the LCD screens of the photographers ahead of me.

When I checked the playback, I scrolled back through my images with my former art teacher's words ringing in my head as they had done since I hallucinated her face on the ride to the waterfall in Luang Prabang: *You have no artistic vision*. My Angkor Wat images felt like a step in the right direction. I kept scrolling all the way back to the images from the waterfall, and the photographs that popped out to me were the images of the mother and daughter in the rowboat in Ha Long Bay, the father teaching his son to cast a net in Vang Vieng, and I finally stopped on the image of the two sisters selling water at the base of Death Mountain. Then I remembered why I loved photography — its ability to stop time — and that felt more like my vision. To capture these beautiful moments of people who love each other unconditionally, moments I know too well that may never happen again.

Once the sun had risen, and the tour buses had begun to pile up in the parking lot, I bought a fresh mango shake and sat in the shade of a tree, looking out across the moat. After my night with Miles, I spent two more days in Phnom Penh before heading through the country to a city called Battambang before making it to Siem Reap with Jade, Lana, and the Swedish girls. When they asked how my date went, I was sparse on details. I couldn't face Jade if she knew the truth. I was still reeling from what happened on the terrace, and I wasn't sure what to make of the fact that I hadn't heard from him since. He must have been embarrassed by what he said and how he acted. Not only for his poor choice of words out on the terrace but how he opened up to me and showed me his vulnerability despite his recent heartbreak. And perhaps that I didn't say yes outright rubbed some salt in that open wound. And then I slapped some more proverbial salt across his face. I did overreact a bit. Because…maybe I did love him back.

I wanted to be able to talk to someone about it, but I had no one. Tears pooled as the devastating realization set in that I couldn't reach out to Audrey. She didn't turn up that night in Vang Vieng, or since. Maybe the afterlife was like prison — you get one phone call. Or perhaps I really did just hallucinate what happened in the desert. But it felt so real, and I wanted so badly to believe that she was out there, that she existed in some form, so I didn't feel so damn lonely anymore.

Then, as an orange-robed monk strode past me, I remembered something that Jade had said. In her quest for all things spiritual, she had studied the various religions that we had encountered from Hinduism to Sikhism to Buddhism, explaining their beliefs to us. She said that Buddhists believe that suffering is caused by the desire for permanence in earthly things, and I couldn't help but think of not only how I clung to the idea of Audrey's permanent existence but also how my parents did, and the suffering it brought to us all.

After Audrey died, my parents turned her room back from a library to how it looked while she still lived there. The photos of her were rehung on the light grey walls, her desk was stacked with her favourite books, and the soft blue cotton sheets were turned down, waiting for her to come home from a long day and slip under them. Audrey's urn stood on the middle of the mantle in the living room, a constant reminder of the void in our family. While no one should ever have to bury a child, I wanted them to accept that she wasn't coming home. I wanted them to be able to let go of her. They couldn't live their lives while they were still waiting for her to walk through the door. They refused to sell the house that was too big for just the two of them. They refused to go on vacation. I wanted to believe that her spirit lived on somewhere, but truly, she could only exist in our hearts and memories. If they could understand, perhaps they could regain some feeling of control over their world and be able to move on with their own lives. I had to, as well.

As the image of her urn stuck in my mind, an idea blossomed: I will ask them to bring Audrey's ashes to Australia, the place in the world she wanted to see the most, nut never got to. Then it will be time for us to let go of her together.

***

On our last day in Siem Reap, our Nordic friends had signed us up for a Khmer cooking course on a rooftop restaurant situated on the famed "Pub Street". And yes, Pub Street is exactly as the name sounds, nothing but restaurants and pubs, including the token Irish bar and our favourite, "Angkor What?!"

As a young Cambodian woman with long black hair and ebony eyes laid out bowls of aromatic spices, coconut milk, eggs, green mangos, fluffy rice, and utensils on the long wooden table, I asked Jade a question that had been niggling at me.

Doing my best to feign nonchalance as I grated my mango, I said, "Did you know Miles was in a serious relationship recently?"

She stopped rolling her spring roll. "I heard, but I didn't know any details."

"Why didn't you tell me?"

"Oh, about Celia?" Lana said.

How did Lana know about Celia?

"The first time he and Celia broke up, look at what happened to you. I was afraid that history was going to repeat itself."

"Lana, why didn't you tell me?" She looked at me and glanced at Jade.

Of course, Jade told her not to say anything.

"Please don't fall for him again," Jade said before Lana could answer.

Before I could tell her that I wasn't a little girl anymore, Mira's voice entered the conversation. "Are you talking about Miles?" I looked at her and nodded. "He said he's heading to Koh Samui."

"When did you talk to him?"

"Yesterday, when we were at the computers."

I didn't know why I was waiting for another apology. He had already apologized for what he said in the heat of the moment. He wasn't perfect, and neither was I. He had laid bare his intentions, and the ball was in my court. It was my turn to step up and make the next move.

"Is he going to the Full Moon Party?" Haad Rin Beach was only a short boat ride away from Koh Samui.

"He didn't say."

I wanted to talk to him. I wanted to tell him yes, I did want to go to Singapore with him and start a new life. But to tell him over Facebook or email was too impersonal. I wanted to tell him in person.

"You're going to Koh Samui next, right?" Once she nodded, I ran to my bag and pulled out my notebook. Tearing out a sheet, I scribbled a note:

> *Miles,*
> *I'm sorry about Phnom Penh. Meet me under the Full Moon at Haad Rin with your shovel and I'm yours.*
> *Love,*
> *Harper*

"Can you give this to him?" I said folding it up tightly and extending my hand towards Mira.

She smiled, tugged it from my grip, and slid it in her pocket and resumed making her Khmer curry.

***

The next day we traveled to Bangkok, and two days later we bid the Swedish girls goodbye under the bright lights of Khoa San Road. Then Lana, Jade, and I boarded a bus heading south, with all roads leading to the Full Moon Party.

Chapter 22

Date: March 27, 2010
Koh Phangan, Thailand

When the lines of the ferry were tied, we hoisted our backpacks onto our backs and stepped onto the pier, still weary after our night bus from Bangkok to the port of Surat Thani. I tried to nap on the ferry, but a squall had kicked up, rocking the vessel like a toy boat in a tub during a toddler's bath time. As I stepped onto the pier of the infamous Thai island of Koh Phangan, I began to regain my equilibrium. The one good thing about seasickness is that it never lasts for too long once you're planted back on land. And the land we just stepped into was paradise. Wooden Thai longboats and sailboats floated on vivid turquoise sea on either side of the pier facing the oncoming breeze. Before us lay an island of rolling hills, limestone karst cliff-faces, and forested headlands. It felt as if I had stepped into one of the paradisiac wallpapers that had been plastered on the walls of my old apartment.

Since all of the guesthouses on Koh Phangan required an advanced booking of a minimum of five nights, we didn't have to bother with the song and dance of searching for one. Though originally peeved that we would only be able to stay for four nights and eat the cost of the additional one, a guaranteed place to rest our sleepy heads was a blessing.

On the days leading up to the Full Moon Party, I prepared myself for the big night, physically and emotionally. I joined the sun worshippers on Haad Rin to ready my tan, spent hours at the spa getting manicured, pedicured, scrubbed, massaged, and waxed as hairless as a mole rat. Every day, like a compulsive masochist, I checked my Facebook hoping that perhaps he had read my note and wanted to tell me where to meet him. But nothing. There had been activity on his page, and I could only hope, that maybe, just maybe, he had read my note and planned to find me and surprise me with the proclamation that he forgave me.

On our third day in Koh Phangan, the day before the Full Party, we explored the island away from Haad Rin by moped. During one of our stops, at a sliver of beach with a palm tree hanging just over the turquoise sea reaching towards the horizon, I decided to confide in the girls.

"So I didn't tell you everything about my date with Miles," I said, pushing a coiled shell in the sand with my big toe.

"That was obvious," Jade said, lighting a cigarette. "He did something bad, didn't he?"

"He asked me to move to Singapore with him."

Lana clapped her hands and squealed. "What did you tell him? Oh my God, how romantic! But wait, why didn't you get nookie that night?"

"Because I didn't say yes," I said, taking a seat on the grassy ledge overhanging the threshold of the beach.

"Good," Jade said with smoke billowing from her mouth as she sat downwind next to me.

"But I didn't say no, either."

"Great!" Lana flopped on the other side of me.

"Look, I want to be with him." I refrained from saying that I needed him to forgive me for that to happen. "Jade, I know you can't understand, and you don't agree with it, but I need you to be there for me. You both are like my sisters, and I crave your support."

Jade blew out a long stream of smoke and gave me a smoky kiss on the cheek. "I'll be there to support you. I always am, and I always will."

With her words, I put my arms around the backs of my two best friends, the two girls I would be lost in this world without, kissed them on their cheeks, and, in silence we watched the light of the sun dance on the rippling sea.

***

Date: March 30, 2010

With the full moon headlining a chorus of stars in the night sky, I climbed into the back of the jumbo tuk tuk with Jade, Lana, and a thousand fluttering butterflies in my stomach and we made our way to the big event. I struggled to steady my breath as the vehicle jostled us about, our neon body paint glowing in the blue light embedded in the tuk tuk's ceiling. We passed a bucket of vodka and Red Bull back and forth and finished it when we arrived at a parking lot behind Haad Rin beach.

On a normal night, the beach held a few hundred revelers, but on the night of Full Moon, tens of thousands of drunken backpackers make the pilgrimage. Riding the tide of neon-painted bodies through the town we decided that liquor was our top priority, and given the entrepreneurial spirit of the Thai people, it was not in short supply. Heeding the sound advice of the guidebook, we purchased bucket packages of mixers and top shelf liquor with caps tightly sealed from a proper shop on the edge of the beach, rather than the moonshine disguised as premium liquor from the vendors on the beach. With buckets of vodka Cokes filled to the brim, we stood on the threshold of the beach and looked out to the madness we were about to walk into.

"Hold onto your buckets, ladies," I said gripping my handle, "it's going to be a wild night."

Haad Rin Beach was crescent shaped, with white sand stretching perhaps five to eight hundred feet in each direction to lush headlands, and one hundred feet in front of us to the gently lapping waves. A huge sign spelling "Full Moon Party" in flames stood before us. Bars lined the beach, each blaring pulsating house music, DJs clashing with one another as black lights strobed, illuminating the thousands upon thousands of partygoers. It was chaos in paradise.

"I'm never going to find him," I said as I scanned the beach. Most of the party was concentrated on the southern end of the beach and trickled down to the northern end. It was an overwhelming sight, as was the thought of being lost in that crowd.

"Yes, you will," Lana said giving my hand a squeeze.

Then a thought tightened the knot in my stomach: this was so not Miles's scene. The seed of doubt that had been planted in my mind began to bloom. What if he didn't show up? The vision of our life together in Singapore, my vision of having it all, began to fade.

After establishing the point of arrival as our meeting point if we got separated, we took our buckets and dove into the crowd. As we made our way club by club and bar by bar, towards the frenetic southern end of the beach, we managed to stick together for a while. Stopping at a club with a platform made from picnic benches pushed together, we pulled each other up and Lana flirted effortlessly with every guy in a twenty-foot radius while Jade swayed and lost herself in the music, and I took every opportunity to assess each blond-haired man who passed through my line of sight.

Then, as "Sex on Fire" roared from the speakers, a shock of inky black hair bounced in the distance.

It couldn't be.

I craned my neck trying to get a better look but, as he turned, I lost my footing and tumbled from the platform onto the soft sand. Jade and Lana jumped down to pick me up.

"I'm fine, I'm fine," I said as I climbed back to the platform.

I looked out across the crowd scanning each head but nothing. That mop of black hair had vanished.

Get a grip, Harper.

I had to forget about Xavier. I had to accept that I would never see him again.

It wasn't until nature called me that we split up. I disappeared into the bar, through the back and waited in a long line of ladies with dinner plate pupils, still dancing to the music for the bathroom. Once I was at the front and one of the two stalls opened up, I dashed in and squatted over what was little more than a hole in the ground. Upon leaving the bathroom a fight had broken out in the line between two girls. Once fists started swinging, I took a detour 'round the back of the bar and walked between tall bushes and a series of crude structures until I could find my way to the beach. Once I stepped back onto the sand, I lost my bearings. It all looked "same same but different." Looking around all I could see were writhing bodies and vacant eyes. It was a sobering feeling not recognizing a single face. Some guy picked me up and spun me around. After I swatted at his back, he finally put me down. Scared and thoroughly disoriented in the crowd, I couldn't figure my way back to the platform.

Instead, I headed away from the southern tip of the beach, back towards the middle, where our meeting point was. Once the girls noticed I was missing, they'd come looking for me. Pushing through the swarms and avoiding the flaming skipping ropes, I fended off advances from drunk guys and made my way to the water. The tide had receded, and the water was shallow. Out at the water there was much more open space as the party was concentrated towards the threshold of the beach. With my toes in the wet sand, I navigated past littered cups and buckets, boys peeing out in ankle deep water, and couples making out in the surf. Relief washed over me as I stumbled across my girls sitting at the water's edge along with a few familiar faces.

"Hawaii?"

"Hey, Canada," Chad said with a warm smile as I strode over, knelt down and wrapped my arms around him before hugging Kelly and Felix.

"Dude, this party is crazy, right?" Kelly said after eyeing up a group of scantily clad girls walking by.

Then I noticed that Jade was washing an open wound on Lana's leg. "Oh my God, what happened?"

"I couldn't talk her out of giving the fire jump rope a go," Jade said shaking her head.

Lana took a swig from her bucket, giggled and squealed, "I can't feel it!"

I looked at the boys and rolled my eyes. She will in the morning. Then when I met eyes with Felix, my thoughts returned to my quest. "Hey, have you seen your Swedish girls? They should be here."

A smile spread his lips like a boy unwrapping a BB gun on Christmas morning. "Really?"

"Yeah, they may be with a friend I'm looking for. Wanna come look with me?" I said, ignoring Jade's disapproving look.

Felix nodded, and we turned and wandered towards the northern end of the beach. I figured if he were there, it was probably at the quieter end. We popped into every single bar on the stretch, and while I knew finding him would be, as they said in Thailand, "diving for a needle in a giant ocean," the fear set in that he really wanted nothing to do with me.

The newly edited version of my five-year plan I envisioned in Singapore, touring the continent, camera in hand, on the weekends with Miles at my side, biding our time until we were both settled enough in our careers to start a family, was slipping from my grasp.

As we stood over two partiers passed out on a plastic table in front of a row of beach-side vendors with signs reading, "Fuck It Bucket"' and "Boiled Bollock Bucket" it struck me: I wasn't thinking like Miles. He wouldn't be at a place like this. He'd be somewhere quiet, somewhere classy. I beckoned for Felix to follow me off the beach and into town. But "classy" in Haad Rin was a relative concept. With my sandy feet leading me, I wiped the sweat beading on my brow, and sized up all of the bars as we meandered through the streets. Most were filled with men with sleeveless shirts chugging beer, scantily clad females taking body shots on the bar, football and hockey flashing on television screens above them. Then one called to me.

Lanterns hung from the ceiling above palm trees potted in ceramic pots, bathing the dark wood entranceway in a soft glow. I peered through the large windows that paneled the front walls. Two men who were not splattered in paint or wearing neon muscle shirts held cues and leaned against a massive pool table. The bar was long and dark, and a bartender strolled back and forth in front of a liquor collection stacked to the ceiling. This was a better bet. I looked at Felix and said, "Let's try here?"

I pushed the door open and let my eyes adjust to the dim light. I glanced at the booths, but no one looked familiar. Then as I scanned the back wall past the pool table, sandy blond hair caught my attention.

Miles.

He had come.

Time slowed down as I stepped towards him. Happiness bloomed through me. This was it. The moment my life was going to change. The moment that I, Harper Rodrigues, got a happy ending in Thailand that didn't involve money for sexual favours.

All is well.

Across from him, Elin sat with her leg hooked around another man's leg. I turned to Felix to see if he had noticed. I felt for him as his smile slipped. I stopped, placed my hand on his shoulder, and said, "There's always Mira."

He bit his lip and nodded. Then his eyes widened, fixated on something. I turned Mira glided across the floor on long dancer's legs towards the table. I stepped forward again, ready to thank Mira for her help and then to fall into Miles's arms. But then, as if in slow-motion, my brain unable to process what it was seeing, she lowered herself into his lap, threw her arms around his neck and pressed her lips against his.

I screamed in my head: *Get off him! Get off him! Get off him!*

Then my mind froze, unable to speak, unable to form a coherent thought, unable to hear anything more than the blood rushing in my ears. Without my consent, my feet carried me forward as my body trembled, jaw pulsing, red spots raging in my vision.

Elin saw me and called Mira's name. The gangly over-processed blond peeled her lips from his and looked up at me. Instead of remorse, a smug smile curled her thin lips. Miles glanced up and stiffened, his wide eyes sticking to me like glue.

"Oh, I was supposed to give you this," I read on Mira's lips as she reached into her pocket. She pulled out a beat-up folded piece of paper. My note. My muscles tensed as it took everything I had not to lunge across the last remaining steps and rip her bleach blond hair from her head.

How could I have been so naïve to trust her?

She slid from his lap onto the chair next to him before he plucked the note from her fingers. He dropped his gaze and read the note as he was supposed to have days ago. He raked his fingers through his hair, rose to his feet, and slowly approached me as if I were a wild animal ready to charge.

"I'm so sorry; I thought you were done with me."

"So you just find the next ready, willing, and able girl?" If he meant what he said to me how could he move onto the next girl so damn quickly?

He rocked back and forth on his heels, seeming to struggle to get his next sentence out. "I can't be alone," he finally said, his admission knocking me off balance. "I'm so sorry, Harper. I want you. I want it all. I want Singapore. Please. We can go now."

And as he looked at me with pleading eyes, I no longer saw the confident man whose approval I needed, the confident man who seemed have it all, the confident man who starred in my teenage fantasies. I saw a scared and insecure little boy. A scared and insecure little boy I had lost all respect for. A scared and insecure boy I could not love.

"Now," I said, shaking my head. "Now I'm done with you."

And with those words, I felt the hypnotic hold he had cast upon me eight years ago lift. I turned, took Felix by the hand, and, with tears in my eyes, I pulled him back to the beach. I was mad at myself for being so naïve, to trust her, Hell, to trust him. He wasn't a new person. He was the same scumbag who took advantage of me on a beanbag in a frat house and broke my heart, only older, but no more a man today than he was then. At that moment, I decided no more boys. I could only be with a man.

Pushing the sand with my toes next to my mopey Hawaiian friend, I wiped my face with shaking hands, trying to stem the torrent of liquid anger. I had wasted too many tears on him. It was time to stop. But each time I tried, a new wave surged through me. I needed to be numb. I needed to find the girls. I needed to be numb once I found the girls. So as I stormed through the beach back to our meeting spot, I stopped at a stall selling moonshine and threw some Thai *baht* on the counter. My last memory of the night was imposter Smirnoff vodka burning its way down my throat.

Chapter 23

Oh God, where am I?

Pain jackhammered my head, and I struggled to open my eyes. Though hard, whatever cool surface I was lying on was a welcome reprise on my overheating skin. Peeking through the lashes of my left eye, I recognized the stained light blue linoleum flooring. I was lying on the floor of the bathroom in our guesthouse room.

Gross.

I tried to push myself up, but a weight held me down. It was then I realized that I was not alone. Forcing my other eye half open, I looked down to see a hairy arm on top of me.

Who is this and what did we do?

I tried to piece together the night and sent a search party into the depths of my consciousness, but it returned empty-handed. It all ended with that damn moonshine. I picked the hand up and rolled over to see whom it was attached to.

When I looked at his face, I was convinced I was still dreaming, or my moonshine had been laced with some kind of hallucinogenic.

"Xavier?"

"Morning, mon étoile." His leaden eyes met mine as he sat up and held up a bottle of water.

I pushed myself to upright, took the water bottle from his hand, and, though it was room temperature, I chugged it all in one go. I never took my eyes off of him, afraid that he was nothing more than a delusion of dehydration and would vanish once I finished the bottle.

"You're here," I said, reaching out to touch the soft skin on the inside of his forearm. He was real. "What are you doing here?"

"You remember nothing of last night?"

"Did we…"

"Of course not." I then realized that I was still wearing my dirty tank top splattered with neon body paint. "I found you in the surf nursing a bottle of vodka near Jade and Lana and took you home. I wanted to stay and make sure you were okay."

I cringed thinking of how sorry I must have looked as I wiped the surely smeared painted orange flower from my cheek with the back of my hand. Then it dawned on me. I *had* seen him.

"I thought you weren't coming to Thailand."

"I wasn't, but after Goa I couldn't get you out of my mind. You said you were coming to this Full Moon party, so I booked a ticket and left Leo."

"You came after me?" Xavier had crossed a continent to find me — Miles couldn't even cross a hotel.

"I had to see you again," he said, reaching out and running his callused fingertips down my cheeks.

The soft light that filtered through the gauzy curtains highlighted every angle of his beautiful face.

The constellations of freckles, his full pink lips, those storm-grey eyes. Just looking at him made all of the drama from the night before fade away. Gently brushing the hair from my face, I leaned in, determined to kiss him guilt-free for the first time. My heart drummed, pumping desire through me from my marrow to my fingertips as I felt his breath on my parted lips. But then…

"Harper?" Lana burst through the door.

"Yah?" I replied without moving as his lips hovered over mine.

"Oh God, sorry guys, but we have to go."

It was like déjà vu.

"Can you give me a few minutes?" I turned to look at her. She looked like she had been dragged through the party face first — smeared with neon paint, mascara pooling in her eyes like a sad panda, clothes stained with God only knows what.

"Oh, honey, I really wish I could, but we missed the first ferry and we have to make the next one in twenty minutes if we have any chance of making it to Bangkok today."

"Stay," he whispered.

I wanted to. I wanted to so badly but I couldn't.

"I can't. I have to make my flight to Sydney tomorrow afternoon to meet my parents."

It would take three hours to make it back to the mainland and ten to twelve hours to get back to the city.

Xavier helped me to my feet, and once the world stopped spinning, I tried to organize my life that was strewn about the room by shoving it into my backpack and daypack as quickly as possible. He carried my backpack as Lana limped and Xavier and I trundled behind fresh-as-a-daisy-because-she-doesn't-drink-herself-into-oblivion Jade through the guesthouse gardens, up a hill and to the road. She hailed a tuk tuk that was passing by and we piled in. The run, the heat, the humidity, the jerky movement, the engine fumes, and, of course, the alcohol still coursing through my system all hit me at once. I folded forward to set my head on my daypack perched in my lap as Xavier rubbed my back.

The tuk tuk stopped at the end of the pier, and we spilled out with our stuff and ran towards the ferry as its lines were being untied. Jade sprinted ahead with our tickets in hand. As I ran, the adrenaline kicked in, killing the pain pounding in my head. The ferry workers held our hands as they helped us cross the gap between the vessel and pier. I wanted to speak to Xavier, who stood on the edge, but the workers were intent on taking our backpacks from us to add to the pile at the stern. As the engines roared to life, I pushed through them to the port side.

"Harper!" he called out, but I could barely hear him over the engines. "Meet me in New Zealand. Leo said you're going next month."

"How can I find you?" I yelled back, the gap between us growing as the ferry lurched forward.

He ran along the pier and shouted, "Give me your last name, I'll find you on Facebook."

But as I called it out, the horns blared, deafening any sound within a one-hundred-foot radius. And when they finally fell silent, twenty feet of turquoise sea lay between the end of the pier and me. He raised his hand to cup his ear, but as I called my last name again, the ocean had grown twenty more feet and the ocean breeze threw my words back into my face.

He couldn't hear me.

I called my name in vain over and over until he became a speck dwarfed between green mountains and blue ocean, and then he disappeared from sight.

Chapter 24

Date: April 2, 2010
Sydney, Australia

By the time we made it through immigration and baggage claim in the Sydney airport, the bags under my eyes weighed me down as much as the ones hanging from my body. After leaving Koh Phangan I spent the bus ride back to Bangkok replaying the image of Xavier in my mind. As I fiddled with the charm on the bracelet he had given me, I thought about how I wasted my time looking for Miles when I could have been with Xavier. It was what I shared with Xavier that I was hoping to find in Miles. I was so busy chasing the past that I lost the present.

I should have seen through Miles, I should have known that he would never change. But I was glad that I could finally put my infatuation with him to rest. Though I should have stuck to my plan to focus on the competition instead of him. I had entered the eleventh hour with the deadline for the competition tomorrow. Over twenty of my images had been put into my maybe pile, and though I heard it whispering, I needed my artistic voice to start shouting.

After a night in a roach-infested hostel on bustling Khao San Road, Lana and I spent our final half hour in the city searching through all the Xavier's and Leos on Facebook. But there were thousands upon thousands of accounts listed with those names. We had neither last names nor networks to help narrow down our search. There was a chance to find him in New Zealand but with no way to contact him, doing so would be impossible.

"Hey, whatever happened between you and Chad?" I turned to her as I logged out of Facebook.

"Ships passing in the night," she said with a ghost of a smile.

I winced, hoping my poor display at Full Moon didn't get in the way of a love connection. However, I admired her ability to shrug it off, as if to say if it didn't happen, it wasn't meant to be. She didn't stress about it, she didn't whine, and she didn't try to force it. That seemed to be the key to her ability of keeping perpetually positive. And so, with little choice but to accept that Xavier and I would also be nothing more than ships passing in the night, I begrudgingly swallowed the stinging disappointment of never seeing him again.

In Australia it was time for our motley crew of runaways to split up. Lana and I said goodbye to Jade before her connecting flight to Brisbane.

"Enjoy your yoga teacher's training course, Miss Hippy," Lana teased.

"I'm only doing it for exercise purposes," Jade said, gently slapping Lana on the arm. "My body's going to be sick when I'm done."

"And who's going to see it?" Lana replied.

Jade stuck her tongue out at Lana and then opened her arms for a hug. "Have fun you two. And Harper, please give your parents my love."

Then, she merged with the crowd of travelers all heading in the direction of the gate. Lana and I exited the airport and shared a taxi to downtown Sydney.

"Keep in touch, let's have wild adventures after your parents leave," she said, as the taxi deposited her at the bus station. She was headed north of the city to spend time with a couple of cousins. I nodded and hugged her farewell. Then the taxi continued its way towards the harbour.

As tired as I was from late nights and long-haul buses and flights, I was bursting with excitement to see my parents. Though I had been away from them for semesters at a time in university, I was never this far away from them. University was only a few hours drive away. After my taxi pulled into the glass-covered entrance of the Sydney Hilton, I piled on my bags and squeezed through the glass doors into the sprawling beige marble foyer. I scanned the foyer, and my eyes landed on the sitting area to the left. Arranged on a dark grey rug stood brown leather couches and small circular coffee tables. In a loveseat holding hands sat the two people who meant the absolute world to me. Time slowed as I looked at them as if they were mirages. My mother's olive complexion wore worry lines from years of stress, and I was sure the past months had added another few. That stress had also added more greys to my father's dark hair.

When our family was whole they were so full of life, even Audrey and I could barely keep up with them. My father had worked his way up the government department while studying capoeira three times a week while my mother ran the PTA at our school and volunteered at an animal shelter. But when we received The Call, he never went back to capoeira, and my mother resigned from the PTA. Since that day, it seemed like the life had been sucked out of them, and they were operating as shells of their former selves. My father had always talked of taking the family to Brazil one day, but after his last international flight — the flight to bring home Audrey's body from Bolivia — South America was never spoken of again.

My mother seemed to leap from the loveseat and ran towards me, arms open, while my father walked behind her. I dropped my daypack, and she hugged and kissed me as if I were a soldier returning from war, covering my face in red lip prints. Once she finally let go, my father hugged me as if he thought he would never hug me again.

Mom wiped her tears. "We've missed you so much." She clutched my hands in hers and stretched my arms out wide so she could get a good look at me. "You look like such a traveler."

And it was true. I wore purple parachute pants, a stained tank top, ratty flip-flops, and forearms covered with bangles and bracelets. It was an outfit I wouldn't have been caught dead in months ago, but I had never felt more like myself.

"Let's get you settled in," Dad said, picking up my daypack.

My mother hooked her arm in my elbow, and we followed him through the marble foyer and into the elevator. In the elevator, she let me go and joined my father, both facing me with wide eyes and wide smiles. I was grateful that they had each other. They had been together since their first days of university and were still as in love as they were then. When I saw their hands clasped like newlyweds, I realized that perhaps my desire to marry Adam was rooted in my desire to have a relationship as strong as theirs.

When the elevator opened, they led me down the hallway and into a room far too spacious for just me. Windows as tall as me overlooked the city, a cloud-soft double bed was pushed against a decorative wood paneled wall, and the floors were covered in carpet that squished under my toes. A pang of guilt pinched me — they must have spent a small fortune on this trip.

"We didn't have to stay here, I sent you a list of budget hotels," I said, setting my backpack down on a cornflower yellow couch.

"Darling, this is the first vacation we've taken since Audrey died. We wanted to treat ourselves," my father said, kissing me on the top of my head.

I stood staring at them. My mother's smile hadn't cracked since our hug in reception, and my father seemed to be able to breathe deeper. The energy about them had shifted drastically from the last time I saw them.

"We'll let you get settled in," my father said, glancing at his watch. "Ready to explore in twenty minutes?"

He was practically bouncing, and a light behind his eyes that had been extinguished three years ago flickered.

"Sure," I said, pulling them both in for a group hug.

With that, our long overdue family vacation could begin.

***

Being at the bottom of the world, seasons had been turned upside down, so while I had always associated April with spring, I had to remember that it was fall. And I wasn't in hot and humid Southeast Asia anymore. When we left the hotel, the sun ducked behind a blanket of clouds, and the cool air nipped at me, forcing me to pull a sweater over my bare arms. Sydney was a clean city, free of heartbreaking poverty and pollution that had plagued all of the other cities Lana, Jade, and I had experienced on our journey. Though I was excited to see a new country, as we walked through the big city streets towards the harbour, I couldn't shake the discontent bubbling under me. It was all too familiar: the western faces, the recognizable languages, business suits, high-rise offices. I had always fancied myself to be a city girl, but now I realized that it was because I didn't know anything else. After these months spending time in warmth and nature, I felt as if I had found myself, I felt as if I were living my truth. If

I didn't win the competition, I wasn't sure how I could go back to city life.

Audrey had always wanted to visit the Sydney Harbour, and as we stood on the walking path the greasy smells of hotdogs and French fries from food vendors wafted through the air while tourists milled about. Fighting the flat lighting, I turned my camera on the street performers juggling and wobbling on unicycles. I laughed as I looked back on the playback as my mother accidentally photobombed a set, grimacing at a sword swallower. Even though only three of us held hands watching a painted Aboriginal man playing a longer-than-I-was didgeridoo, a warm breeze blew over us, and I had a strange feeling, a feeling like I had in the desert in Pushkar, that our family was complete.

As we walked, I told my parents of our adventurous stories, editing out the parts that would make them try and convince me to go home early with them. They loved my tales of the cycle trip to Luang Prabang, gasped at the story of how Jade ran off and Lana's failed attempt at keeping the business afloat, and were saddened to hear that Adam and I had broken up.

"You're both young. You'll both find who you're supposed to be with eventually," my mom said while my father patted me on the shoulder.

I nodded, but I still couldn't shake my worries that I would be alone forever.

Taking a moment to sit and drink in the surroundings, we settled onto an empty bench with a clear view of the famed Opera House, its white curved shells rising from the rippling water like scales on a giant sea serpent.

"You weren't planning on going to Singapore, were you?" my mother asked with that gossip glint in her eyes. "I ran into Miles Cooper's mother, you remember him, right?"

"Yup. I do," I said, raising my camera to capture the Opera House. I framed the image so the architectural wonder filled the top half of the image, and its reflection on the undulating water filled the bottom half.

"Well, she said that he was moving to Singapore and might do some traveling in the area. I mean, I know it's silly to think, the continent is so big."

To tell or not to tell?

"Oddly enough, I actually did run into him."

"I hope nothing happened between you two."

"Nope, nothing." I turned, met her eyes, and forced a slight smile to hide my clenching jaw. "Just ran into him a couple of times."

Her eyes narrowed, seemingly to debate whether or not to call bullshit. She could always tell when I wasn't telling the whole truth. Her mouth opened but closed again when she seemed to remember my father's presence, though he was more interested in catching up with his work emails on his Blackberry.

"Did he tell you about his engagement?" she asked in a hushed tone.

Engagement?

"Not exactly. He did tell me that Celia left him when his father ordered him to open the Singapore office."

"What a liar," she said shaking her head.

"Liar?" I blurted the word out, hoping that she couldn't read my mind.

"Well, through the Toronto grapevine, I heard that he was cheating on Celia. He had some girl in New York he would see," she raised her hands to make air-quotes, "on 'business trips.' Celia became suspicious, hacked into his email account, and found months of correspondence. And the emails had nothing to do with the contracts."

My mouth dropped open. I had lapped up everything he had said about what running into each other had meant to him, and almost abandoned my trip to be with him in Singapore. Where, no doubt, he would have done the same thing to me as he had done to her. Even in university, he always had a reputation of being a ladies' man, but I, along with, so many other girls, gave him the benefit of the doubt. It was like when a waiter brings you a hot plate and tells you not to touch it, but you want to touch it anyways, and you do and you burn your finger. But, in my case, I never learned the first time.

"So rumour has it," she continued, "when the news broke, his parents were furious, naturally. There was a lot of damage control to be done, as Celia's family are major clients. To try and protect the business, they cut Miles off, shipped him off to Asia, telling him that he has to make up for the damage he did by opening the office there."

"It is rather ironic given his father's fondness for…" Now it was my father's turn to make air-quotes, "…'Email correspondence' with other women. I, for one, am glad you have nothing to do with that boy. I always knew he was trouble."

I leaned back against the bench, stunned as I let my parents' words sink in. It all made sense, and was even angrier with him than before. Before I could forgive him for being a pathetic man-child, but I could not forgive him for being a lying and manipulative man-child.

***

The next morning, we set out to ogle sea creatures at the Sydney Aquarium. We wandered from tank to tank pointing out fish we remembered from *Finding Nemo*, but my parents seemed to walk a little slower today. I thought perhaps it was because their sleep schedule was off or perhaps there was no way to maintain the level of excitement they displayed yesterday, but I knew it had more to do with the date. There were two months that made my parents walk a little slower: December and April. Respectively, they were the month of Audrey's death and her birth.

I was still going to hatch the plan I thought up that morning at Angkor Wat, but I needed to tell them the reason I asked them to bring her ashes with them. And I had to be careful with bringing it up.

Once my mother requested we rest for a while, we returned to the hotel. After ensuring that they just wanted a break from walking and were not quite ready to nap yet, I asked for their assistance in choosing images to submit to the Awesome Adventures competition. The deadline closed in mere hours. I sat at the desk in their room with my laptop in front of me, my parents peering over my shoulder, and Audrey's urn sitting on the desk. The entire family was present as I flicked through all of my edited images.

"These are lovely. You have a talent, darling," my mother said as I narrowed down my favourite twenty shots to ten.

I flip-flopped back and forth, moving images from my *yes* pile to my *maybe* pile, and back. After Googling the images of the winner and runners-up of the past years, it seemed there was no rhyme or reason as to why they were chosen. They varied between portraits, to architecture, landscape, wildlife, underwater, and macro. Digitally stalking the winner of the previous year once more, I noticed that he had a particular style. Just like Steve McCurry, his artistic voice sung in well-defined range throughout his body of work. As I stared at my own images, I remembered that I wasn't Steve McCurry, nor would I ever be. I was Harper Rodrigues, the one and only. Rather than emulating another artist, or trying to figure out what the judges wanted, I thought it best to showcase the work that spoke to me. The work that I saw myself in.

And so, I consulted with my Facebook page, Flickr portfolio, and blog posts to see which style of images had the most likes and views. Unfortunately, since the entries had to be previously unpublished, I couldn't actively seek out confirmation from the masses. It seemed that the images where I captured the unspoken connections between people, those loving moments, captured in time, garnered the greatest response.

Beginning my top three with my parents' help, I chose the image of the frustrated fisherman teaching his son to cast a net in the river in Vang Vieng. It would also count as a landscape shot, as behind the pair, across the brilliant green rice-fields stood the towering limestone cliffs. Next to enter my final pile was a shot of a mother and daughter in a rowboat in Ha Long Bay. They both sat amongst a pile of fruit seemingly painted by all of the colours of the rainbow. The mother held an oar in each hand and leaned forward beaming with pride at the child, barely old enough to begin school, counting coins and notes in her tiny hands.

Lastly, we chose an image of the sisters who sold water at the base of Death Mountain, the bold elder kissing and squeezing her bashful younger sister. I had enough of them to make a flipbook, but I had edited the image that captured the moment where smiles were widest, and you could feel their pure unadulterated joy just by looking at them. That image was declared the favorite and in unison my parents gave what sounded like a nostalgic sigh as they looked at the image of two sisters who shared a love that could traverse time, culture, geographical boundaries, and even death.

These images spoke to me, and in them I saw what was most important in the world.

I struggled to upload the images and fill out the entry form as my fingers trembled. Pushing out the worrying thought that my images may be stolen, and I was consenting to being used again, I stared at the "submit" button, covered my eye with my left hand, peeked through my fingers, and pressed it. Relief and fear washed over me as I was redirected to the confirmation screen. It was over. It was all done. The culmination of my work and nearly all my life savings. They would announce winners in one month. All I had to do was wait.

Breathing out the breath I had been holding in, I looked up and said to the Universe, "Please, please let me win."

I pushed the chair back, rose to my feet, stretched my arms above my head and shook out my jitters. My mother smiled as she sat up in bed, remote in hand, flicking through the television channels.

"So what are you going to do when you get back home?" Dad asked, folding his shirts on the bed.

Et tu Brutus? Why did no one ever listen to me?

"I'm hoping to win this. Keep traveling, keep taking photos." I turned to face him. "Can't we just leave it at that?"

He piled up four shirts in varying shades of blue and said, "You have to start thinking about getting a job. Darling, you must be realistic."

Realistic? I did everything I was supposed to do, business degree instead of art school, real job instead of giving my passion a chance, a relationship with a loving and stable guy, and it all gave me depression, guilt, and a severance package.

"Why is it so unrealistic to want to live my life doing what I love, regardless of how stable it is? I know what I want to do is unconventional, but why can't you just support me?"

"Darling, you're an adult," he said putting his hand on my shoulder. "It's time to start acting like one."

I shook his hand off. "One minute I'm your little girl, next I'm an adult, which is it?"

At the end of a long breath he said, "Your sister..."

"Is dead," I blurted out.

"Harper!" Mom yelled.

I didn't mean it to sound so blunt and insensitive, but I knew things about what Audrey wanted to do with her life that they never knew about.

"Audrey is never coming home."

Guilt rippled through me as Mom broke down in tears. Clutching the remote control to her chest she shuddered and sputtered a cry only those who grieve for their children know.

"You're upsetting your mother." His voice was stern and glare harsh. "And me."

I pressed my hands to my face. It was all coming out so wrong. I wanted to help. But maybe sometimes like when a broken nose heals badly, it needs to be broken, reset and only then it can heal properly. I padded across the soft carpet and sat on the bed next to her.

"I'm not trying to be cruel," I said, placing my hand on her thigh. "But you guys need to let her go so you can live your lives. Our house is too big for just the two of you. If you sold it, you'd have money to retire with. But you won't sell the house because you can't let go of your old life when she was in it."

Dad held his hands on his hips and huffed, "You don't know what it's like to lose a child."

"No, I don't, and I hope I never will, but I do know what it's like to lose my sister. Audrey meant everything to me, too. But she lived a stable life dreaming of more and never got to do any of it."

Mom put her hand on mine and began wailing. I knew I had to keep talking. I had to finish what I wanted to say.

"Mom, I don't mean to upset you I really don't, but I need you to know, you both to know, that she is here. Not in a physical sense, but she's here," I waved my arms around me as if someone were going to take them from me. "She's everywhere. Always. Do you remember on the first anniversary of Audrey's death how you got a strange urge to call me?" She sputtered and nodded. "Mom, I was about to do something very bad to myself, and I know in my heart that Audrey contacted you and told you to call me. I know what I'm about to say will sound even crazier, but I spoke to her when I was in India."

"You what?!" both of them said in unison.

I looked up at Dad. "Please don't freak out, but I kind of drank this drink in the desert and then I talked to God, who took the form of a mountain and then Audrey spoke to me as a voice in my head."

That, too, didn't come out quite like I had hoped.

He gave me that look I knew too well from when I broke his golf clubs. "You... did drugs?"

I refused to change the topic. "And do you know what she said to me? 'I'm with you always.'" His arched eyebrow remained in place. "Don't you see? She's not coming home. She's not even in that urn. She's in here." I drummed my palm on my chest above where I thought my heart was. "She exists, but we have to change what we think her existence means."

Thankfully my mother had stopped crying, and my father stopped looking at me as if he were going to ground me.

"Go on," he said, both voice and eyes softer.

"So I have a proposal. Please keep an open mind to what I'm about to say." It was the product of the epiphany I'd had at Angkor Wat. "So her birthday is next week, right?"

"She would have been thirty," my mother whispered, her eyes finding my father's.

"And you know how I asked you to bring her ashes?"

My father raised an eyebrow as if he knew what I was about to say and already disapproved.

"She always wanted to see the world. If she were alive, there would be no better gift to give her. So on her birthday, I want us to scatter her ashes in the ocean and let the currents carry her around the world."

"Absolutely not," Dad snapped.

"Wouldn't you prefer to think she was happy somewhere, having fun adventures rather than having a constant reminder of our loss staring at us from the mantle?"

"It *was* her dream," Mom mumbled, her eyes still fixated on my father.

I looked up at him too struggling in vain to keep the tears at bay. "Please just think about what I've said. I'm not trying to hurt you. I love you both so very, very much, and I want you to heal. And, yes, I want to heal, too."

Dad stood rigid and unyielding as a statue for what seemed like an eternity. My mind cleared as I watched him, hoping that he would listen to me and try and understand what I was saying. Then he brought his hands to his eyes and crumpled like an origami figure in the rain onto the bed. Sitting at my mother's feet, he reached out for us as he sobbed. And that afternoon, we cried until we fell asleep, napping together as a family like we did when Audrey and I were little girls.

***

April 8, 2010
Cairns, Australia

Five days later we chartered a boat from the tropical city of Cairns and headed east skimming over the flat calm turquoise water towards the horizon. With the sun as our guide, the clouds held vigil on the most beautiful day you could ever hope to see. And on the day she would have turned thirty, my parents and I held each other weeping for our loss and celebrating her short and beautiful life as we sent Audrey on her grand and eternal adventure around the world.

***

April 11, 2010
Cairns, Australia

When it was time to say goodbye to my parents, my father seemed to have one less grey hair and my mother, one less wrinkle.

"Harper," my father said after he put his suitcase in the taxi. "With regards to your career, we do support you and we do hope you do win this competition. We just want the best for you, and I'm sorry if it comes off like we're being hard on you. I don't want you to struggle like we had to."

I wrapped my arms around his neck, and this time we both had trouble letting go of each other. Deep down, I think I always knew my parents' motivations. Most times our parents are hard on us for a reason; they've had their fair share of disappointments and failures, and they want to see their kids succeed in life. Sometimes they are simply unable to see their child's dream, but you just have to follow your heart and listen that little voice inside that says, "Yes, I can."

"Keep us updated on everything, honey," my mother said with glassy eyes, holding her tears at bay. "Please be safe."

"I will. I'm a big girl," I said, wiping tears of my own.

God, I was going to miss them. And I was so grateful that they confronted their fears and flew halfway around the world to see me and see for themselves that the world isn't such a scary place.

"You'll always be our little girl."

"No matter how old I get, I'll never stop being your little girl."

"And if you ever speak to Audrey again, tell her the same."

I reached out and gently placing my hands over their hearts. "She already knows."

After we smothered each other with hugs and kisses they slid into the taxi. I ran after the taxi down next to the Cairns Esplanade waving like a wild woman, as they waved back through the rear window. Finally I stopped and stood watching, gasping for air, until the taxi faded from sight.

Chapter 25

Date: April 17, 2010
Arlie Beach, Australia

Waves lapped against the single hull of the former racing yacht as we motored out of Arlie Beach and headed for the Whitsunday Islands. After my parents left, I boarded a dive boat bound for the Great Barrier Reef and stayed on the wonder of the world for three days, completing my PADI Open Water Certification, a very generous gift from my parents. As I descended into the deep on my first dive, my heart felt as if it would burst from my chest. The skin-tight wetsuit constricted my movements, my breathing was stunted, and reef sharks slunk past me. Halfway through the descent I gave my instructor the "something's wrong" signal and indicated that I wanted to ascend. He pulled out a whiteboard and wrote, "What's wrong?" After he scrubbed it out, he passed me the board, I wondered what to respond. I wanted to say, "Everything," and then list it all: tight wetsuit, unnatural breathing, sharks, but instead I settled with the truth: "Scared." He scrubbed out my writing, scribbled something down and turned it around: "It's okay. I'm here."

When I read those words in my head, I heard Audrey's voice. I wasn't alone. Audrey's spirit was with me, watching, guiding, learning.

All is well.

I nodded, and he tucked the whiteboard back into his BCD. He then gave me the "OK" sign and gestured for me to take three longer breaths, and by slowing down, I adjusted to the breathing apparatus and felt more at ease. I gave him the "OK" sign back, and when he gave the thumbs down signal, the sign to descent, we continued the dive. And with each dive, I felt more and more at ease until I was convinced I was part mermaid.

During the certification, I received a bonus from my fellow divers, a crash course on underwater photography. The cost of the equipment needed is astronomical, but I added it to wish-list along with the Hasselblad.

Too afraid to spend the night alone, once back on land, I took a night bus down the coast to meet Lana in Arlie Beach, which is a bit of a misnomer, as it doesn't have an actual beach but has man-made lagoon instead. I stayed the night in a crowded party hostel on the warm and sunny seaside tourist town, and Lana arrived on the dock just in time to board the sailing vessel. We greeted each other with squeals and hugs and caught up on our missed time as we were shown our cabin.

The yacht ran eighty feet in length, and the hull was constructed in cool white fiberglass, with panels of wood that ran the length of the deck, weathered by age, sun and salt. The captain, first and second mate and sixteen passengers, including Lana and I, were scheduled to spend the night together. The first mate rewarded Lana's flirtation by assigning us the big double bed in the cabin at the bow. Aside from one other double bed in another cabin behind the galley, all the beds were indented in the hull and were as narrow as a coffin — and looked just as comfy.

As we settled in, I noticed that her wound from Koh Phangan was scabbed over and healing quickly. After brushing her teeth, she told me tales of exploring beige-sand beaches, jungle trails, and tanned surfer boys in Byron Bay with her two cousins Alexis and Odessa. I was happy to hear that she had time to reset and think about her career options for the near future. She wasn't in denial about the realities of re-entering the real world, but I still was.

After unpacking, we headed back up to the deck for the safety briefing with the others and took a seat with five girls in our age bracket. Introductions were made, names were forgotten and we simply became the Canadian girls and the Chilean girls. As with most days on the tropical coast, the sky was cobalt, the sea was turquoise and the temperature was perfect for tank tops and tanning. Once the captain cut the engine the first mate invited five passengers up to assist with setting the sail. The boat leaned as the salty ocean breeze filled the sail, and we rode the forested coast until we entered a channel between the mainland and archipelago of the Whitsunday Islands.

Clouds set in when we berthed at a dock on one of the islands. Everyone disembarked and trailed behind the first mate along a dirt path in the forest to a lookout point above the famed Whitehaven Beach. Hues of sapphire, sky blue, and turquoise sea mixed with the pure white sand swirled in the currents through the meandering waterway, between untouched emerald-coloured islands into the horizon. It was perhaps the one must-see tourist attraction I could capture without a single body spoiling the landscape.

After my mother's revelations on Miles, I had been dying to talk to Lana about it, but I had to be patient and bide my time until we had a chance to separate from our new friends. Through the afternoon, Lana and I socialized with the other passengers, swam, and learned about sailing and our sacred Aboriginal surroundings. I took photos of our friends, loving being able to capture these moments of complete and utter joy. We were having the time of our lives. Even though many of these friendships may not last long, they'll always exist in my images. After eating dinner cross-legged on deck, everyone broke out the goon wine. It was prohibited to bring glass aboard, so instead we bought boxed wine, leaving the box on land and packing just the foil bag. As the Chilean girls drank and forgot that neither Lana nor I spoke Spanish, I motioned to Lana to scoot to an empty spot near the bow to continue our catch up.

"Have you heard from Miles?"

I shook my head.

"What an asshole."

"You don't know the half of it," I scoffed and proceeded to repeat what my mother had told me about his cheating and his lies. As she sucked from the plastic spout on the foil bag, she shook her head, gasped, and her mouth hung open at all of the appropriate times.

"Oh, honey," she said, reaching across to put her hand on my knee. "I know you're angry, but you really dodged a bullet."

"Ugh, the worst thing is I ate up everything he had said about fate and all that crap."

"You wanted to believe it. We all want to believe those things."

"Lana, after he told me that, he stole my camera I could actually rationalize the gesture as romantic, not sociopathic." I was so angry with him, but more so with myself. "He used me, and I let him."

She started waving her fists around in front of her body.

"What are you doing?"

"See these red flags? They're not me cheering you on."

"Shut up," I said, laughing. I dipped my hand into my pocket, my fingers closed around a matchbook, and I threw it at Lana.

"Well, you'll know next time to spot these things better." She picked up the black pack of matches from the deck and tossed it back at me. "And if a guy breaks your heart once, he's likely to do it again."

As I held the slick black card in my hand a realization struck me. Given what the word "matches" meant to us, Miles had literally handed me a red flag that day in Laos. And after that, all the other signs were flashing like neon lights in my face. I just interpreted them through smudged rose-coloured glasses.

With the goon wine taking effect, feelings I had been trying to suppress bubbled to the surface. I told her how angry I was at Mira for what she did and how a coal of irritation burned for my father's lack of support. But most of all how I couldn't shake the anger at myself for all of the mistakes I made with Miles and Adam. And how guilty I still felt for hurting Adam.

"Everything happens for a reason," she said, rubbing my shoulder.

I know she was trying to help but that saying felt like nails on a chalkboard. After Audrey died, it seemed some people had the right words, and others had the wrong ones despite their good intentions. Telling me that my sister's life was cut so short, and my family was hurting in a way I wouldn't wish upon my worst enemy, happened for a reason made me want to punch them in the throat. But I was a lady, and I would only imagine doing it instead.

"For what reason did this happen?"

Lana gaped and lifted her hands, searching for words to rationalize an explanation.

"The reason, doll, is that sometimes you made bad choices," an unfamiliar female voice called out from the stern.

"Excuse me? This is none of your business."

An older woman closer to my mother's age pushed herself to her feet and padded down the deck towards us. "Talk that loudly, and it becomes everyone's business." The silver-haired Aussie took a seat a few feet away and held up her foil goon back to cheers. "The name's Avalon." I held up my goon and eyed her suspiciously. "Look, doll, shit happens to us. All of us. And, yes, for a reason."

"Please, by all means, tell me the reason that my sister was murdered."

"The same reason my son and husband were hit and killed by a drunk driver." With those words, guilt rippled through me. It was so easy to forget that everyone was fighting a battle of their own. She took the spout to her lips and then looked out to the darkness. "Life can be cruel and unfair."

"How is that a reason?"

"How is it not? When people say, 'Everything happens for a reason,' they assume that it means it happened for a good reason. No one says you have to like the reason, or even ever find out the reason. What I felt after the day I lost my son and husband, and every day since, has been a struggle. There is the crushing grief, and burning anger, but you truly realize that life is chaos, and there's nothing you can do about it, and you feel so out of control of our own existence. That, for me, is the worst part."

She was right. That's why my grief counselor encouraged us to set goals for ourselves, to regain the perception of control. But, even then, chaos rears its ugly head and derails your plans and goals.

"The key, I find," she continued, "is to give it a reason. You can't go back in time, you can't change what happened, but you have the power to reframe it and let that shape your future. If you want it to have a good reason for happening, give it one."

"What do you mean, give it one?" I asked zipping my hoodie up tighter as the cool night air licked over the deck.

"After a year of wallowing in my own depression, I woke up one day and read the paper. A drunk driver killed two innocent motorists in my town, just like what happened to my Jake and Charles. The drunk driver was eighteen. He was a child himself and would have to life with it for the rest of his life. The worst part was that it was preventable — he left a party and drove home thinking he was fine to drive. When I read this, it was like a light bulb switched on. I started a non-profit along with others who had lost loved ones to drunk driving accidents, and my daughter and I set up an education campaign in my town and set up ride-shares. Eventually secured sponsorship of a large corporate brand to acquire a bus and driver as a late-night shuttle service so no one had to drive drunk or get in a car with a drunk driver. We've done great work, and if that saves even one life, my son and husband did not die for nothing."

I bit my lip wondering what I could do. I had never thought of setting up a charity.

As if reading my mind, she continued, "You don't have to set up a charity, that is simply what spoke to me. I know people who have regained their sense of control by channeling their grief into personal projects like painting and writing. One widow in my charity took up sculpting after her husband died and now makes a living by selling her work."

I dropped my eyes to my polished toes and let her story and words wash over me. No matter what happened with the Awesome Adventures competition, I had to continue my photography. I never really realized that it was more than a love, more than a passion, more than a goal. I felt a sense of control when looking through the viewfinder. I felt a sense of purpose by capturing the stories I saw in the world, and my sharing them with people who were unable to see places for themselves.

"Thanks," I mumbled and looked up at her, "for the perspective."

"No prob, doll. Oh, and may I offer some advice in regard to that pompous boy you keep moaning about?"

I smiled and nodded. "Why not?"

"You set your expectations too high. Never forget that God gave boys two heads and only enough blood to run one at a time."

Lana and I laughed. I did get carried away with my daydreams.

"So forgive him, and forgive yourself," Avalon said.

"Forgive him?" Was she crazy? "And let him off the hook?"

"Forgiveness isn't for them. It's for you. Your anger will eat you alive. Trust me, I know. I wanted to hunt down the man who destroyed my family through his poor choice to get behind the wheel after a night of too many beers, but after fighting my therapist, I finally gave in. I realized I'd be a slave to my past and would never move on. I looked him in the eye the day he was sentenced to jail and told him that I forgave him. It was hard, one of the hardest things I've had to endure, but I felt as if I dropped a backpack full of bricks I didn't realize I had been carrying around each and every day."

I took another swig of goon wine and thought about what she said. After Audrey had died my mother joined a church. She was looking for something to believe in, and I could never understand until that moment why she could forgive Audrey's murderers. I thought she had been brainwashed, and a year ago, on what would have been Audrey's twenty-ninth birthday, she made me say out loud that I forgave them. Though I only did it to make her happy, I did feel lighter, and every day hurt a little less. My father didn't understand my mom's choice, either, I know he will never forgive them in the way my mother could.

As Avalon's story rolled in my mind, I realized that we weren't that dissimilar, she was just further along in her journey through grief than me. She was someone who endured unimaginable pain, and while you're never the same again, she seemed to have come out on the other side. I couldn't move on with my future if I was stuck in the past. I convinced my parents of this in Sydney, but now I needed to listen to my own advice.

"Well," Avalon said, pushing to her feet with a groan." It's time for this old bag to hit the hay. Sleep tight, girls."

"Good night," Lana and I said in unison as we watched her head back down the deck towards the stern.

"Oh, and as for your parents," Avalon said, stopping just four paces away. "I suppose this goes to any of you younglings listening, live your life accepting that they will always worry about you. Take it from me, parenting is not easy, and the first forty years is always the hardest."

I smiled as she gave a wink, turned and disappeared below deck.

"Should we go socialize with the other girls?" Lana asked.

I nodded, and as much as I wanted to sit and think about what Avalon had said, I had taken enough of Lana's time for my own needs, and it was time to give back. We stood with our goons and joined in the drinking game "twenty-one" in the cockpit.

***

The next day we sailed back to Arlie Beach, soaking up the sun. Along the way we anchored off the shores of untouched islands and went snorkeling along the pristine coral reefs. After the boat berthed back in the marina we disembarked and said our goodbyes.

After meeting back up with the new friends we had made on board for dinner, we hung out with the Chilean girls for a night on the town. Most of the girls found hook-ups and Lana stole a kiss from the club's very cute DJ. While getting some fresh air on the balcony overlooking the man-made lagoon, I met a bronze skinned, raven-haired guy from Spain, and though he was very cute and very insistent, I couldn't bring myself to take it past flirty words. He wasn't Xavier.

***

Three days later, Lana and I arrived in Hervey Bay. We signed up for a self-guided tour of Fraser Island, a natural wonder, and at seventy-five miles long and fifteen miles wide, it held the record of the world's largest sand island. Joining the Chilean girls we had met while sailing, we rented a 4x4 jeep and spent three days exploring the forests, lakes, creeks, mangroves, and even the rusting carcass of a wrecked ship. For the two nights we spent on the island, we camped in tents under the stars.

On the last night as the sun was setting, I wandered away from our campsite at the threshold of the beach and sat alone on the top of a grassy dune. I spotted and kept my eye on an opportunistic dingo. With some time to myself, I let Avalon's words sink in, and I honored my decision to forgive and let go. With darkness falling, stars became visible and twinkled against the dusk. I looked into the sky and said, "Miles, I forgive you. Mira, I forgive you."

It seemed that forgiving others was easier than forgiving myself. But after seeing my parents, I could bury the guilt I had for leaving home and making them worry. No matter what I did they would always worry, and I had to continue to do my part to let them know I was alright. Forgiving myself for the hurt I caused Adam was the next step. When I saw Jade had healed from that asshat Cliff's infidelity by letting Arturo into her life, I had to remember that he would heal too. He may never forgive me, but that was on him.

And so, I opened my mouth and whispered to the stars, "Harper, I forgive you. I am ready to let go of the shadows of the past and receive the happiness of the present and the future."

Then I sat, basking in quiet acceptance. What has happened has happened.

***

Through the next day as we continued to sightsee and made our way back to the mainland, I had that odd feeling that I was missing something. It wasn't until we made it back to the hostel in Hervey Bay, and I accounted for all of my belongings, that I realized that I had left my guilt behind. And I didn't miss it at all.

Chapter 26

Date: April 28, 2010
Christchurch, New Zealand

Lana and I reunited with Jade on our last day in Brisbane, the evening after leaving Hervey Bay. Over a cup of tea, we caught up and then slipped into bed for the night. Early the next morning, we boarded a flight bound for chilly Christchurch, located in the South Island of New Zealand.

As we checked into the hostel in the center of the quiet city, we asked for information on the various car rental and bus options to see the island. The receptionist, a Dutch guy in his late twenties, handed us a binder from a shelf behind the desk. We flicked through the pages, and about halfway through, Lana screamed something that vaguely resembled English. Bending over, she furiously riffled through her daypack. Jade and I exchanged confused looks with the receptionist, and Lana bolted upright with a crumpled piece of paper in her hand.

She slammed it on the desk and smoothed it out and said, "Leo said in Goa that they were going to do one of these buses."

With soaring hopes, I practically elbowed Jade out of the way to get a better look. It was a brochure that had been bent in all the wrong places, with pictures of buses with various names and logos, information and dates. Scrawled in red pen were the dates, April 26th, April 27th, April 28th, and April 29th. The titles "Stray Bus" and "Kiwi Experience" were circled. My pulse hammered wildly at the thought of seeing Xavier again.

"Which one?" I said, flipping the brochure over, hoping to see more of Leo's writing.

Lana bit her lip and looked at me. "I don't remember."

I fingered through the binder until I found the pages on Stray Bus and Kiwi Experience. Both companies detailed near identical itineraries, but each offered a dizzying number of sightseeing options.

"He said something about 'hop on hop off,'" Lana said, running her index finger down the pages.

That narrowed it down slightly, but Stray alone had eight routes mapped for each of the South and North Islands, twelve that encompassed both islands for "hop-on-hop-off" passes. The Kiwi Experience boasted thirty-three routes for their "hop" passes.

"We'll never find Xavier and Leo," I said pressing my hands to my face. "What should we do?"

"If I were you ladies," the receptionist answered, even though I hadn't directed the question to him, "I would take the Stray Bus. The Kiwi Experience is for the eighteen-year-old gap year kids."

After paying for our dorm room, we took the binder from reception to a bench in the courtyard. Under the orange glow of a streetlamp, we debated what to do. Christchurch was a quiet little place, and as we sat one-hundred feet across from its famed cathedral, the autumn chill nipped at our skin, and barely any souls passed by. Jade puffed on her cigarette and put forth her argument in favour of renting a car and using the itineraries as a guide. Lana, however, wanted to choose a bus, and the more we debated, the more she was sure that Leo had said the Stray Bus. The dates, he listed weren't in our favour. The Stray busses left on dates with odd numbers, the Kiwi Experience left on dates with even numbers, and given that today was the 28th, our only option was to take the Stray Bus that left tomorrow.

In the end, we compromised that we would take the Stray Bus leaving the nearby town of Greymouth tomorrow on a pass that recommended eight days, and then we would rent a car for the North Island when we got there.

***

Early the next morning, under a blanket of cold fog, we boarded a bus bound northwest to Greymouth. After leaving Christchurch, we made the journey slicing through the body of the South Island. I stared through the rain-flecked windows as we passed through emerald-green mountains covered in dripping dense forests. Just shy of four hours later as we arrived in Greymouth, the sun finally clawed through the clouds.

As we ate our lunch al fresco at a café in the charming mining town, I was glad that I hadn't thrown out the jacket that kept me warm in Agra. In less than an hour, we were due to board the Stray Bus. Meaning, in less than an hour, there was a possibility that I would see Xavier, and I could barely talk with the anxiety closing my throat. But Lana was so excited at the prospect of seeing Leo that she couldn't stop talking: *I can't wait to do ABC to Leo, and I wonder if he'd be interested in trying XYZ.*

All the while, Jade, now more zen than ever, tuned her out and scanned the rugged mountain landscape instead.

As I pushed my food around rehearsing what I would say when I saw Xavier, (I didn't get much further than "Hi") Jade looked at the sun and then asked, "What time is it?"

I looked at my watch. "Shit, it's two fifteen, we're late."

Lana leapt to her feet, grabbed her backpack, and swung it on her back, in the process knocking the solid wood bench clean over. By the time Jade and I put it back on its feet and secured each other's packs, Lana was halfway down the street. We trailed behind her and when I saw the orange bus with the word "Stray" splattered across the side I nearly saw my lunch again. What if Xavier was on there?

What if he wasn't?

After we showed our printed tickets to the young woman wearing an orange shirt that matched the logo, we stored our backpacks in the underbody storage compartment, and I froze as my foot hit the first step. It wasn't until Jade nudged me that I took the next step and then the next. I greeted the driver and turned my attention to the rows of seats, scanning the occupants for raven hair framing a devastatingly handsome face.

Blond hair, blue eyes girl. *Damn*. Brown hair, brown eyes, boy. *Damn*. Red head boy. Damn. Black hair grey eyes…girl. *Double damn*. My eyes locked onto each face, but when they reached Lana's pouting lips at the back, I had to accept that Xavier was not on the bus.

Maybe he didn't come to New Zealand at all.

The bus was half full. Passengers dotted around the seats, and cliques had already been formed. I took the row in front of Lana to spread out a bit. Jade took the row in front of me. The doors closed, and the bus lurched forward. I chastised myself for failing to manage my expectations, particularly since I couldn't shake the disappointment. Lana's disappointment, however, lasted until she met eyes with the ginger-haired guy at the front of the bus.

As the journey south down the western coast began, the rain fell again, first as small droplets, then as fat chunks splattering against the pane. My breath fogged the glass as I watched the world pass by. Mountains rose into the sky like the humps of a giant sea serpent covered in tangles of ferns, moss, bushes, and trees. As I held my breath at the sheer beauty of the river estuaries meeting the sea at rocky waterways, I pulled out my camera, but I couldn't capture the scene properly though the rain-flecked glass. Flicking through the playback, I thought of the contest.

When you decide to enter a competition or start a new venture, the further away and more abstract it seems, the more confident you feel about your chances. Months ago I was so sure of myself, so sure of my abilities, but now all I could do was think about how I could have made my work better. The rice fields were oversaturated with colour in the Vang Vieng shot. I forgot to use the thirds overlay tool for the Ha Long Bay shot. And the shadows are too harsh in the images with the girls from Death Mountain, weighing down the feel the image was supposed to evoke. If only I had stayed away from Miles in Southeast Asia like I had planned to, I could have focused properly on my work. I could have spent more time researching the latest retouching techniques and really mastered the manual settings on my camera. I had mere weeks to wait for the announcement of the winners, and the more I thought of the outcome, the thought of winning transformed from a probability to impossibility.

The thought of failing at my dreams crushed me.

Our guide, Emma, broke my ruminations as she announced our itinerary for the next stop, Frans Joseph. She sent a clipboard around so interested participants could sign up for such adventures as ice climbing and glacier walks. Lana, Jade, and I signed up for a glacier walk, but as we arrived at the hostel nestled in a forest at the foot of the glacial mountains, the rain started pouring. We spent the next two nights huddled in the hostel's common area, the continuous downpour killing any chance of making it to any of the excursions.

The rain began to let up once we left Frans Joseph. As we continued our way south we paused for a tour through a lush dripping rainforest, endured the whipping wind chill at a pebble beach, and stopped for pictures at a breathtaking vantage point as we drove through the fiord land. After one night singing karaoke at a hostel near Lake Wanaka, we finally made it to Queenstown.

***

Date: May 2, 2010
Queenstown, New Zealand

"We're almost at fifteen-thousand feet." I could barely hear my skydiving instructor over the roar of the tiny plane's engine. "Your friends will go first, and then we'll go last."

"What if the parachute doesn't open?" I leaned back and yelled."

"Have a little faith in me," he said patting me on the shoulder. "As they say in America, this ain't my first rodeo, darlin'."

"I'm Canadian."

"What?"

"Never mind."

I guessed if it didn't open, there wasn't much I could do except but enjoy the ride with my new best friend, Sam, strapped to my back. My parents would be so mad at me if this was the way I went out.

On our third and final day in Queenstown, the girls and I decided to go skydiving. Queenstown was called The Adventure Capital of the World, so we figured, when in Rome. It was one of those things that seemed like a good idea when your feet are planted firmly on the ground, but when you're stuffed like sardines in a tiny propeller plane fifteen-thousand feet up, you begin to question your sanity.

I craned my neck to look out the window, and the ground looked really, really far away. There was no way of backing out now. I had a guy strapped to my back whose job was to get us out of this plane at fifteen-thousand feet. And I had paid him to do so. I looked at the other girls; Jade's eyes were shut as she meditated while Lana leaned back into her hot instructor's chest. Maybe that's why she had suggested it — it seemed to be a great way to get close to a total stranger in such a short amount of time.

Jade's instructor gave a hand signal, patted her on the shoulder and together they scooted across the floor towards the open panel in the side of the plane. We waved and a second later she was gone. Lana and her instructor shuffled towards the side, waited, waved and then disappeared into the sky. It was my turn next. Struggling to get our bodies to work together, Sam and I eventually shuffled across the plane and I dropped my legs over the edge and made the mistake of looking down.

Had circumstances been different, say, it was a leisurely plane ride to see Queenstown from the air, I wouldn't have minded the view. But now that I was seconds away with nothing but fifteen-thousand feet of air between myself the ground, I had my issues with the altitude. Before I could protest, Sam pushed forward and we were air-born. I swallowed my stomach back down my throat as the freezing air assaulted my eyes. I had opted not to pay for a cameraman, largely because of the cost, but as I squinted and tears streamed across my flapping cheeks, I was glad I didn't have any photographic evidence of it. No one should have to endure seeing my face like that. I have no doubt it was the stuff of nightmares.

Sam patted me on the shoulders twice, indicating that I un-tuck my arms and stretch them out into the "banana-back" position we practiced on the ground. We had reached terminal velocity, the speed at which we were no longer accelerating and were falling at a steady pace, and as I looked down, I could appreciate the landscape. It was then I wished that I had my camera but bringing anything along was a big no-no. A snowcapped mountain range stood next to a large Z-shaped lake with Queenstown built on hits shores. Around the town stood green grassy fields reaching to the horizon in all directions. From the ground it was a charming little ski resort town, and its name was bestowed upon it as it was considered a town so beautiful it was fit for a queen. At that point, I had no more thoughts of whether or not my parachute would open, it was too late to worry about it anyways. Adrenaline coursed through my veins and pure joy rippled through me. I was staring death in the face with a smile so big it hurt my cheeks. And I had never felt so alive.

Suddenly I was jerked upright, and I let out a loud squeal. Once the parachute was pulled, my sixty-second free-fall was over.

"See? Have a little faith," Sam yelled in my ear as we floated back to Earth.

He made small talk and pointed out points of interest but the words, *have a little faith*, echoed in my mind. After years of convincing myself that my grand adventure with my two best friends was never going to happen, I was nearly at the end of it. After years of convincing myself I would never feel happiness again, I now felt as if I were overflowing with it. After years of wishing to speak to Audrey again, I felt her presence with me every moment. Everything I wanted eventually came to fruition. I just had to be patient.

As we descended from the sky, the little cotton bud sheep in the farmlands grew and grew. We landed with a thud back on the grassy field, and as Sam uncoupled us, he pulled me in for a hug, and I laughed off my bout of terror from before.

***

Still buzzing that evening, the girls and I set off for our last night on the town with our dorm-mates, five Japanese girls who hopped on the bus in Frans Joseph. In the near freezing night air, we made our way through the town from World Bar to Winnies, and then to Buffalo Club. Given the poor choices I made while drunk, I decided to only have one drink at World Bar, only because they were served in white ceramic teapots, and who doesn't like a little bit of whimsy? At the rest of the bars, Jade and I ordered water, requesting it served in a highball glass with a cocktail straw. Lana kept up with the Japanese girls with some pretty aggressive drinking. Once we left the Japanese girls at Buffalo Club, Jade decided to go back to the hostel, and

Lana and I made our way between the ski-chalet-style buildings to Loco Cantina. A sandwich board stood in the glow of a lamppost advertising an open mic night.

It was then I heard it. A note, a voice, carried by the wind. I looked at Lana, she heard it, too. Someone was singing a very familiar acoustic arrangement of "Sex on Fire".

The walls of my stomach caved in, and my legs suddenly felt as wobbly as a drunken giraffe. Xavier was here. He was actually here. Fantasies of what he would do when he saw me, what we could do for the rest of the night, began to play in my mind.

Manage your expectations.

Lana squealed and grabbed me by the wrist, dragging me inside. Welcoming the warmth, I pulled my gloves off once she let go of my hand. Loco Cantina was a large space with a long bar, crowded with bodies on one side, the walls on the other were accented with painted corrugated tin paneling. We pushed through the crowd to find the stage at the back. I could barely hear him over the blood rushing in my ears. Over the sea of heads, I saw him. Sitting on the edge of a stool, strumming a guitar, his eyes closed, lost in the song.

"Come on, let's get to the front," Lana said, leaning into my ear.

Then my expectations swung in the opposite direction: what if he thought he'd never see me again and was with one of the groupies at the front? I don't know what would crush me more: the disappointment or the embarrassment.

"No, there are too many people." As I spoke those words, an arm snaked around Lana's shoulder.

She turned, gripped Leo by the lapels of his jacket, and pulled him in for a kiss. When they finally let go of each other, he waved at me and motioned for us to follow. He took Lana by the hand, and Lana took me by mine. To my horror, we pushed to the front. The memory of approaching Miles in Koh Phangan and the ensuing disaster flashed in my mind.

Nestling into the crowd, I ignored the girls who were not so subtly pulling down their tops to show off more cleavage, vying for his attention. But his eyes remained firmly shut. And so I pushed my insecure thoughts out and melted into his languid and lyrical voice that was as rich and smooth as velvet, with memories of Goa flooding my mind. The exquisite touch of his callused fingertips and the way he smelled of summer and tasted of sin.

And now he was in front of me. And I could finally inhale him guilt free.

His voice was as soft as pillow talk when he crooned the final words of the song. And when the last word had fallen from his lips, his leaden eyes opened, meeting mine instantly. A mixture of surprise, relief, and something a little darker flashed in them. I bit my lip and dropped my gaze to the wood-paneled floor as the crowd broke into applause.

"Thank you," he said with a nod to his new fans before resting the guitar against the stool.

His eyes found mine again, and he crossed the stage, stepped from it, and closed the gap between us. Before I could utter a word, my lips softened under his. As he pulled away he gently tugged my bottom lip with his teeth, stealing my breath.

"Hi," I exhaled as that curious feeling unfurled in the pit of my stomach. "I...ugh...Liked your performance."

Smooth, Harper, real smooth.

He tucked a rogue strand of hair behind my ear, looking at me as if committing each and every feature of my face to memory. "That song always makes me think of you."

My breathing became ragged, and I wanted nothing more than to feel his hands on my skin. It was then I realized we had lost Lana and Leo.

"Did you take the Kiwi Experience?" I asked.

He nodded. "Stray?"

Of course, we took separate buses. And, of course, we would have to separate so soon after finding each other.

"Yeah," I said with a sigh, "we leave for Christchurch first thing tomorrow morning."

Seven A.M. to be exact.

"Let's not waste any time then," he said, taking my hand and kissing my knuckles. "Dance with me."

At this point, the DJ had taken over for the live performers, playing Top 40 hits. Xavier led me to the center of the dance floor, then pulled me hip-to-hip as Akon's "Right Now" pulsed. We teased each other with each song, moving close to the corner. Despite my sobriety, I was still drunk on adrenaline and became bolder and bolder. I turned and grinded into him for "Rude Boy," he took a fistful of my hair and brushed the shell of my ear with his lips for "Best I Ever Had," and when the DJ slowed it down for Jeremiah's "Birthday Sex," I took action.

I whispered in his ear, "It wouldn't happen to be your birthday, would it?"

His lips moved to a spot where my ear met my neck that made me shudder. "For you, it can be."

"Want to go celebrate?"

As if a primal urge took over, he pressed me against the wall and covered my mouth with his. Instinctively, I arched my back and pushed my lips into him, the tightening in my stomach almost too much to bear. He pulled at the belt loops on my jeans as my fingers found the tattoos on his strong arms. When the desire to celebrate pushed at my zipper, he rested his forehead against mine, his eyes liquid with desire.

"Come back to my hostel."

He pressed his lips to mine once more, placing a feather soft kiss on my bottom lip, a kiss so gentle yet so erotic I couldn't stand that we had to wait any more time.

**

With fingers interlaced, we practically ran to my hostel, ignoring the bitter chill of the freezing air. However, as we kissed and wandered the halls we couldn't find anywhere secluded. The hostel life was not conducive to privacy. The fluorescent lighting eliminated any possibility of shadowy corners, and the constant flow of human traffic made solitude an impossible find.

Though we couldn't find anywhere to be alone, we weren't ready to let each other go for the night, so after stumbling into the kitchen-cum-common-room on the second floor, we decided to play a round of pool. But it only increased the sexual charge in the air. We teased each other, flashing skin, bending over, and posing seductively to distract each other, and stole kisses between shots. He beat me three games to two. And after the deciding game, we were alone in the common room.

I leaned against the table, looked up through my lashes and purred, "So what now?"

He stepped forward and pushed me onto the felt, his hips between my thighs. I whimpered with the feathery strokes of his tongue on my swelling lips. He pulled a fistful of my hair with one hand, and his other hand ventured beneath my shirt. His lips skated down my neck, igniting the skin along the way. I leaned back, relishing the pleasure, when I spotted the camera.

"Xavier."

He nipped at my ear at the sound of his name. "I've waited so long for this."

"Xavier. Stop. Please."

Respecting my plea, he pulled back, his hair an absolute mess. I pointed up to the camera in the corner of the room above his head. He flashed a wolfish grin so dark I considered letting him devour me there and giving security a show.

"There must be somewhere private," I whispered, even though we were alone in the room.

Without breaking eye contact, he took my hands, kissed my knuckles, and pulled me from the table and checked the floors we hadn't before. Even though the halls were now empty, privacy was still impossible to find. The utility closets were locked, the bedrooms were full of sleeping bodies, and every inch of the public spaces were under the scrutiny of Big Brother.

"There is one place where there are no cameras," he said, leading me down the hallway. He paused outside of the men's bathroom door.

"You're not serious." I was *not* the kind of girl to have sex in a public place.

Was I?

"We don't have to do this if you don't —"

Before he could finish his sentence, I dragged him through the door and into the nearest stall.

Chapter 27

"God, I missed you," he whispered. I stifled a moan as I unzipped his hoodie. "Shhh, someone will catch us."

A stall in the men's communal bathroom at nearly five in the morning certainly wasn't the romantic setting I had hoped for our first time. My eight roommates, however, would have been less than pleased if I brought him back to my bunk bed.

As clothes fell, the warmth of his hands on my body offset the cold Formica of the stall door against my back. His lips skated from my chest to the threshold of my panties with his rough stubble tickling me. Hooking the silk with his thumbs, he tugged them down. I stared down at his beautiful almost boyish face framed by the shock of inky black hair. I had been longing to rake my fingers through it. My eyes followed the trail of etchings of lyrics and music notes and stanzas on his golden skin down to the tight lacing of muscle across his torso. He was more beautiful than I remembered.

He sat on the closed seat stark naked at full salute. He reached into the pocket of his jeans that lay on the floor and produced a foil wrapper. It was then that I paused.

This was really going to happen. I never thought of myself as the girl who would have sex in a bathroom stall at five in the morning with a guy I barely knew.

What am I doing?

I froze as he placed his hands on my ass and gently pulled me forward. Leaning in he kissed me on the sensitive spot ever so slightly inside of, and ever so slightly south of, my hipbones. First the right side, then the left. I tugged on his hair and bit my lip to stop from crying out.

He looked up at me, his eyes dark and lidded, and then he completely devastated me with the words, "I adore you."

Fuck it.

I grabbed the wrapper and tore it open for him.

His strong arms wrapped around me as I sank into him. He hissed through clenched teeth as I took his lips between mine. Waves of pent up desire rippled from my marrow to my curling toes with the first rock of my hips. He sucked on that sensitive spot on my neck I never knew existed, and I shuddered and dug my nails into his back. Then…

BAM! BAM! BAM!

Both our bodies froze as the stall shook, the sound reverberating through the entire room.

"Look, guys," a familiar monotone voice bellowed. "You have to leave. You can't do…that…in here."

I recognized the voice as the awkward guy who worked reception late night. Though I had only interacted with him once when I lost my key after a night out at World Bar the night before, I suddenly felt embarrassed at my actions. Even though the vodka orange I had at World Bar had long since left my system, they were the actions of a drunk and horny teenager. Still intoxicated with adrenaline from skydiving, I had lost total control of myself. Then I was brought straight back to myself at nineteen years old on a beanbag with Miles and a terrifying thought echoed in my skull: *Now that he's had me, is he done with me?*

I raised myself off of him and reached for my clothes, covering my nakedness with my hands.

"Hey," he whispered, resting his hand on my forearm, "what's wrong?"

"Nothing," I lied, feigning a slight smile.

We dressed in silence. Our interrupter stood in the hallway, making sure we heeded his instructions. I shrank under the weight of his judgmental eyes, wishing the ground would swallow up one of us. Passing him, I made a beeline for my room at the end of the hallway, unable to pinpoint the epicenter of the tremor of emotions shaking me: shame, anxiety, fear?

After my night with Miles I didn't hear from him for seven years, and that was only because he was looking for company in his new circumstances. Xavier didn't come to New Zealand for me — he and Leo already had planned this destination long ago, would he too move on to the next girl? After all, I was leaving for Christchurch in less than two hours.

"Harper," Xavier said, pulling me back gently by the hand before I made it to the door. "I'll be in Wellington next week. I have to see you again. I can't lose you."

There was something about looking into the eyes of my partner in crime that lessened my feelings of shame. And even after plummeting to Earth from fifteen thousand feet, I had never felt more alive than I had in that stall with him. "Find me on Facebook. Harper Rodrigues on the Toronto network."

And then he left me at the threshold of my dorm with a deep kiss that made my head spin.

***

Needless to say, I had some explaining to do when my alarm sounded an hour and a half after I crept into bed, still wearing my clothes from the night before.

"Nice hickey," Jade said winking at me.

I pulled a mirror from my makeup purse and saw a large purple bruise on my neck. My face turned a complimentary shade of red as a dirty little smile carved my lips.

Thankfully, as the girls begin their inquisition, Lana strolled through the door. Hair mussed, and wearing smile that didn't crack, she was more than willing to recount her night. After packing up, we made our way to the reception. As I handed my key back to the guy who had caught me in flagrante in the men's bathroom two hours ago, I couldn't meet his eyes. I simply slid it across the desk and turned around.

On the bus, in between naps and sightseeing stops at sky-blue lakes, I had nothing but time to think about my night before. Even though the insecure thoughts that he would forget about me niggled at me, a louder, more confident part reminded me that unlike that night with Miles, I was in control of the situation last night.

And if Xavier did forget about me, then it would be his loss.

And then, as if on cue, my mind began to wander to the logistics of how we would make a long-distance relationship work and what our future children would look like...

Eight hours later, we arrived in Christchurch and bid our Japanese friends goodbye. The following day after catching up on missed sleep, the girls and I ate brunch and wandered the city seeking native Maori culture at the Canterbury Museum, window shopping on the high street, and following a friendly local to a great 'fush and chips' joint.

Later that afternoon, Jade and Lana and I stopped in the café next to the hostel for green tea and coffee. I ran up to the room to grab my laptop, rejoined them at a table next to the window, sipped my foamy latte, and logged into Facebook. A tremor of nerves shook me when I saw the friend request and message waiting for me from Xavier Northam.

> Harper, I'm so glad I found you. I had so much fun with you last night. When are you going to be in Wellington? I'll be there in four days. I need to see you again.

The time was stamped as lunchtime today. He wanted to see me again. Then a new fear crept in. The paradoxical fear of getting what you want. The paradox created by the fear that you may lose what you want and the ensuing pain. Pain I knew well. Before responding I clicked on his name, and his profile popped up. In his profile picture, he sat on a cliff overlooking Palolem, guitar in hand, wearing nothing but board shorts. And then I saw his date of birth.

"He's how old?" I blurted out. Jade and Lana snapped up at me. I knew he was a bit younger, but I had no idea how much so. "Xavier didn't just graduate university. He's nineteen."

His face was youthful, but the thick facial and body hair added years to him. Damn that Mediterranean blood. The kid must have been born with a five o'clock shadow.

"So?" Lana said with a cheeky smile.

"So? He just graduated high school. He's a teenager."

Lana's smile grew dirtier and dirtier.

I handed through almost clenched teeth. "Did you know they were this young?"

"Leo might have said something about being on a gap year before university back in Palolem, and I might have enjoyed the whole cougar thing."

My eyes shot daggers at her, and my mouth hung agape.

"What?" Don't look at me like that. Younger men have more stamina and are far more eager to please."

"Why didn't you say anything?"

"I didn't think it was a big deal. You were trying to ignore him then anyways." She took a sip of her latte. "Don't tell me you're going to let that ruin your romance."

Instead of responding, I thought I would get a second opinion.

"Jade, would you sleep with someone that young?"

"I'm celibate again," she said as a smile quirked her lips. "But I think absorbing his youthful energy could be a good thing for you."

I said nothing more, logged out of Facebook, and slid my computer across the table to Jade so she could use it. They couldn't understand what I was feeling after my past experiences. After Miles I decided that I was done with boys, I needed a man and there was no way that a nineteen-year-old could be mature enough. But even if he was, we were at such dramatically different stages in life. I wanted a career and family as soon as possible.

He couldn't give me the future I want, so what was the point?

Twenty-five-year-old woman, nineteen-year-old boy. I could only imagine what he and Leo were telling his friends about us. And I had the hickey to remind me every time I looked in the mirror.

***

The next morning, we boarded a train bound for Picton at the northern tip of the South Island. With the gorges, hidden valleys, and a volcano spewing out a towering plume of smoke, the rugged eastern coastline was a breathtaking journey. Unfortunately, I couldn't ask the train to pull over so I could take pictures, and so with nothing to distract me, I convinced myself that I could take things no further with Xavier. As much as I liked the idea of him, I had my future to consider, and I couldn't waiver from my five-year plan. My regained sense of control had been my lifeline since Audrey's death, I feared to think what would happen if I lost it again.

Once we made it to Picton, we hopped on a ferry and motored through the spectacular Cook Straight. We stood on the upper deck, inhaling the crisp air as archipelagoes of unspoiled evergreen islands gave way to shimmering blue sea and after three and a half hours we saw the cityscape of Wellington and entered the harbour.

To our great fortune, Lana's Australian cousins owned an apartment in Wellington, and its tenants had moved out the month prior, leaving it empty, and they allowed us to stay in it. Though the capital city was famous for its blustery weather, we happened upon a series of warm and sunny days. After the chill of the South Island, it was a welcome break. Still unsure of what to say to Xavier, I ignored the niggling thoughts of replying to him as we soaked up the sunshine exploring the city's botanical gardens, museums, and quirky boutiques. I liked Wellington. I liked New Zealand, in general. The cities didn't have that big city overwhelming feeling; they had charm, energy and sprawling green spaces.

During the three nights we spent in Wellington, we decided to rent a car and make our own itinerary for the North Island. Lana's cousins had mapped one out for her when she stayed with them — tomorrow we would pick up the car and drive to Taupo, and then Rotorua, Waitomo, and Bay of Islands. Our road trip would finish in Auckland in time to catch our flight to Fiji.

I bit back the depressing thought of that day. After four days in Fiji, it will be time to fly home, and my adventure will come to an end. I'd have to go home, rejoin the real world, grow up and find a career I could tolerate and someone to love.

Unless I win the Awesome Adventures competition.

Again, that paradoxical fear returned: what if I did win? The girls were heading home — could I travel by myself? This trip had been a big step for me, but the fear of traveling alone was paralyzing. If I scored the opportunity to join their photography team, I wouldn't have to worry about traveling alone. But that was a big *if.*

***

Date: May 10, 2010
Wellington, New Zealand

On our last day in Wellington, we bought wraps from a food truck and ate them on the seawall at the edge of the harbour.

"So we'll pick up the car tomorrow and get moving?" Jade said before taking a bite of her falafel wrap.

"Fine, but can we please go out tonight?" Lana pouted as we dangled our legs above the water. "If I stay in one more night, I'll go crazy. Leo arrived today, and he said he's going out to this bar. It's not far from the apartment."

Jade stared at her feet. She hated going out. I joined her watching the waves off the seawall.

"Harper, you're really letting Xavier's age get in the way?" Jade said. I shrugged. "The least you can do is tell him to his face that you don't want anything to do with him. It's not just girls who get hurt if you sleep with them and don't talk to them after."

Guilt twisted in my gut. I had acted towards Xavier how Miles had acted to me after we slept together — unforgivably selfish. As I chewed my falafel and stared across the shimmering water, I decided that if I was going to end things because of his young age the least I could do was act like the adult I thought I was.

***

That night as Lana and I navigated the streets through the quaint and quiet city, my drumming heart woke the butterflies in my stomach. The coward in me wanted to run home and send him a Facebook message that I wanted to end things. I wasn't sure if I could trust myself to say what I needed to say. I couldn't understand why, but every time I was in his presence, it felt as if a string was tied between us that tightened and tightened, pulling us closer. And once that string became taught, I lost control of myself. And losing control was my greatest fear.

We reached a road where revelers spilled form the bars' patios onto the sidewalks. Across the street, a large red "X" was splattered on the wall of a tall cream-coloured building. It was the hostel that the Kiwi Experience bus would take their passengers.

"This is the place," Lana said, pulling me through an open door.

341

The bar was dark and full of bodies writhing to house beats. The front wall was paneled with windows and all others with dark wood. We pushed through the crowd and made our way to the solid wood bar counter. Behind the three bartenders more bottles I could count were stacked against an aged mirror that took up half the wall.

"Hey," I heard a voice next to me say. I turned to see a cute guy wearing a business suit standing next to me. The two top buttons of his crisp light blue shirt had been undone, and the knot of his silver and navy tie hung just below the second button. He looked like he had just come from a long day at the office. His aura screamed, "responsible adult." He looked like the kind of guy I believed I was supposed to end up with. "I'm Greg," he said with his hand outstretched.

"Harper," I replied.

But before I could take his hand, another landed on my shoulder. I spun around and met the tempest building in Xavier's stormy eyes. "Why have you been ignoring me?"

I paused, fighting the urge to kiss him.

"Let's talk," I said, brushing past him and following the dark paneling to the quiet hallway near the bathrooms. As I leaned against the wall, his lips pressed into a thin line. "What happened in Queenstown was…fun…but we have to leave it at that."

"Why?"

"Because you're too young for me."

"Bullshit."

"I'm twenty-five, you're nineteen."

"Who says I'm too young?" I didn't answer. "All this time I believed that you were this amazing girl who knew what she wanted from life and made no apologies for it."

I bit my lip, realizing that he saw me for who I wanted to be. He saw me for my best self, despite all of my insecurities and flaws.

If only he were older.

"You're nineteen," I pleaded with him to understand. Understand that I found emotional security in my five-year plan. Understand that he was too young to be a part of it. Understand that I was scared that he would hurt me. Understand that I was afraid that, like Miles, he too was using me. Girls threw themselves at him every time he stepped off stage, and what if one day he might decide that he had what he wanted from me and was ready to move onto the next girl.

"It's just a number."

"You're a boy."

He lunged forward, pinning me to the wall with his strong body. "I am a man," he growled in my ear.

I moaned at the hot feel of his tongue pushing my lips apart. A rush of sensations knifed at me as my body begged for him to finish what we had started in Queenstown. I whimpered as his lips released mine. He grazed my neck with his callused fingertips, igniting a trail of sparks.

"My hostel is across the street," he said, his hot breath ragged in my ear. "Let me prove to you that I am a man."

Chapter 28

My heartbeat deafened me as he pulled my top over my head in the empty hostel room. With each kiss, deeper and more frenetic, I wanted more. I needed more. Each time he removed his hands from my skin, I was left wanton and wanting. With each breath, I inhaled his scent. Like an addict, as I received each dose of him, I craved him more.

Bathed in the orange glow of a lamppost filtered through a sheer curtain at the back wall I fell backwards into the soft mattress of his bottom bunk. Sitting up, I reached for his belt buckle and desperately fiddled with it, and his jeans, until both were lying on the floor. He dropped to his knees, and with his lips grazing my neck, he unhooked my bra. I lay back and pulled him into the bed, his broad shoulders bearing down on me as his hips pinned me down. A dull ache between my legs became unbearable as I pushed against him, torturing myself with the friction. He pressed his lips to mine as he dominated me. My hands swept over his back, my nails digging into his flesh.

Releasing me, he pushed himself back so he was kneeling between my thighs and hooked his fingers under the elastic of my panties and tugged them.

Meeting his gaze, I raised my hips slowly. Once he had pulled them past my feet, As I rested my ankles on his shoulders and watched his face as he let his eyes rake over my naked body. Adulation burned in his darkening gaze.

My breath caught in my throat as he began trailing kissing from my ankles, down my calves, past my knees, torturing the sensitive skin of my inner thighs. And when his lips descended upon my demanding flesh, my hips rocked and I whimpered, clutching at the sheets as waves of pleasure pulsed through me.

"I need you, now," I choked out when the feeling became almost too intense. As much as I wanted more of what he was doing, we didn't have much time.

Keeping his thumb on me, he reached into his bag under the bed, and I heard the distinct crinkle of a foil wrapper. For an excruciating second, his skin left mine, and then the air left my lungs when his lips were on mine, his body pressing me into the bed. He hissed in my ear, and I covered my mouth to stifle a moan as I pulled his hips to mine.

"You are amazing," he said, stilling for a moment, his voice running like a feather down my spine, and in that moment I felt cherished, treasured, adored, and I had never before felt so connected to another person.

As he thrust slowly, I could feel him in each atom of my body, from my marrow to my fingertips. Feeling him deeper and deeper, every fiber of my being hummed with pleasure. My body begged for more of the delicious assault of sensations, and at the same time, release from them.

I hooked my leg around the top of his ass and pushed his shoulders until he turned to his back. Though it was a position I never thought I liked before, with Xavier, I instinctively transitioned into it. We kept eye contact, and the intensity made me feel so vulnerable, and I loved it with him. With the callused tips of his dexterous fingers finding my needy knot of flesh, years of pent up frustration built, begging for liberation. I melted into him as I rocked harder, deeper, and as I cried his name we both found release. Trembling as the aftershocks vibrated again and again, I collapsed onto him. His arms folded around me, and as we lay in silence, his heart pounding against mine.

As my breath returned to me, I realized that I had allowed myself to completely lose control. I dropped the guard I had put up since my night with Miles all those years ago, and facing my fears, I laid myself bare to Xavier in more ways than one. And as vulnerable as I felt, I loved every second of it.

In that moment, that was more important than worrying about the future.

"We're renting a car and driving to Taupo tomorrow. Come with me," I said, returning back to Earth, rolling onto the bed.

He kissed me once more. "Of course."

Though I felt more reassured of his affections, there was something I needed to do. Maybe had I employed better communications skills with Miles in Southeast Asia I would have known his intentions.

"Xavier," I said, sitting up, pulling the sheet to cover my bare chest. "I need to get something clear: I like you."

"I was hoping you did."

I smiled and pinched his arm. "Whatever it is that we are, I need to be the only girl in your life. If this is about sex and you have girls on the bus waiting for you, then that's fine. But you need to tell me, and this ends now."

He sat up, gently clasping my chin between his thumb and forefinger and ghosted his soft lips against mine. "There is only you. Ever since that day in the coconut grove in Goa there has only been you."

Then I lay back, sinking into the mattress, and let him prove again that not only he was a man, he was a man who adored me.

Chapter 29

Date: May 11, 2010
Lake Taupo, New Zealand

Of all the ways to pass the time during love drives, kissing was definitely my favourite. Once Xavier's first roommate returned and got over his shock at finding us in bed together, I took a cab back to my apartment to find Leo and Lana asleep on the couch. After a few hours of sleep, Jade woke me so we could get to the car rental place. When Leo was in the bathroom, I sat down on the couch next to Lana, who made no attempts at covering her nudity.

Stretching her arms above her head she asked, "So what did you tell Xavier in the end?"

"Prove to me that you're a man."

Her eyes flashed. "And?"

I bit my lip and glowed pink at the memory. "He's pretty damn manly." She threw her arms around my neck and giggled. "I invited him to Taupo. I hope you don't mind."

"Of course not, and I don't think Jade will object, either," she said, releasing me from her breasts.

"What if we can't fit both the boys in the car?" Money was tight, and we had no choice but to rent the cheapest car available, which meant it was going to be small. I wanted Xavier there, but I didn't want to stand in the way of Lana and Leo.

She sighed and clasped my hands between hers.

"Honey, I have seen you in such a deep depression I went to bed every night praying that you would be around when I called you the next day. And you know I'm not the praying type."

I never told her that that day almost came once.

"I have never seen you so happy, and so if the car can't fit both of them, I want Xavier to be there instead of Leo. You deserve happiness more than anyone I know."

"Thank you."

Jade's voice began in the hallway and joined her when she rounded the corner into the living room. "So let's get packing and…Dammit, Lana, can you put some clothes on, please?"

"Morning ladies." Leo stood behind Jade in nothing but boxer shorts, giving her another fright.

After breaking the news to Leo that he might not be able to come with us, Lana gave him a kiss to tie them over until the Kiwi Experience bus arrived in Taupo the following day. With our backpacks on our backs, we bid our apartment farewell and took a cab to the car rental place where we were given a beat-up Nissan sedan probably older than we were. Our three backpacks filled the trunk, leaving room for only one more person and their backpack in the backseat.

After picking Xavier up from the hostel we set off, leaving the city behind, driving the empty country roads through vineyards and farm fields full of sheep. We put his backpack behind the driver's seat and cuddled on the seat behind Jade, who sat shotgun. We were drunk on each other, leaving inhibitions and common decency in Wellington. Halfway through the trip, however, the girls broke us up by moving his backpack into the middle of the seat. The separation was delicious torture, and we promised to make up for the kissing we lost in those hours when we arrived in Taupo.

But we would only have two nights together. After Taupo, Jade, Lana and I would head on to Rotorua, and he would board the Kiwi Bus to Auckland where he would fly to Fiji. And I missed him terribly already.

Arriving at dusk, we settled into the Nomads hostel in a six-bed dorm with two guys from Israel. Though we had paid for two beds, Xavier and I nestled into the bottom bunk next to the window together. After eating dinner in a burger joint around the corner with Jade and Lana, the Israeli boys joined our group for a drink at a bar across the street from the hostel.

"Lana, do you have the car keys?" I asked once I had knocked back my glass of water.

She reached into her pocket and held them up. Batting her lashes and feigning ignorance, she asked, "Where are you guys going?"

"To go watch for shooting stars," he said, giving me a cheeky wink. "Completely innocent intentions, of course."

Lana dropped them into my outstretched palm. "Have fun."

***

After leaving the small town, we found a secluded spot on the shores of the nearby lake. In a forest clearing, the moonlight danced on the water as Xavier played his guitar, singing an original song I had never heard before. When his fingers turned their attention to my body, we watched the stars fall until the sun rose.

***

The next morning, I woke up in my hostel bunk, cuddling face to face with Xavier, who was still fast asleep. I nuzzled into his warm chest as the cold morning air that penetrated the windowpane nipped at me. I thought of today's date and a restless energy pulsed through me. I would hear from Awesome Adventures about the competition results any day now. Careful not to wake him, I untangled our limbs and rolled over to face the room. Everyone was still sleeping. I reached to the floor and grabbed Xavier's hoodie and my laptop. Sitting up, I pushed my arms through the sleeves, opened my computer, and refreshed the email browser. There was nothing from Awesome Adventures, but one from my father:

> Hello Darling,
>
> Your mother has advised me that the money in your account will barely last you through the next two weeks. I have taken the liberty of speaking with an old friend who has agreed to give you an internship at his advertising agency, Excel Advertising. You

can start the week you return. I know it's not photography, but you can at least be creative.

You're welcome.

Love,

Dad.

I closed the laptop, hoping it would erase the email and the truth within. Leaning over, I placed my laptop under the bed. I was grateful that my father cared so much to help me out, months ago it would have been exactly what I wanted. It fit with my five-year plan perfectly — creative corporate career with room for growth. But now the thought of corporate life filled me with anxiety.

"Morning, mon étoile," Xavier's voice rasped.

I looked down and met those beautiful eyes peering out from a thicket of sooty lashes, leaned over, and kissed him. He grabbed a fistful of hair and pulled me in closer. We then proceeded to kiss, cuddle, squeeze, repeat. God, I was going to miss those lips.

"Gross guys," I heard Lana's voice before being assaulted by a flying pillow.

I flipped her the bird and kept kissing.

"Alright, you two, it's time to get up," Jade said poking me in the back. "We don't have much time here. Let's get moving."

It was then I realized how much time had passed. With him, it was like the world, and time itself, melted away.

"Can we get Burgerfuel burgers again?" he asked with a wide smile as he sat up.

"Okay sweetie, but I don't think they do kid's meals."

His eyes widened, and he launched a tickle attack. "Perhaps they'll accept your senior citizen's discount."

I squealed like a tied hog and wriggled trying to get my arms free to slap him. Once I accepted that our age difference was nothing but a number, it turned out to be wonderful for banter. As he hovered over me we locked eyes, and the energy shifted. Everything other than him, the room, the sounds of shuffling room-mates, melted away. Nothing else existed but him. And given the dreamy look in those stormy eyes, I knew he was with me, wherever we were. It was a bittersweet moment where we realized that we were hopelessly infatuated with each other, and if only things had been just a little different, this could be every morning.

"How about I make you dinner tonight?" he said kissing my knuckles and pulling me out of bed. Desire pooled in my stomach as I thought of a second meaning for his words.

"I'd like that," I replied patting him on the ass.

After showering together in the large single shower/bathroom across the hallway, we dressed for the day, then grabbed Burgerfuel burgers with Jade and Lana before taking the car to Huka Falls. I fought my smile as Xavier interlaced our fingers as we followed the girls down the parking lot. Lana's pace picked up once we noticed the Kiwi Experience bus. Signs led to a narrow path, and the narrow path led to a pedestrian bridge perched between the forested banks of a canyon fifty feet wide with swirling white and blue torrents. I stopped to frame images of the rolling river narrowing to mist above the waterfall in the distance. As I leaned against the black metal railing on the opposite side of the canyon, a rambunctious group of boys headed our way from the direction of the falls.

"Xavier!" Leo called out as he came bounding over.

"Hey man, long time," Xavier replied with a grin.

Before he could acknowledge Lana, she flew into his arms, wrapping her legs around his waist. They devoured each other's faces while Jade kept her focus on the river, and Xavier and Leo's friends started whooping and clapping. One guy, with unmistakable flame-red hair, gave me a shy wave. I blushed and raised my hand to Xavier's roommate who had walked in on us in Wellington.

"Coming back on the bus with us tomorrow?" Leo asked once he and Lana had pried themselves apart.

He nodded.

I swallowed my disappointment at the word "tomorrow". He was flying off to Fiji for a gig, and I wouldn't see him for another week and a half. And after that I would only have two nights with him. Unless I won the competition. Even a runner-up prize would give me enough money to extend my trip for another two weeks. My funds were vanishing faster than anticipated.

"You, me, our rental car, tonight," Lana said to Leo with her most dominating voice before turning to Jade and me. "Is it okay if I take the car tonight?"

"Sure," Jade and I said in unison.

I was happy that she would get a night alone with Leo.

Xavier squeezed my hand. "Let's go see the falls?"

Ignoring the smirks and stares of his teenaged friends we continued down the path, the gravel crunching with each step. At the end of the canyon the swirling torrents spilled over a thirty-foot drop, feeding into a river below. Blue and white jet boats full of raincoat-clad passengers zipped down the river and performing donuts at the foot of the falls. Following a sign, we pushed through ferns and tree branches through an overgrown dirt path until we reached a hot water beach on the river's edge. Steam rose from the shallow water pooling between the brown sand and rocks. He took a seat on the sand and pulled me to sit between his legs, both facing the river. I was grateful for his warmth now that the sun ducked behind a cloud. Listening to the faint shrill calls of birds, he nuzzled into my neck, and I stroked the hand that rested on my knee.

"At the risk of ruining the moment, I have to ask…" he said before pausing.

His disclaimer unnerved me. "Go on."

"What happened in Goa? You ran from me the morning after the Silent Disco."

I had to tell him the truth, despite my fear that he would see me in a different light. I sucked in a deep breath and turned to face him. "I was engaged at the time."

The memory seemed so far in the past.

"Oh?" he said, surprise flashed on his face.

"Yeah. He was my first relationship, and I loved him. I hated cheaters, and I tried to avoid you, but it was like there was this crazy pull between us. And when I woke up that morning, I thought we slept together, and it was one of my worst fears realized. But since we met in that day in the coconut grove, I think I realized that while I did love him, I wasn't *in* love with him."

"What do you mean?"

I lowered my eyes and fought through the shame.

"I feel things with you that I never felt with him. Things I wanted to feel. Things I needed to feel. And when I felt them with you, I realized that I couldn't marry him."

"Did you tell him what happened?" he said, pulling my chin so that our eyes met.

I chewed on my lip and nodded. "We broke up a couple of weeks afterward."

A montage of expressions flashed in his face.

"Please don't look at me differently," I said, wishing that I could change the past. "I'm still me."

"I don't," he said with a soft kiss on my bottom lip. "At least you found out before you married him."

As I forced a smile, a cold autumn wind swept over us, and I shivered and held him tighter.

"Come on, let's head back and get you warm."

***

Arriving back at the hostel before dusk fell, Lana dropped us off and continued with the car to find Leo. Back upstairs, I popped to the bathroom in the hallway and when I walked through the door, Jade and Xavier were standing in the back corner of the room. They then turned to look at me, both wearing mischievous expressions. What were they up to?

"I'm just heading out for a bit." He kissed me as he walked past me and out the door. It was then that I noticed he was holding a small duffel bag. As he swung the door open, he said, "Be ready for seven."

I looked at Jade. "What's going on?"

"Nothing," she said, although her poker face was crumbling. "Why don't you wear this tonight?"

She pulled out my red dress from Goa and a black cardigan. I didn't fight it. I knew Xavier had put her up to it, and I appreciated her support. When the Israeli boys came back to the room, Jade asked them if they wanted to go out for dinner and drinks.

"*You* are going out tonight?" I asked, failing to mask my disbelief.

"What can I say, I feel like dancing," she said with a wink.

Once Jade and the Israeli boys left me in the room alone, I slipped the dress on and pulled out my makeup kit. I dabbed on a finger full of manuka honey lip balm I had picked up in a gift-shop in Wellington and swept two coats of mascara on my lashes. As I pressed shimmering cherry-coloured blush onto my cheeks, there was a knock at the door. A watery sensation spread down my limbs. My young lover made me feel like a nervous teenager, and I loved it.

Maybe I was absorbing his youthful energy.

I pulled the door open, and Xavier stood in the hallway with a small bouquet of red roses in his hand and a grocery bag at his feet. He wore a clean black long-sleeved t-shirt, dark blue jeans and grey sneakers. His hair was styled and his stubble had been shaped.

A shy smile crept across his face as he exhaled. "You're so beautiful."

"Thanks," I murmured back. It was my turn to be shy.

Extending his hand, I took the bouquet. I brought it to my nose and inhaled the scent.

"Bring them," he said, stepping forward, pressing his lips onto mine. "We'll need them."

After he tossed the duffel bag he had taken with him earlier onto the bed, he took me by the hand, picked up the grocery bag, and, with the other, pulled the door shut. He led me down the narrow hallway and one flight of stairs, through the lobby and into the communal kitchen. Jade sat on a barstool at the corner of the metallic island that stood in the middle of the space between the row of stoves and the dining area.

"It was a fight, but I saved the space you wanted," she said with a wink as she hopped off the stool and walked by.

"Thank you, Jade," he said before turning to me. "Luckily for us, the hostel isn't that full, so I think we'll have the kitchen mostly to ourselves."

He led me to the tall stool and helped me into it. "I picked up pesto tortellini with tomato sauce. I hope you like that."

I nodded as he began to unpack the grocery bag, and sunk into the stool when I realized that this was perhaps the most romantic gesture anyone had ever made for me. "Is there anything I can do?"

Leaning in, he stole another kiss. "No, just be beautiful."

An assortment of knives, utensils and chopping boards were laid out on the corner of the island. On the stove sat a pot with steam billowing through a crack in the lid. When he left me in the room, he must have been prepping the kitchen. All he had to do was turn the water back on for the pasta, chop the onions and red peppers to add to the bottled sauce to cook. When he turned his back to me to open the door of the cupboard, I let my eyes wander down his body.

"See anything you like?"

My cheeks seared when I realized he had caught me staring at his ass. "Just enjoying the view."

His smile darkened as he placed two wine glasses in front of me. Reaching up to the cupboard again, he grabbed a tall glass and took it to the sink. After filling it with water, he dropped the stems of the roses into it and placed it next to me. Picking up a corkscrew from the accessory line up, he uncorked a bottle of red wine he had bought when we stopped in at a vineyard on the drive from Wellington. Pouring two glasses, he set the bottle down and took both glasses, handing one to me.

"To us," he said, raising his glass. "To our missed connections in Goa and Koh Phangan, and to finding each other in New Zealand." I raised my glass and locked eyes with him. Before we clinked, he added, "And Fiji."

I bit my lip as we touched glasses. The girls and I would be heading to Fiji in fourteen days. I wanted to leave with him, but I couldn't afford to change my ticket. Tilting the glass back, I swallowed the wine along with my disappointment.

"Not bad," he said, swirling the wine in the glass. "Perhaps I should have let it air first."

"How do you know so much about wine?" He had flashes of cultured maturity that made me forget his age.

"We French drink wine once we're weaned off our mother's milk," he said, laying the onions and red peppers on the chopping board.

"So you haven't been drinking long then?" A teasing smile tore my face in two.

He shot me a look that told me I was going to be punished for my teasing. I looked forward to it.

As the pasta boiled, he chopped the vegetables and heated the sauce, and he teased me with a torturous game of closing the space between us, then pulling back out of reach without a kiss. Punishment. Even though people milled about in the kitchen, as far as I was aware, we were alone.

"Open your mouth." His eyes glowed with devilish promise as he held a sauce-filled wooden spoon in front of my face.

Two can play at that game.

I grasped his forearm with my right hand, and as I took the spoon in my mouth, I slid my hand down, and then dragged my fingertips along the back of his hand, eye contact unbroken. He sucked in a breath. Placing the spoon down, he cradled my face with both hands, pushed his hips between my legs, and kissed me with such sensual softness that my body begged for more. I pulled at his belt loops and opened my mouth trying to satisfy my need for him. But then he pulled back.

"You're hungry," he said running his thumb over my swelling lips.

"Tease," I hissed.

His lips tilted in amusement. "I can't let the sauce burn," he said as he spun around to check the pots on the stove.

Let the damn sauce burn.

He continued to season the sauce, drained the pasta, cleaning and packing away as he cooked.

"Et, voila! Dinner is served." He gestured over the bowls of tortellini and sauce like a magician who had just pulled a rabbit out of a hat. His face beamed with pride, his unrestrained smile betraying his youthfulness.

He took my hand, steadying me as I slid off the barstool. He hooked his arm in mine and led me towards the dining area. In a very affected French accent, he said, "Right zis way, mademoiselle."

Ever the gentleman, he pulled out a chair for me at a table for four. Once I was seated he made multiple trips setting up the table with the wine and glasses, water, cutlery, serviettes, and the bowls with the pasta. As I inhaled the tomato sauce steam, I realized how hungry I really was.

Making his way back from his final trip to the kitchen, he announced, "And the piece de resistance," as he set the bouquet of roses in the center of the table.

We clinked glasses with a toast and began eating. He was an amazing chef. With only a few ingredients from the store and the seasonings in the communal spice rack, he threw together a dish that was both delicious and comforting. I had longed for a home-cooked meal. I relished every single bite, knowing that a night like this with him was unlikely to happen again. And that simple fact made me appreciate it even more.

"That CD you played in the car last night," I said, blushing as memories of what we did in the car while listening to that CD replayed in my mind. "I like it, who are they?"

He washed his mouthful down with a sip of wine. "An indie trance band called Moksha. After last night, I'll never listen to them in the same way. They're playing a gig in Fiji at the end of the month, I'd love to take you."

We met eyes briefly and said nothing more. I pressed my lips together and forced a weak smile. We both knew there was a big possibility that I would be back home by then.

"Have you heard from the competition yet?" he asked, changing the topic to our only hope of me being able to take him up on his offer.

I shook my head. "Any day now. So what's next for you, after you go back to the real world?"

"I'm going to start university in the fall back in England. My mother and stepfather insist I get a degree, so I'll study music."

I nearly choked on my tortellini with the words, "start university." I had graduated university three years ago. We really were at such different places in our lives. Thankfully, rather than discussing the sad reality of leaving this world behind, we hid in our happy little bubble of denial and the conversation changed directions.

"So you said you did your PADI certification in Australia?" he said, reaching across the table for my hand. "How was that?"

I told him all about Australia, scuba diving on the Great Barrier Reef, sailing the Whitsundays, and camping under the stars in Fraser Island. "Oh, and when I was with my parents in Cairns, we scattered Audrey's ashes in the ocean."

He squeezed my hand tighter and said, "How do you feel about that?"

"Better. I knew it was the right thing to do for the family, and for her." I paused as my words caught in my throat. I missed her terribly, and had to get used to life without any trace of her physical existence. Letting go of how life used to be is never easy, even when it's the right thing to do. Feeling tears pooling in my eyes, I changed topics, "So tell me of your adventure making it to Koh Phangan."

"I was in Sri Lanka at the time, and I found a cheap flight to Bangkok through Kuala Lumpur, but I kept getting bumped off the flights. I spent two days in the airport. I arrived the day before Full Moon and thought I wouldn't make it." He stood and collected the two empty bowls as I stared at him wide-eyed and speechless with disbelief of what he went through to try and find me. "Seeing you was well worth the trouble."

As I rose to my feet, he gently commanded me to let him take care of everything. I sat watching him clear up the table and washing our plates, glasses and cutlery, the sadness of our separation already setting in. Once he was done, he took me by the hand and let me upstairs.

"Wait here," he said as he opened the door.

With a kiss, he stepped behind it, and I stood inspecting a spot of chipping paint on the white walls. It was a perfect night, and he was almost too perfect, and there was something about perfect that scared me. As if it were all too good to be true. After Miles, I feared the flaw that lurked under the veneer of perfection.

The door opened again, and my fears melted when I saw his face. He took my hand and pulled me through the threshold. The room was dark, lit by a single candle. Our little sliver of a bed was strewn with the petals from the rose bouquet. "We'll have the room to ourselves for another two hours."

As I lay naked on the bed, bathed in the flickering glow of the candle, I asked something of him that I was no longer too shy to request. "Speak French to me."

***

The next morning, we awoke again in a tangle of limbs. In respect for our roommates, we had dressed and cleaned up the petals before they came in. I rolled over and grabbed my computer and opened my email browser. There was an unread message from Awesome Adventures waiting for me, the subject title read: Awesome Adventures Travel Photography Competition Results. A watery sensation rippled through me. Part of me wanted to close it and nestle into my bubble with Xavier. But a bigger part of me needed to know what my fate was.

Chapter 30

Date: May 13, 2010

Miss Rodrigues,

Thank you for submitting your work to the annual Awesome Adventures Travel Photography Competition. Unfortunately, your work has not been selected as a winner. We will showcase the winners on our website on May 30th, 2010.

Please like our new Facebook Page to keep updated on future competitions.

Kind regards,

Summer Greene,
C.E.O.
Awesome Adventures

I fought the surge of hot tears pooling in my eyes as I stared at the monitor, re-reading it over and over again hoping the words would magically change.

They didn't.

"Morning," Xavier said, giving me a poke in the ribs. I was in such a state of shock that my body didn't register it. "What's wrong?"

He pushed up to his elbows, and I held the screen in front of him. His eyes scanned back and forth and then found mine. "Oh, mon étoile."

I closed my computer and placed it on the floor as the tears broke free. When I turned to him, he wrapped his arms around me, and I sobbed as quietly as I could into his chest. He stroked my hair, and I listened to the beating of his heart, soaking his shirt through.

Adam had been right, I didn't stand a chance. My father was right, I wasn't being realistic. How could I have been so naively confident to think that I could win? I didn't have the equipment. I didn't have the technical knowledge. I wasn't good enough. I probably never would be good enough to make it professionally. And in two weeks' time, I'd be heading back to Toronto, having wasted my life savings on a pipe dream as a total and utter failure.

By the time I had cried myself numb, our roommates were waking up. As I rolled out of bed, I caught a glimpse of myself in the window's reflection: my face was swollen and red, and the remnants of last night's mascara pooled under my eyes. Just then, Lana burst through the door, hair mussed and glowing. She stopped in her tracks and her face turned serious.

"What happened?" She looked at me and then narrowed her eyes at Xavier.

"I didn't win the competition," I said, trying to hold fresh tears back.

She then closed the space between us, enveloping me in her arms. "Oh honey, I'm so sorry."

Before I knew it, there was another pair of arms on me. Jade had joined the group hug. Once they let me go, I breathed a heavy sigh. I had only hours left with Xavier, and I refused to let this ruin what little time we had.

"How was last night?" I asked Lana, wiping the last tear to escape.

"Fucking fantastic." She glided to her bottom bunk and flopped into it. "Literally."

Her happiness was infectious, and a smile pulled at my lips. Even though it was just a whisper of one, it was more than I thought I would get that morning. I walked over to Jade, who was folding clothes on her bottom bunk, getting ready for our departure. "Thanks for last night."

"Of course," she said back.

"How was your night?" I fought the guilt that she had gone out even though she hated it.

Jade poked the tanned hand hanging from the top bunk. "We painted the town red, didn't we?"

Her question was answered by the guttural groan of one of our Israeli roommates who had way too much to drink the night before.

"What time are we leaving?" I wanted so badly to suggest that we stay another day, but Jade wanted to get moving. I had asked too much of her already.

"After lunch," she said stuffing the folded clothes in her backpack. "Hear that, Lana?"

"Uhhh huhhhh," Lana hummed back with a big smile on her face, no doubt playing back the montage of last night's antics with Leo.

Once showered and dressed, Xavier and I walked to the natural hot spring about twenty minutes away. After he helped me into the boiling water of the pool next to the river, we slowly sank into it, letting our skin adjust to the heat. I wrapped myself around him, and we barely spoke as he held me, the word *failure* still ringing in my head.

"I'm going to miss you so much," I told him, finally breaking the silence.

"I miss you already," he said.

I held him tighter, and my head spun at the speed and strength of how attached we had become to each other. We barely knew each other, and he flew thousands of miles, putting himself through such an ordeal to find me. And as I was about to say goodbye to him, it felt as if we had been lovers for years, not days. But there was something that didn't sit right. There was nothing special about me. I was your average, run of the mill, idealistic, twenty-something of no exceptional beauty or talent. The email I received that morning drove the latter point home.

So what was it that he saw in me?

Once our fingers began to prune we walked back to the hostel and I packed up my stuff. As he loaded my backpack into the trunk, and when Lana took the seat behind the wheel with Jade sitting shotgun, I decided to ask, "Why do you like me so much?"

Before he answered, he held my face and gave me the most devastating kiss of my life.

"You're amazing. You're strong and vulnerable. You have passion in your life."

I knew he meant my photography and without thinking, I shook my head.

"Don't measure your worth based on some competition. Harper, you inspire me. When we met, I could barely get a word out. You saw my writing, it was terrible. But the lyrics I'm writing now…You have to read them."

And there was the kicker. I stepped back as the wind left my lungs.

"You're using me for inspiration?"

First my job, then Miles, and now him?

"No." He reached for my hands, but I pulled them out of reach and gripped the handle of the back door. "Harper, no, that's not what I mean."

I slid into the backseat and slammed the door shut. I knew it was too good to be true. Xavier knocked on the glass.

"Don't you see, you're my muse?" he said with both hands splayed against the window.

It wasn't that he cared so deeply for me — it was what I could do for him. Or more specifically, what I could do for his music. And the sex was the icing on the cake. After Miles, I refused to let anyone else use me without my consent.

I met eyes with Lana in the rear-view mirror. "Drive," I ordered, keeping my eyes straight ahead. I had to get out of there. I had to get away from him.

"Harper, are you sure you want to —"

Before she could finish I repeated my command. "Drive…please."

***

Date: May 14, 2010

Rotorua, New Zealand

I pulled the neck of my shirt over my nose to block out the sulphur smell and raised my camera. Peering through the viewfinder, I tried to line up a shot of the bubbling volcanic mud pool. We had passed into Hell's Gate that morning, but I felt as if I had been in hell since we left Taupo the day before. After leaving Xavier's figure shrinking into the distance, I told the girls what he said, and when they both began playing devils' advocate I asked to not talk about it. I didn't want to think about him, or how we left things. Everything had been so perfect up until the revelation. I hoped that I could distract myself from thinking about Xavier by throwing myself into my photography, but after losing the competition, I felt like what was the point of it? I was going home in two weeks and would have to save my money just to get back on my own two feet again. It would be years before I could save enough to travel out of Ontario again. I know I could drive the area, but how could I call myself a travel photographer if my book was full of images from home?

"Excuse me," a voice woke me from my day-dreams. I looked up from the bubbling mud to see a man and a woman. "Would you mind taking a photograph of us, please? We're on our honeymoon."

I nodded and lowered my camera so it was hanging around my neck. I took the small silver Canon point-and-shoot from him and stepped back to frame them with the blue sky, and green hills on either side in the distance. They stood in front of the wooden railing with a large rust-coloured pond behind them. As the lens focused, he put his arm around her and pulled her closer. As I pressed the shutter, a plume of acidic water shot from the pond, startling them. I kept snapping as they jumped and screamed and then fell into each other laughing. They repositioned, and we got the posed shot. Handing the camera back to him, he took a moment to flick through the playback.

"These are great," he said showing the comical series of shots to me.

"Wait, scroll back," his wife said. He skipped back three shots, and she said, "That one. That's the one."

It was a moment of them, looking at each other with a spark in their eyes reserved for lovers.

"These are better than our wedding photos," he said. "You could do this for a living."

I laughed and replied, "Maybe one day," before saying goodbye.

That image remained burned in my memory and reminded me of why I loved photography. And reminded me that even though I didn't win the competition, I still had a voice. And there were options in the photography world other than travel photography.

Feeling ever so slightly better, I decided that I had to make the most of what I could while I was still out of the country. I had gained nearly a thousand followers on my Facebook page and received hits from around the world on my Flickr and blog, so I felt I needed to keep it going. And despite my disappointment, I knew I wouldn't feel this way forever. That was the thing about bad times, as I learned with my battle with grief and depression: they're like a tunnel, and you have to keep putting one foot in front of the other, trudging through the darkness with the faith that there is a light out there somewhere, and one day, with some work, you'll come out on the other side stronger, more mature, having learned lessons to take forward for when you face the next tunnel.

I had to honour my feelings while at the same time practicing gratitude. Each night in Mumbai, hundreds of thousands of homeless beggars find their beds on the cold concrete of the city sidewalks — I, at least had a home to return to. And a loving one at that. In Cambodia, landmine victims make the most they can of their lives after losing limbs, feeling lucky to have survived at all — and I had my health and all limbs intact. And with each happy ending joke made, there is a prostitute in Thailand who has to give sexual favours just to feed herself. I had options and the world's oldest profession would never be one of them.

I knew I always had so much to be grateful for, but after this experience, for which I was also grateful, my eyes were opened to the potential fates I could have been born into. Though, as I had learned in grief counseling, we are all allowed to experience our emotions as they come and we can't shame ourselves, or others, with the knowledge that others have it worse, but as I keep walking through this tunnel, their stories remind me that the light is out there. And when I acknowledged it, I could see a pin-prick of light in the distance, and they reminded me to keep walking, inspired by the strength of each person I met in a less fortunate situation who held happiness in their hearts. If they could do it, I could, too.

***

Date: May 16, 2010
Waitomo, New Zealand

After two days in Rotorua, Jade took the wheel and with Lana riding shotgun we headed west to Waitomo to see the glowworm caves.

"What's next for you guys after this?" I asked, trying to ignore the handprint on the window that I had left on my night with Xavier.

"I think I'm going to work as a yoga instructor back home," Jade said, keeping her eyes on the road ahead. Her tone then turned serious. "I have something to tell you guys."

"Uh huh…"

"My name is Jade Robinson, and I am a hippy."

Lana and I gasped in mock horror.

"I had my suspicions," Lana said, rubbing her shoulder. "How do you feel about this revelation?"

Jade swatted her hand away. "I always knew, but I just didn't want to be like my parents, they're just so weird. But I can be a different kind of hippy, a mainstream one."

It turned out that once Jade stopped trying to fight who she was, she found what she was looking for: herself.

"Oh," she added, "I'm going to quit smoking too."

Lana and I cheered and clapped.

"Well," Lana said turning around to look back at me, "I think I'm going to go back and finish school. I'm going to get a business degree."

"That's great!" I reached out for a high five.

"Yah, maybe I'll go for my MBA afterwards; I hear debt's the new black," she deadpanned.

Turns out the failed yogawear business led Lana to realize that she had a keen mind for business. I was so happy that they both had futures that they were excited about. Maybe my failure was directing me to something better, too.

***

After being strapped into rock-climbing harnesses and rubber boots, Jade, Lana, and I took turns abseiling on a rope and pulley system into a dark gorge. Trudging through freezing the freezing water of an underground stream, we followed our guide into a network of caverns. Thousands of iridescent glowing strands hung from the ceiling, and though we were deep under the earth's surface, it looked as if we were standing under a brilliant night sky. I couldn't fight how romantic it felt. And when my toes were numb, frozen from the cave water, I wished someone were there to rub them and warm them. There was one person I could think of, but I was still too mad to talk to him. And the more I thought of him, the angrier I was that I missed him.

***

Date: May 18, 2010

Bay of Islands, New Zealand

I had avoided the Internet since leaving Taupo and the morning after checking into our hostel in the Bay of Islands, I decided to give in and see what, if any, messages were waiting for me. Part of me wished that Xavier would forget about me and find someone else to be his muse, but the other part hoped that there would be a message from him. I couldn't understand why I cared for him so much and hated him at the same time. I hated most that I couldn't just get a grip on my feelings and feel one way about him.

Nerves overcame me, and instead of checking Facebook first, I looked at a celebrity gossip site, and then my email. I had three unread emails from Meghan, my former boss's assistant, the subject title read "job opportunity." I pressed my face into my hands. I would have to accept the reality that I would have to go home and rejoin the real world. But I left the emails unread, deciding to deal with the real world when I was back in it.

I sucked in a breath when I saw the Facebook notifications blinking with two messages from Xavier Northam:

> May 14
> *The taste of your lips sent me high,*
> *But this addict is now in withdrawal,*
> *The further you run, the closer I need to be,*
> *Each moment we spent I wish were an eternity.*
>
> May 15
> *If only for a second, you were in my arms,*

I could hold you close and inhale your scent,
I'd take you to ecstasy and kiss your skin,
Committing sins I would never repent.

These were the lyrics he was talking about. I checked the time and closed the browser without responding. I didn't know how to respond; I could barely string together an email let alone a response to poetry. I didn't know what to say. So many emotions flooded my mind. I was scared, still afraid of being hurt, scared of doing something that hurt him, but mostly afraid of the heartbreak of having to walk away from him after getting even more attached to him in Fiji. If I missed him now, I couldn't imagine how the finality would feel to leave him in Fiji.

***

The next morning, we booked a tour to the northernmost tip of New Zealand, Cape Reinga, and Ninety-Mile Beach. A bus picked us up from the hostel, and we drove through the warm northern countryside next to the meandering cost, the cobalt blue bay dotted with emerald green islands to the beach that stretched past the horizon and mountainous sand dunes. As we drove, Xavier's lyrics rang in my consciousness. I could practically see his perfect mouth as he sung it, and hear his raspy growl, and feel his voice shaking the innermost parts of me.

After dinner that evening I opened my laptop again to read the poems, and another message was waiting:

May 19
You have my heart

You've seen my soul
I've shared your bed but I need more,
My Beautiful Runaway, please stay.

And the next day when I was uploading photos to my blog after spending the afternoon on a boat bay spotting wild dolphins in the bay another message notification popped up:

May 20
My sails are full, my soul is empty,
A void I never knew was there
If you could stand for just a moment,
I could show you my soul laid bare.

***

Date: May 20, 2010
Auckland, New Zealand

I hadn't heard from Xavier since leaving from Bay of Islands and arriving in Auckland, our final destination in New Zealand. As we wandered the city streets, stocking up with freshly baked chocolate chip cookies from Mrs. Higgins Cookies, and staring across the city towards the green hills and blue water bay on the horizon, I worried that Xavier had given up on me. I hadn't responded to a single message, and he would have been forgiven to think I had given up on him.

After packing up on the day we were due to leave for Fiji, I checked my messages and my core melted as Xavier finished the song:

May 22
You may be carried by the wind,
But I'd cross oceans and deserts,
Following you to the Earth's end,
Its four corners can't contain my love within.

You have my heart,
You've seen my soul,
I've shared your bed, but I need more,
My Beautiful Runaway, please stay.

Guilt twisted as I truly realized the extent of my overreaction in Taupo. Xavier was nothing like Miles, who used me to comfort his solitude. Xavier was nothing like my boss who used me for my ideas. The lyrics Xavier wrote *were* about his feelings for me. He truly did care about me in spite of what a total nutjob I had behaved towards him. I was embarrassed by how I had acted, and I was scared that he might wake up and not want me anymore, favouring someone more level headed instead. Certainly, if I was his friend, I'd tell him to forget about that crazy older girl who flips between hot and cold more times than a Canadian summer. And then it hit me...

Wait, did he say, "love"?

I reread the stanza, and then stared at the word. Was this love in the general sense like I'd tell the girls I loved them? Or was this Love with a capital L. Was he *in* love with me?

There was a final message: Please check your email.

I felt lightheaded and struggled to control my fingers as I pulled up a new browser and logged into the email account listed on my Facebook profile. The email contained an audio file attachment. Pulling the Skype headphones that were plugged into the tower onto my ears, I double-clicked on it. Windows Media Player opened, and Xavier's voice rumbled through the headphones:

> *Harper, I wanted to tell you in person, but this is the best I can do. You inspire me, for who you are, for the reasons I told you back in Taupo: you're passionate and vulnerable and strong. You inspire me to do better. But what inspires my writing is what I feel for you. My love for you is what smashed my writer's block. I know we barely know each other, but I fell for you the moment I laid eyes on you. We live a lifestyle where we have to make quick decisions and follow our instincts. I can't explain it, but something, like a voice, kept telling me to go after you. And each moment we spent together, I fell deeper and deeper for you. We come from different worlds, and we'll only have two nights together, but I'm not ready to let you go. The pain of watching you leave me at the end of those two nights rips my heart out, but there is no greater pain than regret. And I would regret it forever if I didn't see you one last time. Please, please, come to Fiji. I'll be on Malolo Island. Bure 5.*
>
> *Je t'aime, mon* étoile.

I leaned back in the chair with my eyes wide as the realization washed over me.

Oh my God. He is in love with me.

Goa flashed in my mind. When we met, he asked me if I had ever felt "mad and passionate and all-consuming" love. That's what he needed to feel to break through his writer's block. That's what inspired him to write. That's what inspired him to keep seeking me out.

This is crazy.

It was crazy of him to fly from Sri Lanka to Koh Phangan on the hopes that he might find me at the Full Moon Party. It was crazy to pull him into a bathroom stall, and then push him away because I was scared, then pull him in again because I couldn't fight the attraction, and then yet again push him away because I was afraid. Maybe the reason why I've been acting so crazy towards him is that I'm afraid that I'm in love with him, too. I fear most losing control, and what is more out of control than being in love?

Oh my God. I'm in love with him.

I had to find him. I had to see him.

This was the kind of love I had waited for my entire life, and it made no sense whatsoever. He was the total opposite of Adam. My usual type was the older dependable guy who made me think of nesting and baby names, but he was a way too young tattooed musician. We had no future, but even if I could only live it for two days it was more than what some people get in a lifetime. And I knew I would regret it forever if I didn't go after him.

Chapter 31

I opened the message to respond to him, but as I placed my fingers on the keyboard, Jade rushed into the room.

"Harper, we have to go now."

"Can I have a few minutes?"

She shook her head. "We need to get the car back to the rental place and deal with that before we get on our flight."

I checked the clock. More time had slipped away from me than I realized. Deciding to message when we landed in Nadi, I logged off Facebook and followed Jade down the hallway into our dorm room. In the back corner, Lana was furiously stuffing the last of her belongings in her backpack. I helped Jade hoist her overflowing backpack on her back, and she helped me with mine. Then we dashed down the hallway, tossed our key cards on the reception desk, descended one floor in the elevator, and crossed the street to the three-story parking lot. Once our bags were stuffed in the trunk, Jade took the wheel, I slid into shotgun, and Lana hopped in the backseat.

"Alright, New Zealand, thanks for the memories," Jade said turning the key in the ignition.

But instead of the engine humming to life as it usually did, the car made a sound like a retching puppy. She turned the ignition off and on five times, each time the engine sounded sicker and sicker.

"What's wrong?"

"I don't know, the engine isn't turning over," she said, trying one more time. "Dammit, Universe"

"Sounds like the battery is dead," Lana said pulling herself forward between the front car seats so her face was between ours.

"When you guys took the car, did you leave the light or stereo on for a long period of time?" Jade asked turning to face Lana and me.

Lana bit her lip and kept her eyes forward. "Define long period of time."

"Lana," Jade said in a scary motherly tone.

"She's asking for a friend." I glanced at Lana, who was trying to conceal a smirk. Xavier and I played that Moksha CD on our night by the lake, so I wasn't going to let her take all the blame.

"What can we do?" Lana asked. "Can we call the rental place to come get the car?"

I opened the glove compartment, pulled out the information booklet the rental place had given us, and scanned it. "The only office open at this time is at the airport, and this says that for engine problems we need to call Triple-A."

Jade gripped the steering wheel and kept her eyes forward. Checking the time, I forced myself not to panic, so I pinched the bridge of my nose and then tried to mimic her zen-like ways.

"I'll go back to the hostel," Lana said, pushing herself back and sliding towards the door.

Needing to move, needing to feel as if something was getting done, I decided to go with her. Jade stayed on the lookout for someone in the parking lot to help us jump the car. We ran back to the hostel lobby, and the receptionist found the number for Triple-A in the phonebook for us. I shifted my weight from foot to foot as I watched Lana make the call. After waiting on hold for what felt like an eternity, she finally spoke into the receiver, explaining the problem and our location.

"Thanks for your help," she said, her eyes meeting mine. Though her tone was polite and upbeat, there was something about the unusually large size of her eyes that made me nervous. "If there is any way he can be quicker, that would be much appreciated as we are trying to catch a flight tonight."

She then hung up and turned to me. "So there's good news and bad news. The good news is someone is on the way. The bad news is there is only one person working the city tonight, and there are a bunch of people in the line in front of us. They can't give us a precise time. They estimated it could be within two hours, could be more."

"Two hours," I said, seeing my time with Xavier vanish. It was nearly five-thirty and we had to be at the airport at seven if we had any hope of catching the flight. It would take over a half hour alone to get there, and we would have to find a gas station along the way to fill the tank. Not to mention dealing with the paperwork at the rental place.

Running back across the street, we relayed the message to Jade. She looked at us and said, "What do you want to do?"

Lana and I both had boys waiting for us in Fiji. If we missed the flight tonight, we would not have enough time to get to Malolo to see them.

"Let's just wait for the Triple-A guy, the rental place will have to understand that we're getting it back. I doubt it's the first time this piece of junk has broken down," Lana said, looking at me to see if I agreed.

I looked at my watch. We just needed to make it to the airline check-in counter an hour before it closed to make the flight. Even if the car were to miraculously start working again, time would be tight. "Okay, let's go wait on the road and look out for him."

Jade stayed behind with her yoga teacher's course book on the lookout for anyone who could give us a jump, and Lana and I made our way down to the street to make sure the Triple-A guy found us. The street was quiet with barely any traffic. A taxi with its light on sped down the street, and I toyed with the fantasy of hailing it down, but the fear of traveling alone wouldn't let me. The three-story car park stood behind us, and a five-story office building with few lighted windows stood ahead of us. To the west, the halo of the setting sun glowed orange against the darkening sky.

"Have you spoken to Xavier?" Lana asked, leaning against a lamppost.

"He sent me the lyrics he was talking about." I looked down and kicked at a wad of gum. "He said he loved me."

"Well, that was obvious. And how do you feel about that?"

"Scared." I looked up and met her gaze. "Because I think I'm in love with him."

She squealed and threw her arms around me. I sighed and hugged her back.

"We can't have a future. This will all come to an end in a few days, for good."

"Honey, don't worry about the future, all that exists is the present."

"Wow, Jade's yogi-ness has really rubbed off on you."

She gave me a soft punch in the arm, "I rarely think about the future because you know what I've learned? After shit went down at the station, and I thought my life was over, things worked out well with getting interviews and even a book offer. And even though my broadcasting days are over, I'm excited for what's next, but I'm not trying to get attached to a future, or even think that far ahead. Everything always works out eventually, so don't let the fear of the future rob you of a wonderful present."

"You and Jade should really consider getting back in the hippy business together, tank-tops with motivational slogans," I teased.

She punched me in the arm again. "Just think about what I said. Leaving him at the end of those two days will suck, but the sadness will fade, and you'll have amazing memories to giggle at when you're old and grey."

My hopes rose with each car that turned onto the street, only to fall when I recognized it as anything other than a Triple-A truck. Though we played round after round of Animal-Vegetable-Mineral to pass the time, anxiety pulsed as I checked my watch every two minutes. It was past six-thirty and there was no sign of Triple-A, and Jade hadn't called down with good news about getting a jump.

"If we don't leave in ten minutes, we'll miss the flight," I said, fighting the tightening feeling in my chest.

As I said that a cab turned onto the road, it's orange light beaming from the roof.

"Take the cab," Lana said.

"What about you and Jade?"

"We'll just make the flight tomorrow and stay on the mainland."

"What about Leo?"

"Harper, I like Leo, but I don't love him. I won't regret not being able to see him, but I will regret it if you don't go to see Xavier."

I shook my head as my throat felt as if it were closing in on itself. "I can't go alone."

"Why not."

"I'm scared."

She raised her hands and said, "Consider the hot sex you'd be giving up."

The cab was a hundred feet away and approaching quickly. I could make the flight; all I had to do was raise my hand and flag it down. What was I afraid of? I had traveled from Cairns to Arlie Beach by myself, but I was already familiar with Australia and had hostels pre-booked. I had been prepared to fly to Singapore by myself, but that was just an idea, an abstract and distant possibility. Even though this trip raised my confidence, the memory of Audrey's murder still haunted me. Through the past few months, I had my girls, we had safety in numbers, and so the thought of arriving in an unfamiliar country by myself in the dead of night with nowhere to stay scared the shit out of me. I couldn't go alone. Going alone wasn't part of the plan. And I couldn't help but feel like if I went alone, I would be flaunting Audrey's death. How could I survive, and she didn't get the chance to?

The taxi hit the fifty-foot mark.

And then a voice rang in my head, clear as day. "I'm with you always." As a warm breeze caressed my face, a strange sensation took hold, just as it did in the desert in Pushkar, and I felt as if someone was holding my hand.

An image flashed in my vision of Xavier and me laying in the shade of a palm tree on a white sand beach, with the warmth of joy and love washing over me like the rising tide. It was what I fantasized about each time I dove into *Tahitian Heat* and stared at those paradisiac posters on the walls of my old apartment.

It was a reality waiting for me on the other side of fear.

Just before the taxi passed us, as if I had stepped out my body, I raised my hand and called the taxi to stop.

***

Date: May 22, 2010
Nadi, Fiji

The plane landed on the Fijian capital airport runway with a thud, and as I looked out of the window, unable to see past the glow of the wing lights, I wished I had the girls at my side. The airport was small and dusty, and, save for the handful of passengers on my flight, empty. We hadn't booked a hotel for the night, and I had no idea where to go or what to do, but thankfully a group of Australian girls let me tag along with them. We shared a minivan taxi and after driving through sandy roads flanked by palm trees and broken lampposts, more buildings began to appear. The main street ran a little longer than a Toronto city block, and most of the buildings stood only two stories tall. The windows on the second story were covered in bars, and metal roll-down shutters were pulled over the storefronts on the ground floor. Not a single soul walked the dark streets.

The taxi dropped us off in front of the only building with light glowing from its barred windows. The skeleton staff of the guesthouse greeted us, and after the five Aussies had checked in, I paid for a room and booked my ferry ticket to Malolo for the following morning. My plan to message Xavier was derailed when I was informed that the Internet had stopped working that afternoon, and I had to hold out hope and believe that I wasn't about to walk into a very awkward moment. With time to think on the flight, I knew I would regret not going, and that regret would be worse than any heartbreak. If he had moved on, my heart and ego would heal with time, and I'd look back on him with rosy retrospection as I did Miles and commend myself for my courage for going after him alone. But regret remains and festers, kind of like herpes of the soul.

The manager then showed me to my room, and I was left alone for the night. The room was claustrophobically small but clean enough, with white tiles worn from age and walls stained by dripping rust water from the air conditioner. Pushed against the back wall stood a double bed with a faded floral comforter, flanked by two bedside tables. Thankfully it had an ensuite bathroom, so I didn't have to leave the room. Fearing intruders, I dead-bolted the door and pushed my heavy backpack against it, barricading myself in.

After barely sleeping a wink that night, both for fear of being murdered in the night and of facing possible heartbreak the following day if I survived, I scarfed down my complimentary toast and butter and coffee and then made my way to the ferry. The manager arranged for a taxi to pick me up, and after driving out of the tiny capital city, and drop me off at the threshold of a beach. The driver instructed me to wait on the beach for the ferry. I took my bags and made my way to the nearest empty beach lounger. Facing the vivid turquoise ocean, the white sand stretched into the horizon on either side of me. Lining the beach stood a string of guesthouses and hostels, and I took note of the name of the one closest to me. If the girls stayed there, I could find them easily when I returned to the mainland.

It turned out that the "ferry" was just some guy's boat, no larger than thirty feet in length, clearly used for fishing in between taking passengers between the Yasawa Islands. With my heart in my throat, I boarded the vessel and sat on the roof with ten other people, all headed to various islands in the archipelago. We left the main island and for half an hour we skipped over the water between islets and sandbars, which was such a stunning shade of turquoise it almost glowed, until we approached an island with a long wooden pier extending into the water.

A group of six Fijians stood on the end of the pier wearing grass skirts and floral shirts, three with full-sized guitars, one playing a ukulele, and the others clapped as they sang, welcoming us to Malolo. The island was small and densely forested, surrounded by rocky coastline and reefs in the shallows. As each passenger stepped onto the pier, we were draped with a flower lei and handed a purple-pink cocktail with a skewer of fruit poking out from the ice. I was so nervous I knocked my drink back faster than I could say, "Bula!"

Worried my legs were going to give out on me as I walked the pier, I stopped to steady myself at the threshold of the sandy path that led to the reception area. The path took me past a rectangular pool, filled with guys and girls splashing about. As I made my way to the reception desk, I scanned each face, not recognizing a single one. To the right of the reception was an open-air dining hall that faced the ocean, and to the right of that, a common area, with ping-pong tables and hammocks, the roof held up by wooden columns.

Like the pool, it was swarming with backpackers, but none were Xavier.

"Excuse me, where is Bure Five?" I asked the woman who stood behind the reception desk.

She extended a long finger and pointed back towards where I had come, "On the other side of the pier."

After thanking her, I retraced my steps and found bure one, then two, and so forth. At the end of the line of bures, and past a hammock suspended between two palm trees, sitting on the edge of the coastal rocks, I found number five. Like the others, it was a hut with cream-coloured walls made from concrete and its roof made from palm thatching. Anxiety knifed at me, and I began to see spots as I walked to the flower-lined path to the door, and I reminded myself to breathe. The sliding glass door was open, and sheer curtains billowed into the hut. I took a moment to collect and calm myself and knocked on the glass three times.

No answer.

I popped my head through the open glass door and held back the curtain. The interior was spacious. A couch, love seat, and glass coffee table stood in the corner to my left, and along the right wall ran a counter with a sink, stove, and fridge. A closed door broke the wall opposite me, and I assumed the bedroom was beyond it. Before I knew it, I was padding across the white tile into the room.

Then, the clicking of the bedroom door startled me. I froze in place, my eyes glued to the door, holding both fear and hope in equal measure. The door swung open, and there he stood, raven-haired, skin washed bronze from the sun, eyes piercing, wearing nothing but a white towel hanging dangerously low at his hips.

His brow knitted, and his lips curled. "You came?"

I nodded, then straightened my back. "Am I interrupting something? I mean, are you here with someone else?"

He closed the gap between us and took the day-pack that hung from my chest, gently placing it on the floor. Cupping my face in his hands, he tilted my head up, so my eyes met his. "As I've said before, there is no one else."

"I love you," I blurted out without thinking. His eyes softened, and his lips parted. "And I'm sorry. I'm so sorry for how I've —"

Before I could finish my sentence, his lips claimed mine.

***

For two days we explored the island, and by night each other, professing our love with urgent whispers in the dark. At the end of each day as the sun tucked itself into the horizon, I sat with Leo, who was disappointed that he would not see Lana, and we watched Xavier perform his set. He sang the songs he had written, the songs that his affections for me inspired, always ending it with that rendition of "Sex on Fire." And on our last night, we lay in a hammock bathed in starlight as I listened to the waves crash and his heart beat.

***

We barely spoke on my last morning in Malolo. Up until then, we spent each moment basking in the denial that I had to go home. After drying off from our last shower, we dressed, and he took me by the hand through the sliding glass doors saying, "I want to show you something."

I shielded my eyes from the glare of the sun, and he led me through the bushes behind the bure and to the threshold of the resort property. Reaching into his board short pockets, he pulled out a small padlock and unlocked it.

"In Paris there is a bridge known as the Love Lock Bridge. Lovers from around the world write their names on the locks and secure them to the bridge with the intention that no matter what happens to them, what they shared still exists somewhere."

He pulled a permanent marker out from his pocket and wrote our initials on the lock, drawing a heart around them. Then he attached it to the chicken wire fence and locked it. Tears pricked my eyes as I bit back the thoughts of how unfair it was to finally feel this way, and have it end so quickly.

"Hold out your wrist," he said.

Not sure which one he meant, I held them both out. He took the clasp of the bracelet he had given me in Goa between his fingers and released it. From his pocket, he pulled out, and held up, a small key and strung it on the bracelet. With a barely audible *clink*, it hit the Ohm charm. He then closed the clasp around my wrist, and I felt hot tears pooling in my eyes.

"What we shared will always be," he said taking out a length of string and stringing an identical key on it, tying it around his neck.

When he dropped his hands, I reached up, taking a fistful of his hair and pulled his lips to mine, wishing the moment could last forever. As he sucked on my bottom lip, I lost control of my tears.

He enveloped me in his arms and held me steady as I cried into his chest. "There's no way you can stay?"

I shook my head and looked up. "If there were a way, I would not be getting on that plane tonight. I can't change my flights, I have no more money left."

Regret set in as I thought of the unnecessary expenses I had made along the way — the SCUBA certification, the dress for my date with Miles, the sailing and camping excursions, bribing the cops in Pushkar, and I still had to pay the girls back for Triple-A and the cost of them having to buy new plane tickets. Had I been a little smarter with spending I could have stayed an extra week or so. I was just so sure that I would walk away with the prize from the Awesome Adventures competition. How stupid could I have been?

"I wish I had the money so you could stay with me," he said, squeezing me tighter. "The resort is paying me in accommodation and food and I only have enough savings to get myself to my next paying gig."

I looked up at him and forced a smile, "C'est la vie." As he let me go, I glanced at my watch. "The ferry arrives any minute."

He pressed his fingers to his eyes for a moment, then interlaced his fingers with mine and led me back towards the bure. He carried my backpack to the pier while I took my daypack. As we stepped onto the wooden paneling, the ferry was docking, the welcome band played, and once my backpack was secured on the boat we kissed until the captain threatened to leave me behind.

"Please don't forget me," I said as I looked up at him from the bow.

"I never could," he said with a slight smile.

The engine sputtered, and we kept eye contact until I could no longer make out the features of his face. I kept my gaze fixed on his body as he shrank to a speck in the distance, clasping the key that hung around my wrist, and kept staring long after the island had disappeared, my heart tearing with each passing moment.

I barely noticed when the boat pushed itself upon the beach on the mainland. Once my feet touched the sand, reality set in, and my heart shattered.

I took my bags and trudged up the beach towards the guesthouse, finding Jade and Lana on a row of beach chairs. When they saw me, they placed their cocktails on the small plastic tables between them and ran over. Jade took my daypack and paused, resting her hands on my shoulders. She pressed her lips together, sighed, and pulled me in for a hug. When she released me, Lana swung her arms around my neck. I then followed them to the chairs.

"How was it?" Jade asked as she lay back.

I inhaled a deep breath and tried to put together the words as they caught in my throat. "It was perfect."

But as the words came out, so did a stream of tears.

Pressing my hands into my face I repeated to myself: I am grateful for these past months, I am grateful for the support of my family, I am grateful for the most wonderful friends I could ever ask for, and I am grateful that you brought Xavier into my life even though it hurts like hell to leave him.

"So what's next for you?" Lana asked.

I paused and stared off across the sea. "Move back in with my parents and start all over again. My dad lined me up with an internship ad his friend's advertising agency." At first, I felt a pang of rage as my bubble of denial popped, but I thought of that speck of light at the end of the tunnel. It was out there somewhere. "I'm not going to give up on my photography. I'm going to keep learning, keep practicing. Maybe one day I can branch out on my own."

"Good for you," Lana said, and Jade nodded in agreement. "Don't give up on your dreams, this was your first stab at it and no one makes it on their first try."

She was right. Just because I had failed once didn't mean I would never succeed.

All is well.

We still had about twenty minutes before the taxi was due to pick us up, so to keep my mind off of the crushing disappointment of leaving, I took my daypack to the guesthouse patio bar and asked if they had Wi-Fi. After being given the password, I sat on a barstool with a fresh bottle of water and pulled out my computer. After checking my Facebook, unable to re-read Xavier's messages, I scanned the news, and then a celebrity gossip site before checking my email. The email from my former work colleague, Meghan, was still waiting for me. I was heading back to the real world, and so I decided that it was best to get started on reintegrating into it as soon as I could. Four more unread emails were waiting for me. Curiously, one was sent by Rob and Jack from Madcap Travels. Ignoring the others, I clicked it open.

Hello Harper,

It's Rob and Jack from Madcap Travels. Your former colleague gave us your email, we hope you don't mind. We were appalled to hear about what happened with your being let go, especially since we informed your boss that we preferred your vision for our marketing campaign and felt that you were the best candidate for the job. We cancelled our contract with your former employer shortly after.

A few weeks ago, we stumbled across your blog and Facebook page and saw that you were not all talk, you implemented and executed the vision you presented to us, and to say we were impressed is an understatement. We would like to hire you to be a content creator for the site and will pay you upfront for the work you have already done with the understanding that your images and blog posts will be moved to our platform. We would also like you to run our social media pages as you travel and will pay you accordingly.

If you are interested, we would like to get started as soon as possible, and once you name your price, we can move forward with purchasing your existing work and transferring you the money.

Please advise if you are interested — we really hope you are!

Kind regards,
Rob & Jack
Madcap Travels

I stared at the screen with my mouth on the table and smacked myself for not opening Meghan's email when I had seen it a week ago. Now I had two options, and one offered me exactly what I had wanted. My dad's offer would put my original five-year plan back on track. It was a great opportunity, a stable job, and I could get back in the dating scene, and so the prospect of having a family in the next two years wasn't out of reach. But with Rob and Jack's offer, I could continue my vision, keep traveling for the summer, but I had no idea what would happen at the end when Xavier has to return home. Love waited for me a ferry ride away, but I knew I couldn't keep him forever. My dad's offer was a safe one, and I'd be taking a big gamble on the unknown if I took Rob & Jack's.

"Harper," Jade's voice brought me back to Earth. I looked up, and she and Lana stood on the threshold of the beach and patio, backpacks and daypacks secured to them. "The taxi is here. It's time to go."

I turned back to my computer and hit reply.

Chapter 32

With tears and smiles, I kissed the girls a bittersweet goodbye. I loved them as if they were my sisters and mourned the end of our adventure. Standing and waving in the street until their taxi disappeared into a cloud of dust, I felt a renewed sense of independence. Though nervous stepping into an unknown future, I decided to accept life as it came. I had spent so much time, effort, and anxiety rigidly planning my life, and even the best plans can, and will, go awry. I also realized that I had misinterpreted goal setting — it isn't about the goal but taking pleasure in the process of trying to reach a goal, whether it ends in success or a lesson. I learned so much about myself and my craft as I strove to win the Awesome Adventures competition, but almost sullied my amazing journey with being too focused on the grand prize. Maybe one day my images will grace the cover of National Geographic next to Steve McCurry's, or maybe they won't. But I am sure that his journey to greatness began with a decision to start, and his journey to greatness was rife with failures and lessons. And where life takes me is where I'm supposed to go.

As I made my way to the water's edge, I decided that I was done with my five-year plan. I was done planning for happily ever after, I wanted to live for happiness in the present. After all, the present is all that exists.

When the sun hung low in the sky, the last ferry left for Malolo, and I managed to squeeze aboard. Pink, orange, and gold clouds splattered the sky as the boat berthed at the wooden pier. With the gentle evening breeze rustling the palm fronds, I followed the path towards his bure.

My stomach tied in knots as I knocked on the open sliding glass door. After several uncomfortable seconds, I heard the creaking of rope behind me.

"Harper?" I heard his voice, and at the same time, I saw a silhouette rising from the hammock outside of his bure. I set my bags down, leaning them against the cream walls, and when I turned he was so close I could feel the heat radiating from his body. "You're back."

"I'm staying," I said, finding those stormy grey eyes.

He enveloped me in his arms and kissed me, pressing my back against the glass. One hand splayed across my lower back, but there was something in the other. When he released me, I reached for it. It was a book. My cheeks seared when I recognized the cover.

Tahitian Heat.

"You left this earlier," he said as I tried to hide my embarrassment. "It's given me some ideas."

Then, he threw me over his shoulder and carried me inside the bure to show me his new ideas.

***

Date: May 30, 2010
Malolo, Fiji

When word reached home that I was going to continue to travel and had a job that would pay me to do so, I received an email of support from my parents. It was an email that filled me with joy, and I will always remember the moment I read it. While waiting for Xavier to return from playing his set, I took a break from updating my blog in the hammock, and as a warm breeze washed over me, I read their words:

> Darling Harper,
>
> We are so proud of you for going after your dreams. Even if you came home, we would have been equally proud. Thank you for getting us out of our comfort zone and giving us the incentive to come to Australia. Your mother and I have been bitten by the travel bug, and when the housing market improves, we want to sell the house and retire somewhere warmer than Canada. Maybe buy a boat in the Caribbean or a condo in Rio. Who knows?!
>
> Please be safe on your travels, but we know your big sister is always watching over you.
>
> Love,
> Mom and Dad

"Hey, put your computer away." Xavier's voice broke my concentration as I stared at the screen. "Come, Moksha awaits."

Closing my laptop, I bit my lip and looked up at him. "And then we can watch for shooting stars?"

I stood and he pulled me into his arms and his lips covered mine. Whimpering as he withdrew, he gently pulled my chin so my eyes met his, and I wished that I could have him right then and there.

He smiled, and with that voice I could never tire of hearing, he said, "Mon étoile, we can watch for shooting stars all night."

***

The moment I decided to continue my adventure, I released the vice grip of control I had over my life and surrendered to the whims of the Universe, knowing that it will send me not only great things but also things so bad that I could never hope to make sense of them. Control, after all, is nothing but an illusion. As I reflected on my journey across the world and gave thanks for the irreplaceable people in my life, I realized the point of this wild ride called "life": to experience the ups and downs, to explore our world, to listen to those voices inside guiding us to who we are and towards the discovery of our purpose. It is up to each of us to find our own meaning for our existence, and the events that occur in it, and to discover the passions that keep us awake at night and pull us from our beds in the morning. Some people, like Audrey, are taken from this world before having the chance to truly live. And I learned that I shouldn't feel guilty that I was blessed to still be able to. Living my life wasn't flaunting her death; it was honouring the precious gift of life.

I believe the Buddhists have something going with the idea of embracing impermanence. Life is a beautiful tragedy as each moment we are given an opportunity to tell someone we love them, to do what we love, to find what and whom we love, because someday, on a day we may never see coming, it all has to end. So I decided to pour my soul into my art and chase every day as if I would not be given another, because another is never guaranteed. Every second between our first breath and our last is nothing more than borrowed time, and every experience earned during that small amount of time becomes a part of who we are, and gives us memories to look back on and be grateful for, especially during the hard times. And, ultimately, memories are all we ever truly possess.

Before Xavier became one of my fondest memories, we had an entire summer to run wild. And for that summer, we laughed without restraint, loved without shame, and lived without fear, not just in honour of my sister's memory, but for everyone who never had the chance to live their dreams.

The End

Thank you for reading.

I hope you enjoyed Runaways. If you did I would be forever grateful if you left a review on Amazon.

Acknowledgments

First and foremost I would like to thank my parents. If I did not do this first and dedicate the book to them, my mother would yell at me. But seriously, I couldn't have published this novel without their unwavering support and encouragement. They have supported all of my crazy ideas I've had in life, believing more in my success at times than I did. I would like to thank my friends who believed in me, and the ones that read my book and provide feedback - Heather Willens, Kelsey Bacon, Kimberley Fisher, Chloe Kempe, Heidi Hess, Sophie Claire Francis, Lizzie Sheard, Sarah Summersgill, and Jackie Stevenson. I would like to thank the developmental editor that helped me rewrite it in 2015, Sara Lovette, my final copy-editor, Parisa Zolfaghari, and the book cover designer, Caroline Teagle. Thank you to my brother Paul for helping me one evening with a photograph for the cover that didn't end up being used (and thank you to Helen and again my parents for holding up our makeshift studio).

A very special thank you to Ashley Aitken, Sarah Summersgill and Jesse Mitchell who were the best travel partners on the trip that inspired me to write this story. I'd also like to thank everyone I met on that trip and in my journey in life who inspired the events and characters of the story.

Thank you to any and everyone who encouraged me to put this story out into the world.

Dreams really can come true.

About the Author

Writer, traveler, content creator, master of random jobs, avoider of the 9-5. In 2010, Rachel Sawden set off on a trip around the world hoping to be given a sign of what to do with her life. That sign never appeared. It turned out the entire trip was the sign. When she returned to her home in Bermuda, she began to write about the countries she traveled to because she was still obsessed with them and had run out of people to listen to her drone on about her trip. She turned a life-long personal challenge of 'write a book' into *Runaways*, her debut novel. She has continued to travel, take photos, and write ever since.

Follow her on Instagram: @rachelsawden